ALSO BY FRANCIS SPUFFORD

I May Be Some Time
The Child That Books Built
Backroom Boys
Red Plenty
Unapologetic
Golden Hill
True Stories & Other Essays

LIGHT PERPETUAL

A Novel

FRANCIS SPUFFORD

SCRIBNER

New York   London   Toronto   Sydney   New Delhi

Scribner
An Imprint of Simon & Schuster, Inc.
1230 Avenue of the Americas
New York, NY 10020

First Scribner hardcover edition May 2021

For information about special discounts for bulk purchases,
please contact Simon & Schuster Special Sales at 1-866-506-1949
or business@simonandschuster.com.

The Simon & Schuster Speakers Bureau can bring authors to your live event.
For more information or to book an event, contact the Simon & Schuster Speakers Bureau
at 1-866-248-3049 or visit our website at www.simonspeakers.com.

Manufactured in the United States of America

1 3 5 7 9 10 8 6 4 2

Library of Congress Cataloging-in-Publication Data is available.

ISBN 978-1-9821-7414-9
ISBN 978-1-9821-7416-3 (ebook)

for Bernice

Lord Street to Cripplegate

The last word would belong, not to time, but to joy
PENELOPE FITZGERALD

They are all gone into the world of light
HENRY VAUGHAN

Everything was available in Sidcup
KEITH RICHARDS

t + 0: 1944

The light is grey and sullen; a smoulder, a flare choking on the soot of its own burning, and leaking only a little of its power into the visible spectrum. The rest is heat and motion. But for now the burn-line still creeps inside the warhead's casing. It is a thread-wide front of change propagating outward from the electric detonator, through the heavy mass of amatol. In front a yellow-brown solid, slick and brittle as toffee: behind, a seething boil of separate atoms, violently relieved of all the bonds between that made them trinitrotoluene and ammonium nitrate, and just about to settle back into the simplest of molecular partnerships. Soon they will be gases. Hot gases, hotter than molten metal, far hotter; and suddenly, churningly abundant; and so furiously compacted now into a space too small for them that they would burst the casing imminently on their own. If the casing were still going to be there. If it were not itself going to disappear into a steel mist the instant the burn-line reaches it.

Instants. This instant, before the steel case vanishes, is one ten-thousandth of a second long. A hairline crack in a Saturday lunch-time in November 1944. But look closer. The crack has width. It has duration. Can it not, itself, be split in two? And split again, and again, and again, divided and subdivided ad infinitum, with no stopping point? Does it not, itself, contain an abyss? The fabric of ordinary time is all hollow beneath, opening into void below void, gulf behind gulf. Every moment you care to define proving on examination to be a close-packed sheaf of finer, and yet finer ones without end; finer, in fact, always and forever, than whatever your last guess was. Matter has its smallest, finite subdivisions. Time does not. One ten-thousandth of a second is a fat volume of time, with onion-skin pages uncountable. As uncountable, no more or less, than all the pages would be in all the books making up all the elapsed time in the universe. This book of time has no fewer pages than all the books put together. Each of the parts is as limitless as the whole, because infinities don't come in larger and smaller sizes. They are all infinite alike. And yet somehow from this lack of limit arises all our ordinary finitude, our beginnings and ends. As if a pontoon had been laid across the abyss, and we walk it without noticing; as if the experience of this second, then this one, this minute then *this* one, here, now, succeeding each other without stopping, without appeal, and never quite enough of them, until there are no more of them at all—arose, somehow, as a kind of coagulation (a temporary one) of the nothing, or the everything, that yawns unregarded under all years, all Novembers, all lunchtimes. Do we walk, though? Do we move in time, or does it move us? This is no time for speculation. There's a bomb going off.

This particular Saturday lunchtime, Woolworths on Lambert Street in the Borough of Bexford has a delivery of saucepans, and they are stacked on a table upstairs, gleaming cleanly. No one has seen a new pan for years, and there's an eager crowd of women round the table, purses ready, kids too small to leave at home brought along to the shop. There's Jo and Valerie with their mum, wearing tam-o'-shanters knitted from wool scraps; Alec with his, spindly knees showing beneath his shorts; Ben gripped firmly by *his*, and looking slightly mazed, as usual; chunky Vernon with his grandma, product of a household where they never seem to run quite as short of the basics as other people do. The women's hands reach out towards the beautiful aluminium, but a human arm cannot travel far in a ten-thousandth of a second, and they seem motionless. The children stand like statues executed in flesh. Vern's finger is up his nose. Something is moving visibly, though, even with time at this magnification. Over beyond the table, by the rack of yellowed knitting patterns, something long and sleek and sharp is coming through the ceiling, preceded by a slow-tumbling cloud of plaster and bricks and fragmented roof tiles. Amid the twinkling debris the tapering cone of the warhead has a geometric dignity as it slides floorward, the dull green bulk of the rocket pushing into sight behind, inch by inch. Inside the cone the amatol is already burning. Shoppers, saucepans, ballistic missile: what's wrong with this picture? No one is going to tell us. Jo and Alec, as it happens, are looking in the right direction. Their gaze is fixed on the gap between the shoulders of Mrs. Jones and Mrs. Canaghan where the rocket is gliding into view. But they can't see it. Nobody can. The image of the V-2 is on their retinas, but it takes far longer than a ten-thousandth of a second for a human eye to process an image and send it to a brain. Much sooner than that, the children won't have eyes any more. Or brains. This instant—this interval of time, measurably tiny, immeasurably vast—arrives unwitnessed, passes unwitnessed, ends unwitnessed. And yet it is a real moment. It really happens. It really takes its necessary place in the sequence of moments by which 910 kilos of amatol are delivered among the saucepans.

Then the burn-line touches the metal. The name for what happens next is *brisance*. The moving thread of combustion, all combustion done, becomes a blast wave pushing on and out in the same directions, driven by the pressure of the livid gas behind. And what it touches, it breaks. A spasm of deformation, of dislocation, passes through every solid thing, shattering it to fragments that then accelerate outward themselves at the forefront of the wave. Knitting patterns. Rack. Glass sign hanging from chains, reading HABERDASHERY. Wooden table. Pans. Much-darned brown worsted hand-me-down served-three-siblings horn-buttoned winter coat. Skin. Bone. The size of the fragments is determined by the distance from the centre of the blast. Closest in, just particles: then flecks, shreds, morsels, lumps, pieces, and furthest out, where the energy of the wave is widest spread, whole mangled yard-wide fractions of wall or door or flagstone or tram-stop sign, torn loose and sent spinning across the street. The blast goes mainly down at first, because of the shape of the warhead, through the first floor and the ground floor and the cellar of Woolworths and into the London clay, where it scoops a roughly hemispheric crater before rebounding up and out with a pulse that carries most of the shattered fabric of the building with it. A dome of debris expands. The shops to left and right of Woolworths are ripped open to the air along the slanting upward lines of the dome's edge. A blizzard of metal jags and brick flakes scours Lambert Street, both ways. The buildings opposite heave and sag; all their windowpanes blow inward and stick in the walls behind in glittering spears and splinters. In the ground, a tremor pops gas mains and grinds the sections of water pipes apart. In the air, even where there is no abrading grit, no flying rain of bricks, a sudden invisible jolt of intense pressure travels outward in a ring. A tram just coming round the far bend from Lewisham rocks on its rails and halts, still upright; but through it from end to end passes the ripple that turns the clear air momentarily as hard as glass. At the very limits of the blast, small strange alterations take place, almost whimsical. Kitchen chairs shake their way a foot across the floor. A cupboard door falls open, and hoarded pre-war confetti trickles out. A one-ounce weight from the butcher's right next door to Woolworths somehow flies right over Lambert Street, and the street beyond, to fall neatly through the open back upstairs window of a house in the next street beyond that, and lodge among the undamaged keys of an Underwood typewriter.

No need to slow time, now. There's nothing to see which can't be seen at the usual speed humans perceive at. Let it run, one second per second. The rubble of Lambert Street bounces and lies still. The hollow howl of the rocket's descent is heard at last, outdistanced by the explosion. Then a ringing stillness. No one is alive in Woolworths to break it. All of the shoppers and the counter girls are dead, on all three floors; and everyone in the butcher's on the left, and the post office on the right, except for one clerk with both legs broken, who happened to be leaning forward into the safe; and everyone in the tram queue on the pavement outside; and all the passers-by; and anyone standing by the window in the houses opposite; and all the travellers on the Lewisham tram, still upright in their seats in their hats and coats, but asphyxiated by the air-shock. Then, only then, from those furthest out in the circle of ruination, the first screams. And the sirens. And the fire brigade coming; and the middle-aged men and women of the ARP stumbling through the masonry with their spades; and the teenage boys and old men of the Light Rescue Service arriving, with their stretchers which they scarcely use, and their sacks which they do. And the attempt to separate out from the rest of broken Woolworths those particles, flecks, shreds, lumps and pieces that, previously, were parts of people; people being missed, waited for, despaired of, by the crowd gathering white-faced behind the tape at the end of the street.

Jo and Valerie and Alec and Ben and Vernon are gone. Gone so fast they cannot possibly have known what was happening, which some of those who mourn them will take for a comfort, and some won't. Gone between one ten-thousandth of a second and the next, gone so entirely that it's as if they've vanished into all that copious, immeasurable nothing just beneath the rickety scaffolding of hours and minutes. Their part in time is done. They have no share, any more, in what swells and breathes and tightens and turns and withers and brightens and darkens; in any of the changes of things. Nothing is possible for them that requires being to stretch from one instant to another over the gulfs of time. They cannot act, or be acted on. Cannot call, or be called. Do, or be done unto. There they aren't. Meanwhile the matter that composed them is all still there in the crater, but it cannot ever, in any amount of time whatsoever, be reassembled. That's time for you. It breaks things up. It scatters them. It cannot be run backwards, to summon the dust to rise, any more than you can stir milk back out of tea. Once sundered, forever sundered. Once scattered, forever scattered. It's irreversible.

But what has gone is not just the children's present existence—Vernon not trudging home to the house with the flitch of bacon hanging in the kitchen, Ben not on his dad's shoulders crossing the park, astonished by the watery November clouds, Alec not getting his promised ride to Crystal Palace tomorrow, Jo and Valerie not making faces at each other over their dinner of cock-a-leekie soup. It's all the futures they won't get, too. All the would-be's, might-be's, could-be's of the decades to come. How can that loss be measured, how can that loss be known, except by laying this absence, now and onwards, against some other version of the reel of time, where might-be and could-be and would-be still may be? Where, by some little alteration, some altered single second of arc, back in Holland where the rocket launched, it flew four hundred yards further into Bexford Park, and killed nothing but pigeons; or suffered a guidance failure, as such crude mechanisms do, and slipped unnoticed between the North Sea waves; or never launched at all, a hiccup in fuel deliveries meaning the soldiers of Batterie 485 spent all that day under the pine trees of Wassenaar waiting for the ethanol tanker, and smoking, and nervously watching the sky for RAF Mosquitoes?

Come, other future. Come, mercy not manifest in time; come knowledge not obtainable in time. Come, other chances. Come, unsounded deep. Come, undivided light.

Come dust.

t + 5: 1949

Jo, Val, Vern, Alec

Miss Turnbull blows the whistle and it's time for Singing. This is Jo's favourite thing at school and she's quick to the painted line on the tarmac where Class 5 always forms up to march back in, but the rest of the playground accepts the end of morning break more slowly, even though it's drizzling. The teacher has to blow the whistle again, and one more time, before the skipping games and the fighting games and the football matches all reluctantly dissolve, and the gloomy canyon between the sooty red height of Halstead Road Primary and the tall sooty wall around it settles into something like order. Tinies on the right, Classes 2 to 7 ranked line by line over to the left, getting gradually taller and more truculent, till at Class 7, over by the end wall, the boys are standing like miniature men, shoulders shrugged, in postures of extravagant boredom, and the girls are doing scaled-down versions of their mothers' disdain. Back in the Class 5 line you can see some of this, but the imitations are less perfect and less continuous. The nine-year-olds have less front; can still have their dignity melt suddenly into excitement or silliness. Snotty noses. Scabs. Impetigo. The dirty necks and scratchy scalps of the kids from houses with no bathroom. New Health Service specs in tortoiseshell or pink plastic.

"Settle down!" bellows Miss Turnbull, and there is a sort of hush, bolted temporarily over the restlessness of the playground. The colour of the hush is a hard grey, thinks Jo, like a tarnished spoon, with scratches of brighter noise trying to wiggle up over it, which are the subdued sounds of the children as they fail to stand still. Outside on the street a lorry grinds out a gear-change, under the bridge at the street's end a train rushes by: a scuffing of rust brown at the hush's edge, and then a long feathering liquid streak of purple across it. She does not have these thoughts in words, but entirely in pictures. And the pictures of the sounds she is hearing run in her head without stopping all the time she is awake, never detached from what the world is like for her, so she has not yet wondered whether other people have them, any more than she's wondered if other people can see the sky. "Class One," calls the teacher. "Class Two. Class Three." In they all go, each class splitting to go separately through the BOYS and GIRLS doors, only to reunite immediately in the corridor inside.

"Oi, dopey, wait for me," says Val, and grabs her hand: a familiar tug, a familiar drag.

Singing is in the Hall, which must have had a quite grand pitched roof once. There are shields carved in the brick up at the top of the walls which say LONDON COUNTY COUNCIL on them, one letter per shield. Jo looks at them when they sing "When a Knight Won His Spurs," and thinks of armour, and dragons. But above the shields now, instead of grand rafters, there is a flat lid, made of temporary-looking raw wood and tarpaper. It means that the Hall stops sooner than you expect, going upwards. It squidges the room down; and it squidges the sounds you make in it down, too. The Hall must have been Blitzed. (That is the reason Jo has been given for every broken-looking thing in Bexford.)

Classroom doors slam all the way up the corridor and Miss Turnbull arrives, closing the double doors of the Hall behind her and sighing. She sighs a lot. She is Class 5's own teacher as well as being on break-time duty today, and one of the older ones at Halstead Road: one of the teachers that Jo's mum can remember from her time at Halstead Road, a long time ago. She has iron-grey hair in a tight bun, and when she isn't talking she presses her bottom lip up into her top lip as if there is something in her mouth she is trying to chew. Everybody says she must look a fright when she takes her teeth out at night. One time, clever Alec drew a picture of her without her teeth, in Handwriting, and passed it on. And she caught him! And he was sent to the Head, but only for wasting time and bad conduct, because Miss Turnbull did not recognise that it was a portrait of her. Jo saw it before it was torn up, and it was not much like.

Miss Turnbull hands out the red songbooks and sits down at the piano with a tired flump.

"Thirty-seven," she says. "Cotswolds." She means: turn to page thirty-seven, because we are going to sing "The Ballad of London River," which begins "From the Cotswolds, from the Chilterns." But she has said it so many times that all the spare words have fallen out. Jo is relieved. When the song for Singing is a sad one, like "Danny Boy" or "A North Country Maid," or a soft one like "Glad That I Live Am I," the boys start fooling about. They didn't use to, but this year they don't seem to be able to help it. They sing stupid words until they get into trouble. "The Ballad of London River" isn't quite as good for keeping the boys happy as "A Good Sword and a Trusty Hand" or "He Who Would Valiant Be," but it is about London, and Class 5 usually sing it proudly, even though it is full of hard words.

Miss Turnbull looks critically at the two rows that Class 5 has organised itself into: the ones who like to sing at the front, and most of the boys at the back, plus the people that she has banished there in previous lessons for singing badly. Jo is in the front, of course, and so is Val next to her, although *she* doesn't like it much, in fact. She is much more interested in what is happening behind her, and keeps twisting halfway round to look. Their household is all-female, and always has been as far as the girls are concerned: them, Mum, Auntie Kay. Dad, who didn't come back from the War, is just an idea to them, not a memory. But though this has made Jo wary of the whole species of men, it has worked differently on Val. Val is charmed, curious, unable to look away; always hovering at the edge of the boys' games, twiddling her hair and trying to join in their laughter. It's the long habit of twinhood that keeps her at Jo's side. Restless—as if she is always yanking these days at an invisible rope joining the two of them—but not able to pull away either. Yet. Beyond Val in the front row, pre-dictably, is horrible Vernon Taylor, christened Vermin Taylor by clever Alec at the back, but not called that to his face, oh no. Vern is very strong; Vern is a bully; Vern has fists like pink sausages, when the butcher bunches them to wrap them up in paper. Vern also has a horrible voice. When he sings, it's croaky and squeaky. Yet Singing is his favourite thing, too, as if it does something to him he can't help. Miss Turnbull sends him to the back over and over, but every time it's Singing he puts himself at the front again. He holds the red book with his big pink hands, and hunches his shoulders defiantly, and squints his nasty little eyes at the words and the notes. Miss Turnbull's eyes rest on him. She sighs. She opens her mouth. She closes it again, and makes her chewing face. She can't be bothered.

"Deep breaths, everyone," she says. "Open up those lungs. *Use* those chests. Bring the music up from your toes. Mouths open all the way. Heads *high* and sing *out*. Steven Jenkins, wipe your nose. With your handkerchief! And one—two—three—four—" She plays the opening bars with heavy hands, and no excitement at all, but it doesn't matter. There are the quick marching ripples of sound from the piano that come before the singing. They are almost silly somehow, like the National Anthem playing at the Bexford Odeon on Saturday morning before the main picture, wearily grand but no

16

match for the roar of the kids in the stalls. Yet Jo can still hear the idea of the ripples coming firm and clear through the plinking of the old upright, saying: here is the river, here is the river, and making spreading rings of green and bronze in her head. Sometimes it doesn't matter that things are silly. Then the music dances on the spot for a moment to tell them to get ready, and they all breathe in, Alec with a comical suction noise like a lift going up, and Class 5 opens its mouths all the way, and sings:

From the Cotswolds, from the Chilterns, from your fountains and
    your springs
Flow down, O London river, to the seagull's silver wings:
Isis or Ock or Thame,
Forget your olden name,
And the lilies and the willows and the weirs from which you came.

Here are some of the things Jo doesn't understand about the song: what the Cotswolds and the Chilterns are, what the words "Isis" and "Ock" and "Thame" have to do with anything, what a weir is. But here are some of the things Jo does understand about the song. She knows that it is happening in a world where all the colours are brighter than ordinary, where seagulls are silver instead of the dingy white of the ones that come angling and tilting out of the river fog, over from the Royal Albert Dock or the Greenland in Bermondsey, appearing silent and marvellous over the house-ends of Bexford, and probably after your sandwiches. She knows that the sounds of the words match, and fit together like jigsaw pieces, even if she doesn't know what they mean. Ock or Thame, olden name, *da-da DA-da, da-da DA-da, da-da DA da-da-da* came. She knows that in its posh inscrutable Technicolor way, it is saying that the river came from somewhere pretty in the country before it turned into the dirty brown flood that washes under the city bridges, and echoes from shore to shore with tugboat hooters, loud enough to shake the brickwork, or the window of a bus, if you're going over the bridge just then. The glass buzzes under your fingertips when the hooters go. It makes your fingers go all numb and soapy. The Thames is an ugly big river, ugly and loud, not pretty, and the song is saying that being big and loud and ugly makes London exciting, and that being exciting is better than being pretty.

And most of all, she knows how you are supposed to sing it. It pounds along to begin with. The first line stomps like a march, *da-da dee dee, dee dee DEE dee*, only at the end, on "springs," it suddenly mounts up to a higher note than you were expecting, to make a kind of platform you jump off from in the second line. "Flow down," it says, and it does flow down, or even fly down, like the seagull; and then like the seagull, when it has done its deepest dip, it banks up again, hovering in the middle of the air and in fact in the exact middle of the five black ruler marks the music lives on, at "wings." And then "Isis or Ock or Thame" and "Forget your olden name" wind it up again. Step by step it climbs till it positively soars on "name," and you think that the last line is going to let you open your throat as wide as a gramophone horn and fly, fly, fly to the end. But it doesn't, it disappoints you, it disappoints you on purpose, dropping down to a dull and tidy-sounding end at "came," only to give it all back even better, when you sing the last line unexpectedly over again. And the second time round, the "LIL-ies" and the "WILL-ows" are notes so high that they are trying to get free from the top of the ruler marks altogether, they are climbing out like men poking their heads out of attic windows, they are almost as high as Jo can manage to sing, and then the verse flies down to its true end with notes so long at "weeiiirrrs" and at "caaaame" that each of them fills a whole bar on its own, and uses up all your breath. Even Vern can tell you're supposed to soar joyfully. Jo can hear him trying to winch himself squeakily aloft, and his voice almost vanishes in a sort of hoarse whistling noise. But it doesn't spoil her pleasure in her own sure, ringing progress, nothing held back, along that last line. The high notes succeed each other in her mind's eye like rays of scarlet and gold.

They are taking their new breath for the second verse—Alec is singing properly now and has forgotten to be funny—when Miss Turnbull's hands falter to a stop on the piano. The Hall door has opened behind Class 5.

"Was there something, Mr. Hardy?" she asks.

In comes the headmaster, bald and inky-black-moustached, prowling. Instantly Class 5 stiffens, because Mr. H is a figure of terror. His office is where The Cane is kept, and by now a fair few of Class 5 have been sent to visit it and him: not Jo, but the fear spreads. He has a pouncing way of asking questions, and he does not make it easy to tell what answer will please him.

"No, no," he says. "Don't mind me. I won't interrupt." But then he goes on, immediately, "Chil'erns. Chil'erns. That's what I heard coming through the door. There's a T in that word, children. Let me hear you all say it properly, please."

"Chil*t*erns," Class 5 choruses, raggedly.

"Louder, please."

"Chil*t*erns!"

"There," says Mr. Hardy, but not as if he is satisfied. "Pronunciation is important, wouldn't you agree, Miss Turnbull?"

"Of course, Headmaster," she says flatly. And it's true that Miss Turnbull frequently corrects dropped consonants and missing aitches, frequently sighs over the F that Class 5 puts in "south" and the V in their "this." But when she does it, it doesn't have this cat-and-mouse quality. There is a tension between the two adults that Jo doesn't understand. Mr. Hardy, Jo notices, is quite a lot shorter than Miss Turnbull. He is standing next to the piano now, rocking on the balls of his feet while he surveys the class discontentedly, and thrusting out his waistcoated stomach. A watch-chain gleams there.

"Carry on, then, Miss Turnbull," he says, not going away. Miss Turnbull plays the rippling chords of the opening again, and much more reluctantly, much more guardedly than before, Class 5 sings the next verse.

The stately towers and turrets are the children of a day:
You see them lift and vanish by your immemorial way:
The Saxon and the Dane,
They dared your deeps in vain—
The Romans and the Norman—they are past, but you remain.

This time around, the long notes at the end fade nervously away long before they should.

"Hmph," says Mr. Hardy, prodding at them all with his gaze. "Would you say that Class Five are making good progress, Miss Turnbull?"

She takes her hands off the keyboard and folds them in her lap.

"Yes," she says unexpectedly. "They sing with feeling, and one or two of them have real promise."

This is more praise than Jo has ever heard her utter, and she is surprised to hear it. She has always thought of Miss Turnbull, in Singing, as a kind of mechanism for operating the piano, completely unconnected to what she herself feels about the music. Class 5 stirs, tentatively trying out the feeling of being on Miss Turnbull's side.

"I'm pleased to hear it," grunts Mr. Hardy, sounding anything but. He brightens. "But do they understand what they're singing, eh? Boy in the front row there." His finger is pointing at Vernon. "'You see them lift and vanish by your immemorial way.' You've just sung it. What does it mean?"

"Dunno, sir," says Vern.

"All right, we'll make it easier. You, girl; girl with the plaits. Who is 'you' in the song, eh?"

Jo feels her mind going blank, all thoughts in it scurrying for cover like mice when you open the kitchen door. There is no way of connecting her mouth with the pleasure in the song that was soaking her through five minutes earlier, no chance of a path between words and all that flying, flowing shape.

"Well?"

Mr. Hardy is looking at her. So is Miss Turnbull, making her chewing face.

"It's red, sir," she tries, trembling. "In your head. When you sing it."

"What?" says Mr. Hardy. "What? It sounds *red*? The girl's an idiot."

Vernon snickers, then stops abruptly. Alec has kicked him in the back of the knee. Jo can feel him swell next to her, a balloon full of trouble for somebody later, pumping up.

"One doesn't expect much round here," says Mr. Hardy to Miss Turnbull, happily. "I know that. But still, this is disheartening, is it not?"

Miss Turnbull sighs.

"Mister 'Ardy?" says Alec suddenly.

"What is it, boy?" says the Head impatiently. He has much more to say. He has barely got started.

"Could you hexplain it to us, sir please sir? That would be hever so kind. It would be hexcellent. It would make us really 'appy, sir please sir."

Mr. Hardy frowns, unsure if the child is in earnest. Jo doesn't know what Alec is up to, except that it's dangerous. But that is not what his normal voice is like. He is the one in Class 5 who gets told off least by Miss Turnbull for his vowels and his consonants.

He can also spell everything, perfectly. His dad is in the print. Their house is full of books, shelves and shelves of them.

"Very well," says the Head. "'You' in this verse is the river Thames itself—"

"Never!" says Alec, as if awestruck.

"—along whose banks the various— Boy, are you being insolent?"

Class 5 have begun to giggle.

"Me, sir? No, sir," says Alec. "I wouldn't fink of such a fing."

"I think you are," says Mr. Hardy.

"Oh no, sir," says Alec. "I'm just so grateful, sir, to hunderstand the song, sir, what we've bin singing all this time, sir. It's like a light bulb's gone on in me 'ead, honest."

More, louder giggles, and even Miss Turnbull, behind Mr. Hardy's back, has got her eyebrows raised and her lips clamped together, as if she is keeping something from coming out.

"Right, that's quite enough," says Mr. Hardy, who has gone red. (But not the bright joyful colour Jo saw in her mind's eye. A duller, nastier shade.) "Out! I'll deal with you in my office, boy."

And he reaches in with one of his sudden pounces, and grabs Alec by one of his ears, and marches out of the Hall with him, deliberately pulling too high so that Alec has to move at a kind of painful sidle-on-tiptoes, already crying out by the time his dangling boots have been hauled through the double doors. Class 5 have stopped laughing, and are gazing after them.

Miss Turnbull clears her throat, claps her hands.

"All right, Class Five," she says, and her voice sounds less tired, "face the front. Shoulders back. Let's sing verse three. One—two—three—four—"

Ben

"Is this your first time, then, son?" asks the man next to Ben's dad. "Pick him up on your shoulders, mate, I don't mind, give him a bit of a view."

Ben's used to people thinking he's younger than he is, because he's little. But it's been a long time, years and years, since he was small enough to be carried, so it takes him by surprise when Dad grunts agreement, bends down, and hoists him high. All of a sudden, instead of struggling to see in a dark crush of coats and jackets, he's up in the air. The back of Dad's cap presses into his belly, and all around, he's looking down on thousands of other men's heads in their caps and their hats and their mufflers. It's a sloping sea of shout, of fingers up and stabbing the air, of fags in the corners of mouths.

They're up at the back of the south stand in the Den. It's just a concrete slope going up in steps. Up here at the top it's high enough to see the railway lines that hem the ground on three sides. Trains go by, over and over. Rattling green passenger carriages, faces like white peas in the windows. Wagons going from the docks or to the docks, dragged in clanking lines by engines that bark out smoke in hard gusts, like big dogs. The cindery clouds join the haze on the far side that's always there, over towards the river. The cranes at the docks always stand in air thick as soup. But it's just stopped raining and the wet has damped the haze down. The grass on the pitch has been washed back to a streaky green. The roofs opposite glimmer where the rainwater reflects the sky, and a wet gleam fingers a path along the top of the SUNLIGHT SOAP sign. The day is brightening. With all this noisy air open round him, Ben follows the brightness up, and up. He sees the London smoke is only a footstool. Above, the rain as it leaves mounts in a curving wall, immense, slate grey, slate purple. An anvil, pulling back. At the very very top, it cauliflowers. It goes to bumps and lumps and smoothed-out tiny battlements too complicated for your eyes, but all crisp and clear. A sky country far away, getting lighter. A rim there almost as burning white as summer clouds. This is wet autumn, though.

"Mark him, mark him!" the man next to Dad is bellowing cheerfully. "Come on, you Lions! Come on, you dozy cunts! Are you *blind*?"

In the green rectangle, the bright-blue Millwall players drain to the right. A sudden flood of Crystal Palace dark-red-and-blue has broken in. Bright blue recoils, gathers, closes in to grip the tip of the attack. At the tip, a tangle, a trip, a thud, a tumble. Two men roll over in a heap. Groans from the stand on the other side, but the ball rolls out, rolls loose. It looks tiny, such a tiny dot to make everyone move around it. Somebody kicks it left. All together the dark-red-and-blue are moving, the bright blues are moving, everyone is running back to the left again, colours pooling and separating as they go. Wheeling round each other. Drawing lines that change every second.

"Pass it!" yells the man, and all the other men nearby have their mouths open too. Opening and closing. Shouting different things.

"Come on, you Lions!" cries Ben experimentally.

"Come on, you Lions!" shouts Dad, and squeezes Ben's ankles.

"Move yer arse, Jimmy!" shouts the man. "Jimmy Constantine, move yer arse!"

"Which one's Jimmy Constantine?" asks Ben.

"Number eight," says Dad.

"The one with the fucking ball, son," says the man.

Dad turns his head.

"Sorry," says the man, and shrugs.

"All right," says Dad. "But son? We don't talk like this at home."

"Yes, Dad," Ben starts to say, but it gets drowned. An enormous deep disappointed *Oooooo* comes up out of every throat on the home stand. Like they've all, together, turned into one big animal, angry or sad. Angry about being sad. Back goes the ball, wallop, way up high, deep into the Millwall half.

"Should have passed it," says the man to himself, shaking his head. "Should have passed it. Useless bastard. Come on, you Lions!"

The ball goes to the right, to the left, to the right, to the left. Dark red washes into bright blue, bright blue surges into dark red. Waves on a beach. Ben went to Broadstairs with Auntie Joan's family in the summer, and they sat him by the ragged line the seaweed made at the top of the sand, wrapped up so he didn't get cold, and he watched the same rushing, never arriving, never getting tired. When the ball's on the right, Dad and the man and all the other men gasp and cry out and suck their breaths in. On the left they roar, they push out big sounds on a note rising up, and up, and up, till *Oooooo!* the wave breaks, and it all runs back the other way. Ben joins in quietly. When he does, he feels the game working his own chest like a squeezebox. You don't have to decide, it just happens. In, out. *Oooooo!* Come on, you Lions!

Up in the cauliflower kingdom in the sky, the top of the cloud is burning white and gold now. The sun is coming through. Shadows swing around. There's a glare in the north-west that makes it hard to look that way.

"Up the wing!" groans the man.

Dark red pushes over to the right again, but this time, when bright blue takes the ball back, someone kicks it long and high to the Crystal Palace end. The dot soars up. It seems to leave the whole shouting, roaring ground behind. It rises up towards where the cauliflower country is lost in glare. It spins slowly across the hazy metal thicket of the cranes. Like it has all the time in the world before it has to come down again. Like it might not come down again, this time. Like the sky might be going to keep it, and the Millwall players and the Crystal Palace players will have to say to the sky, "Can we have our ball back?" Then the sun, breaking through, catches it, and it flares into a point of molten gold, intensely bright. Ben's mind goes still, transfixed. Elsewhere the ball falls, is neatly snared on the run by a bright-blue attacker, is jinked left and right past a Crystal Palace defender, is passed hard and exact over to bright-blue number 8, just arrived at the perfect spot where he can spin and send it at an acute angle that looks almost impossible straight past the keeper and into the corner of the net. *Oh-oh-oh-OOHHH!* cry all the thousand men around Ben, their voices climbing up to ecstasy on steps of anxiety. But Ben's mind's eye is still full of the burning mote of gold, motionless in the air. It shone as if a hole had been pierced through the world. He hasn't noticed the goal.

"I love you, Jimmy Constantine," howls their neighbour. "I love you, you beautiful fucking dago."

"What about that, eh?" says Dad, twisting his head round to look up at Ben. "What a beauty, eh?"

"What?" says Ben slowly, like someone waking up. "What?"

"I thought you'd enjoy it more," says Dad sadly later, on the bus home.

"It was wonderful, Dad," says Ben.

t + 20: 1964

Alec

It's almost gone one before Alec can get out of his overalls, shimmy into his suit, and be off at a run: out the loading bay entrance round the side of the *Gazette* and up Marshall Street to the Hare & Hounds. As ever, after the metallic close-up clatter of the machines, the air on the street seems soft and expansive. The traffic noise comes and goes in gentle waves, as if all the gear-shifts and revving buses have melted together into soft surges. The sky is very high, the breeze when he rounds the corner by the milk bar seems to be telling him how big the world is. How much bigger than the *Gazette*'s little composition room. Quick glance at himself in the window to set himself to rights, pat the hair, straighten the tie; then into the saloon bar, not the public. They're already there, with a fag lit each but empty hands otherwise, laid on the table as if to emphasise their lack of a drink. True, it's for him to buy today, tradition says so, but still: what a pair of skinflints.

"Mr. Hobson!" says Alec, bearing down, hand out.

"Ah," says Hobson, "here we are, then. Clive, this is Alec Torrance I was telling you about. Alec, this here is Clive Burnham from the *Times* chapel."

Hobson has been very good to Alec since his dad died and he and his mum lost the house. He helped out with the apprenticeship; when that was done, he spoke up for him at the *Gazette*; now here he is again, doing his best to sort him out a route to the Fleet Street shifts that pay better than anything on a local paper. Replacement dad stuff, in short, and all in the name of something-or-other that passed between Hobson and his actual dad, way back before the war, as mysterious from the outside as all work friendships are, based as they are on the alchemy of rubbing along with someone day after day. But whatever it was, it was enough to have Hobson keeping an eye out for Ray Torrance's boy these last eight years. He's a creaky, rusty, angular old thing, with a mess of white hair and a suit of undertaker black, lightly snowed with dandruff on the shoulders. First name Hrothgar, astonishingly enough. H-r-o-t-h-g-a-r, Alec's mind's fingers spell out on his mind's keys, just as they now automatically letter-ise every unusual proper name he comes across. *Mrs. Ermintrude Miggs (61). The defendant, Dafydd Clewson. Employed at the firm of Silverstein and Rule, Manor Road, Hockley-in-the-Hole.* Every one its own different little cascade of brass. He looks like a Hrothgar too, does Hobson. Like one of those minor people in Dickens you see leaning out of the smudgy shadows in the old illustrations. Half smudge himself. But Burnham's the one Alec needs to please. He's a different proposition altogether. Smooth, with a bit of weight on him, packed into one of those silvery Italian-style suits, and a face as tanned as someone fresh back from the seaside.

"What'll you have, gents?" he says.

"Just a small whisky for me, I thank you," creaks Hobson.

"Pint and a chaser," says Burnham, not bothering with the pleases and thank yous. "Scotch egg if they've got one." He looks a bit bored; glances round the bar like he's seen better; stifles a yawn.

"Sandwich, Mr. Hobson?" says Alec. "I'm getting one for myself."

"No, no, that's fine," says Hobson. "I'm not on this afternoon, I'll get something at home, after."

Alec fetches the round on a tray. Pint of mild for him, and that had better be all, he thinks; there's the afternoon to concentrate through. Not to mention now.

"Well, sit down, sit down," says Hobson. "Now, I'm putting you two together because Alec is a good lad, very accurate, and he won't let you down neither. His family's old LTS—in the print back to time imm-em-orial."

"Yeah, you said," says Burnham.

"You prob'ly remember, his dad Ray used to do little articles in the *Journal*? Chess problems, cycling notes? Funny stuff."

"Sorry, no, doesn't ring a bell. I'm not LTS myself—I'm national." The London and provincial compositors had merged the year before, and in theory it was all one union now, but the distinction had been in place since Queen Victoria was young, and it hadn't worn away yet, specially at the London end.

"So how'd you come up, then, Mr. Burnham?" asks Alec politely.

"Birmingham *Post*. Anyway, doesn't matter. What matters is, son—and I'm sure you're doing a nice job down here, don't get me wrong—what matters is, you're on a weekly here, and the pace you're used to will be nice and slow. Stuff up, and there's time to fix it, right?"

"I don't 'stuff up,'" says Alec. Hobson gives him a look.

"You don't know that," says Burnham. "You can't know that till you've been there. Till it's half an hour after press time, and you've got nasty little NATSOPAs breathing down your neck waiting at the presses, and the management muttering about overtime and losing some of the run: and then the stone sub says, ooh dear, page two doesn't add up at all, thanks to this piece from our own correspondent in Fuck-Off-tania, which is full of exciting details about the Fuck-Off-tanian situation which no one has ever heard of, and you certainly haven't, and which is one hundred and five words too long. Shorten it, will you? Take out one hundred and five words exactly, without turning the Fuck-Off-tanian report into gobbledegook. And for this task, you do not have time immemorial. You have no time at all. Or a minute and a half. Whichever is shorter. How would you do at that, d'you think?"

Burnham's teeth when he grins are small and regular, like little squares of Formica.

"I think I could do that," Alec says. "I think I might like that. Actually."

"Is that right?"

"Well, we aren't all asleep, you know, 'down here.' There isn't, like, a belt of sleeping sickness you run into soon as you come across Waterloo Bridge."

"Is that right. Is he always this mouthy?" Burnham asks Hobson.

"Alec is not shy about having an opinion," says Hobson. "But he is pretty calm, on the whole, if you don't wind him up deliberate."

Burnham laughs. "How else am I going to find out what he's like under pressure? Look, you know how many people are after shifts on the Street. They're gold dust. They're the jackpot. And you know how much it matters that *we* get to give 'em out, not management. I don't need a hothead."

"I'm not a hothead," says Alec.

"No? Took me, what, thirty seconds to get a rise out of you."

"I think," says Hobson, "I think—that you should get Clive here another drink."

Alec shuttles to the bar and back, reminding himself of how much he needs the shifts, and when he gets back Hobson has somehow made Burnham laugh, and is laughing himself, in a series of rubbery gurgles that sound like a hot-water bottle being folded and unfolded.

"What's up?" he says.

"Nothing," says Burnham, and offers Alec a filter-tip from

his shiny packet. Which is probably a good sign. He has a shiny lighter too. Hobson, though, turns one down, and says he's off to the gents. They watch him go, limping away with his scarecrow gait.

"He's a bit of a character, isn't he?" says Burnham. "Does he always dress like that—you know, like he's just embalmed someone?"

"Pretty much," says Alec. He clamps his mouth shut again.

Burnham sighs.

"We've started off on the wrong foot, haven't we? Look, I'm not taking the piss here. The old git speaks very highly of you, and it's nice, yeah, that you're loyal to him, too; does you credit. But this is a big step up, and I'm trying to work out whether you're up to it. As it happens, it might be quite useful to have someone in the composing room who's got a bit of a gob on them. Someone who'll push back, speak up, help draw the lines that have to be drawn. We've got management trying to take liberties one side, and the buggers in the machine room with their elbows out on the other, all the bloody time. But it needs a cool head, not a hot one—not someone whose mouth runs away with 'em. I dunno if you read up on that Royal Commission stuff? Said we were overmanned and riding for a fall, basically. Hasn't happened yet; there's more people in the print than ever. But it bears watching; it's ticklish. So you tell me what it is about you that's nice and calm and steady, means I could rest easy?"

He doesn't know what he could offer.

"That . . . I need the shifts? I mean, really need them?"

"Nah," says Burnham. "That won't do it. Look at you: you're young. Put the extra four quid in your pocket and you'll, what, piss it away on nights out. Wine, women and song. Collecting god-awful jazz with no tune. Something like that."

Alec looks at Burnham, and he sees someone asking him to

translate into banter everything in his life that's hardest. But perhaps it has to be done.

"No," he says. "I mean, I'm married?"

"Well, you would know best," Burnham says. "Are you or aren't you?"

"Fuck off, all right: I'm married. Gotta little boy, and another baby on the way, and I could *really* use the extra, 'cause we're living with my Sandra's mum, and my mum's in the flat with us too."

"Oh, right," says Burnham warily, looking slightly startled by this deviation from men's talk. "I see. And it's all getting a bit tense?"

"You could say."

This is where he should insert a joke of his own. He should say something on the lines of: by now, the international crisis in Fuck-Off-tania has nothing on us. That would please Burnham. That would be handing him his own joke back with a cherry or a ribbon on top, and everyone likes that. Mothers-in-law, newlyweds, trying to snatch a chance to have sex when three people aren't listening—it's all the stuff of comedy, isn't it? But comedy doesn't cover the bone-deep, unwavering dislike Sandra's mother has for him and everything to do with him. Banter isn't the right style for the way his own mother is shrinking, is reducing, the longer they stay in the flat, as if she isn't sure she's even entitled to the two-foot space she sits in at the end of the couch. Sandra's mum wouldn't have anything from the old place in her precious living space: not the furniture, not the shelves his dad had made, not the books. It all had to go, or nearly all. There's one cardboard box of the books, down in the damp under the stairs into the area. When he looked in it, there was black mould growing on the covers. *Socialism and* Fungus by *Walter* Fungus. Walter Citrine, really. C-i-t-r-i-n-e.

"Okey-doke," says Burnham. "I believe I have got the picture." He pauses; stares at his fag-end; raises his eyebrows, still at the cigarette, in an expression of pained delicacy. "And you wanna get out from under? Get a place of your own, right?"

Come on, thinks Alec.

"Yeah. That's right. There's a house up the hill's coming free next month, and the collector says we could have it. We need three bedrooms, you see, really, if we're not going to . . . well: if we're gonna be comfortable."

Burnham brightens.

"You don't wanna do that," he says, energy back in his voice.

"What?" says Alec.

"You don't wanna do that. Renting's a mug's game," Burnham explains, back on safe saloon-bar ground. "You wanna think a bit bigger than that, and buy something. And—no offence—not round here, if you take my advice. All this Victorian shit? Leaks, tiny rooms, terrible repair, the coloureds coming in. You wanna get out of London, somewhere new, somewhere clean. Us, for example, we got a semi in Welwyn. Brand new, no cobwebs in the corners, bit of garden, green space for the kids, gravel drive to park the motor. And I get to work on the train quicker than you could get there from here, I should think. And it's *ours*."

"That sounds great," says Alec stiffly. "Really nice. But, you know, I'm born and bred in the Smoke. I think I'll prob'ly stick to the old place all the same."

"Don't know what you're missing," says Burnham.

"Chance to support Luton Town and own a hedge, by the sound of it," he says, unable to help himself.

"Cheeky little bugger," Burnham says, without heat. "Cheeky. Little. Bugger. Wasn't wrong about that, was I? Mouth in gear, brain not engaged. Suit yourself, then."

Fuck, fuck, fuck, thinks Alec.

"Look, Clive—"

"Mr. Burnham to you."

35

"Mr. Burnham. Sorry. Look, I swear, I am not normally hard to get along with. The baby's colicky, you see, and we're not getting a lot of sleep. I'm sure you remember that, right?"

"Yeah, yeah. You know what I do when one of ours is poorly? Leave the wife to sort it, and go and sleep in the *spare room*. Pity you haven't got one, isn't it?"

"Touché," says Alec.

"'Too-shay'?" mocks Burnham. The Formica teeth are back. "'*Too-shay*'?"

"My dad liked *The Three Musketeers*."

"Did he. Yeah, I bet he did. Ooh, you'd fit right in at the *Times*—the stuff we have to set sometimes."

Burnham grimaces at him, considering.

"Ah, fuck it," he says. "All right, we'll give it a go. Step by step, mind you. We'll try you for a shift or two, and if it goes all right, all well and good; and if you point your mouth where it doesn't belong, you'll be back here in the arse-end of South London before you can say too-shay. All right?"

"Yes, Mr. Burnham," says Alec. "Thank you."

"And you can forget about the foreign news and all of that. You'll not be let near the pages that change at the last minute; not for years. The way it works is, you start off on the Court Circular, the law reports, the classifieds, the letters. 'The bride was resplendent in a whoopsie of cerise taffeta' style of thing. But even there, you got to keep your cool, you really do. Bastards to the left, bastards to the right; it's not a peaceful spot, is what I'm saying. And you need to be able to handle that."

"I can handle that."

"You better not make me regret this, d'Artagnan."

"No, Mr. Burnham. All for one and one for all, Mr. Burnham."

"First shift next Thursday, then," says Burnham. He raises his voice. "You can come on back now, Mr. Hobson."

Hobson sidles arthritically round the bar from the corner where he's been tactfully hiding.

"All set, are we?" he says.

"We are," says Burnham. "And now I shall be getting back to civilisation. Thanks for the drinks; thanks for the pointer to your mouthy little so-and-so here."

He drains his glass, picks up a pork-pie hat from the bench, and is gone.

"Very good, Alec," says Hobson. "That's excellent. A bit . . . bumpier than I had anticipated, but excellent all the same. A very good result. I'm pleased for you."

"Well, I owe it to you, Mr. Hobson," says Alec. "I know that. You've been fantastic, all down the line, and I'll not forget it. And now I better get moving, too. I'm back on in ten minutes. Shall I leave it with you, to tell the *Gazette* you'll be bringing on someone else?"

"Yes, yes," says Hobson. "But Alec? Sit down a second, would you. There's something I just wanted to say."

"What?" says Alec, thinking that there might be, who knows, a message from his dad for this moment, or something.

"Well," says Hobson, "well." He steeples his long white fingers just in front of his face, tucks his thumbs under his lantern jaw, and uses the innermost two fingers to tap his nose. "What I wanted to say, is."

"Yes?" says Alec.

"What I wanted to say is, look: you've got a future ahead of you in the print, and that's grand. That will see you and Sandra right. And I done my best to help. But you're a bright boy. And I just wanted to say, so I had at least come out and said it, at least once—is this what you really want?"

"What I *want*?" repeats Alec, baffled, his mind already half heading back down Marshall Street.

"I should have said this long ago, I know. And it would be . . . dicey to make a change now, I see that. But you are still young. And what I find myself thinking is, the machines aren't."

"Sorry, you've lost me," says Alec, glancing at his watch and thinking: can he be pissed? Not on one whisky, surely.

"The Linotype. It hasn't changed, my whole life. It's old. It's ancient. And you're going to sit down in front of it, and then you might spend your whole life sitting there, like I have."

"Not a bad life," says Alec, as gently as he can.

"Not at all! No! But heavens, lad, you've got a very good mind, you've got your father's mind, near as I can see, and you could do anything you put your mind to, pretty much; you could do something *new*."

Alec struggles with exasperation. Six years an apprentice, four on the *Gazette*, a decade getting deeper and deeper committed, and now's the moment the silly old sod chooses? All Alec hears, in Hobson's "could," is an appeal to an imaginary world in which none of the last ten years have happened; in which there is no Sandra, no little Gary, no decisions already taken, no paths already followed, no necessity tightening and narrowing. No need to buy groceries. What's that, that other life Hobson is invoking? A figment, a theory, a phantom, for which you'd have to throw away everything real. Silly old sod. But he won't, he won't, snap at him today—not when he's so much reason to be grateful.

"I'm *fine*," he says. "You know I love it."

And he does. When he's back at the *Gazette* he switches on, and while the red bulb glows and the lead in the machine heats back to the melting point, he sorts through the copy: magistrate's court reports, then small ads. "All right, Len," he says to the other compositor, already rattling away. "Didja get it, then?" Len asks. "Yep."

"Nice one," says Len peaceably. Alec waits, knowing that he's just on the cusp of concentration, of the state he's going to be in all afternoon long, where the minutes are crammed and stretched but the hours slip by, and for once, because of what Hobson said, he notices himself sitting there and waiting. He looks at the machine deliberately, and the bulk of it before him is as big as a grand piano stood on end, only not made of sleek and glossy wood but all of greased and intricate metal, exhaling fumes. And it delights him, with its thousand visible parts interlocked, and its multitude of pulses attending on his fingers, and its seat in front which amounts to, yes, an industrial throne. He is enthroned. (Green bulb.) He's king of the machine. His vision narrows down to the copy clip, and the keyboard with its ninety keys in grimy black and blue and white. Each key he presses releases a brass letter-mould from the registers above, where they wait in columns long as piano wires. *Click, rattle,* and the brass matrix chinks into place on a steel rail in front of him at eye level. But there's a short but definite physical delay before the matrix arrives, so by the time it arrives he's long pressed the next key and started the next one on its rattling descent. When he gets a good speed up—left hand spidering away over the lower-case, right hand punching out the capitals, both scampering into the centre to hit punctuation and figures—the machine delivers him the moulds in appreciable arrears, still jingling down in reliable right order, but two or three characters or so behind his racing fingers. Which means he can't check where he's got to by looking at the brass row building up, if he's got any pace at all; he has to hold it in his mind, he has to mark his place in the copy by moving his attention along it like a pointer, o-n-e l-e-t-t-e-r a-t a t-i-m-e. At the end of the line, which is the width of a column, he cocks an ear for the end of the jingling metal snowfall, and soon as it stops presses the line-end trigger that sets the rest of the machine into treadling, reciprocating motion. A bar shunts the row of matrices away left in tight order. The first elevator lifts them to be injected with liquid lead (*hiss*), pulls them out (*clunk*). The second elevator lifts them way up to the summit of the machine and threads them to a continuous screw running its width that carries each just as far and no further than its register of origin, where it drops back to the top of the column ready for reuse (*jangle*). But he's not paying attention to that, having long since typed the next line, then the one after that: not paying attention, that is, except to the complex invariable symphony of noises the machine makes when going at full tilt, the *click-rattle-chink-chunk-scree-hiss-whirr-treadle-jangle* it lays down constantly, in rhythms far more overlaid and syncopated than can be set down in linear order. A womb of mechanical noise, to be monitored with some spare fraction of a busy mind, because a variation or blockage in it could be a sign that Mama Linotype is about to squirt molten metal at your legs. That apart, his mind moves on with his fingers as they dance on ETAOIN SHRDLU, the first and commonest letters on the keyboard; and at his left, hot enough to smell, pristine, new-minted, brighter than the brightest silver, there build up in stacked lines of metal all the words that a moment before were only blurry typescript or pen and ink—until Alec, king and alchemist, transformed them.

Val

I'm too old for this, thinks Val, as she clings wearily to Alan's waist, and the scooter buzzes along like a huge wasp, and the air stinks of petrol, and her head aches, and more and more and even more cherry orchards and cows and other rural stuff go by as they file along the A-whatever-it-is with all the rest of the bank holiday traffic.

"All right?" shouts Alan, grinning over his shoulder.

"Yeah, great," she says. She should have insisted on the train. She should have not worn the pink batwinged mohair sweater, which is picking up flying crud from the road, and which Alan slopped tea on the sleeve of when they stopped for a breather at a snack van in a lay-by two hours ago. She should have not said yes in the first place to going to Margate. He's a nice enough lad and they've been smiling at each other in the Co-op for weeks but he's only nineteen; and when she turned up this morning, as arranged, at the garage by the railway arches, it turned out he was, if anything, the oldest one in the little crowd of boys-with-scooters and girls-with-beehives who're going to Margate. She feels middle-aged compared to the sixteen-year-old dollybirds, and don't they let her know it. They're in the middle of a whole excited tribal thing, and she's not dressed right, and they treat her like someone's interloping auntie.

Alan says something, but a lorry overtakes and the words get lost in the grind and the roar.

"What?" she shrieks.

"I said, we're nearly there! Only another coupla miles! But there's this great caff! Where we always stop off for a bite! Fancy it?"

"All right."

"What?"

"Yes! Great! Whatever you like!"

And in fact they and their particular flock of scooters are already pulling off the road into a car park which is, oh of course, absolutely choked with scooters. The caff is a red-brick building the size of a pub, with picture windows and a married couple behind the counter on whose faces can be read the reserved wariness of those who aren't sure about *young people these days*. But they are still selling them egg and chips and beans on toast and orangeade and transparent cups of milky Nescafé as fast as they can get the till to open and close. They are still making a living from the half-crowns and ten-bob notes of the slightly threatening young. She could catch their eye; she won't. Instead she goes to the ladies while Alan's lot fold excitedly into the company of a mob of other kids who look just like them. There are girls jammed in the loo stalls in twos and threes, twittering and laughing, and she has to push to get in front of the mirror to repair her mouth, next to a sneery little madam who's got so much eyeshadow on she looks like a raccoon.

But when she threads her way back out, and locates Alan over by the jukebox, she finds that another lad has come and joined the group. He's sitting on the plastic chair with his knees wide apart, like he doesn't care how much space he claims in the world, even though the caff is burstingly full and it's making everyone else shuffle up. His only responses to what's being said to him are little tilts of his head, and *uh-huh*s and *mmm*s from bruised-looking lips. He's gazing straight ahead into space with his big dark eyes, as if he's bored senseless; and he's beautifully dressed. No, *beautifully*, in a peacock-blue suit with narrow lapels and drainpipes that must have cost him weeks of wages, 'cause it has to have been made to measure. He's got high cheekbones and feathery black hair and a nasty look, and he's the best thing she's seen in basically forever. Neville-the-louse, before he scarpered, did not look this good. Compared to this one, it is suddenly clear that Nev's wide-boy act, which at the time was all too successful at getting him into her knickers, was only a very approximate and second-rate thing. And poor old Alan, for sure, looks as appetising next to him as a piece of tinned ham, well meaning, sweaty, sitting there all pinkly in his Aertex shirt.

"Oh; there you are," says Alan. "Got you a bacon sarnie. This is Mike—turns out he's from Bexford too."

Mmm, says Mike, looking at her.

"Funny that we've never run across him, really, innit," says Alan.

Mmm, says Mike, still looking.

"Yeah," says Val, looking back. "I'd remember."

Mmm, says Mike.

One of the beehive girls snickers.

"Well; right," says Alan, glancing from face to face. "We should be on our way, shouldn't we, pet? If you don't mind eating as you go."

"I'm not hungry," says Val.

"She don't look like anyone's pet," says Mike unexpectedly. "Not to me, mate." His voice is full-on nasal South London, as if it's being broadcast in sawtooth vibrations from a point between his black eyebrows. When he finishes he presses his lips together and curls them.

"Er, anyway . . ." says Alan.

"No. But. Are you, then?" says Mike. "Are you his pet? Are you, like, a budgie? Or one of them little dogs?"

"No," says Val.

Mmm, says Mike.

"I've got a headache," says Val. "Really splitting. In fact."

"Yeah?" says Mike.

"Yes," says Val; and if she could, she'd like to pull the dirty coil of the ache out of the side of her head, and step up to him, and shove it into his forehead with the heel of her hand, just where the words seem to buzz, so that the sick hollow feeling is something they share. So that both their heads are adjacent chambers of queasy vacancy.

"Shame," says Mike, raising his eyebrows. He gets up suddenly, in a movement as bonelessly graceful as if he were on strings like

43

a marionette, and he holds his hand out towards her face. Just for a moment it's like he's read her mind, and he's reaching out with finger and thumb to actually take the headache, too impatient for her to bring it to him. But he isn't. He's holding out a pill to her, blue and triangular.

"Try that, then," he says. "That'll sort you. Maybe."

"Oi!" says Alan, uncertainly.

But she takes the pill and swallows it straight away, dry, without even stopping to think, tasting the chalky coating as she squeezes it down her throat; and Mike, not looking round, raises his empty hand to shoulder height and shakes his finger at Alan behind him, once. *Nu-uh.*

"See ya," he says, and stalks out.

Back on the scooter, Alan's stiff damp back in front of her again, Val attempts a quick conscience check. She doesn't know Alan, not really. She's not his girlfriend. She's not—she just— But they're going downhill, the white boarding-house stucco of Margate is rising around them, there's a grainy glitter ahead that is the sea, and also the pill (whatever it is) is coming on, express-train fast on her empty stomach. The headache is going, oh yes; the headache is a cloud she left behind her some time, some long time ago; the thing she was trying to worry about likewise slid out of view ages back. This is not a day for worrying. The sun is out. The colours on all the parked cars shine as if freshly glazed and enamelled. Wherever she turns her head, something astonishing and fresh and remarkable snags her attention, and sends her off on a circuit of gloriously rapid thought, from which she returns with a start much later, surely much much later, when the next glint from a dry-cleaner's sign or the crisp crisp aspidistra in a window reels her attention back in. With a spring, with a bound, with an elastic snap and thwunk and hurl as if the whole bright world were a pin-table in a pub, and her thoughts were doinging and flying and here-there-here-there-here-there hammering to and fro between rubberoid bumpers. Or—

Alan parks the scooter on a piece of waste ground already crammed with others. She has never noticed before how the branching mirrors on the scooters give back a flitter of light, a mosaic of little reflected samples of everything around, a smashed ocean ingeniously cached in round-cornered dishes on stalks.

"It's all pinball, innit?" she says.

"You what?" says Alan.

"You look like ham," she says, "nice ham and of course I met you in the Co-op but you weren't on the meat counter you were in hardware, what a shame, but to tell you the truth even if you had been I wouldn't fancy you, no offence but there it is."

"What's up with you, girl?" says Alan, blushing.

"She's had a dexy, hasn't she?" says one of the beehive girls.

"I'm having fun, is all," says Val, "first time today to be honest, you know what Alan, Alan, Alan my old mate, you know what, you should lighten up, you should take things with a bit of what's the word, what *is* the word, it's on the tip of my tongue, don'tcha hate it when that happens, it's like a hole in your brain innit, ha ha, mind like a Swiss cheese, me. Or a colander."

"Fuck," says Alan, concisely.

"You should sit her down somewhere, shouldn't you? Get her some tea or something. You can tell she's not used to it."

"We've just got here," says Alan. "I don't want to be a flaming nursemaid. I wanna get down the front. Can't you girls keep an eye on her? Go on."

"You've got a nerve, haven't you? You brought her—you sort her."

"Go on, please. Just for a few minutes. Go on."

The chief beehive girl looks at Alan in disgust, and spits out her gum onto the back of a finger whose nail is lacquered post-box red. Then she sticks it demonstratively onto the seat of the scooter.

"Steady on," says Alan. "Watch out for me upholstery."

"*Upholstery!*" cries Beehive Girl, and she and her mates scream with laughter.

"Hey," says Val, who has been waiting an inconceivable age for this very boring conversation to finish. "Hey. Hey hey hey hey hey. You know what? Fuck *you.*"

"Oh, charming, I'm sure."

"Val—" begins Alan.

But Val, smiling broadly, steps backwards into the crowd surging along the pavement, and that's all she has to do. The bank holiday flow takes her, and Alan's worried face, and the girl's scornful one, recede on the instant, dwindle to pink crumbs, to nothing. Out of sight, out of mind: immediately her eyes are full again with other stuff, and the crowd bumps her along sustainingly, as if an ocean has taken her by both elbows and lifted her off the shingle, with a pluck and a pull and a sway.

There's the real ocean, actually. All the side streets are pouring people down onto the curving road that runs along the front, and where she turns—where she is turned, carried along by the mass—you can see the pier sticking out into the hot blue water and beyond it, the whole curve of Margate Beach, hundreds of yards of it, and all of it thronged with the spicules of human bodies. On the roadway they sway to and fro, loose-woven and relatively fast, holding up the traffic. Out in the sea the crowd frays into individual clumps of bathers, little kids in rubber rings, grannies holding up their dresses as they paddle their bunions. But in between, the people are packed tight and only sluggishly convulsing: tight as the bristles on a brush. Three zones of density, three different kinds of movement. She sees them all with a kind of contented impatience. Anything she looks at, she feels she's been looking at for a long time, too long. She jerks her gaze onwards and as soon as it snags again it's been snagged forever. But she doesn't want to do anything but take in this day in more and more of these dragging instants.

She sees: the gloss on the papier-mâché cheek of Judy as Mr. Punch swings his stick into it in the booth by the pier-end while the watching children roar wail clutch their heads in consternation. She sees: women five years ten years twenty years no years older than her, swabbing babies wiping noses towelling hair passing sandwiches. She sees: sleeping dads angry dads patient dads reading-the-*Racing-Post* dads. She sees: encampments of families arranged in deckchairs unto the third and fourth generation, temporarily connecting again on Margate sands everything they permanently connect at home. She sees: a pat of bright-yellow vanilla ice cream sticking up from the tarmac between its wafers at the angle of the sinking *Titanic*, having dropped from the sticky starfish hand of a child. She sees: the swaying blue-serge bulk of policemen buttoned hotly into their uniform jackets, patrolling along the roadway one heavy leg at a time. She sees: the paler blue nylon shirts of the police reserves, standing round the vans that brought them, waiting for trouble, each topped with a blue-and-silver Noddy helmet where sunlight winks and burns. She sees: the bristles on the high-shaved pigskin necks of the men forty and older who've come to the seaside in their ties and who're loitering around the police vans like supporters' clubs, stubs of fags between forefinger and thumb, waiting for there to be some scandalous disorder, so they can cheer on order's restoration.

And in between all this, greatly outnumbered in the granular mass of needle-people, particle-people, people packed close like cress growing on a windowsill, little rivulets of young men are moving, clumsily, uncertainly, looking for each other and also waiting. For what? Attention. Without attention they grin sheepishly, bump shoulders, wipe their sunglasses, pass chips to each other, and drop them on the beach and pick them up and try to blow the crunching sand grains off them. With it, though—when the families turn to look, or the older men in ties do, or the police start towards them—they seem to know what to do. Activated by disapproval, they perform fighting in little clumps and clusters. They push at each other in wavering rucks. They knock each other down and roll over and over, disturbing the deckchairs and trying to free their arms enough to aim clumsy punches. Here and there, one acquires a bloody nose. Mums tut and stand up; the men in ties shake their heads tightly; the hot policemen wade in and pull the boys away by their collars, with their arms flapping and their shoes dragging runnels through the sand. It's not exciting to watch. It's like the slow heaving as a pan of porridge comes to the boil. A porridge-boil of an event.

But then, in one of the struggling groups, her eye picks out a different kind of movement: someone in peacock blue who is in the ruck but doesn't seem to be weighed down by it, who is moving quickly, precisely, elegantly. What looks like a metal comb glitters at the end of his deft blue arm, and where it goes it cuts and cleaves a path, and the strugglers divide. Looking down over the railings at the edge of the esplanade, Val sees Mike: and pausing momentarily with the chin of a groggy bloke with a quiff tenderly poised on the outstretched upturned fingers of the combless hand, he sees her seeing. He grins. Something twists and tightens under her ribs, something else throbs and loosens in her groin. Time pulls itself together with a start, and instead of passing as a series of frames held in dragging delay, suddenly consents to flow. Flowingly, Mike spins and leans and kicks the groggy boy underneath his chin with a pointed winkle-picker. Something crunches, probably; there's blood, probably; but it's a little way away and the kick flings the bloke off into the melee and he vanishes as if he'd never been, leaving all her attention filled by the neat sweet movement of the kick, and Mike turning back to her like a dancer, his hands theatrically spread, as if to say, d'you like my trick?

She doesn't know. She isn't thinking about it. She likes *him*. And it must show on her fascinated face, because he steps out of the fight, and lightly, swiftly up towards her, slipping the comb into his breast pocket and dusting dab-dab, dab-dab at his peacock lapels, ignoring as if it no longer had anything to do with him the cries rising behind him, and grinning at her still.

"All right?" he says.

"Yes, thanks," she says. "Headache's gone."

"See you got rid of yer bloke, too."

"He's not my bloke," says Val.

"Does he know that?"

"Yeah," says Val. "He definitely does."

"Then," says Mike, "*then* . . ." Big build-up.

"What?" says Val.

"*Then*, milady . . ."

"*What?*" says Val, laughing.

"D'you fancy some chips?"

"Might do," says Val.

"Ah, hard to get, eh?" he says.

"No," she says, looking at his gazelle eyes. "Really not."

Mike, who has been sauntering next to her, bending at waist and wrist and neck in a mannered way that somehow still looks dangerous, stops.

"What's your name?" he says. She tells him. "I like that," he says. "Proper old-fashioned. None of that Yank shit."

He reaches out his long hand with its neatly trimmed nails to her face. Very lightly, he taps the middle of her forehead, and then the end of her nose, and then the divide of her lips.

"What's that in aid of, then?" says Val, and saying the words

49

opens her mouth, lets his nail and his cuticle and his warm dry skin come a tiny way in, resting there on the pillow of her lower lip. Police vans go by; seagulls ice cream carts gabbering families a grunting bus.

"I'm laying a finger on you," says Mike.

She licks the square end of the finger with the very tip of her tongue. Mike blinks.

"Come on, then," he says. And he takes hold of her. But he doesn't put an arm round her waist or kiss her or hold her hand or anything. He grips her elbow, absolutely definitely, and he guides her, absolutely definitely, off the busy esplanade and up the first side street and off it into a quieter street of little shops, and off that into an alleyway between pebble-dash walls which has got nothing in it but some bins.

"What?" she says, breathless, half-laughing. "What're we—"

But he just puts his hands on her shoulders, absolutely definitely, and pushes her down onto her knees in front of him, on the ground by the bins.

"Yeah?" he says.

She doesn't know what she's supposed to be agreeing to. This is weirdly unlike the known behaviour of interested men. All the others have wanted to touch, to turn handsy, to get in close and slide damp anxious mitts inside her clothes. Neville-the-louse was all hot breath in her ear. But Mike, for whom she has a yes that for the first time might have matched a man for handsy greed, leans back, away from her and out of reach, with his blue shoulders back against the pebble-dash, and his beautiful face averted, and his legs braced, as if he only wants to come near her with the one part of him, the one point of attachment where the pleasures of bank holiday Monday have dilated him and driven him out to meet her. He brings his hips forward and puts a hand on the back of her head and—oh. He wants to push something into her head.

It doesn't take very long. It's salty, like blood, but with a flat taste, like iron.

Mike produces a matching handkerchief to give her, and zips himself up.

"Thanks, love," he says. "Now, what about those chips?"

Vern

Maybe he should have gone for the Café Royal? Vern quails as the taxi door opens, and it suddenly seems a long way across the pavement to the steps of Tognozzi's, and a total toss-up whether McLeish will even get the point of the kind of understated, cripplingly expensive, visited-by-the-Queen poshness that this place represents. Footballers know about the Café Royal. They get taken there with their wives by the management when they win the Cup. There's gold leaf, and bottles of bubbly going *fwoosh*, and a picture for the paper. It's their idea of quality, isn't it—of the high life? Yeah, he should have taken him there; or to do a bit of that kind of nightclubbing where posh meets gangland. Except that subbing McLeish to play baccarat in Soho would mean, potentially, anything happening, at God-knows-what kind of expense that Vern couldn't afford. This is all carefully costed, carefully budgeted and scraped together: his one shot at creating the impression of careless, glad-handing wealth. It's much too late to rethink now. *Just don't cock it up*, he tells himself. Bulky in powder blue with dazzling white cuffs, attended by an aggressive cloud of aftershave, he bustles to the restaurant doorway, McLeish in tow.

"Reservation for one o'clock. Name of Taylor," he tells the

maître d' lurking just within. And he doesn't try to posh up the voice, to hide the South London in it. Nah, the opposite. Vern *can* do officer-class if he wants. It was one of the unexpected perks of national service, that, getting to listen from the kitchens as an assortment of Ruperts and Hugos in the officers' mess modelled the vowel sounds of the Home Counties over and over again: but here and now, elocution is definitely not called for. What's needed is the upward bounce of common-as-muck talent, utterly unapologetic, shoving into the sanctum with its elbows out. Look at him! He could be . . . a barrow-boy photographer shaking up fashion! A lairy young advertising genius! A record company A&R man with his finger on the beat pulse! A junior film producer dashing into the West End from Pinewood! An exec on the rise in commercial telly! He is none of those things: but, as Vern reminds himself under his breath, *they don't know that.*

"Certainly, Mr. Taylor," says the flunkey, having located the name in a bookings book like the kind of photograph album you'd have if your surname was pronounced Chumley or Fanshaw. "Mario will take you down. Enjoy your lunch, gentlemen."

"Spiffing," says Vern flatly, and takes a step or two after the more junior flunkey who is leading the way to the spiral stairs. But, he realises, he has somehow shed McLeish, and when he looks back, from the opulent dimness of the stairwell to the portal fringed with the silhouettes of petals dangling from window boxes, where the daylight of St. James's glares, he sees his guest hesitating just outside. McLeish is glancing up at the facade with his shoulders hunched, doing that unnecessary fiddling with his jacket buttons that always means nerves. Maybe this isn't the wrong choice after all, if he can read this place well enough to be afraid of it. And now Vern can give him the pleasure of stopping being afraid of it.

"Come on, Joe!" he calls over his shoulder. "They won't eatcher!"

And McLeish follows, with a slight duck of the head as he pierces the marmoreal force field of the maître d' but a promising, faint, half-guilty smile on his face.

The downstairs of Tognozzi's is a long subterranean vault, with traces of the art deco jazz den it used to be pre-war, when aristos and blackshirts and aristos who *were* blackshirts did the charleston down here on glass-smooth parquet. But Mayfair good taste has flowed over it since, like a bland and floral tide. It's all white linen now, with little bunches of freesias on the little round tables. Vern feels big as the waiter fits them into little gilt chairs not far from the foot of the stairs: but then Vern feels big everywhere. It's just a fact of life. He waited and waited for growing up to turn him into one of those gracile kids with the spindly legs, but no matter how tall he got, and he's six-two now, he expanded in proportion. At any height, he was always going to be a big, square block of meat, with sharp little eyes in a face as wide as a shield. He goes to the old gym on the Bexford High Road now, not so much for the sparring, which just makes him sweat and pant, as for the hours on the bag and the speedball. He couldn't chase someone up the street but if they'd consent to get in reach he could flatten 'em. And his size has this going for it: it confers a bit of presence, of authority almost, and thus compensates for his age somehow. People don't see he's twenty-three. They see he's *considerable.*

The waiter brings them red menus that also look like heirlooms of the Chumley-Fanshaws. McLeish gives off new signs of alarm as he grips his. The menu's in French, of course. But, again, God bless the Army Catering Corps; God bless watching sergeant-chefs laboriously typing out the mess dinner menu in the Limassol heat. M-i-l-l-e-f-e-u-i-l-l-e-s with sweaty fingers.

"'S amazing the fuss they make in these places, innit?" says Vern, deliberately. "I mean, that top one's liver, and then it's a steak, and then halibut, and then a lobster."

53

"Yeah," says McLeish, and his wrists relax, and his quick black eyes stop darting anxiously about. "Yeah . . ."

"I dunno why they can't just say so."

"Right, right," says McLeish. "You know, I've never ate a lobster."

Fuck, thinks Vern, acutely conscious of the finite contents of the wallet in his left trouser pocket.

"Go on, then," he says. "Now's your chance. They'll do a lovely job of it here, with all your special French sauces for it, and the special cutlery to get in through the shell and that." Held breath.

"Nah," says McLeish. "D'you know what, I'll just have the steak."

"Good plan. Me too," says Vern. He calls the waiter. "Two entrecôtes, please, medium rare, and we'll have a bottle of the sixty-two Côtes du Rhône. If that suits you, Joe?"

"Fine, yeah," says McLeish; and now that the crisis is past, and the waiter is safely receding, and it's clear that he's not going to be caught out failing to understand something, he leans back on the tight little golden throne and spreads his big thighs, and cracks his neck-bones, and lifts his long jaw, and looks about himself, prepared to be entertained. A good-looking lad: black brush of hair, and blue-white London Scots pallor in his skin. "It's quite something down here, isn't it?"

"It surely is," says Vern. "More dukes and duchesses than you can shake a stick at in here. Nob central. And they get famous people and all coming in."

"Yeah?" says McLeish. "Like who?"

"Well, there's you," says Vern, grinning.

"Shut up!" says McLeish, and of course he's right; he's not famous in any way that would compute or even register in a place like this. He's a second-string striker in a fourth-division club, and the Millwall only signed him ten months ago. For a little less than a year he's experienced a strictly local and limited celebrity down in Bexford, New Cross, Bermondsey, where dockers will buy him pints at the price of telling him in exhaustive detail every single foot the team have put wrong this season, and their daughters will give him the eye on Saturday night. But he likes it, this piss-taking by Vern with a dash of flattery thrown in. And he's got used enough, you can see, to the little bit of extra female attention that here too he's glancing around, probably automatically, to see if he's causing any flutters. Nothing doing: the younger ones of the ladies lunching in Tognozzi's today are sleek Mayfair types in their thirties, with their court shoes and their collarless jackets and their thoroughbred knees pressed together slantwise as they laugh. All McLeish's optimistic gaze gets back is an occasional display of nostril. Well, that's not quite true. A couple of nancy-boys on the other side of the staircase who look as if they've just woken up are enjoying him, but best not to point that out.

"All right, the Queen, then."

"For real?"

"Yep. Real and royal."

"Blimey," says McLeish.

"*And* you. Her Majesty—and you."

"Shut *up!*" says McLeish. He is nineteen years old. "My mum'll have a fit when I tell her that."

"Good," says Vern benignly, the bestower of mum-worthy boasts, the founder of the feast.

And, right on time, the waiter is back with a bottle which he splashes into the wine glass on Vern's side for testing—sagacious nod—and then there's the ceremonial pouring, the filling of the water glasses, a ritual of crystal vibrations and gurgles in the face of which McLeish falls silent again.

"Cheers," says Vern firmly. They knock glasses together.

Then, while McLeish is cautiously sampling his mouthful, Vern leans forward, drops his voice and says:

"She might've sat in that very chair. You could be right on top of the royal arse-print."

McLeish chokes and ducks his head.

"Steady on," says Vern. "Don't cough up the vino. It's a quid a bottle."

"You can't bloody say that," hisses McLeish. "Not . . . *here*." He is definitely blushing, and he is darting looks out to left and right as if the Posh Police will imminently step out of the shadows and grab him.

"I bloody can," says Vern. (Though he is himself observing strict volume control, and keeping an eye out for trouble.) "And what's more, I bloody should."

"What d'you mean?"

"I mean," says Vern, leaning back so that his powder-blue lapels and his gleaming bri-nylon shirt, collar size 19, and his turquoise silk tie, together fill McLeish's vision like a cliff face of confidence, "that all this stuff down here—these people—this place—it's all very nice, but it's basically over. It's the *past*, innit. And I'm not bothered about the past. I'm for the future. Look around'jer. Who's the future, down here, eh? I'll tell you, it's not bloody them. It's us. Who's the future? *We are*."

The look he gives McLeish is fierce and full-on. It's the one the speedball in the gym has been on the receiving end of. The boy squirms, but he also swells. He's excited.

Enter the steaks. They come with button mushrooms, round and rubbery, which McLeish abandons when the first one he tries to capture bounces off onto the tablecloth, trailing juices. But the meat yields tenderly to the knife, and emboldened by Vern's speech he ignores the mushroom, chews, swigs the red wine, and actually makes the next move himself.

"So, you're gonna be opening restaurants, then, Vern?"

"Absolutely," says Vern. "Something a bit more modern than

this, I can tell you. Light and air and none of the oh-I-say-how-quaint, if you know what I mean?"

McLeish nods, grins.

"But that's Phase Two. I've got to build up to that. Conquer the world in stages, that's the plan. First comes bricks and mortar. Houses—you can't go wrong with houses, 'cause everyone needs them, right?"

He takes out his wallet and passes McLeish a large cream-coloured business card. GROSVENOR INVESTMENTS, it says, the most solid-sounding name he could think of, with the address of an office over a chip shop on East Bexford Hill.

"You're gonna build houses?" says McLeish.

"Well, not yet. Buy 'em and rent 'em out, that's the plan."

"You mean you'll be a landlord?" McLeish sounds disappointed. More than that—disapproving. "My dad says landlords are all bloodsuckers. Like that Rachman? I saw in the paper where he was setting these great big dogs on little kiddies?"

"No no no no," says Vern swiftly. "All that's over. The new law they just done, that's finished all that stuff off; cleaned it right up." Also, incidentally, the Rent Act has put paid to the kind of fly-by-night building societies from which it would have been much easier for someone like Vern, starting up without any capital, to get his hands on mortgages. But he doesn't say that. He says: "That's my opportunity, you see. All the crooks and the bloodsuckers, they're out of the landlord game, because you can't make money out of it any more."

"But . . . don't you wanna make money out of it?"

"Yes, I do," Vern says. "Yes, I *will*. Because I've got an angle. Think of Bexford High Street, think of the New Cross Road. Think of the middle of Deptford and Lewisham. How many houses there have got a flat upstairs and a shop downstairs? I'll tell you: *thousands* of them. Literally thousands. You can buy them dirt cheap. And who gets the rent from the shop, as well as the rent from the flat? The landlord. Doesn't matter if the old dear upstairs is only paying pennies, bless her. Because the Rent Act doesn't cover the downstairs, it doesn't make the rules for shops. So the money coming in from the shop, right, that's your little gold mine; and it pays for buying the whole property, and then the next one, and the next one, and the next one, till before you know it you own the whole bloody street."

"I dunno," says McLeish uneasily. Vern can practically see the thought he's having. He's picturing Bexford's array of sad butcher's shops, seedy corner groceries, shonky second-hand furniture dealers and mildewed newsagents, and finding it a stretch to believe there's any kind of gold mine to be found in any of them. "I thought it would be something a bit more, you know, *new*. Something, like you said, more—er . . ."

"It *is*," Vern insists. "What this is is the start. On an ordinary street, in an ordinary shop what no one else has seen the potential of. But then, yeah, then comes the exciting stuff. Then comes the shopping centres, and the office blocks, and the—the bloody skating rinks, and the casinos. And the skyscrapers!"

"In *Bexford*," says McLeish. "You wanna build skyscrapers, in *Bexford*?"

"Why the bloody hell not?" says Vern: and then they're both laughing, but it's good laughter, it's audacious laughter, and the ghost of a glorious skyline south of the river lingers in the air.

The waiter appears without being asked, and pours the rest of the wine into their glasses. He takes his time, with some fancy-work where he twists the bottle to catch drips, and flourishes his white cloth about the place. McLeish cools, sits more anxiously again. "Would you two gentlemen like another bottle?" says the waiter. No, bugger off. "No thanks," says Vern, waving him away with a big pink hand.

"So you see"—plunging on before the mood can be lost—"it starts small, it starts practical, but it *is* the future we're talking about. My future; maybe yours too. Because, a lad in your position, you've gotta be asking yourself what comes next, right?"

"That's what my dad keeps saying."

"Sounds like a wise man," says Vern lightly, smoothly, preparing to bounce on with this family testimonial incorporated into the pitch. But McLeish has put down his knife and fork, hunched his shoulders up, and twisted his face into a grimace Vern doesn't realise immediately is supposed to be an imitation of someone.

"Och, think aboot yir future, Joe!" says McLeish in sudden parodic Glaswegian—baritone, geriatric, phlegmy, smoker's-cough Glaswegian, with rumbling pops under it like a Geiger counter gone rogue. "The footie's no' a bad wee racket while yir young, but whit aboot whan yir knees gi' way, eh? Whit aboot whan yir twenty-five and yir bosses think yir an auld man, eh? Whir'll the money come from *then*, eh, tae keep ye in yir shiny wee suit and tie?"

The mimicry is sharper than Vern would have guessed the boy was capable of, and he also can't quite read the level of resentment in it.

"Bit of a ray of sunshine, then, is he?" he says, playing it safe with all-purpose irony.

"Oh, he's not wrong," says McLeish, sighing. "He's just so bloody *pleased* about it."

"What does he think you should do, then, after?"

"Go on the trains, like him. Settle down. 'It's guid work—unless ye think yir tae guid for't.'"

"And you don't fancy it." Safe ground now, for who at nineteen at the beginning of their adventure, their sudden flight, would welcome the thought of crashing back to earth.

"Not much, no."

"Well, you could certainly do better."

"Yeah?"

"Yeah! Course you could. D'you mind me asking how much they've got you on at the moment?" Vern of course knows the answer to this question, to the penny. Finding it out was one of the most important parts of setting today up.

McLeish looks wary, as anticipated.

"Why d'you wanna know?" he says.

"Just as a for-instance. But don't worry, I don't wanna pry. Lemme guess, all right? I'm thinking . . . about . . . thirty quid a week?"

Flattery. The players' strike three years back, also a vital precondition for this conversation, has removed the wage cap that applied for decades, but Millwall isn't rich, and McLeish isn't much of a star yet, and they've got his youth as an excuse, so he's on twenty-six pounds ten shillings right now.

"Thereabouts, yeah," says McLeish.

"Not bad," says Vern. "Good for you. But you know what? In essence, in the final analysis, when it comes right down to it: chickenfeed, son."

"You what?" says McLeish, not sure whether to laugh or be offended.

"I mean obviously, compared to British Rail, that's excellent. Compared to what you could be getting, with the world"—he circles the spectacle of wealth that surrounds them with a finger—"just ripe to be given a squeeze, if you know how; compared to *that*, you're on poverty pay, mate. You haven't got two bob to rub together, really."

"I've got enough that you want some!" says McLeish.

"Pardon?" says Vern, allowing a wrinkle of confusion to appear midway across the slab of his forehead.

"I've got enough that you're after me to put some money in your—you know." McLeish is tapping the business card on the tablecloth.

"What—you think I want you to *invest?*"

"Yeah?"

"Oh Lord," says Vern, trying to look both apologetic and amused (but not too insultingly amused). "No! Oh dear, oh dear. Total cross purposes there, mate. No no no; I've got my backing all lined up. That's all in hand, and to be honest it's coming outta pockets a lot deeper'n yours. No offence."

"You don't want any money from me?"

"No. Obviously I haven't been very clear; sorry 'bout that."

"Then—what . . .?" asks McLeish.

Vern tuts his tongue, and looks modestly down. "Well," he says, rubbing at a non-existent spot on the tablecloth with a forefinger, "I was going to lead up to this, you know, subtly. But fat chance of that, eh. All I'm after—"

At this point he looks up, to give McLeish as planned a double eyeful of sincerity. But instead his gaze snags on a sight behind the boy's head. There, stepping off the spiral stairs with a couple of brilliantined continental smoothies in attendance, is a face he last saw minuscule and fifty feet below him on the Covent Garden stage, pouring out song that soared to the six-shilling seats in the gods, and took him by the heart, and twisted. She looks older without the tragic-heroine outfit, and her face is unfamiliar in its mild off-duty sociability. But it's her. Just there, a few feet away. That woman, there, is the key to a compartment of feeling inside him that he keeps secure even from himself. When he gives himself the opera, he doesn't let the left hand know what the right hand is doing. He goes behind his own back. He slopes off on the quiet to the West End with his own mind averted from the certain knowledge that later he'll be wiping his eyes with his hanky, he'll be sitting up under the golden roof at Covent Garden leaking silently down both cheeks. His eyes prickle now.

He should be launching into this lunchtime's patiently developed *coup de grâce*. All the goads of greed and humiliation and flattery have been deployed. It's time to close. And, somewhere far off, he is still talking. McLeish is nodding. But it's as if Vern has split. A Vern kept locked privately away, a Vern who trembles at beauty, a Vern who does not know what he wants or how to get it, a Vern tenderly incapable, has with truly terrible timing emerged to divide the attention of the Vern who needs at this minute to be driving events to their destined destination with as hard a hand as he possibly can. Out of the chrysalis of the usual him has crept this damp-winged other Vern, who only wants to stare. Who wants to hang his mouth open and gawp. Who doesn't want to speak the lines insisted on by the plausible fat man in the blue suit. Who almost resents him, in fact, with his grubby little scheme. And meanwhile the Vern who has worked so hard is feeling hollow indeed. His strength is failing, his energy is dipping, his delivery of the last part of the pitch going from fiery to watery. Where's the conviction? Where's the belief he should be infecting McLeish with? Gone AWOL. Distractedly lingering over the sight of the diva being served consommé on the other side of the room.

"So, right, it's just your name I wanna borrow," he is saying. "People know you, and I wanna use that to raise the profile of the firm; give it a bit of glamour, while I get it going. If I can do that, I'll put you on the books and give you a cut. Which could be worth a lot, later. When I'm doing the skyscrapers." Ghost of a joke at the end there, but that's got to be the limpest attempt at a closing ever recorded. Surely no one would go for it. Fat chance, Vern. Fat chance. His wavering gaze slips off McLeish's face, and past it: past it so obviously that McLeish can't help but notice.

"Fuck," breathes Vern, more in despair than in awe.

McLeish turns his head to see what the big attraction is. But all he can see is a skinny, foreign-looking woman in her forties with black hair. When he looks back, he finds that Vern has put his hand over his face and is looking at the world through the gaps between the bars of his fat pink fingers.

"What?" he says, somehow compelled to drop his voice to a churchgoing whisper.

"You know I said you get famous people here," says Vern very quietly. "Well, that's one of them. That's Maria Callas."

"Sorry, I dunno who that is," says McLeish.

"She's a singer. She's—how can I put this?" *Her vocal cords are like Bobby Charlton's feet*, he ought to say, or something like that, something pat and funny that will make sense of her to McLeish. But he doesn't want to. He doesn't want to connect these two worlds up; he doesn't want to build any kind of jokey bridge between what he feels when Callas sings "Vissi d'arte" and what he's doing here today. They don't match. He doesn't want them to match. "She's . . . amazing," he says lamely.

"You're a fan, ain'tcha?" says McLeish. The boy is smiling at him. Not scornfully—kindly. Encouragingly. It occurs to Vern that McLeish has probably seen the odd person go tongue-tied and shy when meeting *him*. "You know what, you should go and say hello. G'wan. Now's your chance. She won't mind."

"No."

Coaxingly: "Go on!"

"*No.*"

McLeish holds his hands up in mock-surrender, looking indulgent and puzzled. "Fair enough, fair enough. No one's gonna make yer."

He looks at his chunky steel watch.

"I should get going, really, Vern. So—just my name? No money?"

"None."

"And you won't be doing any of that Rack-man stuff? Nothing dodgy?"

"No."

"All right, then. Don't see what I've got to lose."

"Great," says Vern. "That's . . . great. I've got some papers for you to sign, then."

"Okey-doke," says McLeish. "Gotta pen?"

Vern has a pen. Vern passes McLeish the pen, and McLeish obediently signs there, there, there and there, without stopping, just as Vern would have been busting a gut to induce him to do if he were not in this enfeebled state. Consequently, without McLeish noticing that what he signed on page three was a mortgage guarantee.

"There!" says McLeish. "Fingers crossed, maybe you'll keep me off British Rail. Cheers, Vern."

Vern pays the bill and McLeish leads the way back up the stairs, past the flunkeys, through the mystic portal of wealth, out again blinking into London daylight. Vern does not look back at Miss Callas. Vern uses his last pound note to send McLeish off in a taxi. Wave, wave.

Then he totters away towards the bus stop. He feels very tired. He only has the sixpence left he needs to go home to Bexford on the number 29, and it takes an age, but somewhere along the way, around Waterloo, it begins to sink in that it worked. This morning he wasn't a property developer. Now he is. He stops trembling. At the Elephant and Castle, a gaggle of schoolboys boil up onto the top deck towards his seat at the front but he gives them the look the speedball gets and they retreat. About halfway up the Walworth Road, he starts to whistle bits from *Tosca* under his breath, badly.

Ben

The mist has lifted from the tussocky outer field. Now, instead of the bare trees rising from whorls of slow white, Ben sees from the tall ward window that each stands in a ragged oval of leaf-fall, summer's discarded yellow petticoat. A few last leaves, small as halfpennies or candle flames, cling on to twigs, tugged at by the wind. The Largactil affects a lot of things but not Ben's sight. He can see these fluttering holdouts as clearly across a hundred yards as he'd be able to pick out the separate grains in a palm-ful of seashore sand. (They say it's all one colour but it's not, it's got orange in it, and chocolate brown, and stray flecks of bottle green.) He'd like to stay by the window till the wind plucks one down at least—loses the halfpenny, snuffs the candle flame, sends the yellow speck twinkling end over end to land, indistinguish-able, in the shadow of colour the bare tree casts.

He has resisted Sid-the-postman's constant invitations to play ping-pong.

"No, th-th-th-thanks," he says every time, letting go of his left hand with his right hand, and holding it up to show the tremor. "T-too sh-sh-shaky."

Also too s-s-s-*slow*. They had tried a match once, and with Sidney bouncing about on one side of the table and him on the other extending his shaking bat to return the serve at roughly the pace of a glacier, a Parkinsonian glacier, it could not be called a success.

"Oh, right!" says Sid, equally surprised each time. "Right right right. Gotta ciggy, mate?"

"Mm," says Ben. He does. He lowers two fingers into his

65

shirt pocket and traps a bent Gold Leaf between them. "There y-you . . . *are*."

"Thanks!" says Sid. "You're a pal." He puts it between his lips, mouths it, thinks better of it; sticks it behind his ear, thinks better of it; puts it between his lips, thinks better of it; puts it down on the tabletop next to where Ben is sitting by the window. Goes off to try to tempt Mr. Neave into ping-pong instead.

Ben tilts himself to get the Gold Leaf centred in his vision and dispatches a patient hand in its direction, a wobbling probe elongating and growing less convincingly his own as it gets further away. Yet by a process of adjustments and corrections, he closes in on it, he pins it down, he retrieves it. He brings it all the way back to his pocket and drops it in, ready for the next time Sid asks.

Is this time-consuming? He couldn't say. It does not seem to leave him with less time for gazing at the trees, any more than Mr. Neave's interruptions do, when he comes over to Ben and, tapping on his knee for attention, lays out his documents on the table. Always the explanations, with Mr. Neave. The slightly patronising smile, the reminder that he is an educated man, a trained solicitor, who can consequently be expected to perceive more, to understand more, than a simple bus conductor such as Ben. ("No offence taken, I trust? None intended, my dear fellow.") It is true that Ben does not follow the web of implications Mr. Neave draws from arranging the last letter he had from his wife next to the reply he had from the hospital's chairman when he appealed to him under Section 26 of the Mental Health Act 1959. Or that he quite sees why Mr. Neave then deals out in a circle surrounding them an ever-varying mixture of library fine notices, old menus from the notice-board and certificates from the Gardening Club. It is also true that he does not try very hard. All Mr. Neave needs is a nod and a frown from time to time. Otherwise you can go on gazing at the trees.

Largactil congeals time. It makes everything seem to move very slowly, from one point of view, and yet to make great expanses of time slide by with undetectable sameness, until one day you look out of the ward window, and suddenly it isn't summer. Ben doesn't know how long he has been here. Many days, that's for sure; and he doesn't think he has ever seen the leaves fall before. But thinking about this is difficult, because thinking about anything is difficult on Largactil. It swathes your thoughts, it muffles them, it swaddles them up, as if they were all wrapped in dustsheets like furniture in an empty room: still there, underneath, but with their hard edges and definite outlines all hidden, and difficult to get at, without a great deal of determined fumbling.

And why would you want to do that? Because muffled away under one of those heavy, shapeless wrappings is The Trouble. It has not gone. All the time Ben is awake it can still be heard as a remote muttering, mercifully indistinct. If it were allowed out, Ben is sure, it would swell right back into the horrible, unstoppable circuit of thoughts that had taken over his mind before he came to hospital. Vile link after vile link in a vile chain, going round and round, round and round, never stopping. With nowhere to go to get away from it, because how can you ever get away from your own head; and impossible to turn away from, because how can you turn your back on something frightening? It isn't safe to turn your back on the dark thing, the thing that walks beside you on the road. Only you are the road, and you are the dark thing too. It's confusing. Best not to think about it. Even to glance at it like this makes the muttering louder. Naming calls: so don't name it, don't look, don't think. And Largactil makes this possible.

Ben doesn't like everything here. He doesn't like the nights in the dormitory, with Mr. Neave's mews of distress in the bed to his left, and Derek from the next dormitory bursting in, in search of something Mr. Neave has borrowed, and upending Mr. Neave's collection of borrowings all over the hard floor with a clatter.

"Give me back my Vosene, you bastard!"

"It's not—no, no—hands off—oh, how can you? I need it. I need it. Oh, Primrose, they won't leave me *alone*."

In the bed on his right Mr. Corcoran breathes angrily. Mr. Corcoran is never not angry, waking or sleeping, and Mr. Neave does not borrow anything from him. Mr. Corcoran transferred here from Broadmoor, and Nurse Fredericks has read something about him in the *Daily Mirror*. They keep him dosed up day and night. Dull reddish-blue tides of fury crawl under the bristles of his face.

It's worth it, though, all this is easily worth it, to keep The Trouble wrapped away. Largactil is a kind of bliss that Ben is steadily grateful for. He totters to the OT Room and (very slowly) makes raffia baskets and wobbly pots. He eats pork luncheon meat and baked beans followed by blancmange. He goes outside when the weather is sunny. He tries not to worry about the back wards, glimpsed on his way to the vestibule for outings, where lost souls in too-short pyjamas drift in madness decades deep—and Largactil helps him with that, too. He sits by the window and watches the trees.

Look: each stands in a ragged oval of leaf-fall, summer's discarded yellow petticoat.

But there are some things you can't avoid.

"C'mon, Ben, ward round," says Nurse Fredericks, a large kind tired man who gives out jumpers his wife has knitted, and who has only ever been observed to give anyone a slap under extreme provocation.

"Mm?"

Mostly ward rounds involve the doctors conferring with the nurses about who's been prescribed what, and how they've been behaving. Only occasionally are the patients directly involved.

"They want you in Room 3."

"Mm?"

"I don't know why. Up you get, young man. Chop-chop."

When Ben reaches Room 3, just beyond OT, he discovers with a slow coiling of unease that it is full of people. A horseshoe of chairs has been set out, with an empty one at the head of the horseshoe, next to the briskly smiling Dr. Armstrong: Ben's doctor, in theory, though he has scarcely ever spoken to her. All the other chairs have medical students in them, an unmistakable array of white-coated boys (and a few girls) with notebooks and biros. They must be about the same age as Ben but they gaze at him as if he were a member of a different species. The only reassuring face in the room belongs to Nurse Fredericks, who follows Ben in and, finding that he himself hasn't been given a chair, leans against the closed door, his shoulders outlined against the wire squares in the door glass like a graph of an Alp.

"Now," says Dr. Armstrong brightly, as Ben shuffles across the lino, "this is Mr. Holcombe. Mr. Holcombe is a voluntary patient. Age twenty-two, employment since leaving school as a kitchen porter and then bus conductor. He presented six—no, seven—months ago at his GP's in a state of extreme agitation, asking, quote, 'to be put to sleep.' Questioning elicited no apparent prior history of depression, but complaints of persecution by intrusive thoughts, possibly amounting to auditory hallucination. Diagnosis?" she asks the room.

He is being used as a teaching aid.

"Schizophrenia," says a confident boy with sideburns.

"Correct," says Dr. Armstrong. "But with the usual reservations—yes?—about the breadth of the schizophrenic syndrome and its failure to offer fine classification of specific conditions."

They all write in their notebooks.

"Admitted eighth of June 1964. Initial dose of 400mg chlorpromazine. Trade name?"

"Largactil," says a girl with a brown plait.

"Or Thorazine, yes. Increased to 500mg when agitation persisted, then successful maintenance at 300mg per day thereafter. Behaviour?"

This last question is directed to Nurse Fredericks.

"Ben is no trouble at all," he says. "As good as gold."

"I'm glad to hear it," says the doctor. "And how do you find yourself, Mr. Holcombe."

"F-f-f-fine," Ben manages to say.

"Excellent," says Dr. A. "But gentlemen, ladies, what do you *observe*? You've seen Mr. Holcombe walk, you've heard him speak, you can see how he's sitting. Thoughts?"

They all stare at him. The girl with the plait taps her biro against her teeth. A small, slight Indian student, neat and brown and feathery-eyebrowed, like a sparrow you could pop into your pocket, clears his throat and says: "Tic in his right hand. Quite pronounced."

"Indeed," says Armstrong, and as if her approval had granted everyone permission, they all start to offer suggestions.

"Gait ataxia?"

"Parkinsonism?"

"He keeps sticking his tongue out?"

"Frequent blinking?"

"T-t-t-"

That last one is Ben, trying to say *tardive dyskinesia*, which is what he saw written on his notes when they were left facing him at the nurses' station. He doesn't know what it means and he knows he's not supposed to join in, but the urge to surprise them all is too strong. In fact, though, since he can't get the word out, all they hear is another symptom.

"Speech difficulties!" says Plait Girl triumphantly.

"Mm-hm," agrees Dr. Armstrong. "All symptoms which, if we

didn't already know Mr. Holcombe's medical history, might lead us to suspect—what?"

"Cerebral palsy," suggests the Indian student.

"Yes, or Huntington's chorea. We'd be testing for both of those if Mr. Holcombe presented himself like this for an initial consultation. And yet—and this is what I want you all really to notice—*there is nothing organically wrong with Mr. Holcombe at all.* Every single one of these symptoms is a secondary effect of neuroleptic medication. Mr. Holcombe is a healthy young man. It is chlorpromazine that has done this to him. Yes, Mr. Patel?"

The Indian student has raised his hand.

"He has been unlucky, I think. These symptoms would usually take longer to come on, and affect older patients more?"

"Indeed. Only about thirty per cent of patients have these reactions, and Mr. Holcombe is one of the unfortunates within that percentage who exhibit them particularly strongly." She holds up a finger. "Remember, please, that this is ordinary. Rare outcomes are not outcomes that never happen. They are outcomes that happen all the time to a few people. And as clinicians, we must expect to encounter these people, and to be prepared to care for them."

Scribble, scribble, in all the notebooks.

"So, how shall we care for Mr. Holcombe? The tics, the impeded movement, the interrupted speech: I said there was nothing wrong with him (apart, of course, from the schizophrenia itself) but it would have been more accurate to say that there was nothing wrong with him *yet*. Because . . . ?"

"Because the symptoms can become permanent."

"Thank you, Mr. Patel. So what should we do for Mr. Holcombe? Recommendations?"

"We could switch him to a different medication?"

"Such as, Miss Edwards?"

Plait Girl looks down; she doesn't know.

"Well," says Dr. Armstrong, "we could try him on Fluphenazine or Acepromazine, true, but they are from the same family of drugs, and they all produce the same side effects, and we know that Mr. Holcombe has an elevated susceptibility. Anyone else?"

Patel coughs questioningly, but no one else wants to speak.

"We must taper off his dose, quickly?" he says.

"N—!" says Ben. "N—!"

The noise he has made is more a groan than a word. The doctor frowns at him, but gives him a pat on the arm and goes on talking.

"I think so,' yes," she says. "Not *too* quick a decrease, but a prompt one, in the first place to a much lower maintenance dose, with perhaps some conventional sedatives if the psychotic crisis shows any signs of returning. But you've had a nice quiet few months, haven't you, Mr. Holcombe?" she says kindly, raising her voice as if speaking to a deaf person. "Time to get you home again. You don't belong *here*."

It is possible to be afraid on Largactil, Ben finds. Angry, too. If the emotion is strong enough, it sweeps through the room with the muffled furniture, bumping it and rattling it like a wind, throwing it to and fro while your heart bangs. He throws off Dr. Armstrong's hand—she wouldn't smile at him if she knew what The Trouble murmured to him—and pushes to his feet.

"No!" he bellows thickly, his tongue getting in the way like something half-swallowed. "Naow!"

The students avert their eyes. Armstrong sighs. This is not how she wanted her little demonstration to end.

"Fredericks?" she says. The nurse moves forward, irresistible, and takes Ben by the back of the neck with one wide hand.

"No need for that, son," he says. "Calm down, now, calm down."

"Maybe give him his next dose now, and start the taper tomorrow," she commands. Fredericks nods, and has him out of the door in seconds.

"Honestly!" says the nurse. "This ain't like you at all."

Ben is used to getting his Largactil as foul-tasting syrup in a little beaker. But now it arrives as an injection in his arm, and from the place in his vein where the needle goes in, calm does spread with astonishing immediacy, a blanking numbness that freezes all the rattling contents of his head in place as if they'd never move again, and wipes away too—for now, at least—all the terrors of the future, all that will need to be endured again in solitude.

"You have a sit in your chair," says Nurse Fredericks, "and I'll get you a nice cup of tea."

Look: each tree stands in a ragged oval of leaf-fall, summer's discarded yellow petticoat.

Jo

In the wings at the Pelican Club. Well; the wings. The "artists' entrance" to the Pelican, so-called, is up a Soho alley that smells of men's piss and indeterminate rotting things, in between an Italian grocer's selling spaghetti in long blue paper packets and one of those doorways with many bells where shamefaced men come and go without meeting anyone's eye. You go up the alley, and a door lets you downstairs into a warren of little backstage spaces, many with black bundles of cable snaking about on the floors. Jo changed into her Tearaways outfit in a narrow slot halfway between a dressing room and a corridor, with mirrors in horseshoes of light bulbs on one side but people coming and going behind, and not much privacy. And the wings are another compromise, an L-shaped leftover tucked next to the stage, where people do wait to go on, but where there are also dead amplifiers stacked, and cardboard boxes of flyers for gigs past and gigs yet to come. Part of the roof of the L is made of the green glass bricks that run right across above the stage itself, letting in a watery aquarium light from the pavement outside the front of the Pelican, when it's daytime. Go on early at the Pelican, in the summer, and the glare coming at you from the spots competes with a rainy glitter draped over your hair and shoulders like jewellery.

It's fully dark now, though, and from where Jo is tucked in the angle of the L she sees the stage as it looks when you're performing on it at night. The light strikes down and in from the track running around the little proscenium, and it kindles the air where you are into a radiant wall. Apart from the dancing legs of the front row, in drainpipes and tight skirts, and the occasional dangling hand holding a smouldering fag, you can't see the audience, packed in five feet in front of you: you can only hear them, a hooting whooping sighing swaying presence just outside your tent of light.

In the tent of light is Willy Reeves of Chicago, stamping on a wooden block to make his own percussion and pounding through a twelve-bar on a steel-string guitar, in a way that somehow contrives to sound both heavy and light at the same time. Heavy, as in inevitable; as in blues-logic proving its way through the changes and coming home as certainly as the tumblers of a safe locking into place. Light, as in playful; as in fingers that dance their way in and out of inevitability as if they had all the time in the world, and arrival at the iron-hard conclusion might be an airy impulse. *I cain't hardly*, sings Mr. Reeves. *Tell my baby*. Backstage, he is a small walnut-coloured lech, reeking of whisky and making a stumbling nuisance of himself. Out here, where the democracy of the tight space abruptly shakes itself out into aristocrats and commoners, headliners and mere backing musicians—he's an aristocrat, for sure. The part of the invisible audience who know what they're getting are reverently mute, in a hush of attention, although the hush is edged by some impatient mutter from the rest. This year, proper Chicago blues isn't quite the commodity it was in London. You can get it from pretty-boy white guitar bands now, or a version of it, rather than from old black men. You can get it hipper, better-dressed, more fanciable, more danceably diluted into a solution of rock 'n roll. A lot of the crowd want to get on to that part of the programme.

Jo, though, is with the mute and reverent contingent. She's listening with her ear cocked, hungry for the secrets of how Reeves does what he does. *She done tol' me. Ev'ry mornin'.* She should probably be back in the haze of hairspray, perfecting raccoon eyes with the other Tearaways. She's the new girl, after all, brought in to fill a space left by pregnancy, and she should be chatting with Viv and Lizzie, cementing things. But this is too good a chance to miss. Reeves's chords sound out in her mind, gunmetal grey and blackish-brown like Bournville chocolate, for she still hears in colours, though she knows now that people mostly don't. Her fingers move in the air at waist height.

Someone jostles her. Concentration broken, she glances behind and finds that, guess what, the pretty-boy white guitar band who're due to go on next but one have pushed round the corner of the L too, to get their look at Willy Reeves. They're a slightly motley lot, with a look (suede jackets, jazzman polo-necks, denim jeans with big buckles) that says, to her at least, that they don't know what to aim for, now that the Beatles have claimed smooth 'n cheeky and the Rolling Stones have taken over rude 'n rough. They're called the Bluebirds, if she remembers rightly. A little pathetic in itself: a name so busy creeping up on the Yardbirds that it hasn't noticed it's gone accidentally all Walt Disney, twitter-twit round and round Snow White's head. Mind you, thinks Jo, the Beatles have got one of the worst band names of all time, and nobody even notices any more. She hardly even notices herself.

Took ma chances. Played ma cards out. Needless to say, none of the irritated scrutiny she's giving the Bluebirds is coming back her way. She looks good tonight, she knows she does: the Tearaways have an Honor-Blackman-in-*The-Avengers* thing going, and are all wearing tight black sweaters, tight black trousers and boots with spike heels. Three in a row at the mike, swaying in time, they look kinkily fabulous. But right now, she's girl-furniture as far as these whispering, oblivious boys are concerned. They're locked in the serious business of male-to-male musical adoration. Without even noticing it, the one with the sideburns has backed her against the amp stack. The one with the thin froggy lips has blocked her view of Reeves. The skinny one with the nose has trodden on her foot, then tried to kick it away under the impression it's cabling. She's been absent-mindedly pushed behind a wall of bloke.

"Amazing," breathes Sideburns. "Fuckin' phenomenal."

"Hear the way he sort of *slaps* it, on the six chord?"

"Just like on the LP."

"We've got to learn that."

"Yeah, *you've* got to learn that."

"Well, I will," says Sideburns. "I will. 'S just, he picks it so fast, yeah? Look at that. I can't even— I just can't."

"No such word as 'can't.'"

"No such word as . . . ?"

"Ladies present," says Froglips, gaze unwaveringly fixed on Reeves.

"You swine."

"You filthy *swine*," they chorus, in a strangulated, murmured version of Bluebottle's voice from *The Goon Show*.

Oh, shut *up*, thinks Jo.

Clearly there has been worshipful listening to Reeves's long-players in whatever bachelor pit these idiots inhabit. Blue-and-white Chess Records label going round and round on the turntable, stylus dipped crackling into the groove for three or four bars then lifted out again; fingers on the fretboard trying to puzzle out something sounding the same, nearly the same, not quite the same, memory of the original slipping, lost it. And repeat. Banging on the party wall from infuriated neighbours.

"Hey, he's doing 'Northbound' . . ."

"Yeah . . ."

"I *love* this song."

"Yeah, but you can't play it."

"I can. I *so* nearly can. Except—"

"Here it comes—"

"—yeah—"

"*That.* What was that? On the five chord? That sad . . . thing. I'm looking at his actual hands, and I still can't work it out. 'S nearly a B seventh; 's not a B seventh. What *is* it?"

She shouldn't, she knows. In her experience nothing good at all comes from making the faintest criticism of men's expertise in what men think of as men's stuff. Probably if she had spent the usual amount of time in men's company the urge would have been completely squeezed out of her by now, but the years of nursing Mum in relays with Auntie Kay, while Val went out gallivanting with bloody Neville and his predecessors, made for a lot of evenings on her own. Home from the job in the shoe shop; take over; make the tea and coax it into her; sit by her; measure the medicine, and the medicine, and the medicine. Then alone, either at the upright in the front room, playing from the weird mixture of Dad's pre-war sheet music, or upstairs, slipping the treasures from the record library on Harper Street free of their sleeves, and lowering her own stylus into the valleys of the black vinyl, and making her own experiments in reproducing the sound. "You're like an old maid," says Val. (Thanks, Val.) And it's true that by Val's standards she's about six years late at venturing into the men's world. (And whose fault is that, Val? Who took all the fun and left me with all the duty?) But time alone does tend to get you trusting your own judgement, there being no one else's around to trust. Is this an advantage? Probably not. All the magazines say not, all the wives she's ever talked to say not, bloody Val when she's offering expansive advice says not. You don't ever let men know that you know better. Even if you do. Especially if you do.

But her foot hurts. And Mum is dead. And she's been waiting too long already.

"It's an open A and a finger sliding up the D-string to a seventh," she says.

An almost undetectable pause, and then they resume as if she hadn't spoken.

"Just mystifying," says Sideburns. "It's a mystery of the blues, that's what it is."

"A blues Bermuda Triangle."

"The lost city of the blues."

"A blues enig-*ma*," says Frogface, doing an old-fashioned newsreel announcer's voice.

"You could always ask him, when he comes off," says Skinny.

"Nah."

They pause again. *North-bound, North Side. Reds 'n whites.*

"Don't know what that means either," says Frogface.

"Maybe," says Sideburns, "maybe . . ." He has the air of one labouring to bring forth a discovery.

"What?"

"Maybe it's not a B-chord at all. Maybe it's, like . . . a combination of some kind?"

Jo rolls her eyes in the dark. But to her surprise, Frogface starts to snicker.

"Genius, mate! Just came to you, did it?"

And he shuffles sideways enough to be able to turn and look at Jo.

"How d'you know that, then?" he says. Unlike the others, whose voices are pure grammar-school London, from one of those middle-class zones in Hendon or Ealing or Sydenham where the middle-class-ness overpowers the difference between the city's compass directions, his voice has something warm in it that comes from elsewhere: from west, and further west than Ealing by a long way. A burr. Bristol, maybe. He's a head taller than her. His face is insolent-clever but he's not sneering now; he's leaning in, interested.

"Worked it out," she says, shrugging.

"You play?"

"A bit."

"You like this?"

Shrug.

"Why? Wouldn't have thought it was a chick's kind of thing."

He means, of course, that the blues is men's music. Songs of male misery and male disappointment and male boozing, sung by men with aggressive unprettiness, all sinew and bone, so that the sound itself seems to mimic strength being defeated, independent of the words. That's not the whole story, of course, just the story that boys tend to see. But it's true that, compared to the bone-hard jangle Willy Reeves is laying down now, the music she's going to make when she goes on stage with Viv and Lizzie, any minute now, will sound deliberately light and sweet and girly, apparently woven out of candyfloss, with all *its* muscles concealed. So yes, why? If she likes the one, why is she making the other? The question has answers she certainly won't give here; maybe answers she couldn't give anywhere. Part of it is, she doesn't see why she should choose. Willy Reeves singing "Northbound" is glorious, and the Crystals singing "Da Doo Ron Ron" is differently glorious, and to tell the truth neither of them are exactly her cup of tea, neither of them sound like the music she would make on her own account. *Will* make, some day. And underneath there's another reason, made of silence. It's a reason to do with their house being quieter than any other house in the street, always. Only two kids; no man; and later a sickroom hush getting deeper and deeper. She wanted to fill it, and she did, listening hard to everything she could get, picking determinedly along. Working it out, and working it out, knowing that she would still be missing most of the music until she could make it *with* people. Till Mum died, and she saw the advert for the Tearaways audition, and she dared.

Shrug.

He hasn't lost interest, though. He goes on looking down at her, and puts a hand experimentally on her bum. She twitches it away.

"Get off, I'm listening."

"You really are, aren'cha?" he says, smiling.

Not for long, though. Willy Reeves's set is over, and they're calling for her. The Bluebirds are pushed aside by the stampede required to get the Tearaways on stage. It isn't just the three of them, on vocals. They also need, to get the Spector-ish sound they're after, live, the guitars and the rhythm section and the brass, all played as a favour by blokes they know from the studio circuit, backing musicians like themselves who've turned out to help see if the Tearaways can move on up from backing to headlining. No one is going to get rich tonight. The Pelican's payment for the gig is getting split nine ways. In strict cash terms, they'd all do much better just turning up, prompt and professional and self-effacing, for another session laying down the harmonies for Miss Springfield. But you've got to try, haven't you? You've got to find out if you have it in you to be the one the crowd's eyes focus on.

Now they're in the tent of light. There's the song they want to be a single, but they thought they'd better lead up to it, and get people going a bit first, if they can. So they open with "Mockingbird": home ground for them, at least home ground in their old role as the chicks in a row at the back somewhere. Brian on bass starts up, deep with some echo on; they get the kinkily fabulous hip-sway going; the feet that are all they can see of the audience follow into tentative motion. Viv, slightly uncertain taking the lead, launches into call-and-response, and Jo and Lizzie sing it back to her.

"Mock! *Yeah!*"

"Ing! *Yeah!*"

"Bird! *Yeah!*"

"Yeah! *Yeah!*"

Then a spurt of drums, and Terry and Nigel lift the cornets to their lips and loose a shining blare with crisp corners. And the feet in the front row begin to dance in earnest, and their own hips settle into the groove, and all together they sing:

Mockingbird, everybody! Have you heard,
Have you heard?

The trumpets are golden. The trumpets are golden, and as she head-tilts right, left, right, she discovers out of the corner of her eye that though the wings have emptied of all the other Bluebirds, Frogface is still standing there, and she would swear that he is listening. To her.

t + 35: 1979

Ben

It was the poster that did it, he tells himself. He was having one of his quiet times, with his thoughts only subject to a nervous ripple now and again, like the river surface when the tide is just on the turn, and the Thames does a slow grey boil on the spot, creasing and wrinkling. Manageable.

But then on his day off, the day before yesterday, he was on the Tube, and somewhere when he was changing trains he found himself in front of one of those walls where they've stripped off the top layer of the posters ready to paste up something new, and some of the old layers below have ripped away too in strips and gouges. A Tube-palimpsest faced him: a concave slab glue-stippled, mildew-spotted, a dog's breakfast of previous attractions in thirty-two shades of rotted brightness, showing by the thickness at its edges just how anciently the tunnels are caked with paper. And there on the right a triangle had torn off under which you could see a blocky scarlet capital E and after it a blocky scarlet exclamation mark.

That was all, but he knew what it was. Once seen, impossible to unsee; once recognised, impossible to unrecognise. It was the poster, years gone now but horribly pushing back into the light, for the film called *Survive!* about the plane crash in South America. Which he'd had to dodge and sidle past for weeks when it came out, always aware of every poster for it, glowing red in the corner of his averted gaze. The poster only had words on it, not pictures, and of course he'd only ever seen (or tried to not see) the poster, not the film itself. Because why would you ever go and see something like that? Why would you ever want to look at people *shut up* eating each other? If you had a choice, if you could choose not to. Only the poster, then—only a corner of it now—but that was enough. That was enough to end the quiet time in his head. That was enough to set the fear stirring, and start another round of the endless struggle.

He suspected it at once, too. He stood pierced and pinioned in front of the wall, a slight little man nearly forty years old with eyes big and fearful and fists clamped by his sides, till the next train came in and someone jostled him, and the kind crowd released him into motion again along the Bakerloo Line platform. He shook his head like it was a tin with a dried pea in it, and thought maybe he'd been lucky, maybe he'd shaken it back out. *It's only an old poster, what's there to be afraid of in that?* he told himself, and as he said it he nearly believed that he believed it.

But gradually is how the bad times always come on. A thought he can push away, more or less. Then a pause. An ordinary hour, maybe two ordinary hours, in which he seems to be able to forget without effort that there is anything to worry about, except that in the act of reflecting this—reflecting that he is fine, and unworried—he is of course remembering that until now he had successfully forgotten. (Such intricacy; such compelled sidling about it, inside his own head; such long-practised efforts to prove himself unaware by catching himself unawares, this one time more. And this one. And this one, just to be safe.) Yet when he does remember that he had forgotten the fear, and feels compelled to check he isn't afraid, to make sure he can forget it again, he really isn't afraid, much. No, hardly at all. No, just the faintest trace, really, surely not enough to worry about, for hours and hours, as he traipses to and fro in his head, checking. (Wearing a kind of trail or groove in his thoughts, or that's what it feels like.)

Until the moment when on one of these repeating errands, the tenth the twentieth the millionth, he finds that with a malevolent logic all that tramping through the house of himself to check has somehow in itself tramped something in with it, has brought in on the feet of his thoughts an undeniable smear, a spoor. A speckling of blood, of *shut up* melted fat. And then he has to admit he is afraid. That it is one of the bad times he is coping with here. But surely not a very bad one. *Come on, you, out,* he says to his fear with, still, an almost convincing confidence. And smirking slightly, mocking slightly, it yields possession, it slinks out, it consents to be banished. But every time for less long, and with more effort.

All through yesterday, he trod around the cycle required to push the fear out, faster and faster. He had to get himself well out of it to sleep last night; and this morning the fear was waiting for him the moment he woke up, or after only the most microscopic pause during which the sun fell on his sore eyelids and was merely itself, and there was nothing wrong, as if he were one of the lucky ones. One uncorrupted photon, mate, one instant of easy natural light; that's your lot, that's all you get today. The time before he saw the poster already seemed like another age, a golden one, far away and long ago. On the way to work he was fending, fending, and the fear was jealous now, it didn't like him paying attention to anything but it. Busy fending, he trusted bare animal consciousness to get him to the garage, pilot him across roads, clock in, nod to Trevor, sling the ticket machine over his shoulder, hop up onto the rear platform of the Routemaster. 36C, Bexford to Queen's Park, Queen's Park to Bexford. Oh the mind, the mind has mountains. Cliffs of fall. Hold them cheap if you never dangled there. Hold tight. Hold tight, please.

(Why this? Why is it always this he's afraid of, why specifically is it the thought of cannibalism, of all things, that the horrors huddle round? He has no idea. A long time ago, before he first got sent to hospital, before he left school even, someone showed him one of the old American horror comics that used to go around, and there was a story in there where the pay-off was that the tramps sitting around the campfire were eating a person. You could see that what was roasting on the flames was a person's head and part of their ribcage. The flames were coming through the ribs. But, and here's the thing, it didn't particularly get to him. He went, *yech*, in an ordinary way, and pushed the nasty object back at Vernon Taylor without giving him the satisfaction of being upset. And didn't think about it for, probably, years. It was later on, when he was, what, fifteen or sixteen or so, that certain things got connected that probably shouldn't of. He threw up at the christening do when his Auntie Madge described his cousin Stephanie's baby as "good enough to eat." Out of nowhere: just his gorge suddenly rising and the cake he'd swallowed the minute before geysering back up. And then again in the alley next to a Wimpy bar when his sister brought him along on a double date, a shy fourth, and her boyfriend did this whole *yum-yum-yum* thing of munching up the chip she was holding out and pretending he was going to move on to her finger. The girl who was supposed to be his date, clearly chosen because she was an object of faint pity too, with thick thick glasses, stared at him as he puked. "You're mental, you are," she said, and fled. But once he had seen how alike the food adverts and the film posters were, how the camera lingered on the golden brown of a Findus crispy pancake and then lingered on the golden brown of Sophia Loren, he couldn't stop seeing it. He couldn't stop seeing how close flesh was to meat, he couldn't stop thinking of the vileness of a wanting that would destroy what it wanted, that would enjoy by gnawing, tearing, grinding, chewing, swallowing. Was that him? Was that his desire? Was that what he wanted? He didn't think so, but how could he prove it? He could never quite lay the fear of it to rest after that: and the more careful he was, the more he tried to avoid even the slightest ways in which you could look at girls like food, the guiltier he got, the more unsure of what he might be capable of. And *then* the ancient EC Comics panel of the human barbecue came floating out of the deeps of memory to give a shape to his fear. It fused to it and never let go. He did not want to eat anyone, he was almost certain. He never had eaten anyone. He had never bitten anyone, never licked anyone, never for that matter kissed anyone. Yet what comfort was that? Turn it and turn it as he liked, study the whole question over and over till it made him want to scream, he couldn't ever know for sure that he was safe.)

It's an April morning, blustery and grey and prone to little spitting showers, and both ways on the first trip to Queen's Park and back they make good time, which Ben is glad of. London's traffic has moods. The same time of day, and it can be fluid or clotted, easy or jammed. Today the lights go green as they approach the junctions, the mobs of school-bound kids and work-bound adults slip easily on and off the bus, and the moving weave of the vans and the Cortinas and the black cabs seems light and open, somehow. Trevor darts quick and sure through the gaps between the lanes, through London's gaps, and they fly across Peckham Camberwell Kennington, over the river under a brief oculus in the clouds that strews a rumple of light on the water, and quickly even through the tourist core of the route round Marble Arch, which often sticks. No stickiness now. Ben darts up and down the ridged-wood floor of the two decks, vending tickets in ceaseless motion, making change, giving the double-pull on the cord to the bell in Trevor's cabin when the platform clears, dodging the hot ends of lit ciggies between the smokers' seats upstairs, and balancing, balancing without even noticing, as Trevor's deft kicks to the accelerator bend the gravity inside the Routemaster this way and that. The blue smoke that floats upstairs jerks and reels like one unit, on a sharp corner. *Grark* go the gear-changes of the big diesel. At junctions, at idle, the floor shudders impatiently, and then smooths into a bass buzz, a rumble, a roar as they pick up speed, till the ground under the rear platform flows past in a blurred grey ribbon. And being in such continuous motion gives Ben something different from what's in his head to attend to. So long as he doesn't look down (down inside himself, he means, not physically down, down the curved stairs and out onto the receding tarmac) he can perform a kind of skating from task to task to task. The rhythm of the bus, when it flows, puts a fragile surface beneath him. Each action requires the next action, each bit of compelled speech brings about the need for the next bit of compelled speech, so long as he doesn't stop to think about it. Fares, please. Where to? Thirty pee, please. Got anything smaller. There you go. Hold tight. Move the bag out the aisle, please. Marble Arch!

It doesn't banish the fear. You can tell the fear's there all the time, underneath, gaping. Staying busy just gives him that faint support for his mind. But there's a trap. (There's always a trap. Every good way of being, Ben has found, has somewhere in it a hidden door into nightmare, waiting to catch you out.) With the quick moving around the bus, and the conjuring from it of the thin ice to skate across, the trap is that he might be seduced by the ordinariness around him, the ordinariness of his own actions, into believing for an instant that all is well; that he might then make the grievous mistake of thinking he could appeal to the ordinary world and ask it to protect him. If he was going round the Oval, say, and looking out from the top deck at the curving wall of the cricket ground. *Hey, you red-faced men in SCCC ties glimpsed for a moment at your shepherd's pie through a dining room window. Hey, you space of billiard-table green rimmed with hoardings pasted gold for Benson & Hedges. Hey, you row of squats on the far side, with paint like rotting custard, where grungy banners hang. Hey, all you solid things, all you solid world—aren't I solid too? Couldn't I be here as straightforwardly as you are? Couldn't I just trust the day? What is this cannibal shit, anyway?* Grievous; fatal; because then he'd be looking at the fear dead-on, and none of that reasonable-sounding stuff has the power to send it away. You can't disbelieve your way out of a fear when you are, really and truly, afraid. The fear is stronger than him, always. He knows that. All you get for challenging it is panic. Better to keep on the surface, as long as you can; better to skate on and be grateful for what he can get, as he's grateful now for the swift run up to Queen's Park and back. The second time they go north, things are slowing, however.

This time at QP, the statutory crew break. Cheese-and-tomato sandwich with curled-up corners, milky coffee in a polystyrene cup, fag sucked so hard it shortens with an audible crackle at every drag. Trevor doing the quick crossword and rolling his eyes at the sight of Ben twitching, pacing, stealing glances at the sky as if something might be hiding in the grey folds up there, which he would invite out if he let his gaze linger. *C'mon, off we go. C'mon, c'mon, c'mon.* They go in the end. The diesel gives its judder, and out they lurch between the brick pillars. But meantime the weather of the traffic has changed. The weave has tightened, the gaps have sealed, what was smooth and free-running has gone viscous at best, and by Marble Arch the route of the 36C is bumper-to-bumper, and Ben has nothing to do but wait along with the passengers, alone with them on a stationary red island out in the middle of the four-lane gyratory. A rotund businessman the worse for drink works his way out to the bus through the chinks between the cars, making exaggerated and provoking bows of apology to the drivers. *Honk honk. Parp parp.* Ben offers an arm up and has it smacked away, probably harder than intended. Elephantine pinstripes disappear up the stairs. Ben's trousers are a child's size.

Petrol fumes from the cars around gust in through the rear.

It's a smell that's a taste. It's a chemical smell. It's a burnt smell. It's nearly a cooking smell. *Charred ribs.* He goes up top and sells a 55p ticket to Fatso, who drops his change all over the floor. *Seared flank.* Even for the sake of the distraction Ben's not scrambling about to pick the money up. No one else needs anything. He goes back down. Nothing doing there either. He stands in the little conductor's alcove at the bottom of the stairs and drums his fingers on the upright chrome of the pole. Ching-ching-ching-ching-ching. Ching-ching-ching-ching-ching. *Charred ribs. I'm not going to think of that. Sizzling skin. I'm not going to think about that. Charred ribs. Go away. Arm-fat melting and making the fire spit. O please go away, please please. Charred ribs. Shut up.*

He is thinking of those things, though, isn't he? And once he is, and avoidance has failed, he has to argue, even though he knows it's no good; even though he recognises, and is sick of, and knows the uselessness of, every single thing he can conceivably say back to this *shutup shutup* picture of ruined blistering burning hideous cooked *shutup* flesh. The lights far ahead change, and Trevor manages to creep fifty feet down Park Lane. The trees along the edge of the park thresh. The petrol fumes briefly blow away and then reassert themselves.

All right, says the piping little voice of reason in Ben's head, *those are horrible things, but what have they got to do with you, eh?*

Charred ribs.

You've never seen any of that stuff, have you, not for real, not even in that film.

But here it is. Charred ribs.

No but, it's not actually happening, is it. You're only imagining it. Charred ribs.

It's just made up. It's just in your head.

Yeah, exactly, it's in your head.

So?

Your head and nobody else's. This is your doing.

No it's not. I don't want it, I hate it, I want it gone.

Really? Look at these people. Look at that git in the suit. Look at that girl in the jean jacket. You know the one. Where the buttons heh are under a bit of a strain. Big chest. Lot to button up. Yeah, that one.

Shut up.

You don't want me to.

I do.

No you don't. Her; him. D'you think they're thinking of this stuff? Course not. It's just you. You all alone, you evil man, looking at them and thinking of

Shut up shut up

lips puffed and glazed like pork crackling, eyebrows

shut up!

melted to those little dots like the bristles on a roast

stop

eyes cooked white like the eyes on cooked fish

o please stop

Why? This is what you like.

No it isn't.

Then why'd you think about it? You think about it all the time. You do. It's on you. It's your thing. It's your favourite. You love it.

No I don't.

Charred ribs, mate, charred ribs.

Red, amber, green. Another fifty feet. Green, amber, red. And repeat. And repeat.

I wish I could take my head off and wash it out with a hose.

Well you can't.

At last they reach the front of the queue, and get their turn to be pumped through the clogged valve of the junction between the almost-touching angles of Green Park and Hyde Park. New green on the trees dulled by the fumes as if already defeated;

scurf of litter in gutters and round the bases of lamp posts, left over from the winter's bin strike; the triumphal statues and stuff from the old wars looking down at heel, corroded and tatty or choked in black paint. The flow's not much better beyond, but at least a block of people want to get off, in the blank-walled stretch of road behind Buckingham Palace, and a few more get on, so thank heavens there's something to do, activity that lasts Ben until Trevor pulls left into the slips of the Victoria bus station, where the red double-deckers wait in rows like clumsy race-horses, between the plastic fascias of the adult bookshop and the betting shop and the all-night caff and the tourist-tat place selling plastic bowler hats with Union Jacks on them on one side, and the echoing cast-iron canopy of the railway terminus on the other. Ben remembers this place from childhood as rather grand: a kind of palace for the steam trains, sooty on every surface, of course, but with gleaming boat trains and Golden Arrow expresses idling at the platforms like pampered monarchs, waited on by scurrying porters. Now its grime is glamourless. It just looks tired in there. Or maybe that's him. He is tired. The front of his mind jitters fearfully on, but underneath there's exhaustion waiting like a continental shelf. When days like these finally consent to end, he slips past the sentries of terror into dim depths of fatigue, and gratefully dissolves there. He's yawning now.

Thanks to the clotting of the traffic, they've caught up at Victoria with the buses that should've been ahead on the route, and are now the back one in a row of four 36s. Trevor turns off the engine, and steps out to lean against the cab and have a smoke. It's getting on for teatime.

"Other ones'll be leaving first," says Ben to the chuntering passengers. "Move on up to the 36 at the front if you don't wanna wait. Yeah, you can use the same ticket."

Most get off, leaving only a nun on the longwise bench

seats downstairs who seems as patient as a statue, and upstairs a harassed-looking woman with three young kids who presumably can't face the palaver of moving them. Also the git in pinstripes is still there, slumped red-faced against a window and snoring.

"Oi," says Ben, "wakey-wakey. Victoria!" Nothing. Louder: "Mister? *Victoria.* This your stop?" Still nothing. Ben's not going to shake him, prod him or otherwise touch him; he doesn't touch people, if he can help it. Almost shouting: "Sir! Sir! Is this your stop?"

"Oh, for heaven's sake," rumbles a voice of treacly grievance, without the puce eyelids opening, or the jowls shifting from where they're squidged against the glass. "Go away, bus-wallah. Go 'way. My business where I get orf."

"Your funeral, squire," says Ben, backing off. "Don't blame me if you wake up in the depot."

And this little bit of righteous defiance gives him enough fuel to go down and stand next to Trev and smoke a fag of his own in fierce sucks and endure the couple of minutes till the other 36s have moved off and it's time to get going again. The fear sends needles of dread through him, almost playful. It knows it has him; it can afford to wait patiently to see how he fails next in the struggle to get rid of it.

Off again. Rumbling down through Pimlico to Vauxhall Bridge. Traffic at least in jerky motion. A party of posh kids upstairs, aged fifteen or sixteen, presumably just finished school, all puffing away on Silk Cut and looking as if they're enjoying the conscious wickedness more than the taste. Goodbye to the nun; hello to weary office cleaners coming off a shift that started at dawn, and a middle-aged woman wearing a carefully maintained outfit that hasn't been in fashion for a decade. She raises her eyebrows at the posh boys, but as if she's entertained by them, not tutting at them. They and she get off just before the Thames, at the stop for the Tate Gallery. The harassed mum gets off beyond the river, by Vauxhall station, and she needs Ben's help manoeu-vring the pushchair and her bags down the stairs. He manages to do this without making any skin contact with her *good enough to eat* offspring. And all the while, Ben is working, working in his head, having decided *though you know it never works* to look away from the fear; to starve it of the oxygen of his attention. Every-thing he does, he now does with an extra zeal or maybe just des-peration, grabbing at its scope to fill his gaze. His mind's eye's gaze, that is. To blissfully ordinary eyes, such as other people's, he might seem to be doing exactly the same things as on the north-bound journey, when he was resisting the fear by skating the flow. But this is quite different; a different strategy altogether. Instead of not looking, and asking no questions, he is now actively refus-ing to look. He has turned away from the fear, inside himself, and is making himself go on facing away from it. Mentally fac-ing away. There it is behind him, murmuring away, trying to send around tendrils of *charred ribs* alarm into the edges of his vision. But he won't look, he won't won't won't. He will not think of it. He will not-think of it. He is putting out anti-thought where it is concerned. He is *charred ribs* forgetting it, he is refusing it, he is turned away. He is chanting *la-la-la-la-la-la*. He is winning, he is winning, he is *charred ribs* not winning. The trouble is that it's not safe to turn your back on a frightening thing. Every animal knows this. Every animal would rather be facing the predator than feel-ing it pacing about behind them somewhere, preparing to spring. Not knowing where it is is worse, even, than seeing it closing on you with *charred ribs* teeth bared. If you were walking on a lonely road at dusk and you felt that something was following you, its presence betrayed by ambiguous movements just at the margins of your sight, black shifting on black, grey flexing on grey, you'd turn, wouldn't you; you'd turn to check. You'd swing around, hop-ing to be wrong; and till you did, you'd feel the tug of your fear urging and urging you to, taking priority as the sense of danger always does. This is like that, except, of course, that the lonely road and the monster following, the cornered mouse and the stalking cat, are all in Ben's head, and none of this is visible to anyone else on the bus. There's just the fine-boned little man in the grey polyester jacket with the conductor's badge, quick-stepping about with sweat on his forehead and his eyes as wide as a lemur's. No one can tell. No one can help. It's his head, and he's locked inside it forever and ever, till kingdom come, amen.

And not long after they've passed the Oval again, having deposited the last of the posh central London custom and picked up the wodge of travellers who've come up from the Tube there needing transport east into the Tubeless wastes of the city's lower half, he gives in and turns round. He was right. The fear was behind him, just behind him, and *CHARRED RIBS* it roars in his face.

"Sorry?"

"I said, Peckham Rye."

"Right. Sorry. Twenty, please."

He'd almost welcome it if the fear would actually pounce, if that would be the end of it. If it were possible to actually surrender to it in some final way, and let it (appropriately enough) crunch him up. A willing step forward, and then the whole thing over with. But that's not its way. It isn't substantial enough to make an end of him, only to keep him never-endingly afraid. (Though there are better days than this: a fact he struggles to believe, on a bad day.) Now, stared at, it falters momentarily. Just for a moment, it resolves into its constituent elements, like a looming figure in a dark bedroom that flicks back into being a pile of clothes on a chair. Just for a moment, as if the lighting has changed or something like that, Ben can see that his monster is only made of the ancient memory of a horror comic's page, a teenage anxiety about what it means to want someone, an ordinary distrust gone septic. It's as if a far-off window has opened. Not in this room, nor in the next, but somewhere; down some dark L-shaped corridor, perhaps, and across a landing, and up some stairs, but eventually to a chamber in the house of the self where a long-stuck casement has opened outwards, and let in an unexpected breath of air. *Oh*, says some tiny part of Ben. *Charred ribs?* offers the monster, pathetically. For a second, he could almost laugh.

But the terrible truth is that these occasional moments of release are familiar too. They too are part of the familiar round, the long churning, of Ben's fear, and they do not seem to help much. They certainly do not end it. Maybe they are another of the fear's tricks and traps, maybe they are something else. But they go away, and the struggle resumes. So now, since he is staring at the fear anyway, Ben wearily switches to the opposite tactic, and tries to pin it with his stare: to look at it so unflinchingly, before it can regroup, that it will be unable to account for itself, and be forced to shrivel away. Not that this has ever worked either.

Meanwhile, rumbling up the long straight of Camberwell New Road towards the junction with Walworth Road and the green, they've picked up some unwelcome cargo, a group of skinheads who go tramping up the back stairs in their big boots and occupy the whole front of the upper deck. The normally raucous school-kids who get on at the green and after for their journey home to Peckham take a look from the top of the stairs and prudently retreat, though a couple with Rock Against Racism badges shout something once they're safely on the pavement. Two art student girls in dungarees and a boy with long hair on one side and a clip-job on the other move downstairs. Soon the top deck pretty much belongs to the British Movement, and everyone else on the bus—the hardy pensioners at the back upstairs, the overcrowded contingent filling the downstairs, Trevor in the cab—

is nervously aware of the field of aggro being generated there. Except Ben; Ben, pushing through the crush in the lower-deck aisle, double-tinging the cord for departures, vending away like a contortionist, has other things on his mind.

What are you? What even are you, really?

You know what I am.

No I don't. Or anyway, I don't know why I have to be afraid of you.

Ooh, in't he brave!

I haven't done anything, have I? I haven't actually eaten anyone, have I? You're some pictures in my head, that's all.

Uh-huh?

I'm going to look at those ribs on that fire straight on. Go on, give me all you've got.

Charred ribs?

Hah! Nothing there! You're nothing, you're not made of anything, you're literally just fear.

Charred ribs.

I look at you, and you can't do anything, can you?

Charred ribs.

Ha ha. That's it, is it? You're a one-trick fear, ain'tcha. You poor—

Look away, then.

Eh?

If you're so safe, look away.

I could.

You will. You'll have to, in the end. You're only safe as long as you've stared me into stillness. But you can't keep me frozen, you know that. You'll blink. Your eyes are getting tired already. You'll look away. And then—

Shut up.

Brave Ben. Fearless Ben. Heroic Ben. Whose mind is a barbecue in hell.

Shut up.

I can feel you're going to blink, I can feel it, here it comes, here it comes—

Ben has climbed the stairs without noticing. Has vended, on automatic pilot, two 10p fares to the pensioners tucked at the back. Now blunders forth up the surprisingly clear aisle towards a group he hasn't clocked as anything more particular than his next task, because inside he has indeed blinked, reeled, looked away, and had the fear flash out roaring with the more power for having been temporarily confined, and fill all but a tiny leftover rind of his sensorium with dripping fat, bubbling skin, disgusting smells of roasting flesh, which expertly weave together with the blood smell that really is coming in through the windows just here on the route, where the 36C passes between the massed streetside butcher's stalls of Peckham: and while the British Movement (Bexford branch) idly watch him come, to see if there's any entertainment in the little pipsqueak's attempt to make them pay, he doesn't pay them any attention at all. A crescendo is taking place in his head.

CHARRED RIBS CHARRED RIBS CHARRED RIBS CHARRED RIBS CHARRED RIBS CHARRED RIBS CHARRED RIBS shut up CHARRED RIBS CHARRED RIBS oh please CHARRED RIBS CHARRED RIBS shut up shut up shut up

"Any more *charred ribs* fares, please?"

"No thank you my good *charred ribs* I think we'd rather you *charred ribs* your little ticket machine up *charred ribs* if you would be so *charred ribs.*"

A vague impression of the grinning mask of the largest and oldest of the skins.

"Sorry," says Ben, "I didn't quite *charred ribs* catch that?"

"I said," the skinhead begins again patiently, winking at his friends, "that we *charred ribs charred ribs charred ribs CHARRED RIBS CHARRED RIBS CHARRED RIBS—*"

Shut up shut up shut up, cries Ben desperately inside his head, and then, entangled by the confusion of inner and outer, without even noticing the difference yells out loud:

"Oh just fucking shut up why can't you! Shut up, shut up, shut up!"

There is a moment of startled silence. Then the lead skin rises to his feet, with his shoulders up against the curved yellow enamel of the roof and his head bent over towards Ben's face.

"You what?" he says, quietly, delicately.

Something like a jolt of belated adrenalin goes through Ben, a chemical alert for real-world problems from a system neglected and overruled most of the time in favour of the hateful blizzard blowing in his psyche, but still just about operational and now insisting successfully on his attention. His vision clears. Or rather, what he has been seeing all along is permitted to register. The man whose face is in his face is a rangy, graceful, liquidly moving predator, on whom the shaved scalp does not produce the effect of scabby babyhood which can be seen in his two much younger male mates, or on the pinch-faced woman beside him, shrunken-looking and minimally female in her Aertex shirt, who is staring up at Ben with a peculiar expression on her face as if she recognises him. On him, the suede-fuzzed curves of skull have the heft of a weapon—the weighted, rounded surface at the back of a well-balanced ball-peen hammer, for example. His smile is jovial, his eyes are deep blue and fringed with pretty lashes, and his clothes are perfect for what they are. The wide bands of the red braces, the crisp white Fred Perry shirt, the jeans the exact right shade of blue faded almost to white, the boots tied immaculately with fat red laces. He puts a finger out to the crumpled grey lapel of Ben's polyester uniform jacket, just under the round identity badge with his number on it, and stirs contemptuously at the cheap cloth. The top of Ben's head comes to somewhere under his collarbone. The two of them must be pretty much of an age, but beside this pumped, gleaming, comfortably aggressive animal, Ben is a scrap, a wisp, an anxious little fleck of gristle.

"Yeah?" says the skinhead.

I'm dead, I'm dead, I'm dead, supplies the rusty subsystem of Ben's brain devoted to physical survival, and he's surprised to find he minds the idea. It isn't a relief after all. But he hasn't a notion what to do about it; what to say, to turn wrath aside. His mouth hangs stupidly open, with his vulnerable herbivore's teeth on display.

"Someone's-gunna-get-their, *fuckin*-head-kicked-in; someone's-gunna-get-their, *fuckin*-head-kicked-in," chant the young male sidekicks, happily.

"Oh, leave it out, Mike," says the woman. "Look at the poor little bugger."

Mike doesn't look at Ben. He closes the pointing hand round Ben's lapel, to keep him in place, and turns to look at her instead, sour irritation spoiling his mouth.

"I *told* you," he begins.

But then the Routemaster judders to a halt, and Trevor, who has been watching through the periscope from the cab and looking for somewhere to pull over, jumps down, runs round the back, and is up the passenger stairs three steps at a time. Trevor is six foot three and won a heavyweight title while he was in the merchant navy. He is also a deacon in the Joyful Assemblies of the Holy Spirit: but he doesn't feel he is under an obligation to spell out his commitment to the path of heavenly peace in situations where the greater good would be served by keeping shtum.

"Let go of my conductor, man, and get off my bus," he says: and his voice is a London-Jamaican rumble, full of the bass warning notes of one big beast addressing another.

"Oh look, it's the organ grinder," says Mike, switching his attention with relish to the larger and more promising target. "Or is it? Which is which, eh? Which one's the organ grinder, and which one's—"

"Get off my bus. Now."

"You can't do that, we got rights," says one of the younger boys, too adenoidal for menace.

"Carriage of passengers is at the discretion of driver and conductor," rumbles Trevor, not taking his eyes off Mike. "London Transport by-laws. Hop it."

But the other two skins are strategically irrelevant at this point. Without meaning to, Ben is blocking them from standing up. If they push him, they'll just push him into the immovable obstacle of Trevor. It's all between Trevor and Mike: the other two, like the woman, like Ben, are just audience.

Mike has thrust his face forward, right into Trevor's. He is a bit shorter, but the way the bus roof forces them both to stoop leaves them on a level, nose to nose, brow to brow, Mike's pale warhead of a profile up against Trevor's sculpture in unyielding dark wood. They look as if they're about to rub noses, like New Zealand rugby players do; or like one of those optical illusions where you either see two faces or the vase made by the space between. Trevor's face has got no expression on it but refusal, while Mike is gleeful, enjoying himself to an extent Ben doesn't really get. His mouth is open and his tongue is as red as his braces. The veins on his forehead are standing up. His hand, however, is in his jeans pocket, fishing for a hard lump the size and shape of a Stanley knife.

"Mike, don't," says the woman; and although her voice is drab and exhausted-sounding, it seems to have the power to reach him all the same, twisting his face into a spasm of irritation. Not collected, not self-possessed: a why-do-you-always-fuck-things-up-for-me? expression.

"Fuck it," says Mike, to the floor, and then, into Trevor's face with a shower of spit, "Lucky! Your lucky day! C'mon, then."

As he goes he tries to shoulder aside Trevor, who has stepped back an ironically courteous six inches or so: but Trevor is planted, and gives no more ground to the shove than a plank would. Mike, followed by the woman, followed by the boys, moonstomps his way up the aisle, kicks a dent in the tin of curved stair-guard, and can be heard clomping down and off. There's a muffled cry of "White power!" from the pavement. Then they're gone.

One of the pensioners applauds, not ironically. Trevor wipes his face with a hanky.

"We'll be on our way again in a moment, ladies and gentlemen," he declares to the top deck. Then to Ben, much more quietly, "Ain't you got no sense at *all*?"

"I'm sorry," Ben whispers.

"Man! 'Lucky' was right. I don't know what you said to him, but look: you get yourself in trouble like that, you're getting me in it too, and I don't want to go home with no holes in me."

"I didn't . . . mean to."

"I don't suppose you did," says Trevor. "You'd be the last one I'd figure for picking fights. Off in a damn dreamworld, that's you."

"Oh, come on, driver," says the pinstriped drunk, who has just woken up and sees nothing but the bus crew chatting. "Chop-chop!"

"Hold your horses," says Trevor, but he breaks the gaze he has locked on to Ben's face. "You and me are not finished talking about this," he tells Ben. "At the garage, we are going to have some words."

He sighs and heads back downstairs.

"I was on your side," says the old dear at the back who clapped, as he passes. "Because you coloured fellas have such lovely manners."

"Thanks, darling," says Trevor after a fractional pause, and disappears down the stairwell with his eyebrows raised.

There is a kind of stunned calm inside Ben's head as the Route-master shakes itself back into life and they chug on through the rest of the route. Queen's Road, New Cross, Lambert Street, Bexford Hill, Bexford Garage. The long views back towards the cluttered basin of the city winch themselves free from the rooftops as they make the last leafy-green climb. The squalls of April rain are visible over there as little patrolling smudges, trailing tentacles of darkness over the wastelands where the docks used to be. It's not a total calm inside him: he can feel that the fear is still there, faintly alive down in a sub-basement, and will be heard from again when the real-world shock has had a chance to recede. But it's quieter than it ever is, pretty much, even on one of the good days. Meanwhile, and this is the thing that is enforcing the quiet, he can feel that his legs are like water, his chest is aching, his forehead is damp, his hands are cold and clumsy. His whole weak, skinny, urban-ape body is insisting minute by minute on its reality and vulnerability, is demanding that he notice for once that it is more than a container to tote his horrible thoughts around. It's him, himself: the thing itself, the man itself, the "I" itself, to all of whom something bad nearly happened. *Your fingers are as real as your thoughts*, his fingers are telling him. *Realer, in fact*. It's an astonishing sensation, and to be honest not at all a pleasant one. Because if someone, some fairy godmother, had propositioned him up front and said, *You can have a break from the fear inside, at the price of being frightened out in the world*—well, he'd have taken the deal, wouldn't he, like a shot; and he'd have done it thinking, as he always tends to think when in the grip of his fear, that the alternative to what grips him is some unimaginable, infinitely desirable state of calm. Compared to which a bit of skinhead-induced agitation would be a piece of piss. A straightforward bargain. But it's not like that at all. The thing that has been strong enough to silence those *charred ribs* isn't a perfect peace but another, stronger, more pressing emotion. Perhaps if he wants not to live in his private barbecue hell he has to consent to fill his life up with all the things he'd feel, many not nice, if he let his life have events in it. Large, vague, alarming thoughts stir: perhaps it is the emptiness of his life that gives hell houseroom, perhaps it is even his wish for peace that does it. Perhaps all this time he has been somehow hugging his hell to himself. Like the cruising clouds that smudge the grey levels of the London air, these are ideas without edges, that melt into the general sky as you draw close. And since they are disturbing, as well as hard to hold on to, they will probably blow by, as will Ben's guilt at what he nearly made happen to Trevor.

Bexford Garage. Their Routemaster slotted into the oily-floored brick barn, the toad in pinstripes tottering away baffled, clutching his puce brow and clearly with no idea where he is. Thanks to the jams, the return trip took so long it's shift-end for Ben and Trevor. As soon as he's dropped off the machine and the cash bag in the office and clocked out, Ben makes an attempt to slip away, seeing as over by the exit onto the East Hill he can see Rodney hanging about, waiting to sell him his regular solution to the problems of sleep and the night-time. But Trevor corners him in the red alley between their Routemaster and its neighbour.

"So, what *was* that about, then?" he demands.

"I dunno," says Ben uncomfortably. "I'm not. I. I think I told him to shut up."

"You *think* you did?"

"I was thinking of something else."

"But why'd you tell him that?"

"I dunno."

"No, man, you do. Come on, out with it."

Impossible to explain that he wasn't speaking to the skinhead at all.

"He said something to me. But I'm not sure what it was."

"How can you not—? Never mind. Okay, what d'you think it was, this terrible thing?"

"I wasn't really paying attention, you see. But I think he told me to stick my ticket machine up my arse."

Having said this out loud, having put it out there in the conversation, and finding that fear has flipped over into absurdity, Ben suddenly gets the giggles, and it's infectious; Trevor starts to laugh too, and for a moment they rock to and fro together between the buses.

"Right, then," says Trevor. "*Right*. I see it now. Okay." He swallows his last chuckle. "And you lost your temper, right? Probably out of the blue, just like that, am I right?" He snaps his fingers. "And you're not an angry guy, are you, so I'm guessing you got not too much practice at keeping your temper, or getting it back when it's gone all of a sudden like that. Now, the thing here is . . ."

And he launches into a speech which Ben guesses is probably a version of the advice that Deacon Trevor gives to young fighters at some boxing club or other, about how to keep your cool under pressure; or maybe to his own sons. It's very well meant, and Ben has no idea how to tell him that it's completely off-target. So he just goes quieter and quieter, waiting for the talking-to to end, and for his chance to go. *You and I need to be alone together again*, says the fear. And Trevor sees this, and grows puzzled and frustrated again.

"Where've you gone, man? I thought we was understanding each other."

And it's at this point that Rodney, tired of hanging about, appears at the end of the metal alleyway in his unconvincing tam and his green khaki jacket with ASWAD written on it in marker pen, holding out Ben's regular order of an eighth of Leb in its little baggie.

"Go away, man, we're talking," says Trevor.

"I and I jes' here to do a little business," says Rodney.

"What?" says Trevor.

"Ya know, the holy herb."

"*What?*" says Trevor. "That's the worst Rastaman imitation I ever heard. Where'd you learn it from, listening to records?"

"All right, all right, Grandad," says Rodney, trying to sidle past. "Just tryin' to show some appreciation. Roots and culture, know what I mean?"

"Not your bloody culture. Newsflash! You're a white boy, boy. And take that shit away. You don't want to be messing with this one's head. He's enough of a mess already. Look at him!"

Trevor isn't even looking at Ben himself at this point, he's just getting rhetorical because he's getting exasperated, and while he does so Ben snatches the eighth, shoves a blue fiver into Rodney's mitt in exchange, and scarpers, leaving Trevor making tooth-sucking noises of despair.

Across the road, past the old Odeon, boarded up now, around two corners, loping along on sore feet. The fear beginning to wake up, just as he knew it would *charred ribs* but at last with some medicine in hand for it, a reliable dose of mind-softening ahead to look forward to. Through the door of his sister's house, fumbling with the keys; past her daughters doing their homework in front of the telly; refusing his tea; up the stairs and into his room, and bolt the door. And skinning up with his clumsy hands, and the flame sputtering on the little lumps of resin in the tobacco; and then the oily, thick, oblivious smoke, bringing a pause at last to today's twenty rounds with the demon.

So many days like this.

Alec

"No, leave it, I'll do that," says Alec as Sandra starts automatically collecting up the cereal bowls.

"You sure?" she says, raising an eyebrow. He's making an effort, but he's not normally Mr. Domestic.

"Yeah, fine, my meeting's not till ten and then I'm not on the picket till one. I'm a gentleman of leisure, me."

"Well, all right. Thanks, love."

With a kind of twitch, she detaches herself from the groove of her usual tasks, and goes through into the hall to find her bag and put on her coat. He can hear the slither of fabric over fabric as the coat underneath hers falls off the peg, and has to be picked off the floor. Then she comes back to the kitchen to do her face in the mirror by the door, where the light is stronger. She lifts her chin and turns it from side to side as she does her cheeks, grimacing at herself with that weird objectivity women have when it comes to their own faces. Pout-stretch-blot with the lipstick. A bit sticks to a front tooth and she reaches a quick hand for a Kleenex to get it off. She's got big front teeth, always has had; nicely racehorsey to go with her long, lean body, Alec thinks. He can remember her teeth and his teeth banging into each other the first time they kissed, in the bus shelter by Bexford Park it must be (good grief) twenty years ago. She must be changing with time, he supposes. Nearly-forty Sandra with two teenage sons can't be the same as the eighteen-year-old with the hair-flip. But you don't see it, do you, if you live with someone, if you see them all the time? The changes are too gradual. Or, more than that, the changes are additions not displacements, only ever doing their work on top of memory, in all its layers and layers. The girl doesn't go away, she just gets added to. Maybe it goes on like that, he thinks. Maybe that's what's happening, he thinks, when you come across one of those pensioner couples down the pub who are all handsy with each other. Everyone thinks it sweet they're still so devoted, considering the wrinkles and his arthritis and her having a bum as big as a barrel, but maybe they just don't see those things. Maybe to them, the wrinkles et cetera are details to be brushed aside, because from their point of view they still fundamentally are the courting teenagers who started mashing tongues in the bus shelter in 1925.

"Phwoar," he says gently, joking and not joking, teasing and not teasing, and reaches an arm for her hips.

She gives him a V-sign with her free hand, and skips out of the way. The Co-op checkout calls. She never had to have a job, before. She was busy with the boys, and Fleet Street wages gave them all a pretty good life. They talked about her going back to work, but without ever getting to the decision point. Now, with Alec on seventy quid a week strike pay, they suddenly need her to be earning, and she's kind of enjoying, Alec would say, being back in the world. Having a bigger life than the family. She talks about people on the tills with her who he's never met. But then he supposes he's been passing on composing-room gossip to her for years which makes just as little sense.

"I'm off, then," she says, coming back and ruffling his hair. "Be good."

"Also," he says carefully, "I thought I might try and have a word with the lazy lump upstairs—you know, if he surfaces."

"Oh, love," she says, frowning. "Is there any point going round it again? You just set each other off."

It's true that Alec being in the house more seems to mean more collisions between him and Gary. He and his older boy form an unstable mixture, it seems, liable to combust. The two of them must have depended more than they knew on Sandra acting as interpreter and go-between. Face to face, things go swiftly wrong. But Alec isn't ready to give up on the idea of reaching him; of finding the right tool to jiggle open the mysteriously jammed lock of Gary, who not long ago, surely, was being helped to balance round by the garages on his orange Chopper.

"I will walk on eggshells," he promises.

"Hmm," she says, unconvinced. But she's got to go. She kisses him and departs; and thirty seconds after the door's clicked, and he's dumping bowls in the sink, he sees her head go by above the trellis on the back wall of the pocket-sized garden, taking the short cut down towards Lambert Street and the shops. Just her head, with her straight fair hair flying, moving in quick jerks that mean she's taking her long, downhill, almost-bounding strides, also unaltered (thinks Alec) from the girl who won the hundred yards at Bexford Secondary Modern and moved as if less secured to the ground by gravity than other people. She looked like a gazelle in running shorts. Such legs she had. Has. Had. Whichever. Her expression, though, thirty seconds away from him, has cooled, and gone resolute, and public, and unbetraying.

"*Private faces in public places*," quotes Alec, adding too big a squirt of Fairy Liquid to the washing-up bowl, "*are wiser and nicer than public faces in private places.*"

The sink grows a loaf of foam. Alec roots about in it for the crockery and the cutlery, and brings up each item he finds, one by one, for a careful scrub. He has to run the mixer tap hard to get the foam off again, and even then when he piles the clean dishes on the drainer they all have a slightly bubble-tufted appearance which doesn't look right. He picks up the whole rack and tries to fit it under the mixer tap for a final rinse, but it won't fit on top of the plastic bowl. He transfers the rack to balance on just his right arm, and uses the other to tip the bowl out. He has nowhere to put the bowl, though; if he puts it on the draining board, he can see that it will immediately foam up his post-foam recovery area. He squats and leans, and props the bowl down on his Hush Puppies—half on them, anyway—to try to keep the foam off the floor. He straightens, and with his left hand turns on the cold water to wash out the sink itself, also foam-bound. When enough seems to have gone down the drain, he manoeuvres the draining rack and its cargo under the flow and starts to sluice it. Success! The foam residue washes off the washing-up with pleasing prompt-ness. But he tips the rack too far, and the bowls and saucers at the end start to slide off into the sink, and when he hastily tips the rack the other way, he overshoots, and crockery bounces off the other end onto the floor, while an icy jet shoots out of the under-carriage of the rack and squirts the leg of his jeans. He starts to laugh, and more bowls slide off the rack—bouncing not breaking on the floor, luckily, since they're melamine.

There's a sound from upstairs. Alec looks at the ceiling, and stops laughing. He picks up the mess, replaces the bowl, rewashes more efficiently. He finds a mop in the tall cupboard and sorts out the floor. All of this he does with a degree more clatter than he could have managed. But when the washing-up is really, truly, definitively done, and he squints at the ceiling again, there are no follow-up noises. He turns on the radio on the windowsill and gives the kitchen a dose of Radio 1. Still nothing.

So he puts the kettle on and makes Gary some tea. It occurs to him that he doesn't know how Gary likes it, so he puts in one sugar, as the low-risk, consensus option, and carries the mug to the upstairs of the maisonette. It's dim up there, he discovers as his head rises above the level of the swirly carpet on the landing. With the door of his and Sandra's bedroom shut, and the shade still down in the bathroom to shield Sandra's shower from being on view to the road, and Stevie's door open but the curtain left closed when he went off to school, it's as if the night hasn't shifted upstairs, is still hanging about, a murk as thick as flannel pyjamas only softly punctured here and there by light, and smelling strongly of boy. Really strongly, in fact, now that Alec's nose has been purged by Fairy Liquid and is getting the chance to smell his household afresh. It smells of used Y-fronts and other teenage male laundry, and spray-on Brut 33, and spot lotion, and the general reek of newly exuding armpits and groins. Of, probably, (disgusting word, but useful for winning at Scrabble) smegma. S-m-e-g-m-a. The only feminine thing putting up a fight in the mix is the floral smell of Sandra's shampoo.

Christ, she really is alone in the zoo with us, thinks Alec. *It's a wonder she doesn't reel out of the house in the morning coughing and gagging.*

He puts down the mug on the post at the end of the banisters and opens doors, draws curtains, opens windows, imagining a cleansing gale blowing through from end to end. Out on the other side of the Rise he can see the new green on the big trees starting to cover up the frontages of the big old houses over there. The part they live in is modern infill, presumably where a bomb wiped out the Georgian symmetry. It's the only new bit, and the only comfortable bit. The behemoths opposite are all dusty-windowed multi-occupancy nightmares, full of art students, old people with a hundred cats, and bewildered Nigerians. Though there are one or two being done up—the ones with a Saab or a 2CV parked outside. A little bit of April rain spatters on the tilted glass. The April air, on the other hand, pushes hesitantly inside a few inches, doesn't fancy it, withdraws. Oh well. He's wasting time anyway, he knows he is; his watch says it's nearly nine now, and he ought to be heading for the bus stop himself soon if he's going to make the meeting on time. *Now or never, Dad.* He picks up the mug, knocks on the last unopened door on the crowded landing and, getting no answer, pushes into Gary-land.

In the sweaty dark, ancient-looking suits bought from charity shops hang on walls, plus one, two, three pork-pie hats, equally vintage. There's a record player and a row of LPs but not a single book. The shelves Alec put up have shoes on them. His firstborn child is sprawled under a duvet and, as ever, Alec's first reaction is to be startled by the boy's bulk. Alec is stringy, Sandra is a lovely greyhound. Gary is brawny, blubbery almost, with big slabby shoulders and a seam of flesh around his jaw that could easily grow into a double chin. Who the hell does he take after? Where did he come from, this junior Mussolini?

"Cup of tea for you, son," says Alec.

Gary doesn't answer or open his eyes but he goes still. His mouth is set, his brows are slightly clenched. Alec is almost certain he's awake.

"Gary?"

There's a pause, as if Alec's voice has a long way to go to reach the relevant authorities. Down corridors the message goes, up stairs, till at last it reaches the Department of Irritating Dad, where a functionary will consent to look at it, and sigh.

"What," says Gary in the end.

"I was wondering if you'd had a chance to look at that brochure? From the college? With the list of courses?"

"No," says Gary.

"Well, you should, when you've got a moment."

"Huh," says Gary.

"There's all sorts in there. Graphic arts. Carpentry. Electrical."

"Dad," says Gary.

"You could take your pick. Decide where you wanna end up, and then work out what you need to get there."

"Dad!" says Gary, still without opening his eyes, but with a sort of thick anger gathering in his voice.

"What?"

"I don't *need* to go on a course. I've *told* you!"

"Well, you need to do something, don'tcha?" says Alec, feeling his own irritation kindle helplessly. "You're lying in bed in the middle of the day. If you're not going to stay in school, fine, but then you need to learn a trade. You need to get off your arse and—"

"I'm asleep!" bellows Gary. "I. Am. A. Bloody. Sleep!" And in an infuriated convulsion he draws up his big feet, pulls the duvet over his head and disappears. The interview is clearly terminated. But to make this doubly plain, a second later Gary's arm snakes out and he stabs the On button of his clock radio. Capital Radio at full volume fills the room, Kenny Everett howling like a camp banshee.

Alec retreats. His own anger fills him: his chest is tight with it, his fingers clench. He thumps down the stairs and ditches the tea mug in the sink. It slops as it goes, and he makes himself wipe it up neatly, and squeeze out the cloth, and rinse the mug. But peace does not return, his breath still comes quick and angry, the song, whatever it is, comes through the ceiling. Everyone knows that parenthood changes you: but he'd thought that meant the rearrangement that comes at the beginning of it, when you learn that your life is going to be curled protectively around the kids. He doesn't know what to do with this recent, new rage, where you feel the pattern of hopes and expectations you've had for them all this time start to shrivel and unpick, at their initiative; where they let you know that they don't want, or apparently even understand, what you want for them; where the story of their lives you've been telling yourself, with chances you'd've liked, and a step up you'd've been glad to take, turns out to be nothing like their own story of themselves. The homework carefully done with Gary—the projects, with the little light bulbs and the batteries and the wires—all gone. Gary doesn't want that. Gary wants— Oh, who knows what Gary wants. *Little bastard. Idle, ignorant, ungrateful little bastard.* He's not going to calm down in here, is he; and he should be on his way. Sweater, windbreaker, book in the pocket. But he shuts the front door with a demonstratively controlled click: no slam.

The meeting is in the NUFTO Hall on the corner of Jockey's Fields, just in the lee of Gray's Inn itself. When Alec gets off his bus, he finds himself in a swirl of barristers, wigged and gowned, being loaded into a fleet of black taxis along with box after box of documents. This is the funny thing about this part of London, this particular compartment of the city. At the south end of Gray's Inn Road, you've got this enclosed playground for the lawyers, with its paths and trees and stately facades, like an Oxford or Cambridge college parked in reach of the Old Bailey. But then, as you go up the street, just a couple of hundred yards if that, it turns industrial. There's four thousand people working in the *Times* building—well, when they *are* working—manufacturing the newspapers, and sending out the finished product in lorries. For that matter, you've got thousands of posties working just to the east in the Mount Pleasant sorting office, so there's a definite blue-collar critical mass. And then, when you go *on* up the Gray's Inn Road, again only a few hundred yards, it sinks into the scuzziness of King's Cross. Winos, tarts and petty crims, all being steadily ignored by the commuters streaming on and off the trains. And that's one street, half a mile long. It's like some sort of chart of society, from poshness to the lower depths by way of the factory. But the parts do mix. None of it is all just the one thing. It's the balance that shifts as you travel along it.

And here Alec is at the posh end, where the wigs predominate, and even a strike committee meets in a slightly college-quadrangle kind of atmosphere. The Furniture Trades Hall is one of those Edwardian edifices, like some old town halls or public libraries, that wanted to do grandeur for the people. Its actual hall is like a cut-down labour-movement version of the grand halls next door. Dark wood panels and scruffy plywood chairs.

He is a little bit late. The others on the joint liaison committee are already there, and Terry Fitzneil is tapping his biro on his agenda. He loves an agenda, does Terry. The *Times* dispute is five months old, and though it has quickened lately there is no sign of it coming to an end. But Terry's enthusiasm is undimmed. He seems to be immune to boredom. It's impressive, in a way, like being one of those people you hear of sometimes who can't feel pain. The other fathers-of-chapel from the five unions representing the *Times* and *Sunday Times* staff have got that crumpled look, preset for endurance; they sit slightly slumped, ready for the long haul, even though the meeting's just started. As old Clive Burnham said to Alec, before he emigrated to Australia, "You know what you need most, for a successful negotiation? An iron arse, that's what." Terry, on the other hand, seems as happy as a hamster on a wheel, eyes bright, moustache quivering. His secret weapon for defending his NATSOPA clericals—the typists, the secretaries, the ladies who take down the classified ads—is a limitless willingness to talk. In any sentence of any draft agreement he can find an ambiguity that requires exploration. Slow exploration. Long exploration. Patient exploration. It's a principle he brings to the job of handling the fraternal relations between unions, too.

"Lot to get through this morning, gents," Terry says. "Update on the picketing arrangements; some nice messages of support I'm gonna share with you; news on the situation with the scab edition in Germany; provisional report on the co-op ownership plan, I'm hoping? Where are we with that, Josh?"

"Coming along, Mr. Fitzneil." Delicate point of class etiquette, just there. Josh Eden is there from the *Times* journalists' chapel, a middle-class socialist playing nicely with the rough boys. He gets called Josh, just like the others round the table are Terry, Alec, Pat, George, Ian to each other. But he doesn't get to call them by their first names in return. That would be a liberty. The dignity of being given the *mister* by those who work on the fifth floor is too important, even if this particular member of the boss-class happens to be an ally. Half-included, Josh goes on: "But I think maybe we should talk about the NUJ exec's meeting last night first? There's been a development."

"Well, I was going to get to that under Item 3. Is it urgent?"

"I think so, yes."

"All right, then. I'll just make a note. Hold on."

They wait while Terry's biro moves carefully. Someone lights a fag from the stub of an old one.

"Yes," says Terry. "The floor is yours, Josh."

"Right. Thank you, Chair—"

"*Chair?*" says Pat derisively. "He's not a piece of fookin' furniture, you know."

"Steady on," says Alec. "Can't speak disrespectfully of furniture, you know: not in here."

"I'm just trying to avoid, er, sexism," says Josh.

"I wouldn't say no to a bit of sex, cold morning like this," says an elderly lithographer from SLADE who has somehow become the group's licensed blue joker, probably because his voice is satisfyingly prim.

"Still up for it, then, your missus, is she?" says Pat.

"I'm glad to say that Mrs. Edwards remains the tigress she has always been."

Whistles and hoots for politeness's sake, fairly nominal.

"Sex-*ism*," says Terry reprovingly. He nods to Josh and they subside.

"Right," says Josh. "Well, okay. Well, as I was saying, our NEC met last night, and the German edition was discussed; and I'm glad to say the ruling is that *Times* writers should *not* co-operate with the whole scheme."

"No co-operation meaning no copy?" asks Alec. The journalists' position in the dispute is tricky, because their chapels did reach a new working agreement with Times Newspapers Limited, last autumn, and so they didn't get laid off when the lockout came. They're still working, technically, though there isn't anything for them to write, or hasn't been till this idea of getting a kind of export-only *Times* printed up in Frankfurt came along. Apart from management, the journos are the only ones still occasionally going in and out of the building.

"Yes," says Josh, and a chorus of approval goes round the table. "But, sorry, there's a catch," he continues, raising his voice to be heard. "The national executive say no, but I couldn't quite swing it at our own chapel vote. I'm afraid it was a close thing, but the *Times* NUJ has voted *to* co-operate. Some of us will write for the German version of the paper. You know, people are frustrated? With the general election coming up and everything? They want to get their pennyworth in. I'm sorry, I know it's awkward."

"That's one word for it," says Pat.

"So, wait a minute, what's that going to mean on the picket?" says Alec, leaning forward. The picket concerns him more than it does any of the others, because it's the compositors who took the initiative when the German thing leaked, and it's the compositors and only the compositors who are keeping up the picket on all seven of the building's entrances. "If they cross the line, are they scabbing or not?"

"Not technically," says Josh. "Our constitution says the chapel has the final word, where there's this kind of disagreement."

"Maybe that's something that should be looked into, at a suitable moment," Terry says thoughtfully. "Convene a working group, maybe?"

"We're not the only ones who think local autonomy matters," says Josh, with a flash of defiance. The NATSOPA chapels are notoriously unruly, and have been ignoring their national leadership at will throughout the dispute.

"Leaving that on one side," Alec insists, "what are we supposed to be saying to people *today*? What do my members say to your members, if they try to go in?"

"It was very close, Mr. Torrance," says Josh to Alec. "Very close; and I think a lot of the people who voted in favour are uncomfortable with it, deep down. So I think if you do get people coming in, this afternoon, you could probably get a long way with just, um, a gentle appeal?"

Pat snorts, but Alec nods. A mighty social gulf separates the journalists from the troglodyte world of the printing plant in the basement; but they work with the compositors directly, often, or at least through the wafer-thin mediation of the subs. He knows most of the *Times*'s London writers, to look at if not necessarily to talk to. He's been typesetting their words for the last fifteen years. It's a kind of intimacy; it's something you can appeal to.

"Gentle appeals it is," he says.

Five hours later, and Alec is standing in one of the smallest doorways of the *Times* building, wearing an NGA armband. He's done his stint at the front door, where the picket is at its most visible and organised, and where there's the greatest chance of an argumentative encounter. In fact, bar the odd bit of chanting to do when Marmaduke Hussey came back from his lunch, and leafletting passers-by, it's been without drama. If *Times* journalists are at work today, they're doing it at home. Now Alec has taken over the unpopular job of watching a side exit, and to be honest he rather welcomed the chance to be bored in solitary peace, instead of in company. He propped himself against the crinkled brown mosaic-tile wall of the passageway, sunk his chin onto his chest, and disappeared into Mario Puzo.

Tried, anyway. But there's something insistently, distractingly woeful about the state of the building. He keeps glancing through the locked metal door at the stub of narrow corridor behind it, and the dim stairwell at the end, as if someone might come down. But of course they never do. The building is virtually empty, and rendered odd by its emptiness. It was never attractive, never somewhere with much of an atmosphere. The old *Times* site by St. Paul's was the place for that, the place where you could feel the history, and know that the brickwork had centuries' worth of ink ground into it, all the way back to the dawn of the print, to hand presses and hand-setting. New Printing House Square, the present building is called, to try and claim some continuity, but it's a dull and plain object, with fake arches of the mosaic cladding at the top of all the windows, and the only thing showing it's not just an office block being the huge shuttered doors closing off the ramp from the basement. *And it ain't square either.* It's the shape of a sans-serif capital D, with a patch of corporate garden between the two prongs on the left.

The only thing it had going for it was energy. When the building was full, it buzzed like a hive. A quarrelsome hive, prone to blockage and disruption, admittedly: but even when in a state of frustration or bad temper, somewhere that pulsed with anxious urgency, all day long, accelerating and accelerating as the evening drew towards press time: when, after Pat's NATSOPA boys had extracted their pound of flesh or Terry had forced a clarification of the word "secretary" from some luckless editor, the presses would roll, and the roar and vibration of the great rotating drums would travel upstairs through the whole building, as a shake in the floors, a chattering of pencils left on desks, a standing wave in a cold, half-drunk mug of tea. And then, when Alec came out onto the pavement on his way to the bus stop, in winter dark or lingering blue high-summer light, his part of the process done, the first lorries would just be grinding up the ramp, stacked with bales of newsprint bound for the railway stations, so that tomorrow over breakfast in Greenock and Merioneth people could read Bernard Levin's thoughts on *Aida*, or editorials by William Rees-Mogg containing words like "orotund" and "oriflamme." O-r-i-f-l-a-m-m-e.

Now, instead, the building is a derelict, a hulk. You could see it most clearly back before the days lengthened, when at teatime only a pathetic few strip lights would flicker on, up in the management's rooms on the sixth floor, and the rest of the building dimmed to black. Blackness behind the hundreds of metal-framed windows, concentrating in there while outside it was still grey urban dusk. In the April light, the dereliction is less blatant, but it's still palpable, and miserable. This is a hive without bees he's guarding; a modern ruin; a structure unknitting itself. Entropy has crept through offices and composing rooms. Dust is gathering. There's a polystyrene cup lying on its side at the bottom of the steps that must have been there for weeks. Energy is dying into dullness.

Alec is genuinely uncertain whether it's ever going to come back to life. Management seem utterly cack-handed in their willingness to pick a fight they don't know how to win. On the union side, the unity they can just about maintain in a talking shop like Terry's committee falters into bickering as soon as there's something definite on the table. The whole reason that there's union leverage on Fleet Street is that the product is perishable—that if the *Times* doesn't make it to the newsagents within a window of a few hours, it becomes unsaleable. But where does that power to take the print run hostage go when the paper is closed down by management? What can the compositors and the lithographers and the ad girls and the machine room operators threaten now?

And beyond all that, there's the issue specific to his own union, the technological threat that affects the compositors alone. In any conceivable future, the paper is still going to need printing; there'll still have to be people to operate the presses. (Though, yeah, probably not the five-hundred-odd that Pat claims pay packets for, half with names like M. MOUSE and D. DUCK written on them, thinks Alec, his compositor's lip curling at the dirty ways of NATSOPA.) But upstairs somewhere, management has already bought and installed a computerised system for photo-composition. There are keyboards up there from which you can set whole pages of type, not single lines, without the need for burbling reservoirs of lead, or noisy Victorian clockwork. The NGA position is that they're happy to move on from hot lead to quiet, hygienic screens, so long as it's union compositors who sit at those screens, tapping away. But management has noticed—how could they not?—that this essentially means the pointless retyping of what the journos have typed in the first place. You could put the journos at the keyboards, and give them "direct input," and at a stroke (at a keystroke, ha ha) you'd abolish the compositor. You'd abolish the whole skill that has meant a good living for working men for eighty years. You'd abolish Alec's grandfather, and father. You'd abolish Alec. This is what a management victory threatens. This is what they keep pushing for: not the whole thing at once, they know they won't get that, but little holes to puncture the dam, thin ends to a very fat wedge. Won't you let us . . . have the phone girls input the ads directly, just the ads? Won't you agree . . .

to let the NGA supervise a single journalist keyboarding—just as an experiment? So far all these little probes for weakness have been fended off. Les Dixon, the NGA president, comes faithfully down to Gray's Inn Road once a week to report, and he makes it sound as if it's perfectly possible to hold the line; as if the sergeant majors of the union have safely got the measure of the officers up on the top floor. (Back in the war, he really was RSM Dixon in the Royal Military Police while Marmaduke Hussey was being Captain Hussey of the Grenadier Guards.) Maybe, thinks Alec. Maybe. It's true that the *Guardian* and the *Mirror* have signed up for photo-composition by the union. But alone with the loud melancholy of the building, surrounded by a million grimy brown tiles, it's hard to avoid a melancholy of his own. In this blocked-off inlet of a dead building, the thought is horribly near that his own life in the print, these last twenty years, may also have been a blind alley.

Oh, come on, he thinks, *snap out of it*. Whatever happens, he reminds himself, it has been a good life. He's been able to feed and clothe and house Sandra and the boys. He's been able to pay for school trips, nights at the pictures, a colour telly, a car. Holidays, too: though when they went to Spain, there was noisy boredom from the boys when he tried to get them to look at old churches. Stevie adores Gary, that's the trouble; always has, from when he was a toddler. If big brother does it, he does it too. Oh well, that's a melancholy sidetrack of its own. Alec liked it better last year, when the boys were left to look after themselves for a weekend, in a litter of fish-and-chip paper, and he and Sandra went bed-and-breakfasting in Kent, on their own. It was about this time of year, come to think of it. They went walking round a gravel pit, just the two of them, on a green-and-white day when mist up above matched the blossom on the thorn bushes. Both ways round: as if it was shreds of mist that had caught in the bushes, and as if the pale sky was about to burst out into flowers. A green-and-white world, and him and Sandra hand in hand in it.

Oh, come on, you great softy, he thinks. Thrusts the neglected copy of *The Godfather* into his anorak, pokes his head out of the doorway. Nothing happening. He'll just nip along to the main picket, check everything's hunky-dory.

"All right, lads?" he's just saying as he approaches, when a boy with sideburns whose name he can't remember, not long out of the apprenticeship and fresh-moved to the *Times* when the lock-out began, points at something over Alec's shoulder.

"Ey-ey-ey!" he cries.

Alec turns and a figure is indeed bowling across the road towards the emptied doorway, loose-limbed and slightly approximate but moving with intent.

"Shall we come over with you, bit of moral support?" says the boy.

"No, no," calls Alec as he sprints back, "I know him. More chance if it's just one."

He is just in time to block the entry as Hugo Cornford of the political desk reaches it. He's in his early forties, but burly in that upper-crust way you get when the effects of public-school rugby linger lifelong. He has brogues and corduroy trousers on, and one of those non-functional scarves wrapped round his neck, like an enormous woolly cravat. And judging by his high colour and slightly random movements, he is indeed a journalist who has lunched.

"Buggeration," he says. "I thought there wouldn't be anyone in these little doors. Hello, Alec."

"Hello, Hugo. Sorry, the picket's here too. Anyway, 's locked."

"I," says Hugo, his voice booming in his chest like an echo trying to get out of a cave, "happen to have a key, actually. And I'm coming in. As the bishop said to the actress."

"Well, I won't stop you—" begins Alec.

"*Can't* stop me, actually, legally, I think?"

"—but I am going to ask you to think about it for a sec."

"Oh-kay. Thinking about it, thinking about it, thought about it now; still coming in."

Cornford is much less of a bullshitter when he is sober, Alec reminds himself. He's a foreign correspondent turned parliamentary sketch writer, and Alec has been reading his work for more than a decade now. (Some compositors, maybe most, let the copy flow through their minds untouched by conscious attention, like a stream of Morse code. But not Alec.) Terse, atmospheric, anger-breeding reports from Vietnam; more recently, acidic comedy from the House of Commons, as the Labour government lurches from emergency to emergency. He's good. His sentences are a pleasure to set. He is—at least he used to be—one of those posh Trotskyists, with their own mysterious little world from which they emerge to be a good sport, old bean, on protest marches.

"I suppose you're here to write up something for the German edition," says Alec. "Am I right?"

"For the forlorn rag which is all that remains of a great paper, yes. And why shouldn't I?"

"Well, because this is a picket line, and you're a socialist."

"Am I?" says Cornford, rubbing at his face. "I don't know what that word even means any more."

Not very promising.

"Cigarette?" says Alec, offering his packet.

"No, no, I should get on," Cornford says, and he starts fumbling in his corduroys for a key.

"All right, then, because," says Alec, "the German print run probably won't even happen?"

"Is that right." *Jingle, jingle.*

"Yes. I don't know if you know, but we've got the German print unions looking for the outfit that's doing it, and when they find it—"

"They'll try to shut it down, I suppose? Oh, charming. Very constructive."

"When they *find* it," says Alec, getting crosser himself, "they'll let them know that it's a sleazy ploy to get around a legitimate dispute back in England, and then it'll be up to them whether they want to piss off IG Papier and be blacklisted forever after."

"I see. How dignified. How righteous. So?" He's found his key.

Alec looks at Cornford. It's as if some piece of awkward but previously negotiable understanding has vanished, or been withdrawn, and in its place has appeared, or reappeared, something . . . harder.

"So," Alec persists, "for the sake of something that probably won't even happen, you'll be risking your"—what's the best word—"*relationships* with all the people you work with."

"Work with?" says Cornford, and now he looks hard at Alec, and seems bull-like, threatening almost. "I don't 'work with' you. I get messed around by you; I get held up by you."

"Me?" says Alec, holding the look.

"No, not you personally. I mean you chaps in general; all of you chaps. This last couple of years, we don't even know if you're going to deign to let us bring the paper out. It's touch and go every bloody night."

"That's not us, that's NATSOPA."

"Who cares which of you it is? NATSOPA and the NGA, SLADE and SOGAT: I'm sick of the lot of you."

"Well, this last couple of years," says Alec, "we've turned into the worst-paid workforce in Fleet Street. Did you know that? Management have stuck to the government's bloody incomes policy, and we're the ones who've paid the price for it. Maybe that's why things have got a bit bad-tempered, did you ever think?"

"Don't care; sorry, don't care. I just want to be able to write my stuff, and know it'll be printed. Now can you move out of the way, please?"

I just want to write my stuff. Alec is suddenly able to draw the obvious conclusion from Cornford's agitation, his sense of urgency, and flings it out as a last gambit.

"You've got a story, haven't you?" he says. Deliberately, he grins.

"Yes!" says Cornford.

"And you're dying to get it down, aren't you? You want to tell the world, don't you?"

"*Yes,*" says Cornford. "Come on, Alec, move over."

"Well, if you go in there, it won't get printed, will it. Why not tell it to me?"

Cornford laughs, then he stops.

"Seriously?" he says.

"Yes. Go on."

"No offence, but you're not exactly the audience I had in mind. You're more the subject matter."

"What do you mean?"

"I mean that I've just been to a lunch at the House of Commons, and the times they are about to change."

"We can deal with the Tories," says Alec. "We saw them off last time."

"This is going to be different. They're not the half-hearted patricians you're used to; not any more. And then—and then— I'm afraid you chaps are going to get blown away like dandelion fluff. Gangway!"

Cornford pushes past in a spiritous vapour, jiggles open the door, shuts it behind him, and is gone up the stairs. A storey up, he must click a light switch: a small, bleak patch of fluorescence flickers into existence on the steps at the end of the dead stub of corridor.

Jo

Jo has a little house on the heights. Really, the summerhouse of the grander glass-walled place next door, but separated from it during some kind of marital dispute of the landlord's, and now rented out on its own, with its own little crease in the hillside filled with the deep green shade of pines and succulents, bamboo and yucca: the California green that can make you forget the California brown all around it. The deck is upstairs, on a level with the tops of the branches, and looks west through a notch in the skyline towards the bruise-coloured inversion layer and the mica glitter of LA on the plain below. When she breakfasts out there, it isn't usually morning. Times they are recording, like now, make her almost nocturnal, and once she's got rid of any company—less and less of a necessity these days—and comes blearily outside with a cup of black coffee and a sliced peach taken cold from the fridge, it's around five in the afternoon. The sun is sinking westwards, swollen and bloody, and she sits in a puddle of crimson light, her eyes itching behind her shades. But then the track of the sun takes it behind the canyon wall. The last lip of its disc blazes into a bright line and disappears, and all of a sudden she finds herself in a space of gentle air, long-shadowed, blood-warm. The cicadas are tuning up their instruments, the smog above the city is dimming to pearlescent prettiness, the lights below are just beginning to twinkle out their come-on that never tires. She's tired, though. She pours a second cup of coffee and in the couple of hours that are hers before she is due at that night's restaurant rendezvous, she makes herself fetch out the four-track in the twilight and, with no one to hear, tries to work out a little music on her own account.

Guitar first. This is a song she's trying to come at from both ends. She has a few of the words, and an inkling of the tune, but not the whole of either. What she knows is the colours it should be. It should be grey, silver and brown; the brown, that is, of old wood, or old brick walls, not the warm living brown of skin, which needs a different music altogether. Cold-weather colours that are nowhere on the Californian palette, even in this tender evening glow. So, maybe A minor? And acoustic, of course. She settles the Ovation on her knee, and picks out a basic little pattern in four-four time. Plucks it, rather, with her nails, to give it a melancholy sharpness, an almost tinkling plaintive edge in the sound. Steady, though: she doesn't want to pick the steel strings too hard and turn the sound too country. Hmm.

Round and round she goes, and her intuitions of tune begin to take some more shape and to declare themselves. Something is forming: a structure for the verses (three lines: two short, one double-long) that goes *Dee-dee dee DEE, Dee-dee dee DEE-ee, Dee dee-dee dee dee DEE dee dee dee-dee DEE-ee.* And a chorus, higher, which for three little sets of call and response will make a wistful, tentative, suspended kind of sound, at least the first time she sings through it, but which can then fill out with a stronger push of mournful feeling on the next visit, before soaring out (both times) into a line that will use her full voice. *Dee-dee-dee, DEE-dee; Dee-dee-dee, Dee-dee; Dee-dee-dee, DEE DEE; Dee dee dee dee dee-dee DEE DEE DEE.* Like that, or nearly like that. Something's there, and it has the colouring she wants, grey silver brown, which for her are memory-colours, the shades for things remembered rather than physically present. Is it hers, though? In this groping early stage it's hard to tell apart a melody you're discovering from one you're half-remembering. She thinks so, but tucks a little mental reservation into place so she isn't wholly surprised or disheartened if she remembers a source for it in another song, later.

Right. Catch it, while the catching is good. (The shadows have lengthened out into a sheet of shade, abolishing the gold etching round the edges of the leaves, and the sky is going to dark violet, and the lights of the city on the plain are sparkling brighter in proportion.) Plug in the pick-up. Stretch the leader from a new spool of decent BASF tape through the heads and onto the take-up reel. Fast-forward a little way. *Flip flip flipflipflipflip.* Zero the timer. Turn on track one and check the needle moves with a chord or two. Check tracks two, three and four are safely off. Cue up the combination of buttons for Record, with Pause engaged as the trigger. Breathe. And . . . Pause off. The sweet-tipped melancholy jangle of A minor floats over the darkened paddles of the cactuses and the resinous asterisks along the pine branches. With the part of her mind that isn't concentrating on picking as precisely as possible, she notices how inevitable the tune is already sounding: how meant, how deliberate, this thing that she has been pulling together from who knows what vapour, who knows how. It's necessary, this hardening of the separate parts of a song. Without it, as you turned to a new task, the rest would melt back into the mush of possibility again. And if you need to alter what has already hardened, there is scope to return and soften it again, for a while. She does so now: as she plays back the guitar track, and is provisionally pleased with it, a thought occurs to her, and she goes back and re-records the same thing on track one, only now with a bit of reverb on. Yes, that's right. Though the physical space she's working in is the room behind an open deck, with the French doors open, her pointillist sad steelwork now sounds as if it's happening somewhere bigger and emptier, echoing back just a little from the surfaces of distant objects. From the remembered things, the absent things, the song will name, perhaps. This is how the feel builds, laid physically into the acoustics, integrating sound and idea.

131

If this were proper studio work, not homebrew improvisation, she'd go on to figure out a bassline, a piano line, maybe, on one of an electric piano's lonelier-sounding settings. But with just her and a four-track, the guitar is the only instrument she has space for. She wants the other three tracks for voice. That's where there's most to work out, that's where the heavy lifting of mood needs to go; and she has in mind—half in mind, half-loose and indefinite and out of reach until she has the actual sounds before her and can wind them to actuality—a delicate thing where on two of the tracks she harmonises with herself on a time delay, so that echo between two versions of her duetting in time creates, in another reinforcing way, the empty space, the longing absence of the song. Leaving the last track for her as her own backing singer. A chorus of Jos: two at the front facing each other, and another behind doo-wopping, oo-woo-ing, yay-yay-ing. And all on her terms.

The land is black now, though, and the sky behind is a deep indigo, gauzy, cinematic, looking as if it's waiting shamelessly for searchlights and kettledrums. (That's the trouble with living in the Hollywood Hills. Reality tends constantly towards movie cliché, particularly once nightfall has smoothed away the daytime scurf of Los Angeles, refining all those one-storey breeze-block bodegas and bail bond offices into vistas of tail-lights and skyglow.) She looks at her watch. No time to do it all. But time to begin. If she hurries. If she can manage to keep hurry out of her voice.

Track two. Plug in the mike. Fetch out the pad that's got her criss-crossed first thoughts about the lyrics on it. She can hardly see it in the small leaks of light from the meters of the four-track, but it's important to have the piece of paper there, somehow, even if she's working mostly from memory. It's another solidification, another little handle on something still only half-formed. Sing a little against the guitar track with Record off to play with the levels. That'll do. Remember to press the Simul-Sync button, so the playback she's singing against isn't a randomising twelfth of a second out of sync with the voice—not a delicate game with time, that, but a toe-stubbing trip over time's doorstep, when you get it wrong. Breathe. Breathe. Try to banish the anxieties of the night, and find grey, silver, brown: the sound of missing what is missing, of feeling the distance of all you name, as you name it. For some reason it is getting hotter again, as if the withdrawal of the light has stilled the air currents on the hillside. The LA night presses. Pause off, and Jo raises a voice, a small voice, an unhopeful voice, and sends it winding out into the hot dark.

> *A love unknown*
> *A seed not sown*
> *May grow someday into a flowering tree*
>
> *Next time's the charm*
> *No fire alarm*
> *To smash the spell uniting you and me*

Then the chorus, with the momentum that's gathered so far dialled back into high, wistful to-and-fro. Almost throaty, almost raspy, the feeling near the surface; and as she works on that, pushing deep down away from the surface, as far into irrelevant oblivion as she can manage, where it can't mess things up, the distracting thought that she might (of all things) have stolen part of the tune from Ray Charles singing "Makin' Whoopee." No, no, no. Shut up, mind, and sing.

> *Hanging on*
>   *next time*
> *Depending on*
>   *next time*

And all because
　this time

And then some muscle into the voice: not too much, a marker for how strong this line's going to be when the chorus comes round again, and she's shifted into full-throated angry-woman lament. But some. A change of gear. A filling-out. A gain of force. And naturally a platform for the clever things her second self will be singing against her, here.

. . . you left me singing solo harmonies

Leave a gap, a longer gap than seems natural, to accommodate whatever layering will go in there on the other tracks. If it's too long she can always trim it in the edit. And round again into the verses, but now with power continuing in the voice at a level only a little lower than the last line of the chorus. Push, Jo. Let the diva out. Push rage and heartbreak into the night. Make the silver and the grey, ring; let the brown resound.

Pouring rain
As you explain
We're better off divided, you and me

A moment's hush
And then the rush
Of this time crumbling into history

Something into history, anyway. Crashing? Folding? Drifting? Fading? This time the thought snags her too insistently, and just like that pulls her out of the necessary mood. The song crashes, folds, crumbles, drifts, fades. And into its place the anxiety she's been holding at bay comes irresistibly. Shit. Press Pause. Her watch says she's out of time anyway. Rewind; label the tape NEXT TIME #1 and put it away in the row of others, that little library of ideas for which (it seems to her when she's down) she's always running out of time, or missing the moment, or finding her enthusiasms have moved on from. She will finish this one, she swears. And she has also sworn, she reminds herself, that she will make herself make Ricky listen to something here, while he's in reach. Her fingers dance nervously along the shelf. NEXT TIME isn't ready. He's never, never hearing LOST SOUL. She picks out NOBODY'S FAULT, four-fifths of a piece of cheerful funk about earthquakes.

And after a quick shower, and a brief confrontation with her face in the bathroom mirror as she dolls herself up, she's away, heading down-canyon in the Beetle with the windows wound open all the way. When the night air goes sluggish and stifling here, you can either hide indoors in the aircon, or move through it, making your own breeze. That must be some of the reason why the freeways are busy almost till midnight, these August nights, and at the stoplights on the boulevards there's always a revving, impatient queue. It's not that people have anywhere to get to, they just can't stand staying still. Hot gusts, sage-smelling, blow on her as she corners and corners and corners again on the bends of the canyon road, washing-machine whirr sounding from the engine compartment, headlights skipping and sidling across trashcans, mailboxes, adobe walls, pine roots, the crazy-paved barrier at the edge of the drop and, nearly at the bottom, the carcass of a piano someone dragged outside to be nested in by jays. It's a kind of boundary stone, that piano. It seems to have been there, bleaching, for a decade, since the canyon's hippy glory days. It declared the beginning of the freaks' kingdom, to those going up. The end of it, going down. Beyond, the road straightens and the grade eases, and after only another minute she's crossing Sunset and has joined the red/white flow of the automotive pilgrimage to nowhere. The light streams carry her. The tropical neon swallows her.

The restaurant is in Beverly Hills. Now and again, Ricky will conceive a fancy for really obscure ethnic food, or for some Mexican place that's been written up for its challenging authenticity, and they'll all obediently troop off to Long Beach or Culver City. But for the most part he has a taste for unironic, dependable luxury. He likes cocktails, and steak, and valet parking, and beautiful waitstaff, and maître d's who know who you are and who seat you where you get the right combination of privacy and admiration. So Jo pulls up a manicured drive between uplighters styled to look like Japanese stone lanterns, and has the VW sneered at by a boy who looks like a dilute version of the young Tony Curtis. And then is hastily grovelled to, once it becomes clear that she is somehow part of the entourage. She finds them all in a private (or "private") room beyond the pool, a long low teak cabana blue-lit by reflections from the water, and safely out of earshot of the other diners but so latticed and louvred that rock-star still lifes in various poses are sure to be on view.

She's the last to arrive, or nearly the last. The table is already cluttered with glassware and food, and Ricky is seated halfway up, *Last Supper*-style, flanked by a gaggle of people on his left and a gaggle on his right, all leaning slightly in towards him and paying attention, even as they rabbit on to each other about other things. She doesn't know any of them very well, though they're now into their second week of working together. There's Si, Ricky's new manager, and Si's plus-one, a blonde girl trying hard to fall out of a halter top. There's Johnson, a gruff bassist from Watts whom she rather rates. (He has been responding to Ricky's attempts to soul up the mix with silently rising eyebrows.) There's Rubén, the producer provided by the label; there's Ricky's own favoured producer Ed, present to keep things territorially complicated. There's

Ricky's PA, Melissa, a size-6 New Yorker. There's the engineer from Aurora Studios, invited along every night since the second one, on Ricky's principle that you should always butter up the sound guy, and his assistant, a crop-haired lesbian with an opiate pallor who is well worth listening to when she isn't locked in the toilet. Further out, there's the nightly altering crew of session musicians, in whose number Jo technically belongs, except she doesn't. Closest in—in fact stuck to Ricky's right side like five foot ten of bronze draught excluder—is his current girlfriend, twenty-two-year-old Angeline from Buenos Aires, delivering another instalment of her surely exhausting one-woman show *Continuous Minx*. She shrugs, she pouts, she rolls her eyes. She dibbles in his shirt front with her almond-shaped scarlet nails. The man himself is tapping his fag ash into a half-drunk flute of Dom Pérignon and twiddling his expensively spiked platinum hair.

"Wotcher, Frogface," she says.

"'Ello, J!" he says, looking up. His voice after seven years in America has morphed into a kind of generic expat cockney. It would be easier to deal with him if she could concentrate on how ridiculous that is, and not notice that his face still lights up with reliable pleasure when he sees her.

"What is this, this 'frog'?" enquires Angeline, scowling.

"'S just an old joke, sweetheart," says Ricky. To Jo: "All right, then? Thought you'd stood us up."

"Just trying to finish something."

"Right, right," says Ricky. He doesn't ask what; he never has. "Gotta have you here, though, babes. Can't do without you, you know that."

What is it in her he can't do without: that's the question. What she does for him, what she means to him. All that seemed obvious, once. During the golden year that *Racket* broke America for him and they toured month after month across the continent, the music was something they were doing together. She was with him constantly, on the stage and off, sharing a bed in every hotel from Nashville to Seattle, a bed which was their bed not his bed. In Atlanta they went to a black church together on Sunday morning to drink gospel from the source. In a lodge among redwood trees in Oregon they played with a mandolin all through a midsummer night, till dawn came through the calm red columns in green beams. In the Wichita Hilton he tickled her so unmercifully that she actually wet herself. That year she was . . . something unnamed. But something more substantial than a rock star's girlfriend. Collaborator, musical best friend, sounding board, sharer in the ridiculous adventure of his fame: from San Diego to Boston, almost as inevitable and central a member of the band as him. Only not on paper, and not with any songwriting credits, which turned out to mean that it was easy for her to fall all the way out of the band when she got pregnant (Bangor, Maine, a blizzard day) and he panicked, and needed her to make the threat of permanence go away, and then suddenly couldn't bear to have her around.

But he couldn't bear to let her go completely either. She had her viable small-scale West Coast life, never near the headliners again yet never short of work, and on he went into full-blown celebrity, adding glam-rock sequins to his original white-boy blues. But when he had a record to make, and sometimes when he didn't, when he was just in town, he'd leave a message on her answering machine, chirpy and wistful; and then she'd find herself in a studio with him, or in a bed, and for a little while they would inhabit a painful echo of the past that neither of them seemed quite able to refuse. It wasn't just nostalgia. It would have been easier to resist if so. Reduced, ragged, something still reliably awoke between them. Unfinished business with a long half-life, getting fainter on a slow clock.

Last week, when they'd been working on a raspy crowd-pleaser that she found almost completely synthetic, a piece of plastic soul worked up to make housewives throw knickers at him, he'd caught the scepticism on her face.

"Don'tcha like it?" he said.

"I dunno. It's a bit . . . leopard-skin trousers, isn't it?"

"Oi! What's wrong with leopard-skin trousers?"—grinning, joking, but with a touch of real anxiety in there, too. Her judgement still affected him. He still wanted her approval. He wouldn't do anything at her say-so that he wasn't already planning to do; but he wanted to be reassured about it. It was like being, in this one narrow respect, his wife, with the power to make him feel okay, or not.

Tonight follows a familiar pattern. Food and drink and bullshitting and a line or two, and a swim in the electric blue of the restaurant pool with much look-at-me splashing from Angeline, and a blowjob-length disappearance by her and Ricky, while Si flirts awkwardly with Jo. He has picked up that she is important to Ricky but cannot work out how, exactly. She is not inclined to help him out. Sometime towards 1 a.m., they make the move over to Aurora, Ricky trying to urge her to ride in the stretch limo, she insisting on puttering along behind in the VW. (Jo's principle: never be without your own means of departure.) Another burst of high-jinks before they settle, the transition being marked by the ceremonial playback of last night's completed track, the disco-fied number that put Johnson into the state of silent irony. Then, finally, they can get to tonight's work, a relatively simple ballad-ish thing which, thank God, has the potential to be genuinely touching if done right. It's not by Ricky; it's a cover version, but one chosen quite cunningly to suit his voice. He's always been able to survey his own talent with a detached eye. It's one of the things she finds admirable about him. He puts on the cans, shuts his eyes and becomes serious. She falls into her own familiar groove when working with him, in and out of the picture as required of her as a backing singer, but otherwise without comment becoming part of the little group around the engineer in the control room. When she makes a suggestion to Ricky through his phones, when she stops him and tells him his phrasing's off, he nods contentedly.

By half four they've essentially got the track. Angeline is bored and yawning as they listen to the playback. They need a retake on part of Jo's rising wail in the third verse, and she heads back through the soundproof doors.

"Someone come and give me a note?" she says, and she is surprised, but not totally surprised, when Ricky follows her through, and sits down at the piano, alone with her on the players' side of the glass.

Pling-pling-pling, he goes, on the C above middle C. She finds it, she gives the thumbs-up to Ed, the engineer rolls tape, and she pulls up from her diaphragm, if she does say so herself, just the quiet banshee ripples which will resonate unobtrusively with Ricky's voice. He listens, smiling. Beyond the glass Angeline scowls. She is not without basic radar, even if all her brain cells are devoted to controlling her hips, even if she has no idea why it should be the cranky, uncharming woman of nearly forty who is a rival here. Jo points.

"You're pissing someone off," she tells Ricky.

"Yeah?" says Ricky.

He makes eye contact with Angeline, poises his hands over

the keyboard, and without warning starts pounding the ivories in full-on honky-tonk pub-piano mode.

She was a beauty queen-ah!
From down in Argentin-ah!

Angeline doesn't know much, but she knows when she's being mocked. She flounces out of sight.

"Can you turn off, please, Ed?" says Ricky into his mike. The green lights wink out.

"That wasn't very kind," says Jo.

"Do you care?" says Ricky.

"Nope."

"Didn't think so."

"I was wondering—" she begins.

"I was hoping—" he says at the same time.

"What?" says Ricky.

"No, you first."

"Well," Ricky says, looking down and playing soft chords, "I was hoping . . ."

She knows what he means. She knows what it will be like if she says yes, based on all the other times she's said yes. Twenty-four tempestuous hours of expensive hotel, good sex (because they know their way round each other really well), more or less coke depending on the state of Ricky's habits, and almost certainly some highly pleasurable messing about together on guitar and piano. He always gets a suite with a piano. "Hey, Liberace," she'll say, and he'll chase her around the bed. It'll be fun. And it will end with protestations, and with him sending her home up the canyon in a limo she does accept. And they'll have been pretending, both of them. It will have been a tiny visit to what might

have been, which only works because they look away from the difficult stuff, and ask no questions, and part before the pretending
becomes unbearable. And maybe she will do it anyway, because
she misses it so. But now it will look as if what she wants to ask
him is a quid pro quo, a favour in return for a favour.

"What about . . . ?" she says, nodding towards the sound booth.

"That's not exactly serious."

And what are we? she wants to say, but doesn't. He sees her
hesitation, and doesn't press the point. He has his delicacies.

"What were you gonna ask me, then?"

"D'you ever miss London?" she says, chickening out: but
chickening out into a subject that really has been on her mind.

"God, no," says Ricky, looking surprised. "I was there on tour
in the spring, and it was grim, grim, grim. Dirty and miserable
and kind of, you know, defeated-feeling?"

"So far as you could tell from Claridge's."

"So far as I could tell from the Dorchester, darling. Why?"

"Oh, nothing much."

"You're homesick, aren'cha," he says, with a sharp, diagnostic
glance.

"Well, maybe."

"I get that. I do! But not for London. You gotta remember, it
was only somewhere I stayed for a bit, mostly in bloody bedsits.
But Bristol—yes, I miss Bristol, moy lovurr." A quick trill on the
high notes. "Not often, but sometimes. I'll be in a hotel somewhere, doing my stuff, click-click, flash-flash, hello darling, and
I'll realise, shit, for hours and hours I've been walking through
Filwood in the back of my head. Like a very slow slideshow, you
know, going on behind everything else? And it gets you, doesn't it,
under here." He pokes himself under his ribs. "But you wait, and
it goes away again. You just have to wait it out."

"You don't ever want to go back for real?"

"Can't, can I? 'S not Filwood *now* I'm walking through, whatever that's like; it's Filwood *then*, and the postboxes are taller than my head, and I'm on my way home with a Lonnie Donegan single; and that's the point. That's all gone. Except in here." *Tap-tap.* "I wouldn't find it if I got on a plane, would I?"

"I suppose not."

"You can't go home, babes. You can't go *back*. You gotta go on. Think about it. What's waiting for you, if you get on a plane?" His voice has gone gentle. "Not your mum, love. Tea's not waiting on the table."

"There's my sister."

"The one who's married to the actual Nazi."

"That's the one."

"Tempting, highly tempting. You could go and help them sing 'Deutschland, Deutschland' on the streets of Lewisham."

"Bexford."

"Same difference. No! Stay in the sunshine, love."

He plays end-of-a-tune chords—*dum, dum, du-dumm*—which make it clear that he's ready for the conversation to be over, and for him to get an answer to his question. And something about this, and about his obvious pleasure just now at being given a chance on easy terms to be wise and kind, tips a balance inside Jo, and makes it possible for her to say what she meant to in the first place.

"Can I play you something?"

He blinks.

"Like, of your own?"

"Yeah."

"Course! Anytime, babes, anytime."

"I've got it here."

"Oh-kay . . . Right. Right! Let's have it on."

They go back through the soundproof doors, Ricky wearing a

faint puzzled frown, and she fishes the reel of "Nobody's Fault" out of her bag.

"Something of Jo's we're just going to run through," announces Ricky to Ed, Rubén, Opiate Dyke, Johnson, the other draggled survivors of the night. "Didn't I always say, look out when Jo gets an album together? Didn't I always say, she's gonna do something great?"

They nod, but it's polite, uncomprehending. None of these are the people they toured with in '72 and '73, who saw them in their glory days. Ricky has fallen out with all of those—with everybody, in fact, who knew the non-famous version of him. Except, possibly, her. This lot pick up a few old-girlfriend molecules in the air, and that's it.

"Rick?" says Ed, yawning, before she can get the tape anywhere near the reel-to-reel. "Could we maybe do that later? We've really got to put this track to bed now?"

"Yeah, yeah," says Ricky, clicking his tongue. "I suppose you're right. Sorry, J. Duty calls. But—next time, yeah?"

Dawn finds her at the store halfway up the canyon. It's just opened. Normally she pulls the Beetle over and nips inside only for long enough to pick up some milk, and some fruit from the trays in the shade out front: furred peaches, plums with the purple-white bloom still on them, watermelons striped like circus tents. But today for some reason she buys a cup of fresh coffee from the percolator and takes it outside to sit with it under the vine. All the time she's lived here there's been a mural on the front wall, a Joan Baez-like hippy-chick face, crowned with stars, growing paler and paler as the LA sun wears away the colours. Now the owners have had it repainted. Their glory days are what they plan to trade on forever. Joan's eyes are piercing turquoise again, Joan's hair is a smooth gloss-black waterfall. And above, the sky brightens to the implacable blue of yet another day without rain.

She misses rain.

Vern

Rain is general all over London, falling in a steady dismal downpour on the bridges, on the monuments, on the parks, on the rusting cranes in the docks, on the twenty thousand sullen streets; on the sodden green of Bexford Park and the grey towers of the Park Estate; on last night's vomit, swilling away across the pavements to join the mush of fish-and-chip paper in the gutter; falling too, further out, on the golf courses of Swanley and the avenue named after a flower where Vern is being thrown out of the large detached house he bought before his second bankruptcy.

"Don't forget anything," says Kath, watching as he wrestles a cardboard box and a suitcase down the stairs. "I'm not sending it after you."

"Fuck it," says Vern, "this is an overnight bag and stuff for this week. Half of everything here is mine."

"It bloody isn't, and watch your mouth in front of the girls, thank you very much."

Sally and Becky, aged four and six, are hiding behind their mother's legs.

"Daddy will be back soon," says Vern to them, trying for a voice of reassurance: but he hasn't ever had much to do with them, and they shrink away. Two stocky little girls and one stocky little woman, like peas in a pod. A female family, sufficient without him.

"No, he won't," says Kath. "Daddy is slinging his hook. *Daddy!* When were you ever that? We wouldn't have a bloody roof over our heads if it wasn't for me. You screwed up, I sorted it. So none of this is yours, not any more."

It's true that it was Kath, as the accountant for Albemarle Developments, who talked him into putting the house in her name, "just in case," and it's true that that's what stopped the house getting treated as an asset, and washed away by the debts when Albemarle went tits-up. But he can remember other things being true. There's no point in arguing, not now, but he can't help himself.

"You were just as much in favour of the shopping centre as me," he says.

"Well, I didn't think you'd make such a pig's ear of it, did I."

"It was the bloody interest rates that did us in, you know that!"

"We'd have coped with them if the income had kept up. But it didn't, and whose fault was that? You picked the location. You picked the tenants. You skimped on the insurance. You!"

Vern, pinned by banisters, box, suitcase, feels a familiar wrath congesting him. Kath's sharp little finger is up, poking at the air in front of her, and her face is stony with dislike. But there's something else in it, a kind of satisfaction, a pleasure in being on the winning end, even in an argument about the wreck of their business; and looking at her, he wonders all of a sudden if her getting together with him in the first place ever had much more in it than this same determination to win. Kath in the back office of the estate agent's where he met her, grinning at him. Kath in a wedding dress, triumphing over her sisters. Kath in bed, briskly riding on his bulk, impatient eyes fixed on him. Kath in the maternity hospital, presenting a bundled-up Becky like an on-time payment. Kath's early, decisive pessimism as Albemarle ran into trouble, when he was still telling himself stories of how it could come right. Kath's detachment, Kath's self-protection, Kath's stone face.

She's a bookie's daughter. He should have realised she'd be good at telling when the odds change. Fuck it.

"All right, then," he says. "I'm off."

"You need to give me the office key. Where is it?"

"Dunno," he lies. And he uses a little bit of the rage that is thickening his neck, lets out just enough of it to bull his way past, pluck up a random umbrella, hook the front door open, and stomp off down the path in the wet.

Even the short walk to the Mini is enough to plaster his hair, and damp the corners of the cardboard box, in the cold pelt from above. It's a world of liquid noises outside: pattering from the eaves, guggles from the red-brick path he never got round to weeding, a tireless pissing from the downpipe by the garage. A sheen of water is moving on the driveway. By the time he's wrestled the case and the box into the narrow back seat and wedged himself behind the wheel, his face is so sopping he has to blot his eyebrows with his tie so he can see straight. The Mini feels tiny. It seemed cute once, a neat trademark for Albemarle that a big man in a blue suit should emerge from a little blue car. *Albemarle: Big Things in Small Boxes!* That's what he had in mind to use as a slogan for the company's next stage, when they built the second, third, fourth shopping centre. None of that is going to happen now. Now, the car seems like a tin skin wrapped too tight around his swollen, damp fury. Bastard thing. Bastard life. Bastard wife. Vern rocks and roars, and having nothing else to do with his fat fists in the small space, pounds on the steering wheel. Of course the horn sticks, sending a thin continuous parp of distress winding through suburban Swanley. Some bastard neighbour would poke their nose over the hedge to see what's going on, if it wasn't for the rain. He has to jiggle the steering column to make the button pop back up. Then he puts the Mini in gear and goes.

Traffic hissing on the roads north; the wheels of buses and

lorries sloshing out arcs of spray; tail-lights squiggling and goggling through the rain. The wipers on the Mini can't keep up with the rivulets running down the windscreen. He hunches forward and peers. But everything is going equally slow, and rain can't stop him knowing the way to Bexford. He could probably drive it blindfold. It's the A20 all the way: the Swanley bypass, and then the Sidcup bypass, and then the Eltham bypass, gentle curve after gentle curve of tarmacked no-place, with the green signs for the exits coming up in the gloom like unconvincing promises.

Somewhere around Sidcup he fumbles in the glove compartment and finds the cassette of Joan Sutherland singing *Lucia di Lammermoor*. He saw her do it once, nearly ten years ago, at the point when he'd picked himself up from the smash of Grosvenor and was just working out how to put Albemarle together. He hadn't met Kath yet; that was coming when he started looking for agencies with small supermarkets in their client lists. And here's the whole glorious flight of that voice, bottled, time-proofed, except that the cassette is starting to glitch and fade, except that it makes tiny what once was gigantic. Still it's better than nothing. He left the tape at the end of the mad scene the last time he put it on, so he only has to squibble back through eighteen minutes and there she is again, bloodstained, astonishing, throbbingly distraught. Tenors, Vern has been known to sing along to while he drives and no one can hear the heartfelt mess he makes. But the sopranos, he can't even aspire to. He just listens, and lets Dame Joan do the heart-work for him.

Past Eltham, and the traffic lights begin, puddled red-amber-green on the glass before him. Red-brick walls and closer trees channel the grey light descending from the sopping air, and darken it. As he stops, goes, stirs through sheets of water where the drains have overflowed, the familiar matrix of the city closes around him. The 1930s semis with their triangular raised eyebrows; the Edwardian schools and the brutalist ones; the corner shops now selling lentils and fenugreek; the railway arches filled with little garages; everywhere the plane trees, the sycamores, the horse chestnuts, so wet now they stand like pulpy chandeliers, dribbling and drooling, filtering the light away so the pavements are dim beneath. He's back under the eaves of his London. It occurs to him that this may be the last time he ever makes this particular commute, and mad Lucia sings—

Un'armonia celeste, di', non ascolti?
Ah, l'inno suona di nozze!
Il rito per noi s'appresta! Oh, me felice!
Oh gioia che si sente, e non si dice!

Well, Vern, do you hear a heavenly harmony? His face is wet again, although the car is keeping the rain out. But the answer, to be honest, is no. If he thinks about it—and now he is think-ing about it—he has never felt anything like what Joan Suther-land reports that Lucia is feeling. He wants to feel it, he lingers hopefully in its vicinity, at least when he's listening to opera. But to die for love, to run mad for love: those are not states that have ever come near him. Not in daylight. Not to his waking self. The strongest emotions he knows are the angry ones, the ones in the keys of frustration, or rage. Those have come closest to carrying him away, to overthrowing his usual calculating caution. He had hoped, deep down in some well-concealed compartment, some safe-deposit box of his heart, that being married to Kath might wake up some of what the tenors and the sopranos sing about. But it didn't. Perhaps the big emotions of the operas don't really exist, perhaps they are a game of let's pretend that everyone is agreeing to play. Perhaps they are news from a far country that likewise doesn't exist. He doesn't know.

He also doesn't know, on a practical level, what he is going to do. He has no house, he has no money. Well: not quite true, in either case. There's a small emergency fund waiting for him in the Albemarle office. That's why he has to go in one more time. And the account it's in, carefully off the books, is being fed by the rents from the one property he kept mum about when they were organising Albemarle, and didn't fold into the company's portfolio. It's one of the big old houses on Bexford Rise, a horrible thing, gloomy and ancient, with woodwormed windows and plugs that produce blue flashes and burning smells. But the immigrants and students he's stuffed into it don't expect any better, and they also don't know he's anything but the rent collector. Something, some habit of caution, made him set these things quietly aside, out of Kath's reach. So now he won't be starting again absolutely from scratch. He isn't quite broke; he still has a toehold in property. If he has to, he can even chuck out a student or three and move in himself, though a bed and breakfast appeals more. And all this is better than the aftermath of Grosvenor, when he really did have nothing left, and had to go back to his mum's for six months.

But what he hasn't got is a plan. Grosvenor was supposed to be an empire built on shop rents, and it went wrong when the supermarkets wiped out his butchers and greengrocers. Albemarle was his reaction. It was his way of getting into the bigger commercial spaces the chains were demanding. He went as big as he could, but it wasn't big enough. The only tenants he could get for the Albemarle Minimart were the marginal players, a fly-by-night cash and carry, a franchised dry-cleaner, a non-chain burger restaurant. Now the likes of Sainsbury's and Safeway are all looking for huge greenfield properties. He couldn't play in that league when things were looking promising for Albemarle and he certainly can't now. He's got to the end of what he can think of to do with commercial property, and it's a bust. What the hell is left that's in his reach, except for bloody residential? Oh, he's done some, you can't avoid it, you pick up sitting tenants like fleas just as a side effect of doing small commercial: but it's so dismal, it's such a dispiriting, damp, low-margin business, in a sector squeezed between council housing and owner-occupiers. You have to play the heavy just to keep a trickle of cash flowing. Water-stained ceilings, missing stair rods, endless complaints: he wants glass towers, not that shit.

It's maddening. This should be his time. He listens to the news and he thinks: finally, there's a government that's on my side. The world should be his oyster, the world should be falling into his lap, the world should be finally giving him what he's been reaching for all his adult life. And instead he is parking a Mini in spitting rain in an alley half-blocked by a skip, and fumbling with a lock while balancing the net results of his marriage in a soggy cardboard box. *Spargi d'amaro pianto il mio terrestre velo*: shed bitter tears on your earthly garment, Vern.

The office is dim from the darkness of the day. It has the stale smell of an unused space, and there are mouse droppings on the floor. A watery glow creeps in from the storefront window facing the court of the Minimart, where unlit plate glass declares the death of burger bar, dry-cleaner, cash and carry. The rain outside makes an indistinct drumming, a fuzz of wet noise. He could turn on the light and get some blue-white illumination on the spider plants, the ominous buff envelopes on the mat, the files stacked on the desk. But there's a kind of comfort in the room being like a cave, a dim hidey-hole. Also a small chance that one of Albemarle's local creditors might see lights on. He sets the box down and climbs on a chair. Four polystyrene ceiling tiles along from the left wall, three out into the middle of the room. No reason why Kath should ever have done this, and besides, she's too short to reach, the little bitch. He presses up, and the tile lifts with a squeaky whisper. Sellotaped to the other side of it, undisturbed, are indeed the emergency bank book and a slender packet of brown tenners and purple twenties. Vern feels better just for having them in his jacket pocket.

With the tile out there's a big obvious gap overhead, and he feels an urge to leave it like that, so that when Kath next comes in here the square of black announces: you missed something, you cow. Better not, though. He has learned not to underestimate her capacity to make trouble. If she deduces there's an extra asset she will come after it. But it's difficult. He stands on the plastic chair with the polystyrene in his hands, and it's so brittle, so granular, so friable. His hands can feel what it would be like to crack it in half, and in half again, raining down white crumbs on the unswept floor. And then to go on. To lumber down from the chair and go on breaking things. Trash the place. Turn round and round like an angry bear in this old den of his, sweeping the files onto the floor, overturning the desk, smashing the glass of the cabinet, throwing the typewriter at the wall. Trampling on the paper underfoot. Pissing on it. Making chaos. Shredding and clawing and flailing. The bitch, the bitch, the bitch.

At the thought of it, his breath comes fast and his hands tingle where he's gripping the polystyrene. Better *not*. It feels as if he might fly apart too, if he gives in to the smashing urge—be discovered by Kath in sections, when she comes in, scattered round the office with the rest of the wreckage. He lifts the tile and with trembly delicacy taps it back into place. *Tuff. Tuff. Squeak.* Then he gets down, one tree-trunk leg and then the other one. And stands, breathing, with his hands over the face.

Cup of tea, that's what he needs. There's a kettle in here somewhere. Yes, over there, dusty in the corner, along with most of a packet of Ginger Nuts. He fills it and puts it on to boil, and while he waits, sits at the desk and eats the biscuits one after another till there's sweet grit packing his teeth and he feels better. He watches the rain on the court-side window run down, branching, slow-slow-quick, briefly mercurial when the grey light catches on the rivulets. The puddles on the concrete outside pock and stipple. The rain has slowed to a finer needle-shower, but the soft blatter of it still carries, mixing with the soothing whirr of the kettle.

Of course, there isn't any milk, and when it comes to it Vern doesn't fancy the thought of a milkless mugful, acrid black. But by then he doesn't care, because he's had an idea. Not a big idea, mind you, not the kind you build your next business on. But enough of an idea to get him back in the game, maybe—to force the (he checks) two-thousand-odd quid in the emergency account into rapid multiplication and, possibly just as important, to let the voice in his head that tells his life like a story say, *Yeah, Vern bounced right back*. There's a bloke he knows called Malcolm Deakin who is planning to go all in on council housing when Right to Buy kicks in next year. Funding for tenants who can't get mortgages, then the lion's share of the sale price when the time comes to sell. Deakin's got his investors lined up and everything. The thing is, Vern has looked into this a little bit, from curiosity, and even though the scheme hasn't started yet, and there hasn't been much publicity, the discounts for tenants buying are already available. If someone were to go out on the doorsteps as a kind of unofficial field agent, and sign a few people up now, in advance, he can't see why Deakin wouldn't buy them on. He'd save himself the hassle, and he'd be looking at a guaranteed profit. What Vern needs to do is use his two thousand quid to make deals eventually worth seven or eight thou, and then sell them on to Deakin for an instant three or four. *Boom*. And rinse, and repeat. It'll have to be flats or maisonettes, not houses, with only two thou to start. But that's doable.

Vern thinks it through again, carefully, and then types up a couple of documents to take away with him, pecking at the keys with two fingers. Before he goes, he spreads out the ledgers Kath is most likely to need and pours all the water in the kettle over them. The ink floats off the columns in smears and eddies. *Take that, sweetheart.* On the way out, he locks up, breaks off the key in the lock and posts the stub back through the letterbox. *You can pay for a locksmith and all.* Right: a fry-up, and then to work.

An hour later, and even the solid savoury ballast of sausage bacon egg beans and a fried slice is not quite able to keep him in good heart. He's over on the bit of infill estate that patched the bomb damage on one side of Bexford Rise, about two thirds of the way up, and not far from his hulk of a house, which he plans to look in on later. The needling rain is still falling from the low clouds, fine-bore, penetrating. It has penetrated Vern's brolly. It's one of those cheap fold-up ones. It isn't made for a sustained downpour and, crumpled and dainty in a big man's hand, it doesn't have the coverage either. His head is merely damp, but his shoulders are soaked. The electric blue of his suit has turned to dark, glistening purple. The extra, wet weight ensures that, though his hands are numb, the rest of him is perversely hot. Overflow from blocked drainpipes sends sheets of wet creeping down the brickwork of the blocks.

So far, no one has answered the door in the row of maison-ettes facing the big houses on the Rise. It must be working-age families in here, mostly, and they're the least likely takers for his proposition. He wants the ill, the old, the lonely. But he thought he'd better work through the maisonettes before heading up to the more probable bets on the seventh floor, the level at which building societies start refusing to lend. A maisonette would be a bigger pay-off than a flat, if he could get one. All this he expected;

but it's still dispiriting to stand there in the wet at door after door, getting his trustworthy smile ready, for no result.

The sixth and last door, however, has signs of life behind it and when he knocks it's opened, by a stringy, harassed-looking man of about his own age.

"Yeah?" he says. Or begins to say. While the word is still in his mouth, a huge voice from upstairs breaks in.

"Oi! If you're limping down the street, in new boots so tight they squeak, and your clothes are magnifeek—"

"Gary!" shouts the guy in the doorway, turning back towards the stairs. "Gary! What have I *bloody* told you, and bloody *told* you, about turning down the bloody *music?*"

"When the rhythm starts to speak, from Pacifeek to Atlanteek, move yer aching plates of meat—"

"GARY! Turn off the fucking music!"

"ONE GIANT LEA—"

And the music stops, or at any rate dwindles so sharply it counts as silence compared to what it was before.

"Sorry, mate," says the man, rubbing his hand wearily on his face. "What?"

"Teenagers, eh?" says Vern, sympathetically. But before he can get any further, the man in the doorway leans forward and peers at him closely.

"Good grief," he says. "It's Vermin Taylor."

"You what?" says Vern.

"Sorry! Sorry. Shouldn't stick you with a school nickname: not fair. But it is you, isn't it. *Vernon* Taylor, right?"

"Do we know each other?"

"We went to the same primary school. Halstead Road?"

"That's right. But, so—who are you?"

"Alec Torrance," says the bloke, and sticks a hand out. Vern shakes it cautiously; and now, knowing what he's looking for, when he stares at the face in front of him (frazzled, unshaved) he can see a younger version superimposed or maybe coming up from beneath.

"Yeah," he says, "yeah . . . You were the cheeky little bugger, weren't you? The one who was always winding up whatsisname, the head."

"Henry Hardy."

"That's right. Yeah, you used to leave his aitches off on purpose, didn't you?"

"'Fraid so, yeah."

"And he'd turn red, and he'd go—"

"*At least try to speak properly, boy!*" says the man on the step.

They smile uncertainly.

"Yeah," says Vern.

"Yeah," says Torrance.

But the moment fades quickly away. Bringing the past closer also brings closer the kids they were, the fat boy facing the smartarse. They didn't like each other then, and there's no reason they should like each other now. Vernon hasn't forgotten being Vermin Taylor, or forgiven it. He's glad to see that the clever little bugger has grown up to be a bit of a mess. Home in the middle of the day; bedraggled; shouting at his kids; clothes one step up from pyjamas. Definite whiff of failure there. Perhaps this needn't be a wasted conversation. And the angry bear who was baulked of his wish to mash and to shred earlier makes himself felt. He rises and stretches, somewhere down in Vern, and lets it be known that there'd be some predatory satisfaction in having it be the smartarse that gets squeezed in the urgent pursuit of recapitalisation.

"So, what are you up to, then, these days?" asks Vern, with a different friendliness. "Between jobs?"

"Nah, I'm in the print. Always have been. Typesetter on *The*

Times. Only, you know, we're out—well, not technically on strike, but it comes to the same thing. Have been for nearly a year."

Oh. "Must be tough," says Vern. "Hard times, eh?"

"'S all right," says Torrance, bridling slightly and palpably rejecting the sympathy. "Mind you, I'm not a very good prospect if you're selling something. *Are* you selling something?"

"I am not a fucking brush salesman!" snarls Vern, with no warning to himself that he might be about to lose his temper, no appreciable interval between manipulative calm and totally losing it. Zero to rage in nought seconds.

"Whoa!" says Torrance, hands up in front of him, eyebrows shooting up too. "You're the one standing on *my* doorstep, mate."

"Sorry," says Vern into the hand he has clapped across his face. Big pink clamp, gripping the squidgy mask that is refusing to behave.

Torrance, who had taken hold of the door and was in the process of stepping back to close it, pauses and hesitates.

"And I thought I was having a shit day," he says. "Here . . . d'you wanna come in and have a cup of tea? You're all wet."

Ordinarily, Vern would have discarded with scorn any such hideous display of pity—particularly from some up-himself, overpaid, feather-bedding, Spanish-practising, never-taken-a-business-risk-in-his-life tosser of a Fleet Street Bolshevik. But today he finds himself squeezing obediently through a dark little hall hung with coats and into a narrow little kitchen with a table jutting out from the wall that just has room for four chairs round it. *Titchy-boom titchy-boom* comes the thread of music from upstairs, and Torrance casts an exasperated glance at the ceiling. Rain still wanders down the window over the sink and the view outside is soggy murk. But what Vern notices is that the place, though small, is tidy. Everything is where it belongs. There are biros in a jar next to a phone on the wall. There are photos from family holidays up on a corkboard, and a note about someone going to the dentist. The washing-up has just been done, presumably by the Bolshevik, and the kitchen smells of washing-up liquid and Vim: clean smells, the smells of things working as they should. It looks like the land of lost content, to Vern.

"Sit down, take the weight off," says his host.

"I'll get the cushions wet," Vern says.

"Doesn't matter. Now, here are some Kleenex, and I'll just put the ke—"

"My wife threw me out this morning," Vern tells the tabletop.

"Oh, mate! Oh, mate. Right, scratch the tea."

Torrance fetches down a tumbler and a whisky bottle from a cupboard, and pours Vern a couple of golden fingerfuls. Then he sits down himself opposite, props his forehead on splayed fingers, and clearly prepares to listen.

But Vern doesn't know how this goes. He slurps the whisky, and it does warm him, but he has no idea how to put the mass of today's misery into acceptable form; into any form, really, for as well as the problem of keeping the private stuff private, about the business, there's the underlying difficulty of knowing how to turn any of this stuff into a story in the first place, this stuff about trust, about finding you had no ally.

"She," he tries. "I thought," he tries.

Torrance waits. But nothing else is forthcoming. A puzzled little crinkle appears between his eyebrows.

"Well," he says eventually, coaxingly, "what is it you *do* do, Vernon?"

"Property," says Vern.

"Really?"

More silence.

"I wouldn't of thought there was much for you round here,

then? I mean, it's all council, isn't it. Or—ah, I get you. It'll be that malarkey going on on the Rise you're into, I suppose?"

"What malarkey?" says Vern, wanly.

"You know—the Saab and Volvo brigade moving in. Hugo and Jocasta. Our new middle-class neighbours who just *love* the *lovely* Georgian *architecture*. Them, right? No?"

"What, on the Rise?"

"Yeah, go and look, must be four or five houses, now. But, mate—"

"I've gotta go," says Vern, surging to his feet and jogging the little table.

"Al . . . right, but . . ."

Torrance, baffled, follows him to the front door; tries one last time as Vern unfurls the comedy umbrella.

"Wasn't there something you wanted?"

"Nothing you'd be interested in," says Vern firmly. "Thank you. That was very . . . kind."

That was very weird, Torrance's face is saying plain as pie as the door shuts. But Vern turns away and hurries through the puddles to the alley at the end of the row that leads through to the Rise. It's still raining, but the needles are turning to drizzle, supplemented by heavier splatters of local drops, where a breeze is beginning to stir the big trees of the Rise and to push at the grey cloudbase.

He comes out by the railings, and there they are, the dark hulks of the Rise, marching up on their long slant as far as he can see to left and right. They go all the way from Lambert Street and the park down at the bottom up to the leafy crown of Bexford Hill. There must be, what, seventy or eighty of the things—grand dwellings once, for bankers and brokers and lawyers and doctors and prospering merchants, promising light and space and a vantage point above the dingy anthill where the fortunes had been made to pay for them. Two hundred years later and almost all of them are what Vern has always taken them to be: run-down, mislocated, impractical nightmares, too big to repair or to do anything with except cram with the least demanding of tenants till the day comes for demolition. Everywhere you look there's ingrained soot, cracked stucco, streaks of water damage, black bricks bulging or showing cracks where the pointing has fallen out. The railings have all been missing since they were taken away during wartime drives for scrap, the areas are choked with rubbish. There's the scaly grey of old, old dirt on the windowpanes.

But Torrance is right. Trotting uphill and down again, Vern spots one, then another, then another, of the houses he was talking about. These ones do indeed have parked outside them an elderly green Saab, a mossy Audi, a silver Volvo estate missing one of its hubcaps: not glamorous, not conventionally posh, yet unmistakably the vehicles of the artsy bourgeoisie. The Saab has two bottles of wine and a sack of cement on the back seat. And the cars correspond to houses with scaffolding on them, with paint-stripped or partially paint-stripped front doors. One of these has ground-floor windows brilliantly lit, through which you can see walls painted a fresh white, hung with little grey rectangles of pictures. Another seems dark, and Vern has strolled up the front path to take a squint before he sees flickers of yellow inside, and finds he's looking at a bearded guy in overalls stripping wallpaper by the light of, yes, three candles in a knackered old paint-dripped candelabra, an actual fucking candelabra, the light fitting overhead hanging down broken by its wires.

None of it gives the impression of work with much of a budget behind it. It's enthusiastic amateur stuff. The Saab-drivers are doing middle-class homesteading out here in the wilderness of Bexford. Which means, which must mean, that they love all this;

that they positively want the wonky eighteenth-century grates, and the cracked oak floorboards under the geological sediments of lino and plywood and underlay, and the bowed old lath-and-plaster behind the layers of cheap wallpaper. Want it enough to do for themselves, on the cheap down here, what they wouldn't be able to afford if it had *stayed* posh, if it had remained in good nick over the centuries, as in, say, Belgravia. Which means, Vern thinks, that for every out-and-out bearded architectural fanatic willing to do the job on their own account, there might well be, in fact there almost certainly must be, a whole bunch of slightly less fanatical people with the same tastes, who'd pay to have a house like this sorted out for them.

He stares so hard at the man in overalls, thinking this through, that in the end he feels Vern's gaze, and turns, and jumps, finding an oval blue spectre looming in the wet darkness of his doorstep. Vern nods, and goes away to stand instead on the doorstep of the building he already owns. The umbrella gets in the way, so he folds it, and just ignores the rain as he stares upwards, trying to see something desirable here, something precious. The house looms above him, a crumbling black cliff. Old, old, old, say his own reactions, meaning by that: chewed up by time, used up by time, in a funny way contaminated by time, as if all the lives lived in this heavy rookery for humans, first the posh ones with the wigs and the ball dresses, then all the ever-poorer clerks and labourers and flotsam from around the world, with their coughing children, and their meals cooked on gas rings in dirty corners, have made it impossible for there ever to be a fresh start here, a new beginning, there being so much living and dying already ingrained here, stuck to surfaces like grease, laid down in scungy thicknesses. There's something else too, a horrible rumour that sometimes things—objects—exist on a longer and slower cycle than the living one, that sometimes they outlast us, overshadow us, will still be standing when we are removed as mortal rubbish, however much we'd prefer it to be the other way round, with our frayed possessions discarded but our skins immortal. Ugh. He wouldn't live here. He's definitely going to a B&B. But: antique, antique, antique is what he has to train himself to think, he supposes. He had better read up on what the incomers want, in case he cleans away some grubby old thing they cherish. Or get someone to explain it to him. Perhaps that's been the error of his businesses all along. He kept wanting to make things happen, when he should have found something that was happening anyway, and just gone along with it.

But he will need capital, if he's going to start buying up and doing up the Rise, and Deakin is his best quick source for it, he reckons. So as the rain dies away into drips, and a knot of brightness begins to untie in the clouds, he's back over in the flats, working his way along the concrete walkway of the seventh floor, knocking and knocking and knocking, until eventually one opens, and there stands a beautifully confused-looking pensioner in his undershirt.

"Hello," says Vern warmly. "I represent . . . Featherstone Investments. How would you, sir, like to make two thousand pounds, right now?"

Val

Mike gets headaches. Bad enough ones that they lay him out for half a day at a time, unable to bear the light. The brewery is starting to complain about the shifts he's missing. Today's a Saturday, though, so he isn't needed for work, and he lies in the bedroom at half past ten in a mess of sheets, with his eyes closed tight even against the tiny leaks of November daylight that make it through the slit in the curtains. It's so dim in there by ordinary standards that it takes her eyes a minute to adjust when she takes him in a mug of tea. (White, three sugars.) There are violet shadows under his eyes, marks of weakness for once instead of the bruises and black eyes he brings home which are strength's proud badges: or the monstrous swelling of half his head he brought back that one time that someone hit him with a hammer. He looked like a jack-o'-lantern then, and like one was grinning, still grinning. But now a pain has taken hold of him that he didn't choose and no one inflicted, and it has subdued his face to gentleness. You can see, as well as the delicacy of the coloured skin under his eyes, the tiny crow's-feet lines coming at their corners. Like her, he's thirty-nine, and in these moments when he can't help himself, it shows. Impossible not to feel tenderness, or something like tenderness, standing over his animal length in the sheets, and seeing all that force temporarily laid low. He is the only beautiful thing in her life, as well as being the cause of all the ugly ones. When she makes a clink putting down the mug on the side table, he mumbles "Thanks, Mum." Then she goes back to the living room to go on cutting corned-beef sandwiches under the portrait of Hitler.

She did manage to coax him to the doctor's about the headaches. Unfortunately the doctor they got, Dr. Sharma, was a young Asian woman. Mike was in his work clothes, but she could still read his tattoos. They glared at each other.

"I see you work in a brewery, Mr. Stone," said the doctor. "Do you by any chance drink to excess?"

"This is crap," said Mike. "I'm not letting her put her hands on me."

"Believe me, I have no desire to."

"Shouldn't you at least take his blood pressure, Doctor?" Val tried. "He's talking about seeing flashing lights and all when he has one of his heads."

"I suppose that would be sensible. All right, roll up your right sleeve, Mr. Stone."

"No!" said Mike. "There's nothing wrong with my blood. It's Nordic."

Dr. Sharma laughed.

"Shut up, you Paki cunt," said Mike.

Dr. Sharma stopped laughing.

"I think you'd better leave," she said.

"What'd you do that for?" Val asked when they were outside.

"What?"

"You know."

"Well—it's rubbish, isn't it love; 's all crap."

And he started to do his pavement-clearing strut, with her tagging along behind. Places to go, people to scare. Mike likes people, in a certain kind of a way. He certainly doesn't like being alone, and he has arranged their lives so they hardly ever are. The top two floors of this block of the Park Estate are BM territory, acknowledged, and the flat is constantly full, evenings and weekends, with Mike's crew of junior skins and the girls who hang around them, and the older hard men of the Leader Guard like himself. (Though none of the others are quite as old as Mike.) It's rare that she has a moment to herself, like now, laying out the white squares of the bread to butter for round after round of sandwiches, wrestling open tin after tin of the corned beef they got for virtually nothing when the cash and carry closed. The little keys that you use to wind the cans open do their best to break off, with the slab of red meat and yellow fat inside only half-released. She could turn the radio on, but it isn't worth the bellow of indignation from the bedroom if the song playing isn't one Mike approves of. Instead as she works she watches a seagull diving and soaring in the spaces between the tops of the towers, as if the buildings, and the grid of lock-up garages and shopping precinct down below, and then the whole bumpy carpet of London beyond, were only unimportant blanks surrounding its true element.

Twenty rounds of sandwiches done, ten more to go. Who'd have thought that national socialism demanded so many sandwiches? So much sewing, too. As well as Mike's street clothes, which obviously have to be perfect, she had to make his Leader Guard uniform from scratch. There aren't enough members of the white race's vanguard for the uniforms to come from a factory. They have to be home-made. The blue BM crossed-circle came as a machine-embroidered patch, but she was the one who had to get it to work on a khaki shirt, who had to make the jacket and the armband, to improvise the Sam Browne belt. When she and Mike went to that horrible Birthday do, and the wives looked at each other—all dogs, all with the same bleak sourness she sees in the mirror every morning—she saw that the uniforms were all slightly different. And he can't even wear the thing otherwise. He got photographed in it for his membership card, and now it hangs in the wardrobe in a dry-cleaning bag.

Twenty-nine, thirty: and as she finishes the sandwiches and starts wrapping them up in greaseproof, her little moment of solitude ends too. She hears the whine and clank of the lift, and then the knock on the flat door. It's Mr. Brocklehurst, with his golf club tie and his megaphone.

"Hello, Mrs. Mike!" he says. "Is Himself available? Ha ha?"

"Bit of a late night last night," says Val automatically. "I'll just give him a knock, shall I. Cup of tea while you're waiting?"

"That would be splendid."

She bangs on the bedroom door and puts the kettle back on.

While it reboils she can hear the sounds of Mike putting himself together. Brocklehurst lingers awkwardly. He comes here to pet his tigers, and he has no idea what to say to her. She can't stand him. She can't stand Mike's deference to him, as if he represented something grand and serious, instead of a few middle-class weirdos and a cocktail cabinet full of daggers and helmets. It's been a long time since she took any of it seriously, but at least when Mike talks about it it's got something to do with . . . loyalty; with being proud of who they are and where they come from. You can usually rely on Mike's bright-clean hatred for social workers, lawyers, probation officers, teachers: posh tossers and rich bastards of all descriptions, who were already offensive to him, already stank in his nostrils, before he decided they were race traitors as well. Alone among posh tossers who have had prolonged solo exposure to Mike, Mr. Brocklehurst has not gone down in a welter of blood and teeth, and sometimes Val is slightly sorry.

"What a marvellous spread," he says, looking at the mountain of sandwiches. "Heavens, how well you do do for us, Mrs. Mike."

Do for us. As if she was a char-lady. She hands him the tea silently. He sips it, though it must be still hot enough to scald.

"Yes, yes," he says. "Home-making. The hearth. What it's all about in the end, isn't it."

"Is it?" she says. If he thinks this place is homely he must be blind. Everything here is scuffed and trampled by the ceaseless traffic of big male boots. A knackered sofa faces a knackered telly across a knackered carpet. There's a permanent smell of sweat. It's like a barracks or a boys' club, not a home. "D'you have kids, Mr. Brocklehurst?" She knows he doesn't.

"I'm afraid not, no. Never lucky enough to find the right girl!"

Yeah, just you alone with your collection of Iron Crosses.

A shadow appears on Mr. Brocklehurst's face, as if he fears he has dropped some terrible clanger.

"I was so sorry to hear from Mike that you two can't have children," he offers, shuffling his feet. "Terribly sad. And such a loss to the race, you know, he being the splendid specimen that he is."

Oh. Oh, is that what Mike told you? She supposes it's not surprising he's come up with something along these lines, but it would have been nice to be let in on it. The truth is that the female anatomy makes Mike go all to pieces. It unmans him, which is not a sensation he likes. So on the rare occasions when anything does happen between them, it tends to feature his dick and her mouth; and it's true, you can't get pregnant that way. The thought of explaining this to Mr. Brocklehurst puts a sour little smirk on Val's face. He takes a nervous half-step back. That's a common reaction. Mike may not want her, but she is his, and terror of him puts an exclusion zone around her. She is not to be upset or offended, she is not to be touched.

But then, to Mr. Brocklehurst's relief, the bedroom door opens. The noises in there have been rising: the getting-up noises, the gargling noises, the dunking-of-the-head-in-the-basin noises, the shaking-the-wet-head-like-a-dog noises, the towelling noises, the noises of clothes coming off hangers. The humming. And now here he is, here's Mike risen from the couch of sleep, in Levi's and green bomber jacket, grinning and momentarily posing in the doorframe, for the pleasure of all onlookers. A few blinks are the only sign of the head-in-a-vice ache he's overriding. It's a triumph of the will. And the familiar, ancient dread tightens its knot in Val's stomach. When Mike gets up, the clock of the day is wound, and now it will tick on till the day ends; and the day will only end when Mike has had enough. Enough of a laugh. Enough aggro. Enough confrontation. Enough of other people bending to the force in him. Enough bruising and breaking. All day long, she'll be asking *Is this enough yet? Is this?*

Now the flow of people has begun, it keeps going, and the flat fills rapidly up with what feels like most of the skins in Bexford, the hard-core BM ones and the larger number of casuals who are into the style as a style, into the tribe for the sake of having a tribe. For them, as far as she can see, the swastikas and the Sieg-Heiling are mostly a matter of having a laugh and winding people up. Yeah, if there's a ruck then tribal loyalty will do its thing and they'll fight as Mike's army. But he wouldn't ever pick them for the vicious small-group stuff, the night-wandering in search of enemies to do serious damage to. That privilege will not be theirs; and as a result most of them stand a pretty good chance of growing up and growing out of being a skin—ending up as men very much like their dads, shaking their heads over a pint at thirty about the crazy stuff they used to get up to. For that matter, even the hard core may get over all this, luck and prison and broken bones permitting. Even Peaky and Taff, maybe, Mike's faithful wingmen and wannabes. They've got time to change in. They aren't twenty yet. There was a time when she thought the years might work a transformation on Mike. The usual transformation, from bad lad to man with responsibilities. But Mike won't let himself be changed. Or can't. She knows that now.

Once the number of skins in a confined space exceeds a certain density, they start to collide. The sofa is full of bodies already. A lad holding a mug of tea adds himself by sitting on the back of it and then just letting himself fall into the press as if it were a mosh pit, moonface beaming as he goes, tea slopping, everyone's elbows going.

"Watch out, the arms'll break," says Val, unheard by anyone but Mike.

"Oi!" he roars. "Listen when the missus talks!"

And he lessens the pressure on the sofa end by lifting a size-10 immaculately laced sixteen-hole oxblood DM and booting the last two in the row off onto the floor, jovially but not gently. They sprawl there, and with the pressure released, Moonface with the mug does a complete back somersault, tea flying like a twisted brown scarf, and ends up on the floor too, on top of the mug, which shatters. You can tell that the hard ceramic punch under the ribs must have hurt—it's one of the oddities of shaving a male head that it sometimes lets the little boy show through more clearly in a face—but he's up in an instant, grinning. Mike looks away. *Enough? Not even close.* She fetches a dustpan and clears away the bits of china, one of the boys trying to help until distracted by being put in a headlock by his mates. So far as they think of her at all, she can see a familiar confusion on their faces. What is she, this silent woman of Mike's? She's not a girl, and she's not a mum either: mums do not let you behave like this indoors.

But the small kerfuffle on the sofa has served as a signal to get going, and so bumping, jostling, spreading as they go out into the hallway like a gas expanding, they set off. Mr. Brockle-hurst and his megaphone and his leaflets and two Union Jacks on broom handles go down in the lift; the rest go whooping down ten flights of stairs. She's in the rearguard, as ever, walking down with the carrier bags of food and the small contingent of girl-friends. (Not a category that includes Fat Marge, who's been to borstal. She's an honorary boy.) Being a skin is such a male style that there isn't really a look for the girls to conform to, as such, except for the compulsory truculence. A couple of them are doing a version of the boys' style, but braces and tits don't combine well, and one has got a spiky blonde fringe above massively mascara'd panda eyes—a pretty little thing, that one, only about fifteen, and every time Val looks at her she thinks, *What the fuck are you doing here, love?*

First stop is the market. On Saturdays it's in the long slot between Lambert Street and Talbot Road, a double row of stalls between the gas showroom and St. Saviour's. A lot of the streets around have vanished, ploughed under in the making of the Park Estate, but in here Bexford still looks pretty much the way Val can always remember it looking, changed detail by detail rather than being wiped away wholesale. And maybe Brocklehurst has thought about that—or maybe they've just gone where the people are—because when the mob of them have pushed their way onto the war memorial steps, and they've got Brocklehurst set up between the flags, glaring heads all around his blue blazer, what comes reedily out of the loudhailer, and floats across the stalls selling veg, and the stall piled with acrylic jumpers, and the one doing socks and clock radios, is:

"Ladies and gentlemen, do you even recognise the place you come from, these days? The place you were born? Look around you. Look around you. They're taking it away from you—from you, madam, from you, sir. From all of us!"

And people do turn their heads. But the white shoppers don't look poison at the West Indian and Sikh ones as they're supposed to do. They cluck their tongues and bob their heads and hunch their shoulders and shrink back without actually moving: all body language saying, stop it and leave us alone. And on the dark faces there's a stonier refusal to react, though people are also picking a path through the market crowd that keeps them quietly away from the memorial steps. Val, nodding at whatever the girl next to her is saying and not listening to a word, sees a woman her own age two stalls away, buying plantains. (Which they didn't use to sell on Bexford market, it's true.) Her face is the colour of a bar of Cadbury's Dairy Milk, she's wearing a plaid raincoat, and her hand is on the shoulder of a little boy of about four who is too young to do stoicism, whose face flickers with fear behind the piles of green bananas. The hand is holding him steady. The back of the hand rubs against his cheek. It looks as if it belongs there very comfortably. Shame and envy, envy and shame, flow wearily in Val, and for a moment, yes, kindle to something like the spark of anger Brocklehurst wants her to feel, for why should *they* have what she lacks, and have it here, in front of her, in her place? But she goes on watching them till they're out of sight behind backs.

The only person who does react is the punk boy selling *Socialist Worker* over by South Thames Gas's window full of cookers. He threads around the back of the market to the phone box and makes a call, and a little later, while Mr. Brocklehurst is explaining that the closure of the docks is down to unfair competition from "the coloured countries," the opposition stroll in. Not so much a counter-demo as a counter-mob, in their donkey jackets and ANL badges, wearing boots just as big as the skins', and with expressions Val finds extremely familiar. She glances at Mike and, yeah, sees the same eagerness, mirrored. This is the fun stuff, this is what they're there for, not Brocklehurst's speech. A metal shutter goes down on the shoe shop by St. Saviour's; the nearest stall holders start to pack their stock away.

But before the tooth-baring grins and the pointing fingers and the rest of the male fighting display can wind itself up to actual blows, an elderly drunk comes wandering into the space between, at the foot of the steps. Skinny, with several days of white stubble, wearing an ancient none-too-clean suit, and clearly with several pints in him from the Feathers (open early on market day).

"Get out the way, Grandad, you'll get hurt," says one of the lads in the front row of the antis, impatiently.

The drunk dismisses him with a vague fluttering hand over his shoulder, and points a finger of his own at the skinheads.

"You," he says slushily—he hasn't got the teeth for the consonants—"should be fakkin ashamed of yourselves. Standing here—"

"Come on, move it," says the anti.

"Yeah, fuck off now," agrees Mike. "We're busy."

"—standing *here*," the drunk goes on regardless, "wearing *that*. That!" He's pointing to Peaky's swastika. "When all the men who's've got their names on that wall behind you, they fakkin *died* to keep you safe from that, that . . . *evil* thing, you little prick."

"That's enough, now," says the anti, again. But the one next to him, a curly-haired lecturer type who carefully took off his glasses as he stepped up, though he's holding a plank, is smiling now. He thinks this bit of accidental street theatre is good politics.

"No, let him have his say. Go on, mate; you tell 'em."

"I don't need your fakkin permission," says the drunk, who in his own way is just as belligerent as all the other men there. "Where was I?" he adds, less impressively.

"I expect you was just about to tell us you was in the fucking desert with Monty," says Peaky.

"No, I wasn't, you cheeky little sod. I was in an AA battery on Blackheath, trying to shoot down aer-o-planes that had *that* on the fakkin side of them. And watching London burn. So if you don't like it here, you know what you should do? You should complain, right, to your friends in the fakkin Luftwaffe who blew all the fakkin holes in it. Right?"

"Look, sir," says Mr. Brocklehurst unwisely, "no one is ungrateful for your service. The European war was a tragic conflict, in many ways, egged on by international finance—"

"Fakk off," says the drunk. "I'm not talking to *you*. Who are you? A ponce in a tie." At this, Peaky and several of the younger skins smile helplessly. "No! No! Don't you grin at me! You've got nothing to fakkin grin about. It's you I'm talking to. You are fakkin *from* here, and them names behind you *are* your dads', and your grandads', and your fakkin uncles', and you know what you are doing, with this Narzy nonsense? You are fakkin *spitting* on them. And you should be ashamed."

172

He's almost crying, the easy tears of drunkenness, and everyone is embarrassed.

"Right," says Mike quietly, "if you don't move out the way, you poxy old pisshead, I am going to break your fucking spine."

But the police have arrived by this time, a minibus full of the busies who come pushing into the stand-off with truncheons out. They aren't always necessarily unfriendly to the BM and the National Fronters, or averse to putting the boot in themselves. The big march in Lewisham earlier in the year essentially turned into a gigantic three-sided punch-up, skins and anti-fascists and the boys in blue all whaling away on each other. Here and now, though, in front of this audience of shoppers and called out by one of the shopkeepers or maybe the vicar of St. Saviour's, they are the blue full stop to what both sides were looking forward to. Mike's army withdraws, muttering. Val checks Mike's face, and sees the disappointment she expects. *Is that enough? No!*

And his luck doesn't seem to improve as the day goes on. Mr. Brocklehurst goes back to Surbiton in his Hillman Hunter. Then it drizzles on the rest of them in Bexford Park as they eat the sandwiches, a damping that takes the fun from the game of claiming territory and scaring the black families out of the adventure playground. Veils of wet blow slowly over the slide and the merry-go-round. Fat Marge knees Taff in the balls harder than she meant, and he goes limping off home. Then the girlfriends, getting loudly bored, manage to detach some of the younger casuals, and they go off to do what you can do in a bus shelter with a bottle of Mac Market cider whatever the weather, despite the lure of the footie to come. And then it turns out the match isn't much of a lure anyway. Mike doesn't believe in women on the terraces, so he parks Val in a caff outside the Den along with one of the older hard men's wives: Jeanie, who in fact Val works with in the furniture shop in the precinct below the Park towers. Mike found her the job, of course. He likes her to be where someone he knows can keep an eye on her. Weekday or weekend, they don't have a lot to say to each other. Val hasn't got the currency of family chat to pay into conversation. Now they smoke and drink deep-brown teas and cock an ear to the sound coming out of the Den; and when the men come back, the pissed-off look on Mike's face has only deepened, because the game was an easy 2–0 victory for the Lions against Bournemouth, and maddeningly good-tempered throughout, because who can be fucked to hate bloody Bournemouth. *Enough? Fuck off.*

By this time Val is praying quietly for him to find someone to thump. *Please, please, please. Something soon, and something not too bad.* The evening looks promising: they're going to a gig up in Camden, a skin-friendly band of white boys making skin-friendly music. (Which means ska; which means Jamaican music; which means the hated nig-nogs are also somehow on the twisted quiet being loved, at least for their capacity to produce Prince Buster and Byron Lee and the Skatalites. It didn't do to think too hard about this.) An expedition up to alien NW1, loads of strangers, a pint or three: surely there's scope there to get Mike safely satisfied.

On the Tube going north they occupy the end carriage of the train. Peaky and the lads ensure that no one else gets into it by standing arms outspread at the opening doors at every station, and grinning. Mike seems subdued, though. He doesn't even join in when they spot a possible pooftah on the down escalator at Camden Town while they're all riding up to the surface. The others go leaping and stomping downward to try to cut the target off—he gets away before they reach the bottom—but Mike only stands there, staring at his feet, his jaw grinding. "Is your head still hurting, love?" she asks. "No!" he says vehemently, as if it's a betrayal by her to even ask.

A pint helps. The second pint helps even more. And when they go into the Electric Ballroom he's almost jaunty. There's so many skins in there, BM skins and NF skins and casuals, from every point of the London compass, that it's like a gathering of the clans. Boots and braces, pork-pie hats and Fred Perry shirts and crombies as far as the eye can see, and the stage lighting gleaming on hundreds of naked male heads, surging and shifting together like white crumbs, or like the beans in baked beans. ("There you go, skinheads on a raft," Val says to Mike when she makes him beans on toast for tea. It makes him smile every time.) They're all the same, or nearly all the same, and it's good-humoured. There's a certain amount of shoving and showing-out going on—the Bexford boys move onto the floor like a phalanx, with Mike at its tip, but the inevitable collisions are happy ones, as if everyone on all sides is on their honour not to care when they go sprawling. It's a Home stand with no Away stand, it's an Us with no Them to hate, and it seems to make the big-kids aspect of being a skin come to the fore, as if the whole venue (barring a few exceptions like Val, parked against a fire extinguisher on the back wall) is filled with man-sized nine-year-old boys, having a laugh. In the flow and crush of the crowd she glimpses Mike from time to time, skanking with his shirt off, beautiful in motion as ever, and for once almost innocent in his pleasure at carving a clean line through the world. Maybe, for once, this might be enough. Maybe an actual good time, with no broken skin, will send the beast to bed content?

But then the support act comes on, and it turns out they've got a black singer, which will have been a fine thing on the 2-Tone tour round the country the headline band were on just now: but it goes down like the proverbial cup of cold sick with this audience. Suddenly aggro is back on the menu. They won't let them play. They roar, they boo, they bellow, they throw cans and bottles. The support band retreat, and the lead singer of the evening's big draw, the head Nutty Boy himself, comes out to the mike to reason with the crowd.

"C'mon," he says, "give 'em a chance, yeah? They're great." And then when that doesn't work, "Come on! I *know* you're better than this." And then when *that* doesn't work, he visibly loses his temper. Other members of the band come out and have a try. "You're here for fun, not politics, aren'cha?" says the one who dances about down the front in shades with his chest out. "Well, we're not playing till *they* do," says the saxophonist in the end: and that does it, that causes a groan to run through the whole crowd; and splits it, and reveals that if you subtract the casuals and all the skinheads who really do care most about the music, there isn't anything like a majority in the place for a firm Nazi no. Val can see Mike's head turning from side to side as he discovers he isn't there with a band of pure-bred brothers after all. The openers come back on, and this time the protests are small enough to ignore, this time when the first song kicks off most people politely dance, and the bassline drowns the rest.

Mike isn't dancing. He's standing there, scowling at the stage. He goes on not-dancing when the main set finally begins and the place goes crazy to the rising saxophone wail at the beginning of "One Step Beyond." Now he's on the outside of the tidal pleasure that's lifting the crowd. Now he's just part of a sour little refusal, a Sieg-Heiling sprinkle of holdouts, an outcast from shared joy.

And when the set's done, the lead singer, lathered up with sweat and with the elation of being joy's conductor, looks at the island of Hitler salutes, and sneers. "All right," he says, "I can see what you are. I've got eyes, haven't I?" It's contempt in his voice, loud and plain.

What's worse, when they're leaving, when they're all draining back out onto Camden High Street, it becomes clear that the split in the crowd is reproduced within the troop from Bexford. Most of the lads had a great time. Mike's fury is a minority fury. Whatever their usual deference to him, just now they don't want to hear about how crap it was, not when they're buzzing, they're laughing, they're clomping off into the Tube station. They're fooling about. They're fooling about and being twenty. They're ready to run down the escalator three steps at a time. "Cheer up!" they say. "We'll see yer tomorrow!" Amazingly fast, there's just her, Mike and Peaky left.

"Never mind, love," she says, carefully.

He ignores her.

"Well," he says, "it's not that late. I think we'll go for a little walk"—and he and Peaky exchange glances.

This is not a part of his life she has ever been taken along on, or ever wanted to be. The dread in her stomach clutches tighter.

"P'raps I better go home," she says.

"On your own? Nah," says Mike.

So she has to follow, picking along behind the bulk of them in the orange sodium lights. It's busy, this unknown region of North London, with punters in the kebab shops and the minicab offices, the blue flashing lights of panda cars going by, and a different mix of human beings from the one down at home. Too many of them, considering it's only Mike and Peaky. They turn off into a side street, and suddenly there's nobody around at all, seemingly, just parked cars bumper to bumper, and tall prosperous-looking houses with thick curtains tightly drawn. Also no good for prey. But up at the end there's a little concrete car park, a kind of baby multi-storey with only two levels, and somebody is in there. There's a car down on the lower level with its inside lights on and its bonnet open. Someone is trying the engine and getting nothing but clicks and wheezes from the starter.

"Problem, mate?" asks Mike from the top of the ramp, and the marooned driver looks up. It's a mild-faced, big-eyed, studenty-looking young Indian bloke, all on his own, and smiling uncertainly, for Mike is a skinhead, but Mike sounds friendly, genial. Something warm is stirring in his voice, and Val knows what it is.

"Just a little bit of engine trouble, sir," says the student, and his voice is Indian-Indian, not London-Indian. Perhaps he doesn't know what he's supposed to be afraid of.

"Well, let's have a look, then," says Mike. "Perhaps we can sort you out."

Peaky giggles, but Mike is straight-faced. There was in fact a time last year on the way to Brighton when a family with a breakdown were sent on their way by a suddenly helpful carful of skins, "compliments of the British Movement," Mike having seen on the telly where the Hell's Angels sometimes did that in America, and liking the way it induced first fear and then relief. But that family was white. And that was Mike having a good day.

Down the ramp they go: concrete pillars and concrete floor and concrete ceiling, all stained shadowy orange. Mike and Peaky pretend to look under the bonnet, leaving her for just an instant alone with the student. (Peter Iqbal, she will discover he was called, at the trial.)

Run, she mouths at him. But he goggles at her politely, and doesn't get it.

"Aha!" says Mike. "There's your problem. In there—no, there, mate—right at the back—look—"

And then the bonnet slamming down on the boy's head, and the kicking beginning, and Peter Iqbal hauled up against a pillar so Mike can work on him with his fists, and with every punch Val thinking *Is that enough? Is that?* and Peter Iqbal's face a whimpering mess and Peaky having a go and Peter Iqbal falling down again and more kicking and the noises the kicks make getting more liquid and Peaky getting tired and being ready to stop and Val thinking *Please God let that be enough* and Mike stepping back and Mike's face still working with an undischarged petulance and Mike stepping back in and starting to stamp on him and Peaky saying "Er—mate?" and Mike not stopping and Peaky looking at her and Val swallowing and saying "That's enough now" and trying to grab his arm and Mike who has never once hit her throwing her off and Val bouncing off the Cortina next along and falling on the concrete and seeing under the car Mike's boot coming down and down on Peter Iqbal's head and Peter Iqbal's head not being the right shape any more and blue lights coming too late too late and enough enough enough, that's enough.

t + 50: 1994

Ben

The soft brown hill of Marsha's shoulder is the first thing Ben sees when he wakes up. All he sees, in fact. He's been sleeping tucked in so close behind her that his forehead is against her neck, and the skin of her back spreads as wide as a field, as wide as a map, when he comes blinking up to consciousness. He's seeing it from so close to, it isn't quite in focus. It is a deep caramel blur, stippled with the rose of freckles and the occasional dot of darker purple-black, which at the edge of his vision firms into the clarity of pores, fine down, tiny wrinkles, unrolling away from him around the cushiony curve of her shoulder blade, and seeming as inexhaustible as a real hill, a whole landscape he could browse across, kiss across, pore by pore, brown millimetre by brown millimetre. Blood warms it; it swells and shrinks minutely as Marsha breathes; it belongs to someone, is part of someone who, improbably, wonderfully, loves him. It is not it. It is her. It is all her. He lies in a glowing envelope that radiates from her, as if she is so full of life that it doesn't stop at the literal edges of her but spreads around her, into the sheets, into the pillows, into the cave made by the quilt. She would say that they are keeping each other warm, but to Ben it is a kindness of hers, a gift she is giving and he is receiving. She smells of shampoo and last night's supper.

He lifts his head to look, and though she stirs on the pillow, sleep still has her. She's still within the fraying cocoon of the night, and does not know her mouth half-opens, half-closes; that she grimaces, a tiny bit, and rubs her lips on the blue cotton as if digging gently in it. In the day she is a talker, a doer, a person in motion, whose face shows constant quick laughter, quick irritation, quick bossiness. Only now can he admire her slowed, vague, languorous, with little impulses moving in her round face that come to nothing, but buffer back into stillness before they can expand into real expressions: the outward and visible sign that, within, the kaleidoscope of dream is shifting and sliding the panes of memory against each other, in combinations too strange and fleeting to call out definite reactions. She knows now (a knowledge made all out of ambiguous texture) what she will forget when she awakens. There is far more of her than there's ever time to reckon with in the businesslike daylight. Marsha Adebisi Simpson is in the depths of Marsha Adebisi Simpson. But she is surfacing, getting closer to the light, drawn up, lured up, by Ben's fingers.

He strokes her temple, where the wiry edge of her hair smooths away. She mutters. He draws the line on her scalp between two cornrows. She mumbles. He hunkers down, and addresses himself seriously to her beautiful back. With four fingertips he makes four parallel lines, slow as he can, dragging feather-light down from her right shoulder onto her shoulder blade, trying to move so that he makes only the faintest shivering trail in the down on her skin, teasing the envelope of her warmth. Then he does it again in exactly the same place, with his fingernails gently scratching, denting four paths southward, southward, southward.

"Mm," she says.

And having scrived on her skin with this faint, faint harshness, this gentle abrasion, he turns back to softness again, and traces the profile of her side with a feather-finger that sets little shivers going. Down the soft skin under her arm, across the padding of her ribs, into the dimple of her waist (not a girl's narrow waist but an honest middle-aged one) and up again around the flaring curve of her hip, and (getting to the end of his reach) onto the long roundness of her thigh. A soft touch and then a gentle scratch, soft and then a scratch. It's as if he's colouring her in, under the quilt, with a pencil that glides and shades and another one that etches and points. He's making graphite love to her, or so it feels, 2B love and HB love. Only he's not making her up, she's really there. All those swelling riches, really being discovered. And astonishing all over again.

"*Mmm,*" she says, with much more emphasis, a waking person's emphasis, and presses back against him. Ben stretches round and outlines her mouth with his artistic finger. Her lips have ridges on them like a brazil nut's shell, if you look closely, but much much softer.

"Hello," she says.

"Hello," says Ben.

"Who's that?" says Marsha.

"Ben?" he says, suddenly freezing.

She sighs a bit, and nibbles his hand. Then she reaches an arm back in turn, a strong and unambiguous arm, and holds him against her.

"I know that, foolish man, lovely man," she says. "Don't stop."

"Oh," says Ben.

"Oh," says Marsha.

"Ah," says Marsha.

"Mmm," says Marsha.

"Oh!" says Marsha.

"Oh!" says Ben.

Among the things Ben didn't know, until these last few years, Marsha having not till then taken him in hand and given him the chance to find out, was how after making love with your wife

185

on a sunny Sunday morning in May, and going downstairs to put the kettle on, you find yourself wobbling, almost tottering, on the stairs. So much tension has been taken out of him, it's as if his limbs have been almost unstrung. At elbows shoulders hips knees ankles, the strings are loose. Teetering across the spotless tiles of the hall, he feels like a young foal making its first parley with gravity, not the grizzled fifty-five-year-old he sees crossing the mirror. In the kitchen, it's all bright. Marsha's passion for cleanliness in the café gets even more so at home. The white blaze coming through the blind above the sink gleams on every surface. There are no grimy corners or lost spots where old envelopes or unmatched earrings gather dust. Everything is lifted and briskly scrubbed beneath, every day. You could lick the counter under the food processor or the coffee percolator and it wouldn't taste of anything but fresh bleach. All the cups, all the plates, all the cutlery match. The sound of the water coming to the boil adds a terribly soothing music to Ben's state of discombobulated comfort, and he props himself on the countertop while he fetches down tea things for the tray, in case he dissolves altogether into a puddle of happiness.

Under the circumstances, it seems entirely safe to make this the moment when he checks the floor of his mind for cracks, as he makes himself do at some point, explicitly, every morning. And it is. He stamps, internally, and nothing gives, nothing threatens, nothing cracks or creaks. It's a crystal pavement inside him, metres thick. He is not afraid. He is *not afraid*. It sometimes seems to him that he is losing the ability to be as grateful for this as he should be. He doesn't want to take it for granted. Surely he should be actively glad, positively and consciously jubilant, over such an enormous deliverance? But as the fear has faded, so in proportion has his sense of how far he has come, how much has changed in his soul's weather. He could only really feel the mea-

sure of the change by being back as he was before: the last thing
he needs or wants. Now and again, now, he catches himself shaking his head over his past self as if that man were someone else,
someone mysterious. How *could* he have wasted the whole of his
twenties and thirties, and much of his forties, on fear? And fear
of what, exactly? It had something to do with . . . bones; but he
can say the word now, in his mind, without the reverberations of
dread it used to have. So it leaves him puzzled, and sad, and, yes, a
touch exasperated, to think of the two wretched solitary decades
on the buses, and their thousands of desperately stoned evenings.

The kettle boils. He pours the water on the teabags, mashes
them, slings them neatly in the right bin, adds milk; takes his pill
and puts the bottle back in the cupboard. Then upstairs again. No
toast because Marsha doesn't approve of crumbs in bed. His joints
seem to be reknitting. He rises up to the landing as if propelled
by a friendly gust of well-being, and when he comes through the
door and finds Marsha sitting up with her riches on display, he
feels a wild urge to frisbee the tray into the corner, jump back
between the sheets, and do it (and her) all over again. The Her-
cules of Bexford!

But Marsha, though she pats the bed beside her, has her busy
daylight face on now. Has her glasses on, and is looking at him
over the top of them while she consults her to-do list.

"Jerk chicken," she says. "Ewa Agoyin. Okra soup. Pepperpot
soup. Goat curry. Potato salad. Rice and peas. Cocktail sausages
for the little one. For desserts, ice cream and lemon meringue.
We'll have to get a move on after church."

Always the lists, with Marsha. Always the sense that life is a
campaign requiring meticulous planning. In fact, the chicken has
been in its jerk marinade since last night, the clingfilm-covered
steel tray filling a whole shelf of the fridge, the goat meat is soaking up its herbs and curry powder down where the vegetable

boxes usually are, and the beans have soaked overnight too. She is well ahead of the game, as always. But there are going to be four-teen people eating lunch in the garden at three o'clock, and the shape of the extended family requires her to show out simultane-ously at both Yoruba and Jamaican food. In the café she's feeding strangers, and nothing is at stake but their livelihood. For this, her pride is involved.

"It'll be fine," says Ben. "You know it will."

"It will be fine because we make it fine," she says.

Ben could not say whether Marsha's rescue of him counts as a departure from her usual practicality or an example of it—whether she saved him because she wanted to do something mad for once, or whether she only applied her methodical mind to his floun-dering soul the way she would have reviewed a menu, or gone through her monthly suppliers' bills. He had been going from agency job to agency job in the terrible year after the 36C went driver-only, shifts doing shelf-stacking, warehouse-unloading, washing-up, any old thing so long as it was badly paid. And one day he got sent by the agency to Café Metro in the gentrified bit at the top of Bexford Rise, expecting from the swags and curli-cues of gold on the glass that it was going to be some kind of deal with scurrying waiters in black aprons, where he would be ban-ished to a sink far out of view, only to discover that it was in fact a one-woman band, operated by a small plump brisk dark matron who insisted that he started off by washing his hands, and stood over him while he did it, sniffing disapprovingly at the lingering reek on him of last night's ganja.

"Right, now do the bacon," she commanded.

He looked at the glistening mound of streaky, pale fat and pink flesh surely so close to human meat, and he blenched.

"I can't," he said.

"Why not?" she barked.

He muttered something and prepared to flee.

But rather than accepting this, she put out a hand to his chin and turned his face so he had to meet her gaze. ("Why did you do that?" he asked her later. She said, "You looked like someone who thought no one could see them. But I could see you.") It was the first time anyone had touched Ben kindly in longer than he could remember. Perhaps Marsha was the first person since his mother to have done it. It shocked him, it made his heart pound and his blood ring in his ears. But it also made him feel as if, for the first time in equally long, in a world of tormenting vapours where thoughts were always stronger than things, he had taken hold of something truly solid. Or in fact as if something solid had taken hold of him. He might flap, he might flail, he might panic, but where she touched him he was rooted, he was joined somehow to the strong ground.

"Why not?" she repeated.

And held in her grip as in her gaze, and exhausted by so much despair, Ben did what he had never done before. He burst into tears and told her. Tried to tell her, anyway. Obvious though his horrors were to him, they came out incoherent, and more puzzling than they had ever seemed inside. Yet the relief of even trying was intense.

"I am a bad man," he finished. "I am full of . . . horrible things."

"A bad man," she repeated, but not as if she believed him. By this time they were sitting at one of the little round black tables. She'd had to release him when they sat down, but he had reached for her hand, so as to be able to go on talking, and she was letting him hold it. "You are a bad man. Okay. Tell me what bad things you have done."

"I . . . don't know."

"Are you a murderer?"

"No."

"How many people have you eaten?"

". . . None."

"Are you a thief? Do you go out and mug people?"

"No."

"Do you hurt children?"

"No!"

"Well, then. I will fry the bacon, and you will do all these rolls. And then I expect I had better show you how to work the percolator. Hurry up, we open in twenty-five minutes."

And she took him into her business; and she took him to her GP, to be prescribed anti-depressants; and she took him to her church, to have an evil spirit removed; and eventually, she having been widowed for two years at that point, she took him into her house and her bed and her heart.

"*Why?*" he asked.

"Because I liked the way you looked. A little bit like something that comes out at night, with big eyes, but nice. I'm shallow like that. Don't keep asking, stupid man. I might change my mind. Ach, I'm teasing. *Olorun a de fun e.* God bless you and shut up."

Marsha is a strong believer in Sunday best, and Ben is in a suit and tie and well-polished shoes as they drive over to the Assemblies of Salvation church, based in the old Odeon. That's minimal, though, a bare masculine nod of respect to the day, compared to the full African glad-rags she has on. Today, a puff-sleeved number in violet, green and gold, with matching headcloth, regally folded and tucked till it climbs up nearly to turban height. Most of the splendour will be hidden when she puts her choir robe on, but that's not the point. It will be there, visible to the good Lord. It will also have been clocked by all the other choir ladies.

Pastor Michael welcomes them in.

"Curtis and Cleveland not with you today?" he rumbles, genially.

"All coming over for lunch later. The whole family," says Marsha, head high. "With Curtis and Lisa's new baby."

"Splendid, splendid," says the pastor. "And does he have a name yet, the baby?"

"Theo," says Marsha.

"Ah yes, a godly name. Splendid. Brother Benjamin, how are you?" the pastor asks, enfolding Ben's small hand in both of his large ones.

"Very well," says Ben.

"I rejoice to hear it," the pastor says, and pats his hand proprietorially.

Pastor Michael disliked him, Ben thinks, when they first met, because Marsha as a widow lady with a prospering business would have represented a nice and natural prize for one of the older men in the congregation; who knows, perhaps for the pastor himself, judging by the odd appreciative glance Ben has detected. But all that has been wiped away by the glorious success of what the church has done for him, their stringy bedraggled interloping white guy. Now Ben is an object of pride, one of Bexford Assembly's very own miracles. "Come out of him!" Pastor Michael cried, and either then or round about then, either because of the hurricane of prayer they sent scouring through the house of his mind or at least for reasons that included it—out of him the evil spirit came. Ben has been lost, but now he is found. He has been dry bones, but now he lives. He has been wreckage, but the fiery gale of holiness has blown upon him, cleansed him, ordered him, set him upright, made him a man again. He is a walking, talking evidence of redemption—so it is all right that he is holding Marsha's hand.

Some Sundays are Youth Sundays, with more or less continuous music interspersed with testimonies from the teenagers as they try to tread the straight and narrow way in Bexford among the temptations of crack and the gangs. Some Sundays see the under-tens on parade in their cherubim and seraphim uniforms. Many Sundays have guest preachers, rotating around the Assemblies of Salvation circuit. But today it is Pastor Michael's own turn again, and the service is an hour-long discourse from him, prowling the stage and the aisles with a mike in his hand, sweating and earnest and increasingly hoarse, raising up devotion to a pitch from which the choir can raise it higher still, by means of gospel settings of old hymns, and a touch of Highlife for those nostalgic for Ibadan, and new worship songs from the sacred (but still funky) end of soul.

"Except the Lord build the house," says Pastor Michael, "they labour in vain that build it. Psalm one-two-seven verse one. Except the Lord build the house, they labour in vain that build it. What do they labour in? Vain! Amen. That's right. You can build your house high and down it will fall, if the Lord don't keep it for you. Down it will *fall*. Nothing but a load of bricks. All smashed up. Gone! Doesn't matter how high it is, doesn't matter how strong it is. It could be a ten-storey house. It could be a twenty-storey house, it could be a skyscraper, it could be a mighty tower, and if the Lord don't like it, down it comes. What did the Lord do to the tower of—where? Babel! Amen. He put it *down*. Right down, tumbled down, nothing left. Think of that. Think of all the work the people do, to build up the high tower; all those days with the bricks and mortar, with the wheelbarrow. Now you know—maybe you don't know—when I come to this country, I'm looking around for work, you know, and it's not a very friendly place for a boy from Lagos, you know what I mean? And I got only fifty shillings in my pocket. But my arms are strong, you know, and I get a job on the building site. Man, it's hard. (*Amen.*) Every day I push the barrow, and the barrow is heavy, and the plank is shaking. So I know this, that it's a lot of work to build a house, just a little house, and the more tall the house the more the work. But God can pull it all down! Praise God, he can! And then all that work, all that sweating, it's wasted. They labour in vain. Now that's a hard word, isn't it, brother? Isn't it, sister? You work and work and it come to nothing. That's hard, that's desperate. But do you know why? Yes, you know why. Lord have mercy, the Lord himself tell you why. You forget to bless it. You don't remember, you got to give it to the Lord to keep. Except the Lord *build* the house, it gonna come tumbling down. Except the Lord *keep* the house, you gonna lose it all again—all that work. Your children gonna fail their exams, your daughter gonna get knock up, your son gonna do those drugs. No blessing, and your house, it's like a magnet for the bad luck. A bad magnet for the bad spirits. So, get that blessing! We got to ask for that blessing! Bless us, Lord; bless us in our homes and in our hearts; bless us deep, bless us strong; bless us in abundance. And you know, when we ask, he answers. He always answers. *You could have left me standing there . . .* (Help me, sisters.)"

> *You could have left me standing there*
> *With no one, no one to care*
> *But you promised me you'd be there on time*
> *And you did just what you said*
>
> *(I gave it up) That's when you bless me*
> *(Oh I let it go) That's when you bless me*

(Lord you brought me through, now I'm brand new)
(I said have your way) That's when you bless me

(Oh I'm here to stay) That's when you bless me
(Lord you promised me you would hear my plea)
And you did just what you said

"So you know what to do, don't you, brothers? Don't you, sisters? The Lord told you how to build your house, he told you himself. Matthew seven verse twenty-four. You've got to build your house on—what? A rock! That's right. And you don't build it on—what? The sand! That's right. For the rain descends, and the flood comes, and the wind blows, and it beats upon your house, and if you've got sand down there in the foundation, oh man, uh-oh, that's not good, that's a disaster on the way. Down it falls, down it all falls, clattering and tumbling. But if you build it on the rock, then it don't matter what comes, it don't matter what get thrown at you. Bring it along! Let it all come. Let it rain, let the flood come, let the wind blow. You're okay. You're on the strong foundation, you're on the strongest foundation in the world. 'The house fell not, for it was founded on the rock.' That is a house that is safe from trouble. Don't matter what trouble. Could be any trouble. Let it come: come on, bad luck, come on, diseases, come on, thieves, come on, police problem, come on, unemployment, come on, bad spells and conjuring, come on, anxious mind, come on, wicked heart. Come on, anything! No need to be afraid, sisters and brothers. No need to be afraid at all. Your house will stand. Your house has the strong foundation. Your house is built on—what? The rock! Amen. The rock. And what is the rock? The rock is the Lord Almighty. The rock is his holy word, in his good book. The rock is the Lord Jesus, strong to save. The rock is the mighty Spirit of the Lord God of Israel. That's right. *Because the Lord is my shepherd . . .* (Sing it with me.)"

Because the Lord is my shepherd
I have everything I need
He lets me rest in the meadow's grass
and He leads me beside the quiet stream
He restores my failing hands
and helps me to do what honours
That's why I am safe
that's why I'm sa-a-a-afe
sa-a-afe
in his arms

"Safe today, brothers and sisters. Safe tomorrow. Safe forever after. Praise him for that! Praise his great name. Now that's a lot! Isn't that a lot to praise him for? Amen! But that's not all. That's not all. The Lord don't just want your house to stand! He's got you safe—you, sister, you, brother. But he wants more. He got bigger plans. He want to hold this whole wicked city in his hand. Listen to him! Psalm one-two-seven again, back we go. Except the Lord keep the *city*, the watchman waketh but in vain. You hear? The watchman wakes up in the night and he looks around. What was that sound? Was that a fox, you know, rummaging in the bin for the cold kebab? (You know that sound, eh, sister?) Or was it a burglar, breaking in? He doesn't know, so he worries and he worries. But it does no good. It is in vain, unless the *Lord* keep the city. Unless the Lord take it all in his hand. Now Jerusalem, you know, was a city just like London. It had nightclubs. It had bad areas. It had dealers in wickedness. It had rich people, proud people, unrighteous people, with mischief in their hearts. But the Lord, brothers and sisters, what did he do? Did he want to burn it? To wash it away in a mighty flood? No. No. He went another way to clean up that dirty place. He loved it. He want to redeem it. And he did redeem it. He wash it with his blood. He wash it bright and clean. He make it new. The New Jerusalem, brothers and sisters, beautiful like a bride; think of that. And you know? It's just the same with London. This dirty town, he want to hold it all safe in his hand as well. He want to build it again, on the rock of salvation. He want to make it new and holy. He want to wash the pavements till they shine like diamonds. He want to dress it in a shining robe. He want to bring it all to salvation. Do you think he can? Tell me if you think he can, brothers and sisters. I can't hear you. Yes, he can! Yes, he can! He can take this great city, he can make it new. He can wash it clean. He can redeem it. He can make it sing and praise his name. Praise his name! Praise his holy name! Praise him, Bexford! Praise him, London! Praise him, Ess Eee Fourteen, and all the other postcodes! Praise him with the sound of the trumpet! Praise him with the psaltery and harp! Praise him with the timbrel and dance! Praise him with stringed instruments and organs! Praise him upon the loud cymbals! Praise him upon the high-sounding cymbals! Let every thing that hath breath praise the Lord!"

And Ben thinks, dazed as he always is as the pastor reaches his climax and the choir ascends to ecstasy: I am safe. I *am*, though I don't know how or why. Thank you.

By the time they get home it is twenty to one, and the tasks required to get lunch ready for three stretch ahead of them in unbroken sequence from the minute Marsha gets their church clothes back into their dry-cleaning bags in the closet. She whizzes up the soaked peppers and dried crayfish for the Ewa Agoyin, and starts the smoky business of bleaching the palm oil. Ben chops—onions, spring onions, okra. He washes and sets simmering the new potatoes. He beats up the egg whites for the top of the lemon meringue. He sous-chefs away, in short, making sure that each time she's ready to assemble a dish, the bits are to hand, in drifts of chopped white, chopped green, chopped red, chopped yellow. This is how they work together in the café, and there's a practised speed to it, a comfortable co-ordination of their two rhythms. (It has occurred to Ben that one reason for his peaceful mind, maybe not the whole thing but a contributory factor, is that life with Marsha is so continuously bloody busy, with zero brooding time.) But the quantities they're cooking are bigger than domestic, with only a small home kitchen to do it all in, so the activities are constantly jostling up against each other, and they have to squeeze past each other on their way to and fro in a kind of controlled whirlwind. The feeling is nearer the edge of chaos than it would be in the café, though not of course over it, thanks to Marsha's list. As he crosses behind her, he kisses the nape of her neck. "Get away!" she says, and bats at him with a wooden spoon. But when she next passes behind him, she pinches his bum. She is nervous, he knows; she always is when her sister comes over. Soon he is washing up as well, to keep her supplied with fresh pans.

"Right," she says, when the pie is in the oven, the curry is bubbling, the okra is done and waiting on the side, the Ewa Agoyin is savourously red-black, and the little sausages are popping under the grill. "Barbecue!"

Out goes Ben into the garden with the steel tray of chicken and a bag of charcoal. He drags the barbecue out of the immensely orderly shed onto the little patio, and while the firelighters catch and he waits for the little briquettes to begin to glow, he has a moment to look around. They need not have worried about the weather. It's a lovely day, with that early-summer brightness to the green of leaves and the blue of the sky that makes them look as if they have just been washed. In the border, up against the fence that Ben creosoted a few months ago, the peonies bob in pink globes, the mallows are a mass of blowsy white, cored pink and gold, and the blue lobelia shine out sharp and electric. Everything looks fresh and new. In the sky overhead a plane glints, tiny as a metal cracker toy, and draws a roar reduced to a whisper after it, as it follows the flight path over Bexford Hill towards distant Heathrow. There's always a plane up there if you look, near or far, visible or only betrayed by a line of vapour, but always moving westwards. It's as if—thinks Ben, putting the first thighs and drumsticks onto the griddle—it's as if the aeroplanes were part of the mechanism of the garden; a necessary part. As if this tidy patch of lawn surrounded by its fence, with its brilliant blossoms too many to count and its coiled yellow hose, together formed the bottom half of a machine of bliss, which required for its complete working the dome of sky above, and for the furthest component of its clockwork the timekeeping planes on their celestial track. Patiently they tick from east to west. Or perhaps they are joined to the sky, and it is the sky that is moving, a blue sphere studded with occasional silver that cranks around, and around, and around.

The chicken is sizzling. It's ten to three. "Chairs!" shouts Marsha.

The first to arrive is Marsha's older boy Curtis and his family. Suddenly the hall is full of childcare clobber as Curtis helps five-year-old Ruthie off with her coat, and baby Theo is scooped up from his carry-cot to ride on Lisa's hip, and then held up to be squooched, no hands, by Marsha, who is still in the last convulsions of the cookery. Ben takes the mixing bowl from Marsha, the carry-cot from Lisa. But at once the doorbell goes again, and there on the step are Marsha's sister Gloria, regal in an outfit even more spectacular than Marsha's churchwear, and beaming next to her in a three-piece suit, and holding out a bottle of champagne, her lawyer husband Julius Ojo. Their daughter Addie is parking the BMW just up the road. Gloria gives a slightly stagey cry of joy and hugs Marsha, who still is having to hold her hands up and out of the way of the silks.

"Now, if you're not ready, you must let me help," says Gloria.

"No," says Marsha.

Ben takes the champagne and puts it in the fridge.

"Good man," says Julius, his voice a reverberant courtroom bass.

Gloria offers Ben a cautious, eyes-averted cheek to kiss—she is not sure about her sister's eccentric choice, or maybe she is sure, and not to his advantage—and he gets them all moving through the lounge towards the French windows. Marsha washes her hands, stacks plates. Just in time: up the garden path are coming the late-departed Clyde Simpson's younger brother Otto, a pale-brown guy in glasses with a beret and a raincoat and a jazzman's frizzy tuft of beard, looking very like the ceremonial picture of Marsha's husband on the lounge wall, except for the beret and the beard, and except for the wary expression, which he shares with his partner Margaret, also a teacher. They both look braced and ironical round the eyes, as if already looking down on events from a prepared position somewhere to the rear of their literal bodies. This isn't the look on the face of their daughter Grace, though. Grace is nearly fourteen and big with it, in the awkward place between child and teenager. Today she wants to be a child, and she hugs her auntie, and pushes on straight through the hall in search of Ruthie, who adores her. Ben picks up the coats that have fallen down.

No point in shutting the door again. Addie is coming up the road, twirling the car key round her finger; and in the other direction, under a tree, Curtis's younger brother Cleveland is in sight, with his arms round the girlfriend no one has met yet. Not, by the look of his body language, having a snog; more a case, as he strokes her long fair hair, of calming her down, or nerving her up, for her meeting with the assembled clans. Here they come, Cleveland gently propelling her along. They meet Addie at the gate, and she says something that makes Cleve laugh and the girl smile, and then they're in, twelve—thirteen—fourteen, and that's everyone, the clans *have* assembled. High-achieving pots-of-money Tory-voting Ojos to one side, public-sector on-the-committee-of-Carnival brushes-with-the-law Simpsons to the other; in the middle, Marsha's two boys, the shy accountant and the can't-make-up-his-mind student. Not to mention Marsha herself, showing off to all sides a replacement for dead Clyde who is a spindly, weird, white, mental-patient sous-chef. So many possible disasters. So much that can go wrong.

Marsha serves up like a demon, plate after loaded plate dispatched into the garden. Ben runs about with beers, juices, the champagne, and a huge jug of Fanta tinted pink, which is a Nigerian thing, apparently. In between times he flips chicken. The whole of the backlog that he already barbecued is used up in a flash, and he gets the next lot cooking. The younger ones mingle, but their elders have picked out lawn chairs in separate encampments, Ojos by the French doors, Simpsons towards the shed. And there is no sign of Marsha. Sometimes she needs to be prised out of the kitchen. If he doesn't fetch her now, she may decide to stay put in there until second-helping time, hiding from her own party. In he goes; and as he passes the Ojos, he hears Gloria grumbling about the seasoning of the Ewa Agoyin.

"Well, I think it tastes exactly like yours, Mum," says Addie. "I mean: exactly."

"Well, of course it does," rumbles Julius. "They both learnt it from *their* mother. It's the same damn recipe."

Oh dear.

"Come on, love, come out," says Ben to Marsha. "Everyone wants to see you."

"All right, all right," says Marsha. But she takes off her apron and follows. There is an empty chair over on the other side of the garden, but as Marsha comes up, Addie gets up and pats her own seat next to Gloria.

"There you go, Auntie," she says, and takes her own plate off towards Cleve and Curtis's encampment. Marsha sits down with a bit more emphasis than is natural, doing an impression of a relaxed person.

Gloria lifts her chin towards her receding daughter. "She is doing really well, you know. Already a star in her chambers, they say."

"I'm sure she is," says Marsha.

They watch Addie go: heels high enough to make holes in the lawn, creakingly tight skirt, perfect curves and perfect hair and perfect cheekbones and perfect purple nails. Ben knows, from what Marsha has told him, that Gloria and Julius struggled to have babies, and that Gloria minded bitterly being the child-less older sister while Marsha popped out boys, even if they were slightly inferior boys, conceived with the feckless Clyde. Addie's perfection is supposed to represent a kind of devastating reply. Marsha is supposed to look at the future Adesina Ojo QC, and to mind that Curtis operates from behind a plastic fascia on West Bexford Hill, doing the books for one-lorry haulage firms. And yet the sisters also love each other. And yet Addie, as well as look-ing like some kind of West African goddess of success, is in fact a miraculously nice person, with a considerable soft spot for both her male cousins and no time at all for the status games Gloria tries to play against them using her. She's over there now, flirting decorously with Cleve, ruffling Curtis's hair as broken nights with the baby, and Marsha's food, threaten to send him snoozing off. When she was a little girl, she was worshipfully fixated on Curtis the way Ruthie is on Grace now, and it still shows. The quarrel is stupid. The quarrel is stupid, but Ben has never dared to intervene in it. What would he say?

"How is the café going?" Julius asks Ben. (It's the only question he can ask, Ben supposes, there being no other kind of professional achievement to ask safely about, where he's concerned.)

"Fine," he says. "Really good, in fact. We're thinking of taking on some more people." And this is true. Since they took the plunge and acquired the Gaggia machine that steams and hisses on the counter, they seem to have picked up a lot of trade from the incomers in the Rise's Georgian houses. Café Metro is full of well-off twenty-somethings, reading the paper and happily paying more than a pound for a cappuccino.

"Of course, it's a very small business," says Gloria.

Ben has no idea what to say to this. Marsha's hands are knitted together in her lap. Her empty lap.

"You've forgotten to get any food for yourself," he realises, and retreats to the kitchen to load Marsha a plate. He isn't fleeing; no.

But when he gets back he finds that things have already escalated to the point where the sisters have switched into rapid Yoruba. He doesn't understand a word of it, but Julius's jovial face is strained; Addie, sighing, is heading back over too.

"Honestly!" says Ben without forethought, standing over them with a knife and fork in one hand, a mounded plateful in the other. The two women, startled, look up at him. "Honestly!" he repeats. "You always remember that you like each other in the end. Why can't you remember it quicker? Why can't you just remember it now?"

Gloria starts to say something, stops, looks at her lap. Marsha blushes.

"Hmm," says Addie, leaning forward to study their faces. "Naive—but effective."

Julius starts to laugh. Marsha covers her face with her hand, and groans. Gloria coughs, taps her sister on the knee, and says, "You know, this is delicious."

"Ben cooked it too," says Marsha.

"Well, Ben, this is delicious."

"She taught me everything I know," says Ben, nodding at Marsha; and again everyone laughs, including him, though it is only the literal and absolute truth he is speaking.

After that it becomes one of those afternoons when good-will, once established, goes on reinforcing itself, making a deeper and deeper groove down which the party happily rolls. Ben flips chicken pieces and more chicken pieces; Marsha produces, to applause, the vast pie, covered with soft brown peaks like a merin-guified ocean in a storm; the men settle down and obediently eat, and eat, and eat. After a while Otto comes over, hands Julius a new beer, and starts a conversation with him about cricket. It expands to sports in general and absorbs Cleve. The women, more mobile, perch and travel, perch and travel, passing baby Theo from shoulder to shoulder, and periodically clearing away. Ruth runs about, looking over her shoulder to make sure Grace is following, and when Grace comes to rest, Lisa talks to her about school and makes her feel she has a junior spot among the matriarchs. Margaret hesitates at the edge of the group at first, but Addie draws her in and soon she is laughing and taking a turn with Theo.

Ben watches. He's comfortable like that. Marsha catches his eye across the garden and he salutes her with his barbecue tongs. But Cleve's girlfriend drifts his way and lingers, fanning the spicy-greasy smoke away from her face. (The weather is behaving itself too, bright blue only deepening as teatime goes by and the evening comes on.)

"Chicken?" says Ben, though she's not holding her plate out.

"Oh, no thanks," she says. "I'm a vegetarian." She gazes at the crisped and spiced skin, dripping fat that makes little gouts of flame. "Doesn't it, you know, *bother* you? That you've got, like, all dead things on there?"

"No," says Ben firmly. He looks at her again, and then he gets it: Cleve is busy and she's anxiously presenting herself over here, despite all the evil carnivore-ism, because he's the only other white person in the garden. It's not that he forgets that himself, exactly. His sister was eloquent about it, when he announced that he was moving out to live with Marsha. It came up a lot, in a different way, between him and Cleve, who was still just about living at home then, and let Ben know that he minded, and that he was creeped out by his mother sharing her bed with "an albino fucking spider, man," and that he didn't expect Ben to get any ideas about fatherhood, step- or otherwise. But today he hasn't been thinking about that, just now it's the Ojo/Simpson difference that's been the pressing one. Ben puts down the tongs and applies himself. "So, you're at uni with Cleve? What are you studying?"

She is studying hotel and catering, she says. But she is not sure that it's really right for her. It's not what she really cares about. Mmm, says Ben. Has she found out what she does really care about, because it's not always easy to tell, is it? No, she says, that's right! Maybe, she says, it might be travelling. She feels really alive when she's travelling. Mmm, says Ben, who has never been beyond London's bus map, except to hospital. And there is a place she *dreams* of going, she says, somewhere that sounds completely magical, she says, and that's Thailand. Really, says Ben. Oh yes, she says, it's very spiritual. And of course the food's amazing. Mmm, says Ben.

"Hey there," says Cleve, joining them. "You bending Ben's ear?"

"He's really easy to talk to!"

"Isn't he?" Cleve says, grinning, and it's probably ironic, but he doesn't say it, now, in an unfriendly way. If anyone is being teased, it's the girl (whose name Ben hasn't caught).

"D'you want some more chicken?" asks Ben.

"Nah, I'm good." Cleve pats his stomach and stretches. He's the good-looking one of Marsha's boys. "Looks like peace has broken out, man," he says, surveying the scene by the French doors.

Julius and Otto are smoking Julius's cigars, Ruthie is riding on Grace's shoulders, Gloria has said something which is making Marsha laugh and laugh.

"Yeah, thank heavens," says Ben.

"Mum's looking happy."

"D'you think so?" Ben asks, instantly anxious.

"For sure. Probably," he adds, looking at Ben sidelong, wickedly, "'cause you let her boss you round all day long . . ."

"Cleve!" says the girl, not sure what Cleve means, only that it's a wind-up.

"No, it's not that," says Curtis, who is coming over yawning, having surfaced from his nap and caught the end of what they were saying. He's slighter than his brother, large-headed, mild. There's sleep at the corner of his eyes, there are the yellows and greys of tiredness in his skin. You can see the middle-aged accountant in the thirty-year-old one. "Not just that, anyway. It's because you're not like our dad."

Cleve gives Curtis a glance, not a joking one.

"I know she misses him," says Ben. He doesn't know that, but he's thought a lot about the absent Clyde. The space he left seems unfillable to Ben, so surely it must to Marsha.

"Yeah, well, everyone's got stories about how great he was," says Curtis.

"Well, he was," says Cleve.

"When he was up, yes. Then he was, like, officially, a Fun Guy. *The* Fun Guy. Life and soul. But he was bloody moody too. Sulks that lasted for days. 'Get out of my *face*, boy.' 'Can't we have a bit of peace in here?' 'Ah, don't feed me no more of that African shit.' You remember, Cleve."

"True dat," says Cleve.

"And the good times were mostly when he was out, and the bad times were mostly at home, so Mum had to, you know, soak them up. So you'd get this happy guy, this cool musician guy, with this weary-looking woman on his arm, and all his friends would be like, 'Relax a little, darling, eh?'"

"Like that ever helps!" says the girlfriend.

"Yeah," says Cleve, not looking her way. "And there'd be this . . . *expression* round her mouth, like she was always having to keep, like, a *grip* on her face, yeah."

"Haven't seen that for a while," says Curtis.

"No," says Cleve.

"Because she's not doing it any more. Because Ben here isn't sticking his lip out, like, 'I'm miserable, woman, and someone needs to pay for it.'"

"Well, of course not," says Ben, puzzled. "She's wonderful. Why would I be miserable?"

"Yes, why would you?" repeats Curtis quietly, as if he's proved something. And he pats Ben on the arm.

"Well," says Cleve, and he sounds almost embarrassed. "Well! You know what I'm going to do? I'm going to nip behind the rose bushes, and spark up a J."

"Great!" says the girlfriend.

"Fancy a smoke, bruv?"

"Don't let Mum smell it," says Curtis. "Nope, not for me; I'm trying to wake up."

"How 'bout you, Ben," says Cleve, studying the roses.

How to explain that for him the dope was always oblivion not pleasure, that now he doesn't need his mind wiped. But then he realises that he doesn't have to, he doesn't have to give reasons. He just has to smile at them.

"I'm good," he says.

Much later, when everyone has gone but Curtis and Lisa and the kids, and they're packing up, he's out again in the garden, raking out the barbecue before putting it away. It's dusk, the blue of deep water stretching right around the dome of the sky except in the absolute west, where the last of the light stains a couple of puffball clouds red. There are burned chicken bones among the ashes and for a second something stirs but just as quickly is gone again. He gazes. A rose-coloured scratch is travelling on the blue, high and far. The last plane of daylight. The celestial clock is revolving and bringing on the night. Even happiness can't stop it. Time is his friend now, but it goes by so fast.

Ruthie comes running.

"Grandpa Ben!" she cries, as if she's caught him out in something. "Nana says come in right now!"

Val

Ring, ring.

"Hello, Samaritans."

"I, I. I don't know if this is a good idea."

"That's okay."

"..."

"I can tell you're very upset."

"Yes!"

"All right. Now, I need to just ask you this. Are you thinking about taking your own life?"

"No? I don't know? I'm just desperate. Am I still allowed to talk to you?"

"Course you are. Course you are, petal. You can talk to us about anything. Why don't we start off with you telling me your name."

"I don't want to."

"Okay, that's okay. It's fine if you don't want to. Well, can you tell me what you're upset about?"

"It's so awful."

"Mm-hmm."

"I just can't. I just can't. I'm sorry, this was a mistake . . ."

"Awful 'cause you're embarrassed?"

"Oh, I'm way past embarrassed."

"Ashamed, then?"

"Yeah. Oh yeah."

"Let's see, then—ashamed about something you did, or somebody else did?"

"It's complicated."

"Oh, love, isn't it always? Might feel better if you got it out."

"I don't see why. It'd still be true."

"Yes, it would. We can't change it, whatever it is. Might help you see it different, though."

"I just don't know if I can."

"D'you mind my asking, d'you work nights?"

"No? Why?"

"So you're at home, then."

"If you can call it that. I just can't sleep."

"Mm-hmm. And are you on your own."

"Yeah."

"All right, I'm going to make a suggestion. We're really not supposed to give advice, so this is me officially breaking the rules. You ready?"

"What?"

"Go and make a cup of tea."

"You what?"

"I'm serious. It's three o'clock in the morning, and you're just about to spill your guts to a total stranger. You need a cup of tea in your hand for that kind of thing. It's like medicine, innit. Don't hang up, mind. Just leave the phone, and go and get your tea. I'll be here when you come back. Go on. I mean it."

". . . Okay."

". . ."

". . ."

". . ."

"Hello?"

"I'm here. Got your tea? Milk and two sugars?"

"One, actually. Oh, oh, oh."

"What?"

"You're being so nice to me but you won't be when you know what it is."

"You know what, love? Whatever you tell me, *whatever* it is—I absolutely guarantee you that I've heard worse. Probably done worse myself, for that matter."

"Really?"

"Yes. This isn't dial-a-saint, you know. It's just people helping each other out. Now: deep breath, sip of tea, and tell me what's up."

"Well. It's about a bloke."

"You amaze me . . ."

"Oh, don't make me laugh! I'll start crying again, or the tea'll come out of my nose or something."

"Sorry."

"Well, I used to be married. And I thought it was all right, you know? And we had two kids; we were just, like, a family? A normal family. But he met someone, and he left. And he was good about the money and all that, but he was gone, and it was just me and the kids. And Aidan was about—fifteen, then? And Marie was twelve. And I was really lonely. Least, I thought I was. It was nothing compared to this. Just—*laughable*, compared to this. *Ridiculous*, compared to this. I didn't know I was born!"

"Doesn't sound ridiculous to me. Go on: you were lonely . . ."

"Well—my friends said, you should get out there; enjoy yourself; meet someone new; you're not that old. So I joined this computer dating thing, and—there was, like, a selection of weirdos and disasters, and I would have thrown the towel in, but then I met—Andy."

"Andy."

"Yes. And he was . . . really different from the others. He was so sure of himself. He said things like he was sure they were going to happen—and then they did, usually. He was, like, really calm, all the time? And he smiled a lot."

"Was he good-looking?"

"I thought so. I mean, then. But, you know, I really don't know? Maybe it was all the smile and the confidence. He was really well dressed too. Now I think, shouldn't I have been seeing danger signs? But I didn't."

"Well, you don't really look for them till something goes wrong, do you?"

"No. And it felt like it was going right? I was just really pleased that someone seemed to want me. My confidence wasn't so great just then and this, this was like the sun coming out. So I didn't really notice how fast everything happened. How fast he made things happen."

"But you've been thinking about it lately."

"I've been over it and over it. Because I know I should have seen something. Asked more questions. Something! But I didn't. I brought him round, and he was . . . *charming*, that's the word. He charmed me, and he charmed Marie, he was really clever about it, and he tried to charm Aidan, but it didn't work, Aidan was the only one of us who didn't take to him at all, not even at the beginning. I think he must have smelled something wrong. But I just thought, you know, old dog/young dog, you're just upset 'cause it's not your dad, you don't like having a man about the place, you're a teenage boy and you're having a bit of a squirm about your mum having a boyfriend. I thought it would die down when he got used to him. When he moved in. But it got worse. And Aidan sulking—you know, grunting at Andy over the cornflakes; teenage-boy stuff—it didn't make me sympathise with him, or think, this must be really hard for you, or, what doesn't he like, then? None of that. It made me cross. A tiny bit first, then more. And Andy saw it, and he sort of worked on it, and it always sounded like sympathy, and I got angrier and angrier. Always me against Aidan. Andy stayed in the background. You know, oh you poor love—to me; and to Aidan this kind of quiet, couldn't you try to be nicer to your mum? Oh my, you're really upsetting her. Well, that *I* heard, anyway. Who knows what he was dripping in Aidan's ear when I wasn't around. So then we had an enormous row, like earthquake-size: and Aidan walked out. Went to live with his dad. Fact his dad rang up; he said, 'Angela, what's going on? Aidan's telling me some weird stuff. Are you all right?' But I just told him to mind his own business. Didn't I have a right to a bit of happiness?—that kind of thing. And then it was just me and Marie and Andy. He said, we don't need anyone else. We'll be a little family, just the three of us."

"Mmm."

"*I* thought he might want to try for a baby. I was young enough. But he didn't want to; he closed that idea right down. Now I know why. I didn't then. Oh, do I have to tell you the next bit? Come on, you know where this is going, don't you?"

"I can guess, love. But tell me anyway."

" . . ."

"Go on, get it out of you. Blow your nose and tell me. You can do it."

"Well. Well. The next thing was, Marie had her thirteenth birthday, and Andy took her out and paid for her to have her ears pierced, which she'd been on and on at us to do, and got her these little gold sleepers—real gold, really expensive. Without talking to me. I was quite put out. He said, like it was a joke, don't be jealous, love, I just wanted to show her that she's a very special young lady. And then from then on, he was always talking like that, always, like, hinting that if I minded the way he behaved round her, it was because I was jealous. Or grudging. Or suspicious. Or something like that. And she did start to behave weirdly. She'd always been, you know, one of the good girls at school. Homework in on time, hair always brushed, coloured biros all in a row. Oh God, I miss her. Oh God, I let her down. Oh—"

"Hang on to yourself, love, if you can. Don't get stuck here. Get it all out. Tell me faster, if it helps."

"Well, he was interfering with her, wasn't he, Andy. Of course. Obviously. Anyone could guess that, couldn't they; except thicko here, I didn't. But that's not the awful thing. I mean, yes it was, what he did to Marie is the most awful thing, and I hope he burns in hell for it, and I don't know if she'll ever be all right. But. But . . ."

"But it's not the thing you can't forgive *yourself* for."

"No, it's not."

"So what's that, Angela?"

"It's that I didn't do anything. Not when she started bunking off school. Not when she started cutting herself. Andy made it seem like it was all . . . irritating, you know; all, like, something I ought to be annoyed by. You know, 'Oh, madam's in a strop this morning,' that kind of thing. Always egging me on to be angry not sympathetic."

"Did she try to talk to you?"

"A couple of times, yes. But I just flared up. She was like, 'Mum, I wish it was just us again,' and I'd be, 'Well, I'm sorry, but I'm entitled to a life too'; or later, she went all, kind of, apathetic? Like, limp and depressed, and I'm not surprised, poor scrap, but she refused to wash, and I kept getting rung up by the school, because she was missing again, and it played hell with my work; and I just said—no, I shouted it—'Pull yourself together, girl!' And Andy hung about, smiling and smiling. And now I can see it was so's we wouldn't get the chance to talk to each other. But there were chances. I just didn't take them. I didn't do anything. I didn't notice because I didn't want to notice. I didn't save her, or help her. I just shouted at her. For being difficult!"

"So you didn't stop it."

"No."

"Then how did it end? It did end, didn't it, Angela? This isn't something that's still going on?"

"No, no, it's over."

"What happened?"

"The police turned up out of the blue, and arrested him for something he'd done before. Well, the same thing, in another family where he'd cuckooed his way in. And the WPC who was with them asked me, did he get up to anything like that here, and I said, no, no, of course not; and Marie said in this really strange quiet voice, yes he did Mum, and then again louder, yes he fucking did Mum, and then like screaming it, like it was tearing out of her throat, YES HE FUCKING DID MUM. And the police looked at me like they couldn't believe me; like I was dirt."

"And then it all came out?"

"Yeah. And then they took Marie off to the station to do the rape kit on her; and I said, I'll get my coat and come with you, and she said, no Mum, and she asked the WPC, would you call my dad, please?"

"Oh, love."

"And basically she never came back. She went to her dad's. And I rang up to say, how's she doing, and could I speak to her, to say how sorry I was, and her dad just went, are you joking? Are you joking? Do you think I am ever going to let you anywhere near her, after this? I've written her letters, and she never writes back, and I rang, when I couldn't bear it any more, and they'd changed the phone number."

"Oh, love."

"And I can't take it back and I can't stop thinking about it, and it just goes on and on and on. Ah, ah, aarh aarh *aarh*!"

"Are you hitting your head, love? C'mon, don't do that. C'mon, Angela. Don't do that."

"Why shouldn't I?"

"Because you should look after yourself, love."

"Why? What's the point? They're gone. It's all gone."

"Yes, love."

"And now I know this terrible thing about myself."

"What's that?"

"That I'm the kind of person who'd let . . . *that* happen under her nose to her own daughter. I just am. They're right to hate me. I hate me. Now you hate me too."

"No, I don't."

"Yes, you do. You've been trained to be all nice about anything anyone says, that's all, but underneath you hate me too."

"I really don't, love."

"You must do. I did a *disgusting* thing."

"Yeah, but you can do a disgusting thing without being a disgusting person, can't you?"

"I don't know what that even means."

"Well . . ."

"Look, thank you, you've been very kind, but I don't think you can really help because I don't think you get what this feels like. I don't think anyone can. Good—"

"Angela!"

"What?"

"I do get it, 'cause as it happens, I've been there. Or somewhere very like it."

"What did you do, then?"

"No, love, this isn't about me; this is about you. I just want you to know that you're not alone, you're not the only person who has to live with something really bad."

"I don't believe you. You're just making it up to make me feel better."

"I'm not."

"If it was true you'd tell me."

"Angela, that's not what this call is *for.*"

"I spilled my guts to you. I told you the worst thing I've ever done in my life."

Pause.

"Well, it was about a bloke—"

"You amaze me . . ."

"Hey, I made you laugh. That's not so bad, is it?"

"No, but go on. Please. It does help."

"We're not supposed to."

"Please."

Pause.

Something white flutters in front of Val. Father Tim, the other person on the Samaritans night shift in the crypt of St. Saviour's, is leaning over the hardboard partition of the cubicle holding out a piece of paper. ARE YOU OK? is written on it in marker pen. She considers, and nods. *Really?* he asks, in dumbshow, with hands and eyebrows. She nods again. *Really.*

"All right. Angela? I was married to a violent man. He liked to hurt people. Not me, though. Men. Other men. He scared the hell out of me, and he kept me under his thumb, but I kind of adored him. He was beautiful. Stupid, mind you; very stupid; and scary; but gorgeous. I knew he was dangerous, and I sort of tried to manage it, and to point him where he wouldn't do too much harm; but mostly, I just let it happen. And then one day he murdered somebody in front of me."

"Oh my God."

"Yeah; and I didn't stop it. Just this poor harmless student from Pakistan whose car had broken down, so he was in the wrong place at the wrong time."

"Oh my God. That's horrible."

"Yes, it is."

"What happened?"

"Mike got sent down for murder, and I did six months as an accessory."

"You were in *prison?*"

"Yes."

"Oh my God. Oh. My. God. Did you divorce him when you got out, then?"

"No. No, I didn't. I was still thinking about it, and he just dropped dead suddenly in prison. It turned out he had this, like, dodgy vein in his brain? And it popped, and he was gone. So I never really said no to him, you see, right to the end. I can't say I ever drew a line. And that's why I really do understand where you are now."

"You're, like, a murderer!"

"Nearly. Yes."

"I don't know what to say."

"You don't have to say anything, love."

". . ."

"Angela? Are you still there?"

"Yes."

"Have I shocked you?"

"Yes, you have a bit."

"There's people who've done bad stuff all over the place, love. We walk past each other in the street, and we all say, I'm the worst person in the world, no one gets it, I'm all alone. All of us. And it's not true."

"How d'you cope? What d'you do with it? I mean, you sound all right, you sound sorted out. I wouldn't ever have guessed."

"Well, it was a long time ago for me, love. And it does take time. You just have to keep . . . getting up in the morning, I suppose. And you don't try to feel better by telling yourself lies, 'cause that doesn't work. And you're patient. And you try to be hopeful, even though you don't know what you're hoping for. And even though you can't make it up to the people you've hurt, you look out for little chances of being kind. 'Cause being kind to anyone at all helps bring on the lights a little bit, if you know what I mean. And you wait, and you hope, and you see what happens next."

"Andy's written and asked me to come and visit him in jail."

"Don't do it."

"I won't. Better to have nothing than have that, right?"

"Exactly."

217

"Well, you've been kind to me. Thank you?"

"You're welcome. What are you going to do now, Angela?"

"I'm going to go to bed. What about you?"

"I'm going to blow my nose, and answer the next call, I expect."

"Goodnight."

"Goodnight, Angela."

There are next calls, of course. A Chinese kid from Hong Kong who has stayed awake for three nights straight, panicking about his college exams. Remedy: go to sleep. And a dawn example of the traditional helpline wanker. ("Put away your Kleenex, love, that's not what we're here for. I'm going to hang up now, but remember you're always welcome to ring back if there's something you're genuinely desperate about. Bye!")

But at seven the next pair of volunteers arrive, and she is out smoking a ciggy on the steps of St. Saviour's while the light mounts in a petrol-coloured sky over towards Dartford, and a cold breeze blows the litter about. It is Saturday morning. Father Tim comes out and sits down next to her.

"Ooh," he says, hugging his arms round himself, "is that a packet of Rothmans I see? Can I cadge a Rothie, please?"

"Course you can," she says. He lights up, inhales, and combines the exhale with a stretch and a yawn and a sprawl, ending up leaning back on his elbows and gazing at her smokily from under his fringe. He has one of those posh male faces that stays boyish even when its owner is thirty-something or forty-something, and makes it hard to guess its owner's age. Father Tim looks tired now, after an all-nighter on the phones, but he also, in some essential way, looks untouched: someone, you'd think, swanning their way gracefully through Bexford, and through the years. And yet he and Father Louis, who he shares the vicaring with, and shares the vicarage with too, are known to be people you can call, day or night. Trouble with a rent officer, son under arrest, school exclusion, court appearance, sudden death: any situation where a calm middle-class voice would help, and one of them will turn out uncomplainingly, looking poised in a midnight police station, whether you are in their congregation or not. Mike would have hated both of them, of course. But then Mike's hatred—she worked this one out long ago—would partly have been envy. Father Tim liking men was presumably as much against his church's rules, what little she knew about them, as Mike's desire had been against the rules for a Bexford mod, a Bexford skin, a South London Nazi. And yet Father Tim seems to manage it without violence, without having to be attacking male bodies to get close to them, kicking and clawing and breaking them when he only really wanted to be pushing and nuzzling at them. *When he only wanted to fuck them*, she thinks—and is surprised by how easily that thought comes, now. Poor Mike. Poor me.

"Are you here to tell me off?" she says.

"Nope," he says. "Everyone gets a call now and then which gets to them personally; it just happens, it's inevitable. And yeah, you went way over the line, but you didn't do it self-indulgently, you didn't do it at the caller's expense, you were still thinking about looking after her, and in the end it was all right. If you ask me, you took a bigger risk with the tea thing. You could have lost her right then, you know."

"I just thought she needed to *do* something, something really ordinary, so she could concentrate on that instead of panicking?"

"Yes, and it worked, but you did send her away from the phone."

"I won't do it again."

"Really? That might be a pity. I'm just saying, use your judgement, and be aware. That's all."

"Okay."

"Mmm," says Father Tim. He blows out smoke again, and they look at Bexford waking up: delivery vans backing, shutters rattling up, the smell of frying bacon coming from somewhere.

"So, if this isn't a bollocking . . ."

"Well. No. Um. This was more in the nature of . . . a religious observation," says Father Tim, studying the glowing end of his cigarette and for the first time looking faintly embarrassed. "I know I don't talk about God much, but one of the things He's very good for is confession. I heard the end of your call, and it sounds as if you've been carrying some hard, hard stuff for a long time. And I wondered if I could tempt you to come and join us on Sunday morning, and see if that might help?"

"Me, get religion?" says Val.

"Ooh, that makes it sound very untempting, doesn't it? As if it's some kind of unpleasant thing to *wear*. Or maybe an illness. 'Poor her, she's got religion.' No. To me it's more . . . a way of thinking about what's going on for you?"

"It's very kind of you, Father, but I don't think so."

"Oh well, your loss. Ours too, of course."

He doesn't push it, and they smoke the rest of their fags in companionable peace. Then Father Louis pulls up in an elderly car, waving a fragrant paper bag.

"Croissants!" cries Father Tim, and jumps up from the cold stones as if he's twenty. He looks back as he opens the car door.

"D'you want to join us?" he calls. "Louis always over-caters."

"No thanks," she says. "I'm having breakfast with my sister."

Vern

The dinner jackets are like school uniform. They make all the men look the same. You can't tell—at least from a distance— which penguin suits come from M&S and which from Savile Row. All the display, and all the competition, and all the shadings that tell apart different kinds of wealth, are in the clothing of the women. That blue velvet frock and discreet string of pearls, which clearly does multi-purpose duty for formal occasions: sensible, old-fashioned county posh. The watered-silk Italian jacket and paisley-print scarf: Hampstead. The drop-waisted ivory flapper dress, a beautiful recreation or conceivably vintage: City money. The hourglass magenta satin thing with matching fascinator: recent ascent to the big time, and here a bit of a faux pas. It would have been better suited to Ascot. Vern likes looking but he has no one female on his arm to identify him in turn. He glides along the garden terrace, massively monochrome between the fuchsias, and offers no assistance to the onlooker in working out that his din- ner suit is indeed tailor-made (as it kind of has to be, given how egg-shaped he has become) but tailor-made by Manny Perlstein in the arcade behind Bexford station. He descends the brick steps, one leg at a time, and sets forth solitary and self-contained across the lawn towards the ha-ha. No wife beside him: he never wanted to remarry, after Kath, and these last few years he has preferred to handle that whole side of life on a straightforward cash basis. No daughter either. This isn't Sally or Becky's kind of thing, and he gave up trying to invite them years ago. He is, however, followed at a discreet distance by a waiter. Who, once Vern has selected a picnic spot under a pretty flowering tree, with a view towards the

Downs in one direction and the new opera house in the other, sets him up with lawn chair, folding table, linen and cutlery, and then proceeds to serve upon it the first of many courses.

"Hello," says Vern affably, tucking his napkin into his collar. The party next to him are having a more conventional *déjeuner sur l'herbe*, a middle-aged man and two middle-aged women of the County Posh genus sitting on a rug around a hamper, sharing a bottle of Moët in plastic flutes. They watch, fascinated, as the waiter cooks Vern an omelette on a silver spirit lamp. The blue flame is almost invisible in the June sunlight, but the smell of butter and chervil saturates the air. Vern sips at Pouilly-Fuissé.

"I say," says the man on the rug, "that looks splendid."

"Well!" says Vern. "Why not push the boat out, I say."

"I thought we *had*," says one of the women. "You know, bubbly and nibbles. But, gosh. It looks like you've pushed it out a lot *further!*"

"I don't do it every year," says Vern, factual rather than apologetic. "Wouldn't have been a lot of point last year, fr'instance; place was still a building site."

"Oh," says the other woman, sounding ever so slightly surprised, now that she has clocked his accent properly. "Are you a regular?"

"Haven't missed the opening day of the Festival for, oh, twelve years," says Vern. "You?"

"Now and again," she says. "Not as faithful as you, by the sound of it. But then we always have to drag Rory here away from Twickenham, don't we, darling?"

"Is that right," says Vern. He finishes the omelette and moves on to foie gras on toast triangles, with a salad of chicory and endives.

"'Fraid so," the man is saying, jutting his square chin. "Lovely day out here, obviously: but I have to say, I know it's heresy, but I have to say, I've never really got the *point* of opera?"

He says this comfortably. He says it as if, his whole square-chinned life long, he has been saying confidently stupid things, and the world has reliably responded by saying, good point, Rory old man.

"No, I don't expect you have," says Vern. And since he sounds just as genial saying it, it takes a minute before it sinks in; before the man looks away, and his wife flushes. Vern beams down at them, and applies himself to the creamy unction of the pâté, the bitter crunch of the leaves. But something about the confidence of Vern's rudeness, his comfort as he dismisses them, turns out to have generated a reaction in good old Rory like a Labrador rolling over. He waits politely till the pâté is replaced by beef Wellington on a chafing dish, and the waiter is uncorking a half-bottle of claret, and then clears his throat with an attention-seeking noise, low and submissive.

"D'you mind my asking what line you're in?" he says.

"Property," says Vern.

"Commercial? We do a bit—"

"No, historic buildings." Vern sucks his fingertips, wipes them on his napkin, and pulls out a pair of gold half-moon spectacles through which he considers his neighbours. Probably not candidates to participate in the regeneration of architecturally significant South and East London. They look as if they are very firmly rooted in the Old Rectory, Little Fuddling, and likely to stay there. But you never know; maybe they have London-based offspring with a yen for architraves, and the kind of City job required to pay for them. Vern's empire is still centred on Bexford Rise and its counterparts in Camberwell and Dulwich, but he has recently been doing more in Spitalfields and Shoreditch, from which his clients can walk to their dealing desks. Next will come Borough, all being well. He's got his eye on a run-down eighteenth-century square just in the shadow of the Guy's Hospital tower block, all black brick and white sills, which should respond beautifully to Vern's rigidly cost-controlled, by now standardised spruce-up and restoration job. He should be able to get a hundred thousand pounds' worth of value out of each house there, easy. And from there, the foot commute to the City he can offer will be a stroll across London Bridge. Seagulls, HMS *Belfast*, the Tower, St. Paul's doing its famous thing on the skyline: it's amazing how much his business model is based on selling back to people a sanitised, touristic version of the grimy old city. He's a tour guide, he's a set-dresser. He's a pediment pimp. He's Mary Fucking Poppins. But he's not knocking it. It works. He fishes in his wallet and passes across a business card. THE FEATHERSTONE ESTATE, it says, and then in italics: *Conserving the Georgian Capital*. He had them run up on a hand press by one of his anchor-tenant nutters, a man who takes his eighteenth-century lifestyle so seriously that he cleans his Persian carpets by scattering tea leaves on them, and plays the harpsichord in an actual wig. "The face is Baskerville, of course," the nutter said, "but you'll like this, Mr. Taylor: it's original lead t—" "Yeah, whatever," said Vern. Thick cream card and a slightly wonky handcrafted quality, to press the pleasure buttons of the upper middle class: that was all he needed to know. And indeed, when he hands it over now, Rory the rugby-lover takes it as reverently as he could wish.

"D'you know, I think I've heard of you?" says Rory. Impossible for someone like this, notes Vern, not to talk as if they're conferring something, even in self-abasing mode.

"We get a few write-ups," Vern agrees.

"Yes—something in one of the colour supplements, just recently."

"The *Observer*."

"Yes; extraordinary stuff. Pictures of a chap who doesn't believe in electric light . . . ?"

"That was the one. S'matter of fact, he printed those for me," says Vern, gratified.

"Did he; did he."

"Oh, do leave the poor chap alone to eat his lunch, darling," says Rory's wife, smiling tightly.

"Sorry, of course I will. Well, if you don't mind, I'll just keep this. You see, we have had *rather* a good year ourselves, thanks to Lloyd's, and we've, you know, wondered about the possibility of a—a little *pied-à-terre*, perhaps."

"Have we wondered that?" his wife asks, showing her teeth.

"Yes, we have. So maybe I'll be in touch!"

Vern's mouth is full of bloody beef fillet and flaking crust. It's possible, of course, that this is one of those Hooray Henry men who is idiotic about everything except money, and that Rory through luck or skill has attached himself to one of the few syndicates at Lloyd's which hasn't run into trouble underwriting asbestos or hurricane risks. But from what Vern hears, it's far more likely that the Old Rectory in Little Fuddling has already been inadvertently gambled away, and Rory simply doesn't know it yet. Vern nods gravely, and swallows. The sun brightens the distant hills, dapples his tablecloth, and picks out all over the emerald-green grass the sombre or resplendent figures of his prey. He finishes the beef, and moves on to a lemon mousse, accompanied by a pipkin of Sauternes. Then, of course, the cheeses.

Vern has booked himself a box. Lately, ordinary-sized seats have come to feel rather constricting. And in any case, the point of today is as much to show off the new opera house as it is to unveil the new production on its stage, so why not get the effect at its best? As the five-minute bell goes, he wades his way patiently around a curving corridor of blond wood and finds his door. Oh yes, a very successful treat for the eyes. He has bought himself an elegant compartment at the foot of a vertical wall of other elegant compartments, a pigeon loft for opulence, and filling with the soft becking and cooing of wealth at play. The auditorium is deep, and very steeply raked, with the seats for those of slightly less wealth rising in semicircle stacked above semicircle. As a builder—as a builder obliged by his business model to spend his time among old stuff, and cunning simulations of old stuff—Vern enjoys how unashamedly new the look is. The wood is pale and fresh, the gold paint is bright, the exposed red bricks aren't pretending to be anything but straight from the kiln. He prefers out-and-out modern himself, in steel and glass, like his own flat; but this will do nicely, this is a lovely job, and when he's nudged the comfortably broad armchair around to face front, and settled there with his arms crossed over his belly, he's floating just above the orchestra, mere feet from the front apron of the stage. The company will be singing to him. The lights will go down, and he will eat the music up.

And it is a really good production, that's instantly clear. Mozart is not Vern's favourite—he prefers something a bit more blatant and stormy—but this version of *The Marriage of Figaro* does the light/heavy mixture of the story beautifully. It's a bedroom farce, and it's about true love; it's got jumping out of windows, and heavy-duty redemption; it's a romp, and it wants you to take the love lives of servants as seriously as those of counts and countesses. It goes from silly to heartfelt and nimbly back again, and all of those strings doing their pinpoint golden thing under Vern's feet, for the baton of the man in the white jacket, are the right sound somehow for the mobile moods of it. *Actually buoyant, possibly sad!* say the violins. *Possibly buoyant, actually sad!* reply the cellos. *Whatever you feel*, the woodwinds put in, *it will be quite clear. Though subject to change!* the violins reason. *Though subject to change*, the woodwinds concur.

Figaro the valet is a wry, quick, handsome, curly-headed bass, pulling faces and nipping up and down ladders. Susanna the maid, his intended, is a self-possessed soprano, a bit too skinny for Vern's taste but lovely, no question. The Count, their master, is being played by a German baritone who is very good at a kind of sulky, spoiled sarcasm. His neglected wife the Countess has slightly more old-school plunging-nightgown heft to her, and Vern enjoys the scene where she sighs throbbingly amid her bed-sheets. But all four of them are acting properly, not just trudging to their marks and letting go with the vocal cords, the way some big names used to when Vern started going. All of them have faces alive and communicative, all of them are witty. All of them are singing from somewhere fully inside the story of how the Count, who proudly abolished *droit du seigneur* in his domains, now wants it back again so he can have his way with Susanna on her wedding night. Laughter and indignation and fear chase each other through choruses in which they harmonise their disagreements while they're having them, shaking off technical difficulty like someone smilingly brushing a sleeve. It's glorious, it's masterly. And the set, like an extra compliment to Vern in his box, is made of the same architecture as his London houses, reduced to lines and planes and airy gestures.

Why, then, with all this clever beauty laid out for him to banquet on, does Vern feel a thread of unhappiness tightening inside him, a faint faint signal, growing stronger, that something is wrong? Why, then, glancing back at the rapt and glimmering tiers of faces in the darkness, does Vern feel that, alone among the enchanted, he is being subtly got at by the pleasure he paid for? It's not an abstract disquiet, this. It's not just a thought in his head. It's physical. He feels it as a gripe in his gut, an ache in his neck, a dull twinging in the nerves of his arms. In fact he wonders for a minute if he could be having a heart attack—which is indeed a fear of his. But nothing hurts in his chest, he has no pins and needles, nothing is afflicting him on his left side particularly, which is where they say you feel it. He remains solid. He is clad in slab armour. So what can be wrong, he thinks angrily. What can be wrong when nothing is wrong. Check the inventory: every-thing is all right. He is rich. He has the world where he wants it. He has a Bentley parked outside. He can afford to buy himself any pleasure. He is surrounded by delicacies, none forbidden. Death is still far away (surely). Yet something makes him ache; something coming from the stage. Perhaps it's Cherubino's song. Cherubino the page, played by a girl whose thighs look good in breeches, does comedy philandering mostly, like a for-laughs teenage ver-sion of the Count; but in Act Two he turns plaintive.

Ricerco un bene fuori di me,
non so chi'l tiene, non so cos'è

he sings, and up on the proscenium, where the subtitles are pro-jected, the English text spells out

I seek a blessing outside myself,
from whom I don't know, or what it even is.

Is it that? Certainly the misery eases when the song ends, and Mozart glissades back into farce mode. Cherubino hides in a cup-board; Cherubino jumps out the window; Figaro pretends it was him; just when he seems to be getting away with it, enter a com-edy gardener. All's well again, or at least better. But then, as the act ends, the Count comes bursting in with a pack of assorted min-ions, and suddenly Susanna, Figaro and the Countess are on the far side of the stage facing off against the Count and the minions, singing against each other like two opposing gangs. And the mysterious grip on Vern is back, the mysterious alarm. Over there, the forces of love singing their heads off, over here the gathered musical army of . . . what? Spite, vengeance, age's anger with youth, and at the head of it, on the Count's face and in his voice, a despairing greed. Perhaps it would be better if Vern were seeing it from the opposite cliff face of boxes, so it didn't seem as if the lovers' army were all singing at him. Perhaps that's it: he booked the box in the wrong place, and now he is on the wrong side.

When the interval comes, Vern stumps to the garden, stumps to his waiter, ignoring the paper lanterns in the trees, ignoring the revellers, and those who happen to glance at his face step out of his way. He sits and waits to be served. This time, when the food starts coming, he eats as if he is entombing something. Burying it under shovels-full; spoons-full; forks-full. Mozart can fuck himself with all his fine balances. Vern eats the turbot. Vern eats the cream sauce. Vern eats the pheasant. Vern eats the morels. Vern eats the Roquefort. Vern eats the grapes. Vern eats the truffles. Vern eats.

Jo

"Miss?" says Hayley. "Is it true you used to be a rock star's girlfriend?"

A Year 10 mixed-ability music class at Bexford Hill Comprehensive: twenty-eight faces looking at her without much hope of being excited by anything, but momentarily woken up by the chance of something juicy. Jo has no idea how they can have got hold of this rumour of her former life, unless it was brought into school via Marcus, but Marcus's solution to the indignity of being the offspring of two teachers at his own school has always been a resolute pretence that she and Claude have got nothing to do with him from the moment he goes through the gates in the morning, head high, impervious, lips together in a clamping pout of irony. So it's a puzzle.

"Um . . ." she begins.

"Nah," says Tyrone, one of the cool kids in the back row, before she has settled on how she wants to deal with this. "Someone like that, they wouldn't be here teaching us, would they? They'd be all, like, glamorous, wouldn't they? No offence, miss."

"Oh, none taken, Tyrone," says Jo, milking the general laugh a bit. Tyrone grins. Jo, in her own estimation, looks pretty good at this point, weathered but still trim, dressed and hairdressed with knowledgeable guile about what suits her, and in possession of regular evidence that she's still desirable, at least to Claude. But none of this adds up to attractiveness of a kind that computes for a fifteen-year-old boy. She's not one of the women teachers in their twenties and thirties whose blouses' top buttons are under constant teenage male monitoring. She's invisible to Tyrone except as a mum; except, sometimes, when she can draw him out and hoodwink him into showing his intelligence, as a challenge, someone to cross swords with.

"It doesn't seem very likely, does it, Hayley?" she says.

"I suppose not, miss," says Hayley, crestfallen. She's a lumpy, pale little thing, not in with the cool white girls, or the cool black girls, or the cool Asian girls. One of the nondescripts, the hangers-on; and seeing her face fall, Jo almost feels guilty. Who she's been and what she's done is none of Hayley's business, but it's clear that denying it (or letting it get denied) has extinguished one more little glint of possibility for the girl, has given her one more demonstration that the world is not, after all, exciting. Not likely to burst out into rock stars, diamonds, jacuzzis. At least, not anywhere near Hayley.

Impossible to tell her that, from Jo's perspective at fifty-four, she shares a touching beauty with the cool kids; possesses it just as much as confident Tyrone, or Samantha and her hair-flick, or Jamila and her heavy-lidded Punjabi stare. These just-adult bodies are, all of them, so gallantly recent. Whether they're one of the dewy-skinned lucky ones or are bursting out with zits, their flesh, all of it, is still soft, new, moulded onto their suddenly elongated bones like fresh marzipan. Whether they move gracefully or as gawkily as foals, whether they whack themselves against doorways like poor clumsy Simon over there or arc into pure curves like silent Hamid the football player, there's a quality of surprise to all their steps, to all their occupations of space. *This is me?* their gestures keep asking, whatever else they may be meaning to mean—*this tall thing, not quite under my control? Is it? Or am I just inside it somewhere, trying my best to pilot it?* Sometimes the children they were yesterday can be seen looking out of their faces, amazed. And then a minute later they're making first essays at strength or sexiness, approximate, amateurish, going all in on every bet like the naivest of gamblers.

It's lovely to see; and also hilarious, and also from time to time terrifying, this last element in Jo's response being supplied by her parent's-eye view. Marcus isn't quite there yet. He's only twelve. But all this will happen to him, and while these boys and girls flower, the sellers of brown heroin roam about outside seeking whom they may devour, and all of the hungry adults who, seeing new legs new mouths new eyes, also see something to devour. But you can't warn them, any more than you can tell them in terms that would make sense to them that their transformation is glorious. Youth isn't visible to them, any more than air is. It's the condition of their lives, but it isn't a *thing* that they could imagine not having, and therefore could imagine as being desirable in itself. Jo remembers this—how the interest of male teachers, middle-aged men in the street and in the park, the gardener at the lido, registered only as an inexplicable creepiness.

Don't hurry, she wants to tell Year 10. But they want to hurry. They long to hurry. Everything they are is oriented towards a future which they seem to themselves to be having to wait for forever, enduring the great teenage boredom in which first kiss, first party, first love, approach at maddening snail's pace: but which if you're old enough to count time in decades you know is going to be upon them in a flash, imminent, irresistible. In almost no time at all, possibility will be swapped for actuality. These bodies owned now like masks, envelopes, surprising vehicles, will become their everyday selves. This marzipan flesh will settle and start to collect scars, frown lines, stretch marks. Youth itself will stop being the common, invisible possession of the twenty-eight of them in this room. Bexford Hill is not a rough school by London standards, and contains a good fraction of middle-class kids of all ethnicities behind its 1950s plate glass. Those will thrive, unless they screw up badly enough to fall down one of the big snakes on the social game board. Those, and also the lucky ones, the energetic ones, the organised ones among the strivers, will go off into the long youthfulness of the prosperous, drinking wine and buying lampshades and able to treat turning thirty as a point in late adolescence. For the rest, though, this is it. This first flowering will be the only one. They'll have their bloom, and that's all. By the time they're thirty, time will have stomped all over them. Sorry, Hayley.

"Right," she says, "we've got forty-five minutes, and this week we're spending it on voicework."

Immediate chorus of groans. Singing is lame, singing is embarrassing, singing in front of your classmates and your teacher runs the appalling risk of exposing your raw green soul to the unfriendly world.

"Can't we do steel pan again, miss?" asks Samantha, queen of the white girls. They had a class last week in which, though Jo does say so herself, they got something pretty good going, rhythmically speaking. "That was . . . all right."

"No," says Jo briskly. "Because (a) all the equipment is in the other music room down three flights of stairs and a hundred yards away, (b) the other stream are using it today, and (c) singing is good for you."

Groans.

"What are we going to sing?" asks Hayley. For thirty confused seconds, despite their objections to the whole idea, Year 10 shout out their musical tastes, from Britpop to acid house, each of which is guaranteed to reduce its passionate advocates to despondent paralysis if it comes to actual, out-loud singing. The red National Songbook is decades gone.

"No words at all," says Jo. Then, raising her voice to cut the hubbub: "*No. Words. At. All.* This week we're just using voice as an instrument."

"My body . . . is my tool . . ." croons clumsy Simon unexpectedly—being someone off the TV, judging by the comedy voice. He happens to hit one of the instants of hush and makes more of a splash than he meant to.

"You're a tool, bruv," says Tyrone into the disconcerted silence.

"Tyrone!" says Jo. "We have a volunteer! Up you come. Come on!" She crooks her finger at him, wicked-witch-style, and draws him up from his lair at the back with her teacherly tractor beam. He saunters, tilting the tall cylinder of his hair from side to side, but he arrives. His version of school uniform naturally features a tie only three inches long.

"Congratulations, Ty," says Jo, "you are today's sample human being. Could you turn round sideways—yeah, facing me—and give us a noise? Just say 'ah,' like at the dentist."

"Uh-huh, uh-huh; uh-huh uh-huh; *aaaah*," goes Tyrone. The thing about Tyrone, she happens to know by devious means, is that in the long-lost and long-ago days of about three years ago, he used to sing in his mum's church. He was apparently a "Cherub" in a dear little uniform. And he now possesses a rather pleasant tenor, which he can't quite help showing off.

"Okay," she asks the class, "where's the sound coming from?"

"Er, his mouth?" says Tyrone's wingman Jerome.

"His arse, more like," says Samantha. (There is some history here, possibly involving events as much as a month old.)

"His mouth, yes, but not *just* his mouth," she says swiftly. "That's where it comes out, but where does it start?"

"Down here somewhere," says Tyrone, pointing to a spot at the top of his stomach or the bottom of his chest. "That's what it feels like, anyway."

"His diaphragm," says Jamila, who will be a doctor some day if her family have anything to do with it.

Instant derision.

"I think you'll find that's got something to do with birth control, yeah?" says Jerome.

"Words can mean two different things, duh," says Jamila, with scorn so complete she doesn't even need to lift her eyes from the floor.

"'Diaphragm' is right," Jo says. "It's a muscle just under the V in the middle of your ribs, and you use it to control the air you sing with. If you take in a deep breath, you can feel it moving down to make space. Go on, try it. Everyone, please." Sounds of panting, heaving, exaggerated puffing and blowing, but also real experiment. "Got it? Good. And up above it, you've got a flexible tube that goes up to your larynx here, in the middle of your throat. Your lungs are joined onto it, and your diaphragm controls how much of the air from your lungs goes into it, and how hard the air is pushing. But the important thing to remember is the flexible tube. It's got ridges in it, like a vacuum cleaner hose, and it bends like one, only it's pink and sticky. And that's your musical instrument, when you're singing. Right, Tyrone: remember you're a flexible tube—"

"We keep telling him that, miss," says Jerome.

"We're all flexible tubes for these purposes, Jerome," she says.

"I'm not," says Simon, "I'm—"

"Yeah, thank you, Simon: *no*. Ty, do us your note again, and then bend about a bit, so the tube bends, okay?"

Tyrone gives them the *aaaah* again—it's an E—and twists sideways, backwards, forwards while he does it. They all listen, and they hear the way the sound varies; the way it chokes and kinks and alters in volume.

"You see?" she says. "You want to get the full note, you have to keep the tube as straight as you can. Tyrone, now stand up really straight, please: pretend there's a piece of string from the top of your head down to the floor: that sometimes helps. Good. And now push your shoulders back—not too far, like this—and look straight ahead, with your chin up, but not too far, and give us the note again. Bit louder. Bit louder. Yes, *there*."

A pure, unkinked, full-throated E. In Jo's head, a warm equally pure yellow.

"Lovely," she says. "Can we get a hallelujah in there, Ty?" she adds wickedly, in a lower voice.

"Get stuffed, miss," says Tyrone, but he's smiling.

Jamila's hand has gone up, for a miracle.

"Yes?"

"What happens at the top of the tube, then? Up in your throat?"

"Good question. Complicated stuff. The air that you've got under pressure in the tube makes your vocal cords vibrate, and then the sound gets altered by your tongue and the shape you're holding your mouth in, and finally it gets amplified by bouncing around in all the hollow places in your face."

"So your head's sort of like a speaker, then?" says Simon, not doing a silly voice.

"Yes, exactly. A speaker made out of skin and bone and muscles. But if you just concentrate for now on keeping the tube straight, you get an instant improvement, and that's enough for today. So up you all get, come on, thanks Tyrone, and sort yourselves out, boys over on this side, girls over there, no it's not sexism: and this is what we're going to do."

When she first came back to England, when she first taught anybody anything, the hardest thing was learning to isolate, from out of the mass of things she knew how to do with music, one thing at a time to pass on. One thing at a time, separated, is not how you yourself possess a skill you are sure of. Everything interconnects with everything else, and the natural impulse is to try to impart it like that, pouring it out in a useless torrent. Only bit by bit do you master the unnatural act of taking your own knowledge apart again, and being able to see what needs to come in what order, to build that knowledge in other minds. Every lesson you prepare is madly overspecified to begin with—madly overfilled with stuff the kids can't possibly assimilate. It's astonishing how little a good lesson should contain, if they're really going to take it in. One thing, done thoroughly: that's all you need. So long as it's the right thing.

Not that she expected to teach, when she came home. Or even to stay, necessarily. She flew back to London in the spring of 1980 because Val was on trial, and she wanted to be there in court, no matter how little good it did. Looking around for something to do meanwhile—something that paid—she looked up old friends in the session world and, instead of studio work, found herself drafted along as a freelance extra professional voice for a choir project run by the Inner London Education Authority over in Mile End. It was led by an expatriated American draft dodger a few years younger than her named Claude Newton. He was really good at it, in an intense, glittering-eyed way, and really attractive too, when he turned the same focus on her. Later, it became clear that this was partly because he was at the top of the manic part of a cycle which also included periods of darkness on the scale of a Siberian winter. But everything has the defects of its qualities and the days in Mile End were wonderful. Wonderful enough to off-set the ugliness of the city; wonderful enough to keep her going through the awfulness of the trial, with its gallery of baying skin-heads, and Val in the dock looking like an emaciated goblin. And Val refusing to let Jo visit her. And the *Evening Standard* running a photo of Val on the Old Bailey steps captioned NAZI DEATH QUEEN. She would catch the Tube east, and emerge from carriages reeking with smoke and filthy with litter into a wasteland of tower blocks—and watch Claude coax marvels from children who, to begin with, would barely smile.

"Why don't you stay?" he said. And she did. Everything she cared to keep in LA, it turned out, fitted into three or four cartons, which she unpacked into Claude's flat on Brixton Hill. "Why don't you do teacher training?" he said. "You're good with the kids, you know." And she did, though it took longer than planned, what with her getting instantly and unexpectedly pregnant. "I suppose you want me to get rid of it?" she said. "What?" said Claude. "Why? It was obviously meant to be, babe." She stopped noticing ugliness. She noticed, instead, the way that the heights of South London greened, that pregnant summer. First as a dusting, a shading of the colour of life along the branches of the stubborn trees between the red-brick houses. Then as a canopy, a nodding roof of leaves over the broken steps and uncollected rubbish. She noticed the kicking in her belly. She noticed that something about being in the classroom took away the ominous awareness that had been coming on more and more in the studio, that she'd aged away from what the business of music wanted. The kids in the schools didn't care about any of the stuff she had spent the last two decades doing—they'd barely heard of its biggest names—and she didn't care that they didn't care. It was if anything a relief, to be rid of all that. To replace it with the task of finding, every day, the one thing she needed to communicate.

And then Marcus was born. And looking at his crumpled little head, waxy with vernix, she felt love arrive in thunderclap form, unreasonable and total. It was love for the baby, yes, but it spread. It strewed light like a sunrise. It warmed like fine weather. It helped her persist through the discovery of Claude's disadvantages. It kept her patient—mostly—through the slow, slow reviving of her relations with Val. On the face of it, the existence of Marcus made things worse there, for Val, out of prison and hiding in halfway houses under a blanket of shame, was painfully envious. For two awful years, she tried to get pregnant herself, by the sound of it with all comers; and failed; and failed at not hating Jo for getting what she herself lacked; and was ashamed again for hating her, shame twice over. But with Marcus in the world, Jo had a kind of assurance to call on. Perhaps it was selfish of her to feel that everything was ultimately all right just because it was all right for her. But knowing she could count on a solid happiness made her kinder. It let her wait and hope, and try to help in the small ways that Val would allow her to. And there came a point when he was about four, and had recently been given a football, when Val was with them in Brockwell Park, chain-smoking more than Jo would have preferred she do. "Go on, pass it to your auntie," said Val; and after a surprised moment, Marcus did, and off they ran together towards the swings, kicking the ball backwards and forwards to each other as well as very short legs on one side, and wheezing middle age on the other, permitted. They came back, Marcus giggling, and Val looked at Jo as if to say, *Am I allowed?* And Jo sent back, *Course you are.*

After that she was assiduous, buying him presents that she couldn't afford, living on benefits. When Claude was having one of his spells in hospital, it was Val that Jo could lean on to cover the differences between Marcus's primary school day and her own teaching day. It was Val, at those times, who was standing behind Marcus when they opened the door with the stained-glass panel in it, as she came home, and Val who said, "Shall we show Mum what you've been doing?" *I recognise this*, thought Jo, hanging up her scarf and her beret, and following them along the hall towards the smell of shepherd's pie. *I'm back in the house of women, with Mum and Auntie Kay. Except now there are bits of Action Man on the floor, instead of those cardboard dollies with paper clothes.* It was Val, on evenings like that, who brought her a glass of wine as she played the piano after Marcus's bedtime. It was Val sitting at the kitchen table one particular midnight during one of those times, when they had sunk most of the second bottle, who suddenly told her the story of what life with Mike had been like. Then wept. One thing at a time; one piece of happiness fitting on top of another; one day telling its story to the next.

Now she's got the boys on one side of the room split into two groups, singing a D and F respectively, and the girls on the other side, also split, singing an A and a D. They're not singing their note in unison and then stopping, each group; they're under instructions to sing until they need to breathe and then to start again, staying deliberately out of sync with their nearest neighbours, so that each group is between them producing a continuous note, in a sort of quick and dirty collective version of circular breathing. It takes them a while to get it, and she has to start them off, and occasionally to reinforce each group when they falter, by singing them the note she wants from them. They can't find D, F, A or D by themselves, with the possible exception of Tyrone, but they can imitate, and even with the complication of the breathing and the stopping and the starting, they pick up confidence from hearing the one note they're aiming for sounded out ringingly loud by the clump of people that surrounds them. Soon they can hold their shared note even when she starts to combine them, conducting each group in with a wave of her hand. D—F—A—D: it's a minor chord coming (on and off and on again) from twenty-eight throats, and it sustains, it reverberates, it quivers in the knackered white soundproofing tiles in the music room. But it needs one more element, and she thinks they can handle the multitasking involved. She adds in rhythm. She gets the boys doing a slow *Slap!—clap—clap*, hands going down to thighs for the slap; and the girls, to avoid stereotypes, getting the faster football-ground rhythm, *clapclap—clapclap—clap.*

"Okay," she says. "Now we'll build it all together. I'll conduct you in, one bit at a time. Boys clapping; girls clapping; then the two notes from the boys' side, one at a time, lowest first; then the two notes from the girls' side, one at a time, also lower one first, so we're building all four notes up from the bottom, right? And when we've got it all going, don't stop. Everyone keep singing. Mend it if it seems to be going wrong. Try your best, anyway. Let's see how long we can keep it up. Everybody ready?"

And in come the different claps on top of each other, making new patterns and interference effects, percussive waves bouncing about. And then in she brings the four notes of the chord, climbing as they go. And yes, there's wavering; yes, there's faltering and moments of confusion. Part-singing is difficult for amateurs, even in this incredibly basic form. But through the wobbles, the chord steadies and persists. She's tempted to put in something over the top, some freeform piece of soprano ululation, like Clare Torry's thing on *Dark Side of the Moon*, not that anyone would recognise that. Tyrone's eyes would widen satisfyingly. But she would put them off, wreck their momentary concentration. She'd ruin the structure, not add to it. Instead she just watches: their mouths opening and closing effortfully, the gasps for breath, as for a whole ten seconds, twenty seconds, thirty seconds, forty seconds, Year 10 sustain the chord. Can they hear it, this immense organised sound they are making together? Can they hear the organ that they have briefly become, whose separate pipes are all those sticky pink organic tubes in teenage bodies? Imperfect pipes, made of damp twisted cartilage without a single straight line, pumped up by weird fluttering bladders, and yet capable of sounding a chord that seems to lay hold on some order in the world that already existed before we came along and started to sing. Making an order that matches an order. Music is strange, she wants them to see, and one of the things that is strangest about it is that it comes from our messy bodies. Sing, Hayley. Sing, Tyrone. Sing, Jamila, Simon, Samantha, Jerome. Don't stop till you must. Notice if you can that your temporary orchestra of hormones and still-digesting Big Macs from lunchtime can be coaxed into playing the music of the spheres. If you let yourself be its instrument.

Then the bell goes, and they clatter away laughing.

At the end of the day, she drives home with Marcus. "How was your day?" she asks. "'S all right," he says, staring at the road. This, from her pride, her joy, her last-chance late child who started the whole world anew for her when he came, who once lay so close

241

to her, feeding, that they seemed to her to make one being, milky and whole. But then he angles his dignified, ironic, twelve-year-old head and for a microsecond bumps it against her shoulder.

Alec

"Did you ever read a book called *The Ragged Trousered Philanthropists?*" asks Alec.

"No, Mr. Torrance," says Wayne the YTS trainee, warily. "What's that, then?"

They're prepping bare walls for the first layer of render in an upstairs bedroom in one of the big houses right at the top of Bexford Rise. Big brushes and a bucket of dilute PVA glue. It slops on and then sinks in, leaving only a glisten on the surface. Wayne has been given the PVA to paint on because he's only just started, and Gary hasn't initiated him yet into the mysteries of actual plastering. And Alec has been given it to do because that's all Gary trusts him with, experience having proved that he and a float and wet plaster do not combine productively. (He can in fact also strip off old render reasonably well, with a hammer drill and bolster, but that part of this job is behind them.)

"Call me Alec," says Alec, looking down at Wayne's ginger flat-top as the boy squats effortlessly to do the bits just above the skirting. But it's a lost cause. Gary's the boss; he's the boss's dad. "It's about plastering, actually. Well—building work, all sorts, and painting and decorating, but it's got plastering in it."

"Yeah?"

"Mm-hmm. Probably the only novel in the English language

where the author thought plastering was interesting enough to put in. Mind you, he could've been wrong there."

Slop-slop, load up the brush. Wayne wishes he would shut up, this is clear. He has a hunted expression.

"Anyway, these blokes are doing up a house—they all work for the same firm, you see, so it's one big job—and some of them are really good. Talented, you see. Artistic, even. But to get it done on time, for the price their boss has quoted, they're basically forced to do a crap job. Cutting corners, scrimping on the materials, bodging it up so it looks okay, but it's going to fall to bits ten minutes after they get paid."

"So they're like . . . cowboys, then?" says Wayne.

"No!" says Alec. "That's the point! They're not setting out to rip anyone off. *They're* not the ones who put in the low quote, they're not the ones who're making a profit off the deal. They're trapped by a stupid system. There they are, with all the skills they need to do good work, and their tools actually in their hands, and instead they're fucking it up. They're *having* to fuck it up."

"Yeah, but—"

"And what the book's saying is, that's capitalism for you."

"Yeah, but—"

"Dad," says Gary, appearing in the doorway.

"And maybe you're going to tell me, that was just the olden days. But it's the same now, isn't it? Look at you, fr'instance. You're doing a full week's work, and you're getting ten quid for it. How's that fair?"

"*Dad,*" says Gary.

"But I'm learning the job," says Wayne.

"That's right," says Gary. "Don't mind him, he's a wind-up artist."

"I am not," protests Alec. "I'm making a serious point here. I'm trying to—"

"Dad! Would you please, please, pretty please, stop trying to sign Wayne up for the revolution?" He's exasperated, but it's within the bounds of humour, just as Alec himself is vehement, but not with the old bitterness. It was different straight after Wapping, with his occupation gone, his skill suddenly and forever useless. The humiliation was fresh. He hated taking shifts on charity from his own son, he hated being cut down into a middle-aged dogsbody, good for nothing but fetching and carrying. And he showed it, all the time. Looking back, he's amazed that Gary put up with him.

"Well, you know," he says, meaning the joke to be a kind of apology, "I'm just keeping my hand in. For old times' sake. It's my last day, after all. Gotta leave with something to remind you how bloody awful it was, having me working for you."

"Yeah, thanks for that," says Gary.

"But, but, that book?" Wayne puts in.

"What about it?" says Alec, raising his eyebrows encouragingly.

"If they're doing a rubbish job, the guys in the book, 'cause the quote was too low—that's, like, the customer's fault, innit? They shouldn't of taken the low quote. They paid for crap, so they're getting crap. Right?"

"You bloody Thatcher baby," says Alec.

Gary laughs.

"You done downstairs, then?" Alec asks.

"Yep. Ready to get in here, if you two've finished."

"Yeah, we're good," says Wayne: and it's true, while Alec has been standing there brush in hand, the boy has finished his own share of the walls and quietly moved on to finish Alec's.

"Right, then. Time for lesson number one for you, I think." Gary nods at Wayne.

"We'll help you fetch everything up," says Alec.

"No, no, no need, me and Wayne can do it. You should be moving, shouldn't you? Aren't you doing the handover with mum at twelve thirty?"

Alec looks at his watch. Bugger. Yes he is.

"I better get going, yes," he says. "Well. See you tonight, son. See you, Wayne. Try not to grow up into a total Tory, okay?"

And off he thuds down the stairwell over the huddled dust-sheets, careful not to touch the buttery brown of new plaster that surrounds him, that pales as he gets into the dryer, older work in the hallway to a biscuity terracotta. As they dry, the burnish marks where Gary did his deft swivels and slides with the float edge become mere specklings, faint blushes of red on an apparently smooth surface. Gary does good work.

"He talks like a teacher, your dad, doesn't he?" he can just hear Wayne saying, cautiously, at the top of the house, and Gary replying, "Funny you should say that . . ."

Twenty past twelve. Out of the cool damp cave into August heat outside. Past the signboard saying FEATHERSTONE (in 10,000-point Baskerville) and the white van with TORRANCE BROTHERS on the side (sans serif, but he doesn't know the font). For once, the job is near enough to walk home from. All he has to do is stroll—trot, rather—down under the big avenue trees from the top of the Rise to the point where the estate cuts into the right side of the street. Then the maisonette's just round the corner. (Their maisonette, now, owned by them and not the council. He hadn't wanted to do it but Gary insisted, and operating on benefits, operating on Gary's goodwill, with nothing else to offer to the family economy, Alec didn't feel he really had a leg to stand on.) Leaves still and heavy overhead; only the faintest stirring of the air. He feels the heat as he hurries in overalls. He feels the strangeness as he realises that, unless he takes to DIY, he's not going to be wearing overalls again, ever. Not to work in.

This is the end of him as a working man. Tomorrow morning he'll be presenting himself in the staffroom in a suit and tie. Mr. Torrance, indeed.

"Sorry!" he cries as he lets himself in.

"In here," calls Sandra from the front room.

He can tell she's got Gary's little girl with her straight away, from the particular small-person-present smell in the house: a mixture of lotions and creams, the steam of boiled veg and a hint of used nappy. He missed it the first time round, thirty-two years ago. That was Sandra's department then; he was always off at work in the ink and roar while Sandra did the kids' lives. But he knows it now, intimately, and he feels the familiar bump of delight and boredom together, as he puts his head round the door and finds Vicky on the carpet with legs sticking out of the corners of her little red dress at right angles, and a plastic giraffe held up to her face to be given a talking-to. How can you be bored and delighted at the same time? Filled with love and conscious at the very same point of how many hours there are to get through till bedtime? You just can, that's all.

What he's not expecting to see is Gary's Sonia's dad Tony sitting on the settee as well. They don't move apart from each other as he comes in or anything like that, but he has the impression somehow that they are, as it were, deliberately not moving apart. There's a self-consciousness about them; about them being seen, and being seen by him. Oh.

"I'll just nip upstairs and change," Alec says.

"Better take Vicky with you, love," says Sandra. "I'm out of time. We should get going—Tony's giving me a lift."

"I'm just giving Sandra a lift down," Tony explains, unnecessarily.

"Right," says Alec. "Come on then, Your Majesty, come and help Grandad choose which shirt to put on."

"Can Horton come?" asks Vicky. She must mean the giraffe.

"Of course he can," says Alec. He takes the hand that isn't holding the giraffe, and so it begins, the afternoon at child speed, where every task breaks down into a multitude of tiny sub-tasks. This one is Getting Up the Stairs. They have reached the fifth step by the time Sandra, with purse in hand, is heading out through the frosted-glass front door with Tony. Sandra's part-time job on the check-outs at the Co-op has metamorphosed into something semi-managerial at the huge new Bexford Tesco's, still on the shop floor but moving briskly around sorting out the teenagers and pensioners who run the tills. Her shifts start at one.

"Isn't Grandma coming upstairs with us?" says Vicky.

"No, Grandma is going with Grandpa Tony," says Alec, and wishes he hadn't put it like that. "Wave bye-bye."

"Bye-bye, chicken," calls Sandra as the door closes. "See you later, love."

Two more stairs, Vicky concentrating on the big steps up required. Then she stops.

"Why do you say 'Your Majesty,' Grandad? That's not my name!"

"Because 'Your Majesty' is what you say to queens, and there was a very famous queen who did have your name."

"A queen called Vicky?"

"Well, Victoria."

"I think Vicky is nicer."

"Mm-hmm. *Up* we go."

When they reach the top, Vicky needs the loo, so they do that first; and there's washing her hands, and drying her hands, small fingers and pearly nails wiggling in the towel, and then rescuing Horton, who has somehow fallen into the toilet, luckily after it was flushed; and washing Horton, and managing to stop Vicky from helping with that, and consequently needing her own hands washed and dried all over again. In the bedroom, she doesn't help pick a shirt. She climbs into the bottom of the wardrobe and tries to hide among the dry-cleaning bags.

"I'm a lion," she says. "Rawr!"

"Rawr," agrees Alec. He succeeds in changing his clothes while being-a-lion lasts.

"Now. Have you had your lunch?"

"No. I'm a hungry lion! Rawr!"

"Rawr. Then let's go and see what Grandma made for you. Why don't I carry you this time?"

"No, I want to do it myself, on my legs. Horton wants to do it himself on his legs too." A microsecond's pause. "Where is Horton?" Another microsecond, which is quite long enough for happiness to transit all the way into wailing panic. "*Where is Horton?*"

"Horton's in the bathroom, I expect, petal. Let's go and look, shall we?"

"Horton is *lost!*"

"No he's not, no he's not. Look, there he is." Horton is among the toothbrushes. When Alec passes him over, Vicky is so eager to grab him that Alec gets clouted on the side of the head with him in passing. She presses him to her cheek, trembling. Then the sun is out again as if it had never been eclipsed. Loss is total; then loss is totally cancelled.

"I thought Horton was an elephant," says Alec, unwisely.

"Horton-on-the-telly is a nellyphant," says Vicky with scorn. "My Horton is a giraffe. He has spots."

"So he does," says Alec. "Now, let's go and find your lunch."

"Lunch," agrees Vicky.

They labour down the stairs.

"Upsy-daisy!" says Vicky on each step.

"Downsy-daisy?" suggests Alec.

"No," says Vicky.

Three hours later, Alec is in the park, sitting on a bench with the pushchair beside him, enjoying a momentary respite while the bossy woman with the double-buggy parked at the other end spins Vicky on the merry-go-round along with her two. In between he has fed her her lunch of fish fingers, tried and failed to get her to go down for a nap, sat her in front of a video of *Rosie and Jim*, and had her go to sleep there instead. He meant to ease away from the small, hot weight of her leaning against him and to nip upstairs to check his lesson plans for tomorrow, but he dropped off himself. Now they are out in the high-summer heat, under the glowering sky of city August. He has remembered to put on her sun hat. They have worked their way from the swings to the climbing frame to the see-saw, and now he has a moment to look around him, and even to try to think.

He is, as usual, the oldest person in the park and also the only man. Apart from him, it's all mothers, and young mothers too, busy with the business of fertility. A cloud of oestrogen surrounds him. His presence with Vicky most weekday afternoons has won him a kind of friendly half-admission to the club. He's welcomed, and chatted to, but he is too male to quite belong. Yet at the same time—pass, friend—it's insultingly clear that to them he's much too ancient to count as male in the operative sense of the word. He's not a boyfriend, a husband, a babyfather, one of the maybe desired or maybe resented but definitely visible impregnators who have helped bring about all this burgeoning and swelling. Under the circumstances a bit of middle-aged lechery is inevitable: but also kind of abstract. Self-limiting. Known to be pointless. Rendered remote and theoretical even as it happens, given that you're only shown what you're shown because you're safely neutered. You're allowed in because it doesn't matter. Mrs. Bossy here is never going to whip out her tits, but yesterday a red-haired girl sat next to him with her two-month-old on her knee. She hesitated fractionally, saw that Vicky was running to and fro bringing Alec sticks, and smiled decisively at him. She pulled out a big pale milk-swollen breast and plugged the baby's mouth with a thick tender copper-coloured nipple. The baby sucked away, making little lip-smacking sounds of contentment. Far away, faintly, a part of Alec thought: *I'm not surprised the kid's happy, I'd be happy if I had that in my mouth.* But only far away and faintly. It was like being a eunuch in the harem. Or what Alec imagines it would be like to be a eunuch in a harem. Or what he reminds himself he shouldn't be imagining it would be like, because all that harem stuff is an orientalist stereotype. *Orientalism* was one of the set books on his Open University course.

He has never been unfaithful to Sandra. This is something he is suddenly thinking about, now that there is—is there? can there be?—a chance that Sandra is being unfaithful to him. With Tony, though. With *Tony*. Really? Tony who was dumped by Sonia's mum Jean two years ago, and apparently can't boil an egg for himself. Tony with his red face (though he still has all of his hair, the bastard). Tony whose conversation, all of it that Alec has ever witnessed, is limited to car maintenance. Boring Tony. Helpless Tony. Unbeautiful Tony. What can there be there that would tempt his Sandra, after all these years, that would make that long body draw towards, shift towards, want to shift towards, the pile of Tony on the settee? With his car-coat and his sovereign ring. Probably, nothing. Surely, nothing. Surely he's just misunderstanding something, over-interpreting something, being paranoid about a situation where surely, surely, there can't be any temptation operating.

Temptation, he thinks he knows about. He has certainly felt it himself. On the OU summer schools, in particular. Where, crudely, there were two women to every man and therefore all the middle-aged crumpet you could possibly want. You packed up your suitcase and you went away from home, and for two weeks you were living in a concrete student room on a college campus: an eighteen-year-old's room, with an eighteen-year-old's tiny bed, and it gave you anachronistic ideas when you went to the college bar in the evening. And all the other titchy, uncomfortable cubbyholes were also full of people temporarily cut loose from their lives, and having anachronistic feelings, and acting on them too, quite a lot of them. Seizing the chance. Doing the obvious with the temporary freedom. There was this lady who ran a B&B in Ramsgate who was very willing, very pressing; and she was all plump curves and freckles, the very opposite of Sandra, erotically speaking. And yeah, he wanted to. But he didn't, not so much out of any virtue as from a certain idea he had of his life, and of what it was supposed to be like. (If he remembered rightly, she moved on with unflattering speed to an electrician from Salford.)

How did any of that apply here? I mean, thinks Alec, I suppose Sandra must be as prone as anyone to getting bored, and to those irresponsible moments you get where you wonder about what it would be like with someone else. But—Tony?

Maybe, says a malevolent voice in his head, *it's because Tony can't boil an egg, or run a washing machine, or look after a child for an afternoon. You adapted. You lost your job and you got . . . domesticated. You learned to do women's work. She said she didn't mind, she said she appreciated it: but maybe, down deep, she didn't like it at all. Maybe it's made you less of a man to her. To her too. Eunuch grandad. Neutered Alec, good with the kids.*

Shutup shutup shutup, he says to himself, and digs the fingers of one hand hard into his scalp, startling Mrs. Hyphenated Double-Buggy as she brings her two and Vicky back.

"Is everything all right?" she says, making it clear by her tone that his licence to be fit company may be withdrawn depending on the answer.

"Yeah, fine," he says. "It's just so hot."

"It is, isn't it?" she says, reassured. "Terribly. Might be time to get out the paddling pool when we get home. Dunk the little beasts."

She clearly comes from one of the bourgeois battleships on the Rise. A banker's wife; a surgeon's. *Tut-tut, bit of sexism there*, Alec reproves himself. Who says she isn't the banker or the surgeon, on her maternity leave and taking it terribly, awfully seriously? No reason to assume she's the class enemy's dependant. Give the lady her due, give her her dignity. She may well be the class enemy herself.

"Think I'm going to give mine their snack," she continues. "Would your little girl like some?"

"That'd be very kind. Vicky, say thank you to the lady."

"Than-kyoo," says Vicky, coming forward eagerly with her hand out. But when the top is popped off the Tupperware box, it turns out to contain only sultanas and sticks of carrot. Vicky's hand drops, and she looks piteously at Alec.

"Would you rather have your KitKat, love?" Alec asks, cheering inwardly.

"Yes please," says Vicky, performing good manners without having to be prompted.

Alec fishes out a two-bar KitKat from the multipack in his bag, and, August sun assisting, Vicky proceeds to get chocolatey. The other two watch enviously, carrot and sultana very clearly turning to ash in their mouths. Hah. The care of small people is understood to be a truce in the class war, bringing together people who would talk to each other at no other time. But it's a truce, not a peace treaty.

"I've got two more," says Alec. "Can I offer 'em to your two?"

"Well, I don't know," begins the woman, looking nutritional daggers at him.

"Oh please, Mummy! Oh please!" say her children, bobbing up and down.

Alec cheers inwardly some more.

Unfortunately, a last-minute run back to fetch Horton from his nesting place at the foot of the see-saw trips Vicky over a paving slab and she grazes her knee. It's not a bad graze, just a white scrape with a tiny criss-cross of red in it on the immaculate pink of her kneecap, and the wipes he used to get rid of the chocolate smear on her face take easy care of the blood. He dabs her efficiently with Savlon, puts on a plaster and kisses it better. But partly because it's sore, partly because of the scope for drama in the occasion, Vicky declines to walk back home, or to travel in the pushchair either.

"Carry me, Grandad!" she commands.

So they travel with her sitting on his shoulders, and his left arm clamping her dangling legs to his chest, while his right steers the pushchair along the pavement in a series of wobbling curves.

Nellie the ELephant packed her TRUNK
And said goodBYE to the CIR-cus

they sing together, and Vicky beats time with Horton on the top of his head.

Back at the house, his head aches from the sun and from the giraffe-strikes, and he's got a cramp in his side. Vicky, on the other hand, is recharged. She doesn't want to do drawing, or be read a story, or to play any of the quiet games he can think of. So he puts *Rosie and Jim* back on and she bounces on the settee like a jumping bean in front of it. He can keep an eye on her through the serving hatch, which means he can step far enough away from her to go through to the kitchen, put the kettle on and start making her tea. He can't go upstairs, though, where the lesson plans are calling ever louder. Even being out of sight of her while he reaches down the tin of beans for her beans on toast, or bends to bin his teabag, fills him with an anxious picture of—of—but in fact he never gets any further than the ominous beginning of imagining her damaging herself on some hard corner. The idea is too horrible to permit a clear picture.

"Be careful, love," he calls through the hatch.

"Nellie the CIRcus," she sings, ignoring him and coming to no harm.

The bouncing tires her out nicely, and she lets herself be sat peacefully at the kitchen table to spoon up the little cut-up squares of the toast and the orange beans. It's about half past five. The heat is going off a bit. A pulse of wind shakes the window by the sink, and there are clouds in the brassy sky. Rain would be nice. He sits opposite her, nursing his mug. She's in what used to be Steve's seat, when they were doing the previous version of family in this house. New curtains, new washing machine, but a lot else in the room is just the same, as if it's been waiting to be put back to use. It isn't the same, though, is it? The first time round, it feels like forever; but when it repeats a generation on, you know that the smallness of small people is strictly temporary, that home is a contrivance that only lasts a while. A shelter built of sticks as we go along the road. You can't appeal to the elderly phone on the wall to save you, or the cream paint around the hatch: not when you yourself are about to rip up the pattern of your life and do a new thing. Not when Sandra, God forbid, may be about to tell him— *Shutup shutup shutup.*

"How about that story now?" he says once Vicky has finished, and been wiped and dried.

"All right, Grandad," she says, as if she's kindly doing him a favour. Maybe she is. Grandad and his books; no one else in the family feels the urge, really. He can't excite Vicky about the library as an outing any more than he could get Gary and Steve enthusiastic. But she settles comfortably on his knee.

"Mr. Magnolia has only one boot," he tells her. "He has an old trumpet that goes rooty-toot. And two lovely sisters who play on the flute. But Mr. Magnolia has only one boot."

"I've got wellies," says Vicky.

"Yes, you have. What colour are they?"

"They are yellow!"

"Yes, they are. But poor Mr. Magnolia hasn't got any wellies. Look, you can see his toes."

They reach the end, and Mr. Magnolia is safely rebooted.

"Now," he says, as if an internal alarm clock has gone off and he can't wait an instant longer, "we're going to go upstairs because Grandad needs to look at his work for tomorrow. At the big school?"

"Don't want to."

"'Fraid we've got to, love. Off we go!"

"No."

"Yes, off we go. Come on."

"No!"

"Vicky, yes. Be a good girl."

"*No! Nononono!*"

And all of a sudden the tantrum is upon her. She swells, she goes rigid, she turns red. A volcano of willpower has erupted inside her. Alec should at this point engage in distraction tactics, but he's had enough of patience himself. He just picks her up, a yammering flailing armful, and carries her bodily up the stairs, and into what used to be Gary's bedroom. There he lays her flat on the floor to wail, mutters something nominally soothing, and turns on the computer on the desk. *Do I really want to spend all day every day with kids?* he asks himself. Yes, he does, for all the familiar reasons. And seven-year-olds aren't like two-year-olds. Mr. Torrance the primary school teacher won't be quite the same being, or stand in the same place, as Alec the tetchy grandad.

Vicky's roars subside into sniffles. She is gazing at the screen, he sees. What force couldn't do, the blue glow has accomplished.

"Feeling better, pet?" he says, and scoops her onto his knee. Ridiculously huge tears are hanging on her ridiculously long eyelashes, and he blots them with a pang. Together, they watch Windows start up. She does, anyway; his gaze wanders over his neat shelf of OU binders and coursebooks and set texts. Tools for a transformation he'll have completed at 8:30 tomorrow morning, when he walks through the gates of Halstead Road School with a briefcase. Also, his comfort, his refuge, in a funny way his vengeance. He hunkered down in here with *Ways of Seeing* and Freire's *Pedagogy of the Oppressed* to remake himself and show the bastards.

"Can we do the caterpillar?" says Vicky. She's talking about one of the games the machine came with.

"Yes, in a minute, love," he says, and opens Word. More start-up time; strange whirs and bonks from the hard disk. And Alec thinks: Sandra and Tony, what if it's got nothing to do with sex at all, or not much? What if it's not about temptation. What if she's just . . . lonely. I've been in this room, changing. And the more I've changed, the less we can talk about what's on my mind. We can't have conversations about Paulo Freire; I mean, we've tried, and it doesn't work. So when we talk, and at least we haven't *stopped* talking, it's all about our day, and the boys, and now the grandkids, and what the latest is in the great non-stop soap opera at Tesco, and which of the people I've never met there has split up with which of the other people I've never met. And it's kept us smiling at each other, for sure. But there's this area of me I don't share, and it grows. I've been thinking of that as a loss for me, but of course it's one for her too. She knows there's this big bit of me that's out of her view, out of her reach, now. Maybe, and why on earth didn't I think of this before, there's an equivalent piece of her that's been growing out of my sight, out of my reach? Maybe Tony is just . . . there. When he sits on the settee, he's present. His head isn't off in the clouds.

The file has opened. Bullet points and aims, probably too many of them. Vicky stares.

"What does it say, Grandad?" she asks.

"Oh, boring stuff," he says. "I'll tell you what, let's make the words bigger, and we'll see if we can find a Vuh-for-Vicky."

A move of the mouse, a couple of clicks, and he does what he could never do in his lost trade: blows the font up from 12-point to 72-point to 96-point just for the mere asking. Times New Roman, of course, for old times' sake.

"Look," he says, "there's a Vuh."

Vicky puts out a finger to trace it. Down below, a key turns in the front door: Sandra come home, to tell him he's been imagining things or to turn the world upside down.

"What is it made of, Grandad?" says Vicky.

"Light, love," says Alec. "It's made of light."

t + 65: 2009

Vern

"Where are we going?" asks Vern.

"It's a surprise," says Becky at the wheel of the Range Rover.

"Yes, but—"

"It's a *surprise*, Dad," she repeats.

"You won't find anywhere to park in the West End, you know."

"Well, then, isn't it lucky we're not going there."

"Oh."

"Your old stamping ground, that's all I'm saying."

"You mean *Bexford*? But—oh, never mind."

He fumbles in the glove compartment and finds the CD of Kiri Te Kanawa doing *Tosca* which he uses as an ear-stopper when family life gets too much. Becky rolls her eyes and tuts, but she lets the decibels roll around the pale suede and lime-green metal of the cabin. There's a frown line on her forehead, even with the tight, tight ponytail scraping back skin as well as hair. There almost always is. It's how she seems to go through life, his older daughter, perpetually on the boil, always in a hurry.

They don't know each other at all well. He had seen her, what, once or twice a year, before he got ill? Heard she was getting on okay; helped her out with some of the capital to start up her little empire of leisure centres out in Thamesmead and the Medway towns; felt a faint family pride that she seemed to have a business head on her; had to check her kids' names, to be honest, when writing a Christmas card. Then came the crash, and the hideous downhill unravelling of Featherstone's loans. He shouldn't have leveraged so much: easy to say now, of course, but if the boom had gone on, he knows he'd have kicked himself for leaving anything on the table. Next thing, he was broke. Next thing after that, he was lying in St. Thomas's hospital—on a ward, not even in a private room—recovering from emergency triple-bypass surgery, and there was Becky scowling down at him. "I'm taking you home," she said. "There'll be no more of this nonsense, mind. Look at the state of you!"—indicating his twenty-two stone, stitched with drips and drains.

And indeed, after a year under Becky's roof in Faversham, prevented from putting anything in his mouth that might conceivably give pleasure, obliged to start every day with the vile wheatgrass concoction she drinks instead of breakfast to fight off heredity and stay size 10—he is much thinner. No, that's too mild. He is a stickman of his former self, a diagram of him: spindly, pot-bellied, stooped, forcibly clad in leisurewear since none of his suits fit any more. He is a wraith in golfing trousers. He does not feel at all well. The weight is off the scaffolding, but the scaffolding itself aches and throbs. He teeters round the house on his two sticks, and Becky's boys zoom past him in Lycra on their way to maths tutoring, squash games, paintball, more sessions of mass slaughter on their PlayStations. Is it love that has made Becky put him through this transformation? It doesn't look like it, judging by her face as she drives. More a kind of irritated responsibility. Embarrassment, even, that anyone associated with her can have deviated so grossly from the trim ideal her business sells.

Vissi d'arte, vissi d'amore, sings Dame Kiri. I have lived for art, I have lived for love. Not uncanny, like Callas, but pretty damn good. And a woman with some heft on her, too, a woman with an actual figure. *Non feci mai male ad anima viva*, she goes on, I never hurt a living soul, and London spreads the same enfolding wings as ever around the A20. Further out than they used to be, it's true, and with much of the newbuild sprawl executed in the style that looks as if it's going to be the English default for the new century. Multicoloured ticky-tacky boxes. Bit of wood cladding; snap-on panel of smoky orange; pane of green glass; snap-on panel of sky blue. Back to the wood cladding again. Toy-box architecture. Yet still blending into the great mix of the Smoke alongside the brick and the stucco and the pebble-dash, the concrete and the glass (tired now) that meant new times when Vern was new. Unmistakably London, and at traffic lights and junctions Vern gazes at it through the tinted windows. Gazes at it hungrily—yeah, that's the word—as if his life in it were all still out there, and not liquidated, sold off to competitors, distributed to creditors, by Becky's maddeningly unimaginative accountants. He imagines himself clunking the door open at the next red light, and making a very slow break for home. But that's all gone. There is no Grand King-sized bed waiting for him up on the fortieth floor of Shoremark Wharf, dressed anew daily in smooth Egyptian cotton.

Eltham to Catford. Catford to Bexford. Bexford (without stopping) to Lewisham, and then—

"What's this?" says Vern, looking at the car park of the New Den. "You're not taking me to the football?"

"I thought you deserved an outing. Because you've done really well this year."

Done really well? How old does she think he is? Is she running an invisible version, for him, of the good-behaviour charts she has taped up on the fridge for the boys? Ten gold stars and they get to do go-karting. Lose ten stone and he, apparently, gets to go to fucking Millwall. Always the sports in that house, as if they can't think of anything else to do with a human body except to bounce it around.

"I can't stand for ninety minutes."

"Don't worry, you don't have to. They do this VIP package thing, where you watch the match from the boardroom. I got us two of those."

"Where's the boardroom?"

"Up at the top of the stand, I think."

"I can't climb up there."

"There's a lift," she says. "I checked. And a silver-service lunch beforehand, if that helps." A touch of sharpness in the voice.

"Oh. All right."

Vern pushes at the Range Rover's slab of a door, and manages to open a gap wide enough for him to start the process of slithering down, with a grunt and a gasp, onto his sticks.

"You're welcome, Dad," Becky mutters behind him. "No trouble at all, Dad."

It seems a long way across the tarmac to the grey-and-blue wall of the stadium. They're not aiming for the turnstiles but for a more discreet door. The office entrance, by the look of it. In any case, it's so early for the match that there's hardly anybody about yet. No crowd to cut across, just the two of them labouring along with the South London wind blowing on them—hint of distant kebabs—from a cool grey sky. It's only the end of September but Vern chills easily now. He's glad of the seat in the little lobby where the VIPs are gathering: quite often, by the look of it, people's dads, or other non-habitual match-goers. He is not the oldest person there, by quite a long way, nor the most decrepit. That honour goes to a teenage boy in a wheelchair, one of those full-service whirringly electric Stephen-Hawking-type ones, which can tip and fold and lift its twisted occupant into all sorts of positions at all sorts of heights. But there is also a boy even younger than Becky's two, wearing an obviously mint blue-and-white bobble hat and clearly being given the safest possible version of the Millwall experience by his anxiously posh father.

When the lift lets them out into the corporate penthouse just above the last rows of seating, the others scatter to look at the memorabilia on the walls: the century's worth of scarves, the framed photos of Edwardian dockers, the old Den burning in the Blitz, the carnivorous fans of the seventies with their sideburns, a carefully diverse vista of the present. Not Vern. He goes to the row of windows, and when he gets there he doesn't do more than glance down at the green rectangle of the pitch, surprisingly small from here even though they can only be seventy or eighty feet up. He gazes out, through the gap at the corner of the opposite stand, over the railway and away.

There it is. Enough of it at once, in one glance, in one gulp at the skyline, for you to see how big it is, how unappeasably, inexhaustibly much there is of it; his city, whose jumbled collage of blocks and spires and roofs and stacks never stops changing, never ceases cell by cell to be demolished and then to rise again under the red lights of the cranes, and whose hard angles and crumbling surfaces seem to fend you off, to push you back, but if you know their secret yield a coddled concentrate, a devourable sweetness, veins of rich fat. He loved looking down on it from his eyrie at the Wharf, somewhere, yes, just over there to the north-east, one of those towers sprouted from the corpse of the docks. He was a South Londoner, bred up in Bexford's low red brick. He had made his money—before he lost it again—from primping the city's past. But it was the spectacle of the central city and its eastern annexes renewing themselves that got to him, that spoke the promise loudest. The towers he'd never built himself, maybe that was partly the draw. He'd stand at the floor-to-ceiling glass, shag-pile under his bare toes, Rossini blasting from the speakers, gazing at the rising spindles of concrete, waiting for their glittering skin. Watching the snaking trains, the lines of traffic bumping along like corpuscles. The light coming and going. Sunrise from up there was a smudge of colour swelling the dim band of the eastern horizon, then a roar of brilliance pushing in over the gunmetal flats of the estuary. Sunset a hazy swathing of the west, his own aurora. He wore a silk dressing gown as big around as a wine barrel or, why not, since there was no one to see but the gulls and the helicopter pilots, nothing. London's pendulous figurehead. A lard monolith. A gigantic fuck-you. All gone. All gone; even the flesh. His eyes, to his embarrassment, prickle and brim, and his fumble for a tissue alerts Becky, standing next to him.

"You all right, Dad?" she says, surprised. "Dad! What is it?"

"Nothing," he says, muffled in a nose blow.

"No, what is it?" she insists, and she touches his arm.

"I just miss it," he can't help saying, can't help admitting, weak in the face of solicitude.

"Course you do," she says. "Everyone misses where they grew up." Sentimental, clueless.

"I didn't grow up down *there*," he says. "For God's sake. Bexford's over on that bloody side, over—" and turning, he lifts one of his sticks to try to point out, in the other windows, the ridge the borough straddles. And knocks a carafe, luckily empty, off the set lunch table, which Becky neatly catches mid-air before it can smash.

"Never mind," she says soothingly. "Why don't you sit down?"

He does, and other people are following suit. A hostess-chipmunk in, of course, Millwall-blue skirt and jacket is clapping her hands.

"Hello, everyone!" she squeaks. "Welcome to Millwall. Come on, you Lions!"

"Come on, you Lions," chorus the diners loyally, Becky included. Even the boy in the wheelchair makes some sounds with the right rhythm. Becky jogs him with her elbow.

". . . you Lions," Vern mumbles.

"Now, we've got a great afternoon lined up for you. Can't guarantee we're going to win, but we *can* guarantee you're going to have a good time, with some great football, a fabulous view, a terrific lunch, and some surprises. One of the lads will be up to give you his exclusive thoughts on the match at full time—with any luck, to tell you how we won it, yeah?—and at half-time, we've got our regular Stars of the Past feature, where we're gonna be joined by one of Millwall's heroes from the old days. But I'm not going to tell you who it is, or even when he was on the team, because that's part of the surprise, innit. I'll just say, for the older fans among you, this is someone who's gonna bring some memories, okay? And that's my only clue. Are you ready for your lunch? I bet you are. And here it comes."

In come a small squad of waiters and waitresses toting metal platters and serving spoons. Roast beef, Yorkshires, roast potatoes, cauliflower, green beans, gravy. It's a poshed-up school dinner, basically, or the kind of thing you'd get in a pub carvery on a Sunday, and in his glory days Vern would've been poking at the spuds with his fork and noticing that they definitely hadn't been browned in goose fat or got as crunchy as they might have been. But now, after a year in smoothie-purgatory, Vern is almost desperately eager.

"You going to let me eat these, then?" he says.

"Yes, of course I am," says Becky. "It's a treat. It's my treat for you because, like I said, you've made really good progress this year. And you know what they say, moderation in all things, including moderation, right? You just go ahead and enjoy yourself."

Round come the servers. Becky only lets herself be given one small roastie, and she frowns when Vern looks as if he might say yes to a third for himself. Still, it's a loaded plate, a still life of pleasure in a brown puddle.

"So, tell me what it was like growing up round here," she says

267

brightly as he lifts his knife and fork; and he's so grateful for the unctuousness of the beef, and the flouriness-inside-crispiness of the potatoes, that he actually tries. He has no idea what will interest her, but he dredges around, and fetches up the memory of the old Commer van his uncles used to use for their under-the-counter runs to Smithfield and Covent Garden. A van that smelt like a grocery cupboard even parked under a railway arch. Bacon on wheels.

"Wasn't that stuff rationed?" Becky asks.

"Oh yeah, that was the point. You could get really good prices for it, if you had the contacts—to sell it and to get hold of it in the first place, I mean. Den and Hubert went all over: Essex, Kent, way up to Scarborough once. They nearly got nicked, this one time, coming back into town; got flagged down in the fog by this copper with a flare, when the back was chock-full of cheese and game. 'Where are you gents going?' he said, and Hubert said, 'Delivery to the Ritz, my good man,' and he let 'em through because, you see, the fog was that thick, and Hube knew he wasn't going to be able to see—the copper—what it actually said on the side of the van."

"What did it say?"

"'Taylor and Sons, Plumbers.'"

At this, Becky nearly laughs, which encourages him to go on dredging. She nods and smiles and drinks water, possibly as a way of avoiding having more than a mouthful or two of the lunch. She certainly leaves the cheesecake entirely untouched. The odd thing is that Vern can't make it to the end of the main course, or eat more than a couple of mouthfuls of the dessert either. He feels . . . full.

"Your stomach's shrunk," says Becky with satisfaction. "That's how it works, when you get into good habits."

"Oh," says Vern.

When lunch is over, the VIP package-holders are ushered out of a door into the very top of the stand, where a row of tip-up blue seats are waiting for them. Millwall are at home to Yeovil Town, and there's some kind of complicated grudge issue that Vern doesn't bother to follow the explanation of, about how Yeovil unexpectedly beat the Lions last season, and snatched a promotion chance that was rightfully theirs. Or something. In fact, once kick-off has happened, and he's blinked down at the blues on one side of the small green rectangle beginning to run about with the green-and-blacks on the other side, he doesn't really bother to watch the match. He laces his hands across the almost-uncomfortable sensation in his stomach, and lets his gaze drift. Across the stand opposite—it's a rather thin crowd—into the sky—onto the face of his daughter next to him. She's not watching either: she's texting furiously on her BlackBerry, frown line back in place. Who is she, this skinny, never-motionless woman in her Juicy Couture velour? What has she got to do with him? What does she want? He's been living in her house for a year, but querulous and ill, with his head down, fixed on his resentment over what he wants and can't have back. A faint curiosity flickers. But down on the pitch, the Millwall strikers and the Yeovil strikers miss chance after chance, and the cyclic swell of excitement followed by disappointment, followed by excitement, followed by disappointment again, is kind of soporific. It sets up a soothing dialogue with Vern's stomachful of gravy, and his chin sinks onto his chest.

"Wake up, Dad. It's half-time."

"Yeah? What's the score?" says Vern, feeling he should ask.

"Nil-nil."

"Right, okay."

"Now we go back inside again?"

"Right, right."

"Well!" says the chipmunk, once they've all trooped back in.

Lunch has been cleared, and teas and coffees in blue-and-white china have appeared. "Everything still to play for today! But now it's time for us to take a little journey into the Millwall of yesterday, with our Star of the Past! And our guest this afternoon is someone from a good long time back, 'cause we like to cover all the decades, you know. He played for the Lions from 1963 to 1966, he was a midfielder mostly and a forward sometimes—that's how you put it, isn't it, Joe?—and his shirt number back then was eleven. Let's give him a warm welcome back to the Den—Joe McLeish!"

For a minute Vern genuinely doesn't recognise the name. Or rather, it seems vaguely familiar but he doesn't know why. He is still half-asleep, still swaddled in the rituals of corporate hospitality; and the man to the chipmunk's left is bald and red-faced, with big hearing aids in both ears, so offers no visual cues. But it's him all right, the involuntary backer of Vern's first business, the fresh-faced sucker of Tognozzi's.

"Fuck," says Vern, not loud but with enough intensity to get a disapproving glance from Posh Dad on one side of him and a shushing sound from Becky on the other.

"It's a pleasure to be here, Kirsty," McLeish is saying.

"It's a pleasure to have you, Joe. So first off, Joe, what do you make of the game today? Any advice for the lads?"

Off goes McLeish into fluent footballer-bollocks, which he has clearly not lost the knack of talking with the passing years. The lads are playing with a lot of heart; the lads need to give it a hundred and ten per cent; et cetera. I must look just as different, thinks Vern. More different, probably, what with all this dieting. Why would he know me? He probably won't know me. Vern tries to make himself as small as possible. He ducks his head down, folds his arms on his chest and stares into his cup of tea. All he has to do, he tells himself, is to get through the next ten minutes unobtrusively. Then half-time will be over, and with it McLeish's little turn.

Unfortunately, Becky clocks the way he's sitting, and takes it into her head to worry about it.

"Are you all right, Dad?" she whispers. "D'you need one of your pills?"

"'m fine," he hisses.

"No, you should definitely have one if you don't feel right. Don't be heroic. You know what the doctor said. Excuse me?" says Becky, raising her voice. "Sorry to interrupt but could I just get a glass of water for my dad? He needs his medicine."

"What's that?" says McLeish. He really must be quite deaf.

"Just one moment, Joe," says the chipmunk, raising her voice in turn. "We—just—need—to get—this gentleman—some *water*, yeah?"

"Oh, no problem," McLeish says benignly. "Nae problemo. Are you all right there, chum?"

And now everyone looks at Vern, and as well as swallowing the angina tablet Becky has just thrust at him, he has to look up, meet McLeish's eye and grimace a smile at him and mumble something.

McLeish smiles back, then looks puzzled. He shakes his head for an instant, as if something has got into it and needs dislodging, and goes back to his spiel. But then, with horrible clarity, Vern sees him getting it. It's like watching an alarm clock go off. His eyes go wide, and fly back to Vern's face.

"My God," he says, breaking off mid-sentence. "It's you, isn't it. You—you—*bastard.*" And he sets off up the table towards Vern, lurching a bit, on legs which were once superlatively faster and sleeker than Vern's, but are now, just like Vern's, the legs of a man of seventy.

"Er, Joe?" says the chipmunk.

"What's this?" asks Becky.

"This," says McLeish, arriving with a red finger out, and stabbing it unsteadily at Vern, who has stood up to avoid being stood over, "*this* is the tosser, the con artist, who stole everything I made playing fucking football!"

"Now you wait a minute . . ." says Becky.

"Can everyone please calm down?" says the chipmunk.

"I never stole a penny from you," says Vern.

"What?" says McLeish, both enraged and deaf, both deaf and enraged. "*What* did you say?"

"I said, I never STOLE ANYTHING FROM YOU—"

"You didn't have to! Did you, ya bastard? You just stuck me with your debts. Everything I had, because your firm went tits-up! I had to go back on the railways with *nothing* because of you! And I didn't even know it was happening, till it was too late. Just a brown fucking envelope out of the blue!"

Everyone is staring.

"Well, you should have done," says Vern.

"You what?"

"You should have *known*. What kind of fucking idiot signs something without reading it first? You were a sitting duck for the first person to come along who had half a brain. I just happened to be the one who did."

"Joe!—sir!—" says the chipmunk.

"You were a moron. You were a mug. You might as well have had 'MUG' written on your forehead."

"Dad!" says Becky.

"You *bastard*," says McLeish, but with astonishment in his voice now as well as fury: an almost wondering note.

"What, did you think I was gonna say sorry? *Oh sorry, sorry*," mimics Vern.

"I should fucking punch you," McLeish says. "I should punch your fucking lights out."

"Now, that's enough," says Becky, rising to her feet practically spitting, five foot two inches of angry string. "You leave him alone, he's an old man."

"What?"

"He's an *old man*!"

"So'm I! A skint one, thanks to him!"

"I'm going to have to ask you to leave," says the chipmunk. "Right now, please!"

"Oh, we're going," says Becky. "Right now."

And she tows Vern to the lift, whose doors, at least, open immediately.

"Mug," says Vern, as they close again.

"You shut up," snaps Becky. "Just shut up."

"Oh, that was—"

"Shut *up*," she repeats. She is angry, which he expects, but looking at her, she also has tears in her eyes, which he doesn't.

"Come on, Becky . . ."

"Not a word. Not one fucking word. Do you not get how humiliating that was?"

He shuts up. She stares at the lift doors, face set, and when they open on the ground floor she's out at a furious trot, past the startled receptionist and into the car park. She doesn't wait for him. She marches ahead, and he hobbles in her wake. Behind him the stadium gives the pulse of crowd sound that means the second half's begun. From far up ahead he hears the *bup-bup* of the Range Rover's central locking, and thinks, at least she'll have calmed down by the time I get over there. But Becky is too agitated to stay put. She throws her bag into the car and comes marching back again. When she reaches him she doesn't walk next to him. She circles, she makes glancing little runs at him like an attacking fly.

"Did you ever consider not ripping off every single person you ever did business with?" she says.

And again, on her next pass:

"Do you know who the mug is? Not that poor sod. Me; muggins here, for trying to do something nice for you. I should have listened to Mum. She said you were a poisonous old git."

"Look," he says, the next time she comes in for the attack, "I don't care, all right?"

She stops, she stares. Something changes in her face. Something resolves there.

"You really don't, do you?" she says. "It's like there's nothing left of you but spite." Suddenly, she is calmer.

They've reached the lime-green wall of the Range Rover. Becky cocks an ear.

"Listen, Dad," she says, "they're playing your tune."

He hasn't been paying attention to the noise coming from the Den. That kind of bellowing is not what he calls music. But the home fans are, in fact, delivering the ancient war chant of Millwall.

No one likes us, no one likes us,
No one likes us, we don't care.

Vern laughs, he can't help it. And so does his daughter, but not with him.

"Well," she says, "at least I don't have to do this shit any more. Mum said I should put you in a home, and she was right. Go on, get in."

As they pull out onto the main road he reaches for *Tosca*, but she snatches the CD out of his hand, cracks the driver's-side window and skims Dame Kiri into the traffic.

"We won't have any more of that dismal crap either," she says.

And all the way to Faversham she makes him listen to "Lady in Red" by Chris de Burgh, on repeat.

Alec

Four o'clock on Saturday afternoon. Waiting for his Tube, on the way back from his conference, Alec has one of those moments where you see that the crowd is composed of, is nothing but, individual after individual after individual. The city granulates. He's seeing the leaves not the foliage, the trees not the forest, the spill of separate crystals not the bag of sugar. A Circle Line train—not his—slides into the platform and through its opened doors and lighted windows he sees his fellow citizens displayed as if in a gallery.

A short, jowly guy with a head like a Christmas pudding, wider at the bottom than the top. An immensely tall posh old man in a long coat, nothing left of his hair but white tufts springing from parchment, studying his paper like an ancient tortoise. A plump blonde woman in leggings and leopard-skin mules, whose knees knock in and whose chin points down, turned in on herself. A blue-shoed dandy in his forties, with a white short coat, a white muffler, white gloves, all immaculate, but hair grey-streaked and tangled. A fair young woman wearing fawn, with one of those noses that comes straight down from her forehead, a nasal pier. A dark-skinned Bengali man in his sixties, sitting like one exhausted, who has around his watchful eyes and down onto his pitted cheeks stains of dark on the dark, like bruising. Woman

275

in a puffa jacket, frizzy hair going thin on top, nodding at half the speed with which her friend beside her moves her hands. Melancholic Japanese tourist girl, pink beret standing up on her head like a rising cake, skin tinted greyish-cream with thick foundation, leaning unexpectantly against the window. Brown girl, twentyish, beautiful, whose long black bob curves round her face like a nut's shell. Square-faced pasty white boy, with swags of beard at the corners of his jaw, like a playing-card king's. Pair of Muslim lads in trainers and trackie bottoms, shaved sides to their heads, prayer caps, nudging each other and looking as if they'd like to make a claim to something, but they're not sure what. Black-haired, groomed man of thirty, dark suit and T-shirt, sprawling legs, unconsciously picking his nose as he concentrates on his phone. Slight Asian woman, equally unconscious, who works and pats and stretches her mouth as she reads. Grave, bulky, patient, angry African man, dressed like an undertaker, who grips the rail over his head with thick fingers and glowers. Studious black kid with short dreads and horn-rimmed glasses, legs akimbo, poetry book in hand. Weary grandad with sawn-off grey stump of a quiff and a jutting stubbled ball of a chin, trying to keep hold of a little boy in red in mid-sugar-rush, doing comedy collapses—

And the doors close. *We are so many*, thinks Alec. Every single one of these people homeward bound, like him, to different homes which are to each the one and only home, or else outward bound, to different destinations at which each will find themselves, as ever, the protagonist of the story. Every single one the centre of the world, around whom others revolve and events assemble. So many whole worlds, therefore, packed in together, touching yet mutually oblivious. So much necessarily lost, skated over, ignored, when the mind does its usual trick of aggregating our faces.

And he also thinks: *Right, go away now.* It may be true, this glimpse behind the city's usual scrim of categories, but it is not the vision for dealing with things. You couldn't walk up a rush-hour street, negotiate a bus queue, sit in a theatre, if you were constantly aware of the millionfold press of beings as entire and complicated as yourself. *Stop, please. Give me back my normal, callused apprehension of all these as a pink, brown and black forest, vague in the mass, from which I only need to pick out individual faces when I have a reason to concentrate on them. Begone. Scram.* But the alteration to his sight goes slowly, unwillingly, as hard to shake as the awareness of breathing is when you've once become conscious of the in and the out of the air in your chest. He's still blundering among over-noticed faces when he boards his east-bound train, still ringed around as he sits down with his briefcase on his knee by eyes universally bright and significant because they are all of them the windows through which single souls are looking out.

In the end it's anxiety that pulls him back. The anxiety is centred on his briefcase and on the documents in it. He has just escaped from a day of watery coffee, long-life Danish pastries and (unless he's misread things) veiled threats. Along with fifteen other primary school heads whose last Ofsted report was only a Satisfactory, he's been shown endless PowerPoint slides in which the word "opportunity" repeated. The Department for Children, Schools and Families is pushing academisation. They can't actually force him to cut Halstead Road's connection to the local education authority but they're piling up the inducements, and behind every inducement there seems to be a menace implied. All day long, the bright young civil servants with the laser pointers have been uttering sentences that curdle at the end. "Of course, there's no statutory power to compel this change *at present*," they say. "We can't guarantee that the transitional arrangements *will remain available*." "It may be that existing supports for areas of high deprivation will be judged to be offered most effectively *within the package."* "D'you get the impression," he wanted to whisper to his neighbour, who was prodding her Danish with the end of a pencil, "that we're being told to jump before we're pushed?" But she must have known that already, and maybe she approved.

It's not that Alec is a reluctant player of the bureaucratic game. On the contrary, he has been competing in it with eager skill for more than a decade. This is why, in fact, his colleagues at Halstead Road were happy for him to become headteacher, even though at that point he'd only been in the staffroom for three years, and been teaching for less long than any of them. They knew he actually relished the task of shaking the money tree for the school, and would do his damnedest—old union skills coming in handy—to get the most out of New Labour's generosity while it lasted. It was a pity, he thought, that the Labour government had decided back in '97 to double up on the Tories' regime of testing and league-tabling, instead of abolishing it, but you worked with the world as it was. So he schemed, he networked, he persuaded. He looked for the advantage to Halstead Road in every newly announced initiative. He made assets out of his school's decaying buildings, its high proportion of kids speaking English as a second or third language, its sky-high scores on the deprivation indexes. He conjured the budgets to recruit teaching assistants, specialist mentors, enrichment visits by artists. He got SEAL money, EiC money, EMAG money, LIG money, NDC money, NRF money. Yes, the multiplying acronyms were ridiculous, but laughing at them, getting irritated with them, struck him as a kind of snobbery. A bourgeois affectation. If you were operating where there wasn't private money strewn around the landscape, where the parents were only just coping themselves, where you couldn't count on the PTA offering helpful little subsidies for school trips—what was the alternative? There was a duty to the kids to claw out every chance you could.

"Who'll look out for people like us if we don't look out for ourselves?" he asked a governors' meeting. "Er, 'people like us'?" said a social worker called Liz Boateng. "Working-class people! People who've only got their labour to sell! Honestly, doesn't anyone read Marx any more?" "Okay, Alec," she said, with an ironic kind of smile, and he felt like a dinosaur; like a hypocrite too, with his absurdly gigantic salary.

But he has got the school rebuilt. Alas, it isn't beautiful. If it were up to him the young would be educated in temples to astonishment, every bit as strange and rich as the dragon-scaled houses by Gaudí that he and Priya have been to see in Barcelona. Spires! Weathercocks! Mosaics! Mermaids and angels! Instead of which he has had to settle for fawn cement. But it is new, and it doesn't leak, and there are 234 kids at Halstead Road Primary School and he knows all their names—the Kurdish names, the Igbo names, the Bengali names, the Polish names, the Somali names—and no one is afraid of him, and nobody gets shouted at, and nobody gets hit. And nobody is unhappy? No, he reminds himself; you can't know that. You can do your best to make them laugh, and to see they eat breakfast, and to lead them through the British Museum unintimidated, but who are you to say what's going on inside, which of them privately inhabit a hive of busy misery, impossible to communicate? You're only a teacher, not a magician.

But now the era of new money is ending, thanks to capitalism and its crises, and so with horrible timing is the era of him. Him as a head, anyway. He is sixty-nine years old, and he's already deferred his retirement once, because he wanted to see out the building works. He can't do it again. Next summer he'll be done, ready or not, and there is no one obvious lining up to take over. Even with the absurd salary it is hard to find people who want to take on the fifty acronyms and the guaranteed blame involved in managing an inner-city school. Especially one that has just emerged from an Ofsted ordeal with a grade only one up from the bottom. (Fucking Ofsted. His value-added numbers are excellent but apparently that doesn't count for much.) And now, as well as the cold wind blowing in the post-crash world, there is also this sudden, specific pressure: cut loose from the poor old Bexford LEA, what is left of it, and redeem yourself from Ofsted disgrace as a shiny, rebadged academy. The ideological wrappings round the idea, he straightforwardly detests. All that magic-of-the-market crap; and there's nothing wrong, either, with having one authority for the borough, answerable to voters, making decisions about schools. Yet it's also clear that, in order to cajole schools to academise, the powers-that-be have consented to hang one more fat fruit on the magic money tree. Perhaps he owes it to the kids, and to whoever follows him as head, to say yes. Perhaps, since it's going to be such a big deal in the school's future, the decision has to be left to his successor. He shouldn't tie their hands, should he. But it might be easier to *find* a successor if it were the shiny (et cetera) Halstead Road Primary Academy that were hiring. And there'll be an election next year. Brown may win it but he may not, and if the Tories get back in, God knows what they'll do. Classes of forty sitting on upturned buckets, probably: and they might well snatch away the incentive package for academising, if he hasn't grabbed it while the grabbing was good.

The question goes round and round inside him, blurring his fellow passengers back into the comfortable aggregate, but not revealing the hint of an answer, all the way home. East to Canary Wharf, then up above ground and south on the DLR's Bexford extension. Then up Pevensie Street to the terrace by the common which he and Priya bought on his head's and her lecturer's salary. His feet would still carry him to the maisonette off the Rise, if he let them; he has found himself walking there from the school, on evenings when he's very tired.

"Helloo?" he shouts, entering their whitewashed hall with its Indian art in niches. No answer, but that's not definitive. Priya sometimes doesn't hear him if she's reading. He enters the kitchen but instead of her mass of grey curls arrested over a book on the counter, there's a note. GONE TO ANJALI'S, SEE YOU MUCH LATER. Oh well, probably easier, because his worlds are about to collide, and he needs to be on his way again as soon as he's showered. It's—got to get this right—Gary's Sonia's brother Craig's eldest's wedding. He's missed the actual ceremony, they knew he couldn't get out of his conference in time, but the reception starts at six at the Tudor Tavern on Catford Road, and that he has to be at.

Thanks to splurging on a taxi, he makes it at ten past with his hair still damp. The forecourt of the Tavern is full of cars, including the white Roller the happy couple must've arrived in, and a Torrance Brothers van, and a Costello van too, that being the other clan in this gathering of the clans. Sonia was a Costello, Craig is one, Sandra weirdly enough has become one. Two clans, two vans. Plasterers on one side, builders and decorators on the other. Not that anyone needed to travel by Transit to get to the knees-up. The vans are there as totems, badges, declarations of pride; specially important at the minute, two years into the property crash, with everyone anxious, and the supply of work inexorably shrinking, and both empires reduced sharply in size by lay-offs. For this very reason, Alec is willing to bet, all of the speeches tonight will be full of bouncy optimism, and there'll be a very large float indeed at the bar.

He's right about the bar. In the function room at the back of the Tavern there's a press of men by the long serving hatch through into the pub proper, and they're loading themselves with armfuls of pints, white wines, blue cocktails and alcopops to carry back to their womenfolk at the round dinner tables. The bride and groom are sitting up at the top end, she in cream silk with eyelashes the size of escaped caterpillars, he hollow-eyed and the worse for wear from his stag night, but both grinning helplessly, the way you do; both shining with the astonishment of being, themselves, this moment, standing on the magic pivot, the trampoline of transformation, where your life is being changed and for once you know it. Right then, right there, as you feel the dizzy hilarious bliss of it, the change is underway. Bexford, 1961, the evening of his own wedding day: him and Sandra looking at each other. Wonderingly. With a wild surmise. "Well, you've done it now," Sandra said, mock-stern. "Yes," said Alec, and he remembers he found it hard to get his breath. Also their faces ached from smiling so much. And right now, right here, there she is sitting next to Tony in his wheelchair. She sees him looking and waves— nudges her husband, who waves too, and she points him out to Craig, who points him out to Sonia, who points him out to Gary, and people call out Alec! and Dad! and Grandad! and beckoning arms go up at Steve's table, where a place has been saved for him. And over he goes to them, to join people who are glad to see him, with his usual sensation that he has gone somewhere, in life, and his family have gone somewhere else.

The starter has been eaten and they're onto the mains. Steve has kindly piled up a backlog of food for him.

"Cheers!" says Alec, stabbing a prawn.

"Cheers, Dad," says Steve, saluting him with his pint. After all these years Alec's younger son still looks like a slightly miniaturised version of his older son, shaved head a little nearer to the ground than Gary's, burly shoulders fractionally less burly. Always and forever, Steve is Torrance Brother No.2, number two in the firm as well, and apparently happy that way. "Sorry that your lady couldn't make it."

"Oh, you know how it is," Alec lies. "She had something on at college she couldn't get out of. She sends her best." Priya's actual words being: *Not in a million years.* "Everything go off all right, then?"

"Think so," says Steve. "Well; the registry office bit was fine, but a bit of a wobble with, uh . . ."

"Mm-mm!" says his wife Clare, rolling her eyes significantly at their two kids. Alec has no idea what she means.

"Grandad," says their little girl, "do you like my bridesmaid's dress? It's pink!"

"Isn't it just?" he says. "It's lovely."

"It won't be lovely any more if you get gravy on it," says Clare. "Keep your serviette tucked in. That's right."

They smile at him, and he smiles back, and all of the gap between them that goodwill can cross, goodwill does. He asks about the firm and Steve gives him a bulletin till Clare says she's sorry, she really needs an evening off from their troubles. Then he and Clare chat about schools, the school run, requests at bedtime for complete dinosaur costumes that have to be ready for 9 a.m. the next day, that stuff, it being an understood thing that Alec is, professionally speaking, a kind of honorary woman, able to keep his end up in conversations of this kind. There's a pint by his plate not a glass of white wine but, thinks Alec, it may have been a close thing. He tilts his head towards Clare and gives silent thanks that Steve and Clare live ten miles south and east of the catchment area for Halstead Road, thus keeping things straightforward. He doubts they'd be keen on *his* school, for all sorts of reasons. This is the whitest roomful of people Alec has been in for some time.

"Is something up, though?" he asks Steve, when Clare has shepherded little Alice and Jamie off to the loo.

"It's not—I dunno," says Steve, looking uncomfortable. "You should talk to Gary, really."

"Okay," says Alec, baffled. "Your mum's not ill, is she?"

"No! No, nothing like that. It's just—no, you should talk to Gary."

"Okay."

When the lemon tart is eaten, Sonia's brother Craig's eldest's new husband's best man tings his spoon on a glass and kicks off the speeches. The best man is rude enough to get some groans as well as raucous laughter from the adult bridesmaids, and Craig's nervous father-of-the-bride number is sweet enough to make the older contingent all go *Aah*. They toast the bride and groom, they toast the mother of the bride, they toast the bridesmaids.

"I thought Vicky was bridesmaiding today?" says Alec.

"Yeah, she is," says Steve, looking down at his plate.

"Only I can't see her."

"I expect she's nipped to the ladies," says Clare, with significant emphasis and her eyebrows raised.

"Well," says the groom, "it's brilliant you're all here, we love you all, even you Terry, even after you pulled that stunt with the handcuffs, yer bastard. Me and the missus here—"

"Ooooh!"

"I spose I'll get used to saying that . . ."

"Give it fifty years!"

"Thank you—me and the *missus* here are now going to dance our heads off, and we hope you'll join us."

The DJ has already set up on the little stage at the end of the room, and when the central tables have been pulled back to make a dancefloor, on go the disco lights, down go the house lights, and the tunes begin. Hollow Eyes mister and Caterpillar Eyes missus are the first onto the floor as is only right, not touching, keeping it decorous, but so wholly focused on each other, so wholly directed at each other with their entire bodies, head to toes, that it's as plain what they intend as if they were doing flamenco. Out comes the best man, you-bastard-Terry, with the tallest blondest brides-maid, and their dance is a piss-take of intent, though perhaps it may become real in a few pints' time. And Craig and his wife, giving it some for the honour of the middle-aged, the wife quite a mover, vibrating in her tight white and conjuring the girl who only eighty million heartbeats ago was dancing to Duran Duran in the school disco, but sitting back down knackered after one song. And the younger guests from all over, and among them the rest of the grown-up bridesmaids in a pink gaggle. Except Vicky; he still can't see her. He likes to keep an eye out for her, these sort of events being the main way he comes across her now. She was the first of the grandchildren, and in his head remains perpetually the Vicky who faced him at the other end of the see-saw, every afternoon in the park. No, here she comes, back from the ladies or wherever, hurrying in her pink to the dancefloor.

"Vicky!" he calls, and then again louder, since her head is down and she doesn't seem to be hearing.

"Oh. Grandad," she says, but she doesn't come closer. She lin-gers about as far from him as she civilly can, with her head tilted weirdly back, as if she'd like to keep her face even further away from him than the rest of her.

"I just wanted to say hi," he says, confused.

"Right," she says, and her voice sounds hoarse, scorched. "I'm going to have a dance. Got to dance at a wedding, right?"

"I think this one's a bit fast for me," says Alec. "Ancient knees, you know." He's not thinking about what he's saying. He's star-ing at her. Perhaps it's longer than he thought since he saw her—maybe it's been a year or more. However long it is, something awful has happened to her in the meantime. The pink dress hangs on her like a satin binbag, and the arms that stick out of it are white twigs, with raw patches like eczema. For some reason she has fingerless gloves on. Her face is pancaked in foundation and her eyes are so daubed they look like blotches. It's make-up worn for a mask, but it can't hide her completely, and what he glimpses underneath is . . . shrivelled. A tight-skinned wretched little monkey-face, all bones, eyes too big in proportion, even without the mess of product.

"Vicky!" he says in alarm, stepping forward, but she shrinks back, *jumps* back, leaving him only with a brief wash of a really disturbing smell, acrid and rancid together. The stomach-juice smell of puke, combined with some secretion, waxy and metallic together, that human bodies are not supposed to produce.

"Gotta go," she says, bruised eyes blinking. And she heads into the flashing topaz and the circling glitter-ball motes, to the furthest side of the dancefloor, where she starts to do something that's more like a jerky exercise routine than a dance, and that has no reference at all to anyone around her, or to their boogieing, or (whatever she says) to the wedding in general. She moves like a solitary, manic insect. People give her space.

Alec watches, troubled, baffled. It has been a while, for sure. Maybe he is out of practice with the way she is now. But he's pretty sure that when he did see her last, whenever it was, she was in that late-teenage state of arriving at your settled face. The mid-teens startlement and hormone surge is calming down, the puppy fat is coming off your brow and your cheeks; and, tightening into focus, swimming up and firming up, here's the you you're going to be. In Vicky's case, this pretty girl, a white South Londoner with plucked eyebrows and careful clothes and an expression sitting habitually on the self-possessed/sarcastic borderline. Where's that gone? What undid that?

You should talk to Gary. He looks for him, and finds him at the top table, leaning over Sandra and Tony to say something but glancing up every little while at the dancefloor. Alec's gaze and Gary's gaze cross. *Can I talk to you?* Alec mouths. Gary shrugs, pats Tony and Sandra, and makes his way over.

"Dad," he says neutrally. The music is loud enough that they have to push words at each other, and lean close, but it gives them a kind of privacy, at the edge of the dancing.

"What's up with Vicky?" asks Alec.

"You noticed, then."

"I know I haven't seen you all for a bit, but yeah."

"Sometimes it's nice to fool myself, you know, that people can't tell."

"I'm not 'people,' least I hope I'm not. What *is* it?"

Gary sighs. "Vicky has an eating disorder."

"What, she's anorexic?"

"No, the other one. She eats, but she throws it back up again. Bulimia." Gary says this patiently, tiredly, as if the words are a doom he has had to pronounce on his daughter over and over again.

"She looks *terrible*."

"Thanks, Dad."

"She was fine the last time I saw her."

"Was she? We can't work out when it started. After a bit, you start thinking, was that a sign? Was that? Perhaps it goes way back."

"Come on, no," says Alec, not sure why he's arguing. "She was just this happy, pretty girl. And it can't have been that long. She's only seventeen."

"Eighteen; but, you know, so what. It's old enough to fuck yourself up. Apparently."

"But you can get it sorted, right? She's got her whole life ahead of her."

"*No*," says Gary, with a touch of weary aggression, "apparently I can't sort it. There she is, Dad; still fucked up. She's just eaten a three-course dinner with coffee and mints and puked it all up, and now she's gonna dance like a maniac in case any calories accidentally stuck to her. And then she's going to go all faint and wobbly,

287

and icy-cold, and we'll drive her home, and tomorrow morning she's going to wake up just that little bit more starved than today. Just in time to throw up her breakfast."

"Sorry," says Alec. "Sorry, son. It's just a bit of a shock."

"It is that," says Gary.

"What . . . happened?"

Gary puffs out a breath. "Like I said: we don't know. *She* doesn't know, least I don't think she does. I mean, she broke up with her boyfriend; but that seemed to be all right. She was worried about her A-levels; but so were all her friends. She listened to gloomy music; but, you know, teenagers. She didn't like the way she looked, and she went on these daft you-can-only-eat-porridge-type diets: but, you know, teenagers! It was like she fell over this invisible cliff, and everything went from a little bit bad to impossible without us noticing."

"And she started, what, sneaking off to the bathroom after meals?"

"No, not to begin with. She thought we'd smell it in the bathroom, or the loo. She'd go off to her room with a carrier bag and lock the door."

"A carrier bag?"

"To puke in. Then she'd tie them up, stash them under the bed."

"Oh my God," says Alec.

"Sonia found them, vacuuming. Bags and bags of cold sick. Course, she stopped hiding them after that."

"Oh God, that's awful. I just can't— She's always been so *neat*. Upset if her clothes got muddy. Felt-tips in a row. Puking in a bag? In a *bag*? How could she bear the mess?"

"Apparently, after a bit," says Gary, "the throwing up starts to feel good. It's like a ritual thing. You feel gross until you do it."

Somehow this detail is the worst so far. Children vomit, and you clear up after them. They throw up in the night over their pyjamas and the bedclothes, and they're all pitiful and horrified at the natural logic of things running backwards and their tea reappearing from their tummies, falling chaotically out of their mouths again in chunks and ooze. You clean them up and change the sheets and put everything back in order. Safe, calm order. You sit with them while they go back to sleep. You make it right again. Alec has mopped up Gary and Steve, he has mopped up little Vicky, in the days when he was minding her. The thought of this innocent wretchedness turning into, what, he can hardly imagine, a compulsion, an inside-out greed, an urge so overriding it welcomes the chunks and ooze: that's horrible. Oh, Vicky.

"You should have told me; you should have said."

"What good would that have done, Dad?"

"What about, I don't know, um, therapy? Counsellors? Rehab?"

"Yeah," says Gary. "What about them."

"You've tried . . . ?"

"Course I have. Course I have. I have run around like a blue-arsed fly. Doctors. Psychologists. Counselling services. Expensive houses in the country where rock stars go. None of 'em work if you don't want 'em to work, do they."

"She won't go?"

"Well, she's been to hospital twice. Didn't have any choice. After a bit you just fall over. Then they section you, put you on a drip, send you home when you've put on a pound or two, ready to do it all again. But she won't go to rehab, no, no, no. How," says Gary, and suddenly there's a sob in his voice, "how I hate that *fucking* song." He is staring at the dancefloor with his face set. Gary, capable Gary who never seemed to want anything Alec knew how to give, sounds helpless. Alec catches himself in an instant of tiny ignoble pleasure, drowned at once in shame.

"I'm so sorry," he says. On the other side of the floor the insect dance continues. *But she's so young*, Alec wants to protest. It feels as if it ought to be possible to appeal to her youth against all this. Surely nothing too serious can happen to someone so new, so near to their beginning.

"I'm sure she'll be all right," says Alec. "She's such a lovely girl."

"Everyone says that. Like it can't be much of a problem when she's got all her advantages going for her. But what if it's the other way round? She's got all her advantages, and still she's fucked up. Maybe that means the problem's really bad . . . But yeah; yeah; she is a lovely girl. She is."

"Well, if there's anything I can do to help."

"If I knew what needed doing, I'd be doing it, wouldn't I. But," says Gary with an effort, "thanks, Dad. Thanks."

And he bumps shoulders with Alec—the first time Alec can remember them touching in he doesn't know how long, but a signal of goodwill sent, clearly, from far far away, across a great distance of trouble.

"Oh, here we go," says Gary. The insect has faltered, is folding up. Before she can collapse all the way to the ground Gary has arrived and scooped her up in a horribly little-girlish double-armful, bony legs dangling. "Let's get you home, little lollipop," Gary tells his daughter, who lolls on his shoulder smelling of vomit and a body digesting itself; and there is such an expression of stricken tenderness on his face, he is down so deep in a desperation Alec has not even suspected, he is so far beyond embarrassment as he carries Vicky off through the wedding—that Alec falls back, silent, and after a moment backs off too. His impulse is to go away right out of the room, right out of the building, but that seems like such a confirmation of his total failure with the family that he makes himself withdraw only to an empty table in the dark at the room's edge. From here the points of light tracking across the dancefloor from the glitter ball form a swaying oval through which the dancers shuffle darkly, heads lit in flashes. Round they go, on they go. It feels as if, for the second time today, a hole has appeared in the fabric of things, showing what lies behind. Only this time, instead of a gentle thinning of habit, there's a rip, a gash, and the view through is to a void of waste and disaster. He rests his forehead on his fist, as a dignified alternative to putting his head in his hands.

"Hey, you," says Sandra.

"Oh," he says. "Hey."

"Gary just talked to you."

"Yes; yes, he did."

"Can I sit down?"

"Of course you can." Grey hair now instead of blonde, deep grooves at the corners of her mouth, yet still the same slender being as ever, in the dark opposite him. "Did you know about this?" he says.

"Yeah," she says.

"It's so awful."

"Yes, it is."

"I suppose everyone but me knew?"

"No. No. Gary and Sonia haven't been spreading it about. It's a shock when you find out, isn't it?"

"Yeah!"

"So I thought I'd check you were all right."

"I feel," says Alec, knowing he probably shouldn't but unable to resist the invitation to speak his misery, "as if I haven't managed to do one single good thing in my life."

"Oh, what crap," says Sandra calmly.

"Well—everything I do ends in failure, doesn't it." The paper; the family; the school too, maybe.

"That's different, isn't it," she says. "Everything ends. Doesn't mean it wasn't good. You were a very good dad, you know."

"I never worked out how to talk to the boys."

"Or they never worked out how to talk to you. They're very proud of you, you know."

"You're not sorry you were married to me, then?"

"No!" says Sandra, making a noise of exasperation no different from the old noises of marital exasperation. Bus shelter; registry office; kitchen in the maisonette; darkened table littered with plates and glasses. All the times lie on top of each other. "No, love. Don't be daft. It's not your fault we couldn't make it work in the end."

"I didn't mean to change," says Alec.

"I'm not sure you *did* really, love."

"It feels like I should have been able to fix it."

"Mr. Responsible," says Sandra, and reaches between the glasses to take his hand.

"It feels like I should be able to fix this now."

"Vicky?"

"Yes."

"Me too. I've been all through it with Gary and Sonia. Everything I could think of?"

"Yeah?"

"They'd already thought of it. Every single idea I could come up with. And you know what I realised?"

"What?"

"That this is on them now. Not us. We've done our heavy lifting. They're Vicky's mum and dad, not us. All we can do is hope they find a way. We can't sort it for them. Or for her. It's their problem, not ours."

"It's just such a terrible way for it all to end up."

"*End up?* End *up?* Nothing's over, you berk. Vicky's *eighteen.* She's got the whole of the rest of her life coming."

"I suppose."

"Yes, she has. You've got to believe that. But when she gets out of this mess, you know what? There'll be something else, and something else again, and we won't be able to wave a wand over those things either. Problem after problem after problem, going on forever. It never stops."

"I suppose," says Alec, feeling better, though he couldn't exactly say why.

"Right. So—come and have a dance."

"What? No. It's a bit fast for m—"

"It's a slow number, Alec. Come on."

"Won't Tony mind?"

"Don't be daft."

And she yanks him to his feet, and draws him through the mess of tables into the tilting oval of lights.

"Maybe don't put your hands on my bum, though," she adds, a minute later.

"Sorry," says Alec.

"Behave, or I'll report you to your, you know, your lady." Whether because she's afraid of mispronouncing it or for some other reason, Sandra like Gary and Steve tends to avoid saying Priya's name. Alec, who was not misbehaving but only sliding without thinking into past time, thinks now of Priya. Admirable Priya, up for a conversation about Gramsci whenever he likes; terribly rational Priya, who would fail to see that there was any-thing to make a fuss about here, even if she were told. Priya who would not understand that even if he places his hands with abso-lute propriety, the very act of him dancing close with Sandra has a helpless infidelity to it.

He has his arms round her as they sway along to "Holding Back the Years" and hers are around him. Her grey head is on his shoulder. It's been nearly fifteen years since they embraced, but before that they slept in the same bed for almost forty years.

He knows her body exactly, completely; the nape of her neck, her smell, her long narrow back with its spinal nobbles. Fifteen years is nothing. Time is nothing. Her wrinkles, his, are only variations in a long sameness. Seventy-year-old Sandra, seventeen-year-old Sandra: fundamentally identical. Here with her, he feels reconnected to forever. But she's right, of course. Everything ends. This will. (This already has, legally speaking.) There's no such thing as forever, at least in the sense of there being more and more time like this. Time is running out, and for once, strangely enough, perhaps exactly because he has Sandra in his arms, he can feel that it is. He can feel that the spinning golden carousel of lights that turns here with the two of them inside it, the spinning carousel of light that's held his whole life, will sometime soon tilt away from him, or he from it. Either way it will angle away from him into the great dark, and turn on without him. Gary and Sonia and Vicky will have to cope without him; Priya will have to cope without him; the school, he supposes, will just have to cope without him too.

Not now, but soon. Not for years, maybe: but soon compared to the number of times he has already been around the sun, he and the city of London, a small grey spot on a rotating sphere travelling in a circle through a sleet of rays and particles. Soon compared to that. Soon too compared to the long history that the city has to come, which he won't be around to see. The declines, the transformations, the rebuildings. The green porcelain architecture of future London in *The Time Machine*, which Alec has never forgotten: he won't see that. Or the towers a kilometre high from which it will be possible to see the Channel gleaming in the sun. Or the shrunken half-drowned settlement ringed by steaming paddies. Or the ruins the New Zealander sees, having travelled half the world, as she sits on a broken pillar by Temple Bar. None of that. This was his time, and it's nearly up. And then?

And afterwards? Then there will be no more *then*. After, there will be no more *after*. But for now he goes on turning in the turning lights. For a little while longer, he is dancing with his wife.

Jo and Val

You can tell with all your senses, thinks Jo, that the unit isn't anyone's home, however long the inhabitants live here, including Claude; however likely it is that some of them will die here, including Claude. The carpets are more bristly than you'd choose for a real living room, the lights are more fluorescent, the chair cushions more solid and aggressively orange. They don't exactly have visiting hours but the evening routine is beginning around her. The trolley with the wonky wheel is bringing around hot drinks and little plastic beakers of pills; the day staff are doing their handover and putting on coats. She ought to be going. Claude is visibly tired too. The window is closing for him being able to pay attention, the obsessions are reasserting themselves. He has been asking about Marcus and the radio station, a little random but perfectly fatherly. Now, without any change in his tone of voice, or apparently any sense of doing anything odd, he brings the Trilateral Commission into the conversation.

"Pills, Mr. Newton," says the night nurse.

"I better make a move," says Jo. She drains the lukewarm last half-inch of her tea, and levers herself out of the orange chair. "I'll just go and wash this up."

"You don't have to," says the nurse.

"No, I will," Jo says, from some vague feeling that if she rinses the mug it will make the place a tiny bit less institutional. Symbolically, anyway. She is always glad to leave, always guilty that she gets to walk out while Claude stays behind, medicated.

She carries her mug and his and two teaspoons through into the narrow kitchen that opens off the patient lounge. The instant coffee is in a catering-size tub, the teabags are in a Tupperware box. None of the mugs match. The biscuit tin has a sticker on top that says NEIL'S BISCUITS HANDS OFF. She washes up, she dries up, with a tea towel bearing a picture of Caernarfon Castle. There's a window to the right of the sink that looks back into the lounge, and through it she can see Claude framed in his chair like a badly lit still life. His narrow quivering head, his big incurious eyes, the nurse still standing over him. Probably, the nurse is still there because he has not yet taken his pills. Probably, he has not yet taken the pills because he wants to go on talking. Probably, he is telling the nurse about Henry Kissinger. Yes; the nurse taps the pill pot arrested in Claude's hand, and Claude reluctantly lifts it to his mouth.

And all of a sudden with the last mug still in her hand, a message comes through loud and clear from her psyche: this is an accident. There is no need for her life to have worked out like this at all. So many other possibilities. She could have stayed in LA. She could have had a solo career. She could have stayed in the band with Ricky, if he had been slightly braver. She could have married Ricky—and then, let's not kid ourselves, been divorced by Ricky, and got that ludicrous white wedding cake of a house in Malibu in the settlement, and be living there now, eating egg-white omelettes and all-purple meals (for the anti-oxidants, you know) and showing off her collection of Fender guitars to rock biographers. Chance, that she came back to London, chance that she met Claude, chance that she taught for twenty years at Bexford Hill. How can *this* be her life, how can *that* be her love, if it rests on such accidents? Surely her real life is still waiting to happen. Surely she is still in the wings at the Pelican Club, waiting to go on, or running across the common with Val in her tam-o'-shanter, kicking at leaves. Surely the real thing has yet to come along.

Then just as suddenly, just as clear, she thinks: so what. Nobody chooses who they love. Possessing something, being somebody, loving anyone, it rules the rest out, and so it's quieter than being young, and looking forward, and expecting it all, that's all. The world calms down when your choice is made. That's all. She puts away the last mug in the melamine cupboard, and goes to say goodbye to Claude.

"See you on Monday," she says.

"See you on Monday," he echoes, and watches her as she goes, puzzled, as if she knew something enormous that he does not.

But later, on the bus back from Woolwich to Bexford, it returns. Milder, this time, and more melancholic; a grief, a grievance, not a bolt of disbelief. On the top of the 54, up at the front, where she has always liked to sit on London buses, to get that stilt-walker's sway, that giraffe-rider's ungainly perch above the street. She supposes that at some point, when her hips go, she won't be able to make it up the stairs. For now she can, though, and sits surrounded by changing crowds of teenagers, out for the start of Saturday night. White girls whose thongs show above the back of their low-rise jeans—God, what a stupid fashion—black boys with heads shaved into cryptic sigils, getting on and off in obedience to the invisible frontiers of the postcode wars. Kids young enough, now, to be easily the children of the ones she taught when she first returned, and to all of them her presence is an effective blank. She has no part in their very important games and they treat her as if she were invisible. They chat, catcall, shout, across and around the old woman with the white bob, the melanoma scar, the lips pressed together. Blotted lights of traffic and crossing signals float across the curved glass beside her, neon leaves on black water. Ahead, there is still a faint smear of light in the western sky, sunset remnants fading like a dim lamp behind stained glass. Brake lights stitch the way across Blackheath. Down the hill on the far side, and the panes of dim colour tip up and disappear behind the tree branches on the slope. By the time the 54 levels out at the bottom, the sky to the west—and the east, and the south, and the north—is the plain black static of the London night, fuzzed with sodium. Onward to Lewisham, and then the grind up the long, gradual slope to Bexford.

(Underneath Saturday night, underneath the fried-chicken shops and the billboards and the railway arches, the geology of the city persists on its own timetable, scarcely scratched by the crackle-glaze of brick and tarmac spread over the top. Bexford, Lewisham, Woolwich: permanent-sounding names for gravel beds left behind by the river's random swinging this way and that across a basin of clay between hills, for millions of years during which there were no names, no city, no humans. Here there was ice, pine forest, rainforest, tundra, ice again; over and over, and only in the very last iteration of the cycle, the faint grey thread of smoke rising from the first campfire, the first pinpoint of red in the London night. The city, the great city, is shallow lithography on the clay. The city is a mayfly veil.)

The 54 turns up Lambert Street. Her stop is by the old Woolworths; or rather, where the old Woolworths used to be, before a developer decided to rebuild it during the boom and then ran out of money, leaving a hole behind a board fence and a sentinel crane standing motionless. Jo is so used to the three-storey bulk next to the bus stop that her mind tends to fill its presence back in again whenever she isn't actually facing the empty space, and so she keeps rediscovering that it isn't there. As now, for example, clambering off the bus. Above the fence, Woolworths looms until she glances up, and then dissolves into instant nothing. It's as if the building is flickering in and out of existence. The latest gaggle of oblivious teenagers whirl past, almost spinning her round: honestly, she might as well not be there at all.

What she minds, she thinks, setting off up the hill—what she *minds*, is that there is nowhere to put discord like this. Oh, she has love. She loves her son, and she loves Claude, the mad old fool, and she loves Val, and since she and Val set up house together when she retired, she knows there will be someone waiting for her when she turns her key in the door. All sorts of closeness; but with the way things worked out with Claude, there's no one any more with whom to do that married thing of bringing home your discordant wants, deliberately bringing into the space between the two of you those awkward things which you find yourself wanting but can't have. Can't have, that is, without losing everything precious you do have. When she was younger, in the first years she and Claude lived together and he was still present more than he wasn't, it was the awkward unruliness of desire she'd be dragging, quietly, into the indoor light. You meet a man you fancy, and you take care to mention his name, casually, in conversation at home, so that the thought of him can't exist in a separate bubble of yearning, reality-proof, but must take its chances alongside everyday love: must endure the comparison, and be revealed as thin and greedy and impractical, and pop in the serious air between sofa and kitchen table. Now, it's not wild desire she'd like to carry home to someone who, without even knowing, will make it measure itself against happiness and fall short. It's that she chafes, secretly, like this; that she is finding, just now, when things are hard, how sharply it seems she can still regret the lives not had, the music never recorded, the fame not gained. Old sorrows she thought were long worked through—no, more than that, which she thought were actually abolished by her having had different desires fulfilled—turn out to be still capable, still bitter, able like ghosts to billow up and start talking, if given a drop of blood to feed upon. She stumps up the hill, and the unquiet ghosts say: Why only this? Why this life and not the other? Why this ending and not another? If she were laying herself down to sleep, nightly, in the envelope of warmth made by another body under the quilt, the warmth which is also trust, then the ghosts would surely be laid as well, banished to the far corners of the bedroom. But she sleeps alone.

Number 34 Pretoria Street. Edwardian brick set against the side of the hill, a little wrought-iron gate between box hedges, a path tiled in cracked red and black triangles. A terrace in Bexford, but a cut above the terrace in Bexford where she and Val began, six streets and seventy years away. The lights are on. She turns her key.

Music is coming from upstairs, something in the extended family of drum 'n bass. There are important differences, she knows, but it's not her music and she doesn't keep up with it. Since it isn't her music, or Val's taste either, that means Marcus is over. Ordinarily, she'd be delighted; just now, she feels tired, and doesn't want anything else to happen today. There's a call from upstairs—they must have heard the door—but she puts down her bag and hangs up her coat at deliberate old-lady speed, and goes into the kitchen, and inspects the lasagne through the oven door, and makes a meaningless adjustment to the oven temperature, procrastinating.

"Jo!" Oh, all right.

"Coming."

Because number 34 is built against the hillside, the way into the pocket-sized garden is through a French door in the upstairs sitting room. They've got it mostly covered in decking, and it serves as an external junkyard, neighbourhood pissoir for cats and place for Val to smoke, more like a New York fire escape than a Californian terrace. And not only is Marcus there, so is his boyfriend Lucius Guneratne, a doe-eyed sound engineer whose parents came from Sri Lanka. Both of the Romans, as she and Val call them. And all three of them are smoking, the hot points of their fags brightening and dimming, with Val enthroned on a garden chair and lounging male prettiness flanking her on both sides. Three grins turn towards her.

"You'll never guess what," says Val. "You'll never! Come and listen to this . . ."

But Jo, without a run-up, without any appreciable pause or intermission, is infuriated. The nagging ghosts of what might have been have played at Chinese whispers in her head, waking a more ancient ghost yet. *I've been doing the looking-after*, cries this resentful spectre, *and Val's been having fun with boys. Look at her, sitting with them, sucking up to them, laughing at their jokes, while I do the hard stuff! It's not fair!* It doesn't matter that the Val in front of her is a pensioner roughly the shape of a fire hydrant, with a face as lined as a prune and a chestful of phlegm that pops and crackles as she laughs. It doesn't matter that these boys are Val's nephew and his true love, as queer as a three-pound note. It doesn't matter that by all reasonable calculations Val has less than her, has done altogether less well out of life than she has. Reason has nothing to do with it. It's the complacent smirk she can't stand—the same, dammit exactly the same, as the one that twelve-year-old Val would have plastered on her face as she sat on the climbing frame on the common in a crowd of male cronies, even at that age making sure her dress was pulled up to show off her legs. The same smirk the nineteen-year-old one would be

301

wearing when she sidled in at midnight to a house where Jo had been playing nurse all evening, lipstick smeared, clothes rucked, thoroughly and demonstratively snogged.

"Go on, Loosh, run it again from the beginning," commands Val. She pats the seat next to her.

"Look at you," Jo says bitterly. "Don't you ever learn?"

"What?" says Val.

"It's always *men* with you, isn't it. Always the *men* that come first, no matter what it costs. But you don't care, do you, 'cause someone else always pays."

"Love . . ."

"I mean, Lucius, d'you even know? Do you even know who you're sitting next to?"

The boys look at each other.

"Don't," says Val, urgently. "Oh, please don't, love."

There is such need in her sister's voice that Jo's angry ghost reels and melts, leaving her with no justification but still a headful of bad feeling, a wail of complaint with nowhere to go. She puts her hands in the air and makes a kind of clawing pass over her own skull, a gesture of impotent—something—that ends by her clapping her fingers over her mouth.

"Ma!" says Marcus. "Are you all right?"

But it's Val who steps forward and gathers her into slabby arms.

"Give us a minute, lads," she says. "Go on in for a bit. Please."

Frowning, puzzled, they do go in, and a minute later turn off whatever-it-is.

"I'm sorry," Jo whispers. "I don't know what came over me."

"Never mind that," says Val. "What's up? Did something happen?"

"No," says Jo wretchedly.

"No?"

"No, it was just the same as ever."

"Oh, right," Val says, as if Jo has explained something: though if she has, it must have been in the way she said the words, not the words themselves.

"I just—couldn't—bear . . ."

"Yeah," says Val.

"It's just—so . . ."

"Yeah," says Val.

"It's all . . ."

"I know what you mean, sweetheart," says Val, "I know what you mean."

"Well, I'm glad you do, because I bloody don't."

"Shurrup," she explains. "Shurrup and have a cry."

"That won't make it any better. How will that make it any better?"

"It won't make *it* better. It'll make you feel better, that's all."

Sniff.

Sniff.

"Okay now? Didn't that help."

"Maybe a *bit.*"

"Shut *up.* Have you got a tissue?"

"Somewhere. Yes. Listen, I'm so sorry. You didn't do anything to deserve that."

"Well, not recently."

"It was like . . . *something* started talking out of my mouth."

"No, love, come on, that was you. If I ever learned anything, it was: you got to own up to the ugly. You do. Come on. We wouldn't be sisters if we didn't hate each other just a bit, now and then."

"You mean, you too?"

"Oh God, yes. Mrs. Up-Herself Musician Lady. You're a moody cow. Horrible to share a house with. And you're so fucking *thin.*"

"Well, all right, then."

"I could go on."

"No, that's fine."

"Sure?"

"Yes!"

"Okay. Blow your nose."

"Yes." *Honk.*

"Yeah. But, you know what, if you're ready we should let the boys back out, they'll be worrying. And you know what? You really do need to listen to this track they've done."

"Why?"

"I'm not saying a word. Wait and see. It's okay now," she calls, much louder. "Your mum was just a bit upset over the state your dad's in."

Marcus and Lucius are back as fast as if they've been hiding behind the curtains. She hopes they haven't.

"Poor old Ma," says Marcus.

"Poor old Ma-in-law," says Lucius. "It's like, some things," he adds sagely, "they just build up, don't they? You don't know how upset you are till all of a sudden, you're really upset, innit?"

"Yes," she says, and she finds herself embraced on both sides by gracile male beauty.

"Thank you, thank you. Thank you both," she says. "That's very nice."

"Isn't it just," says Val.

"You dirty old woman," says Jo.

"I'm an antique fag hag," says Val. "I'm not ashamed."

"What's this about some music I should listen to?"

"Well!" says Marcus, detaching himself with the air of someone who needs to make a formal speech. "I was over here going through the vinyl, you know, looking for samples, and I found this cardboard box—"

"I don't remember this," says Jo.

"You were out," puts in Val.

"—with tapes in. Really old tapes, reel-to-reel stuff. And I thought, oh, interesting, because you can get some lovely lo-fi sound off magnetic tape, hiss and stuff, so I took them back to ours, and Loosh worked out how to play them, and Ma, there's—"

"Oh no no no . . ."

"—whole *songs* on them. By *you*. You never said you did your own stuff."

"Well, it never got anywhere. Look, you shouldn't bother with that. It's all so *old*."

She's feeling an anxious embarrassment, not on her own behalf, but for the past self who hoped for things she didn't get, and may be horribly exposed, horribly laid bare, in whatever the boys have found. Some fear too. She half-remembers what's on those tapes: work, it seems to her half-memory now, all bound up with the long decay of her and Ricky, all compounded therefore with false hopes and disappointments. Considering the poison that just now stirred in her, it seems perverse to wake any of that again. No more drops of blood to feed the ghosts tonight.

"That's, like, kind of the point?" says Lucius. "That it's, like, a time capsule?"

"But none of it worked out! None of it went anywhere."

"That doesn't mean it wasn't any good, does it?" says Marcus. "Did you ever listen to any of it again?"

"No, I didn't. Didn't want to; too miserable. Look—"

"But you kept it, though."

"Yes." Equally unbearable to play or to throw away. And then the technology moved on, and she couldn't have played it if she did want to.

"The thing is, we *did* listen to it, Ma, and we liked it, and we thought, treat this right, it could be very *now*."

"Which is weird, yeah?" Lucius says. "In a good way."

"I don't know," says Jo.

"I thought you'd be pleased," says Marcus. "I hoped you would. Obviously we won't do anything you don't want."

She looks at him, and she sees the first sign of the careful resignation with which Marcus has always handled the world not welcoming his projects. Not petulant; dignified. Oh hell, she thinks, trapped by motherly compunction.

"I think you've got to, sweetheart," says Val, reading her like a book.

"Okay, *okay*. Go on, then. Hit me, maestro. Maestros."

The smiles return. She sits down in the vacated lawn chair, but anxiety brings her straight back to her feet, and she's standing as the track begins, making its way outside from the sitting room speakers.

But it's outside sound already. Footsteps first, and faint traffic noise. Engines, brake squeal. Then crackle, a rubble of crackle as if charged dust were being stirred, were snapping thickly with sparks; and arising out of it, like crackle organised, a rattling drum break, dry as a biscuit but with reverb. *BOOM-dubba-da-da!-da!-dah. BOOM-dubba-da-da!-da!-dah.* Bassline threading through it, subdued in the mix so it's like a shake in the ground, seismic. Earth shadowing the drum. Then tentative but reinforcing, building up in layers, swathes from a synth. Electrified air over the rubble. Not one of the smooth-edged imitations of a natural instrument you get now, but blatantly electronic, artifice that can't hide the fact that it's artifice. No doubt to the boys this sounds as ancient as electronica gets, but her ear pins it as a sound out of eighties electro-pop, after her time; in fact, not from the first but from the second geological age of the synthesiser, after the truly early Age of Moog. Somewhere far off in the mix, an ambulance goes by. Of course, it's their sound-city she's hearing, an audio-

London as they've known it. So of course, when they want old they pick the sound of their own beginning, the eighties being as far off to Marcus and Lucius as *Variety Bandbox* on the radio is to her. "Geraldo and His Gaucho Tango Orchestra, coming to you from the Starlight Ballroom . . ." Sound from the dawn, from the oldest just-remembered layer of experience.

But then she hears the looped and sampled voice of a woman singing in the Hollywood Hills, and it's her own history she's travelling in, whatever the boys think they were doing.

A love unknown.

       A love unknown.

              A love unknown.

Next time.

They've bitten off the cut, so the end of the sample comes with an audible rip and it's really really clear this is an arrangement of fragments. All the same, even in fragments, there she is, live and aloud in some other piece of the present, singing into a four-track in a warmer, dryer night. Wasn't there guitar? The guitar has gone missing. The song as it once was—as she never quite finished it—stirs in her mind, tries to reassemble itself, reaches (hooks searching for eyes, oh nearly, oh not quite) for what came after the sample. *Comes* after the sample, for it seems sure that the song is still there, on the tip of her mind's tongue, if not quite in reach. Oh my. Oh my. Not embarrassing, not awful, not trailing toxic failure. That was an artefact of the backward look. This woman singing here, in some strangely nearby faraway, is bitter, yes; angry, yes; but wry about it, and self-possessed, making those sorrows into a thing, a thing not asking for pity. Also, the voice is pretty damn good, if she does say so herself. More of an American lilt to it than it had earlier or would have later; Sandy Denny crossed with Carole King. Nice pipes, lady.

Pouring rain.

                             Pouring rain.

                                                        Pouring rain.

Next time.

Now how are they going to get to a conclusion, or even to anything in the nature of a chorus, an expression full enough to let you put it down and say the song's been worked through? Perhaps it will all be dry bone-fragments of frustration, in this version, sliced-up yearning left unresolved. It's clear that to the boys the song as it was had a lot of sentimental juice in it that needed squeezing out. They certainly have squeezed it. It's implication and atmosphere now. They've taken the heart off its sleeve. They didn't want a narrative, or maybe (the cynic in Jo suggests) they didn't want a woman complaining to take up all that much space. They've turned a woman's whole voice into a sample. But still, they have to make it move, they have to make it arrive somewhere. How—

"We were going for a bit of a chillwave vibe," says Lucius, "but keeping it danceable, yeah, so like, still with some dubstep edge to it?"

"Shut up and let her listen, man," says Marcus.

Oh now, wait. They have done a gear-change, they have kept a cut-up or cut-down version of what she vaguely remembers was the chorus. It's just taken them longer to get to it than she expected, attuned as she isn't to the infinite patience of the dance-floor. Up goes the tempo, forward comes the bassline from the drum break, snip-snip go the scissors of rhythm on the sound-swathes of the synth and the ribbons pick together into something resembling a melody; her melody, she thinks, nearly.

Hanging on
>   *next time*
Depending on
>   *next time*

all because   *all because*   *all because*   *all because*

you left me singing   *left me*   *left me*   *left me singing*

>   *solo*   *harmonies*

With a massive endorsement of bass and synth together on "harmonies." Transcendent, innit. And then a spool-back into yearning fragments, and a descent into rubbly static, the dryness of the drum break, static only. *BOOM-dubba-da-da!-da!-dah. BOOM-dubba-da-da!-da!-dah.* Crackle. Hiss. The unstaged wildtrack of the real London night asserting itself, in the form of a plane overhead.

"Do you like it?" says Marcus, cautiously.

She holds up a hand. If they want professional they can have professional. "Again," she says.

Footsteps, cityscape, static, drum break, synth. Sample. This time round she knows what's coming, she expects the joins. She is developing a view about the details of the mix, another about the pacing, another about the slightly obvious nature of the long-withheld melody. She will have notes to give them later. But at the same time she feels it more, this time around, with the anxiety gone. Next time, next time, says the young voice, singing to her from some other point on the great continent of time, passing her a bitterness awakened into a tune across thirty years; and the voice singing believes in no replacement for what it lacks, not being able to imagine how at later times the lack was filled;

309

and here she is, old, hearing it, and not possessing time enough any more for many next times to happen in, though she can still be surprised, as she is surprised by this new thing turning out to have the time to happen, right now. It ought to be ironic. But it isn't. She hears the time go by, four beats to the bar, ninety beats to the minute. She hears the song, her song, and it's still a song of wanting, of losing, of missing. Only now it is the song of missing what you still possess; what, for a little while longer, you have and hold, but must presently relinquish to the dark, into which will go her song, and all songs; Val's guilt and Val's wisdom; Claude's energy and Claude's madness; Ricky's voice and Ricky's leopard-skin trousers. A stage draped with waterlight like jewels. A baby in arms. A red forest in green sunlight.

One more thing to add. She always meant to put in a second voice, she remembers—to be her own backing singer. Now she can duet with herself across thirty years. As the chorus comes around, Jo throws her head back, straightens the soft tube of her wind-pipe, and harmonises. Solo harmonies for two. Her voices soar, Marcus laughs out loud, and her brown-and-silver song winds away into the night, over the roofs of Bexford, past the scarlet light on the unmoving crane, past the grand houses of the Rise and the hipster coffee shops on the hill, over the burger joints and the takeaways, between the towers of the Park Estate and out over the treetops; voice and bassline and drum break chasing leaves and fried-chicken wrappers, echoing from the surfaces of brick and concrete on which love makes its always temporary claim; from which we constitute a home, we who lift our voices and pass through, pass through.

Ben

Ben's room in the hospice has a window onto a small court of straggly grass. Two-storey brick walls surround it, and the sun only shines directly down into it in the middle of the day. Otherwise it is a shady place, with a neglected square green pool, and a twisting stumpy sculpture gone to moss. But out of sight of Ben, there must be a path into the courtyard and therefore a chink at the corner of the enclosing walls, because sometimes the early light comes raying briefly from the right, low and level. It is doing it now, and the grass has dew on it. All along the line of the sun, a brilliant sea of tiny beads, a million filaments trembling with light.

People say the world gets smaller when you're dying: but there it still is, as astonishingly much of it as ever. It's you who shrinks. Or you who can grasp the world less, who can take hold of less and less of it, until you're only peeping at one burning-bright corner of the whole immense fabric. And then not even that.

Under the sheet a tube goes into his arm and a little pump sends morphine down it automatically. He can press a button for more if the pain gets too much. It doesn't, mostly. But time blurs and moves in jumps. People come and are suddenly gone, he blinks and night has become day or day become night. He loses the thread in the middle of talking, then searching for the next words finds he has left the conversation far behind, hours or days ago.

He pursues his thoughts slowly, across great discontinuities, like someone chasing a bead of mercury that constantly tries to split and roll away.

Marsha and Ruthie and Curtis and Cleve and Grace and Addie are just putting their coats on to go. A nurse feeds him a mouthful of Fortisip and suddenly they're gone. "Is that the MP?" says the nurse. "Mm-hh," says Ben. Swallowing is difficult. Yes, it is; Addie Ojo, member of parliament for Bexford, herself and in the flesh. "And are they all your children?" says the nurse, a slight but polite doubt in her voice, for obvious reasons. "None of them," says Ben. "All of them," he adds. But did he manage to say that part out loud? Suddenly it's night.

Sometimes he's frightened. Sometimes everything seems to be shaking to pieces, idea from idea, bone from bone, matter all flying apart into a broken heap, and then he thinks he can hear a huge sound, a rattling rolling crash he has somehow been living inside.

He tries to put his thoughts in order but the mercury runs this way and that. The different parts of his life: how they seem not to fit together but, he is sure, really do. Really did. How he went round and round in Bexford, one life and then another different one in the same places, the buses and then the café, the horror and then the joy, his sister and then Marsha. Always on the same streets. Only not in a circle, more like round and round in a spiral, rising in place, because didn't he in the end prove to be going somewhere?

Oddly, after all the years when happiness meant not being able to remember what the fear was like, he can now call it to mind again easily, but without being afraid. The crystal floor to his mind is gone but it's all right. He sees the fearful years alongside the good ones, taking their place in the spiral.

An idea is in his head, the mercury consenting to be chased slowly to a standstill. Who knows if it's true. But if the different bits and pieces of his life, rising, lofted as if by a bubble of force from below, are arranged in a messy spiral of hours and years, then mightn't it be the case, mightn't there be a place, mightn't there be an angle, from which you could see the whole accidental mass composing, just from that angle, into some momentary order you could never have noticed at the time? Mightn't there be a line of sight, not ours, from which the seeming cloud of debris of our days, no more in order than (say) the shredded particles riding the wavefront of an explosion, prove to align? Into a clockface of transparencies. This whole mess a rose, a window.

It is morning. It is night. It is morning.

"Ben?" says Marsha, holding his left hand, "Grandpa Ben?" says Ruthie, holding his right hand, but not as if they expect an answer. "*Olorun a de fun e,*" says Marsha. Her lips on his forehead.

Praise him in all the postcodes, thinks Ben.

Praise him on the commuter trains: praise him upon the drum and bass. Praise him at the Ritz: praise him in the piss-stained doorways. Praise him in nail bars: praise him with beard oil. Praise him in toddler groups: praise him at food banks. Praise him in the parks and playgrounds: praise him down in the Tube station at midnight. Praise him with doner kebabs: praise him with Michelin stars. Praise him on pirate radio: praise him on LBC and Capital: praise him at Broadcasting House. Praise him at Poundland: praise him at Harvey Nichols. Praise him among the trafficked and exploited: praise him in hipster coffee houses. Praise him in the industrial estates: praise him in leather bars. Praise him on the dancefloors: praise him on the sickbeds. Praise him in the high court of Parliament: praise him in the prisons and crack houses. Praise him at Pride: praise him at Carnival: praise him at Millwall and West Ham, Arsenal and Chelsea and Spurs. Praise him at Eid: praise him at High Mass: praise him on Shabbat: praise him in the gospel choirs. Praise him, all who hope: praise him, all who fear: praise him, all who dream: praise him, all who remember. Praise him in trouble. Praise him in joy. Let everything that has breath, give praise.

The sun is overhead. The sun is shining straight down. The grass grows bright with ordinary light. Ben sees the light, and the light is very good.

$$t + \infty$$

Come, dust.

Acknowledgments

This one-ounce weight blew onto the keyboard of my laptop because, for the last twelve years, I've been walking to work at Goldsmiths College past a plaque commemorating the 1944 V-2 attack on the New Cross Road branch of Woolworths. Of the 168 people who died, fifteen were aged eleven or under. The novel is partly written in memory of those South London children, and their lost chance to experience the rest of the twentieth century. You can find their names among the other known victims of the rocket in the Deptford History Group's 1994 oral history *Rations & Rubble*. But Alec, Vern, Jo, Val and Ben are invented souls. They do not correspond in whole or in part to the real dead, any more than Joe McLeish ever played for Millwall or you can find the London Borough of Bexford on a map.

I owe thanks and love for this book above all to my in-laws. To my mother-in-law Bernice Martin, sociologist and soprano and quilter, who came with me to Glyndebourne and provided a critical reading of every chapter as I finished it. To my brother-in-law Jonathan Martin, novelist and Millwall fan from the seventies on, who took me to the Den and measured the book against his memories. To my other brother-in-law Magnus Martin, musician, for briefing me on whole-class teaching. To my other other brother-in-law Izaak Martin, for grace under pressure and heroic good humour. To my wife Jessica Martin, priest and scholar, without whom not, in every way: books, life, body, soul, family, art, clear shining after rain. *With thee conversing I forget all time.* I couldn't have written a book in which music figured so large without borrowing from all of them, and being connected to all of them.

I'm grateful to friends who read and commented, especially Alan Jacobs, Kim Stanley Robinson, Adam Roberts and Elizabeth Knox; I'm grateful to all those at Goldsmiths from whom I have learned, colleagues and students alike, and most particularly Maura Dooley and Ardu Vakil. The book was written in Hot Numbers, Cambridge, and the Samovar Tea House, Ely. The world convulsed, idiocy ruled in high places, pandemics gathered strength, and my black coffees kept on coming.

Once the book was done, my agent Clare Alexander applied her usual blend of sensitivity and ruthlessness to its fortunes; Alex Bowler at Faber edited it with a tactful hand; and Silvia Crompton again made the copy-editing process . . . surprisingly enjoyable. (Ellipsis, not dash.)

At the Pelican Club in 1964, the Tearaways are singing "Mockingbird" by Charlie Foxx and Inez Foxx, lyrics © Sony/ATV Music Publishing LLC, used by permission. The choir at Bexford Assemblies of Salvation church sing "Safe in His Arms" by Milton Brunson (1986), and the LA Mass Choir's "That's When You Bless Me" (1989), used by permission. In 1979, Alec is quoting from the dedication to W. H. Auden's *The Orators* (1932), used by permission of Faber & Faber. In 1994, Alec and Vicky sing

ACKNOWLEDGMENTS

lines from "Nellie the Elephant" by Ralph Butler and Peter Hart (1956), lyrics used by permission, and Alec reads to Vicky from the very great *Mister Magnolia*, by Quentin Blake, excerpt used by kind permission.

The book would have been finished sooner had I not taken a detour through the back of a wardrobe. Since I couldn't, as it turned out, thank in print those who helped me with that, let me make my bow here to all of the Friends of Moonwit: AJ, EK, JM, CA, CJ, AM, MM, RW, FC, SP, SA, AR, JB, JP, AR, MWT, CF, WH, PNH, TNH, JL, AC, FCB. You know who you are.

ABOUT THE AUTHOR

FRANCIS SPUFFORD is the author of five highly praised books of nonfiction. His first book, *I May Be Some Time*, won the Writers' Guild Award for Best Nonfiction Book of 1996, the Banff Mountain Book Prize, and a Somerset Maugham Award. It was followed by *The Child That Books Built*, *Backroom Boys*, *Red Plenty* (which was translated into nine languages), and most recently, *Unapologetic*. His novel *Golden Hill* won the Costa First Novel Award. In 2007 he was elected a Fellow of the Royal Society of Literature. He teaches writing at Goldsmiths College and lives near Cambridge, England.